PRAISE FOR

And Only to Deceive

"Newcomer Tasha Alexander almost immediately demonstrates her ability to walk the fine line between history and mystery, throwing her protagonist into a cauldron of intrigue, scandal, and danger."
—*Baltimore Sun*

"The story spans genres, appealing to lovers of suspense, history, and romance . . . historically correct and beautifully done."
—*South Bend Tribune*

"Engagingly suspenseful and rich with period detail . . . provides a fascinating look at the repressive social mores . . . in Victorian high society."
—*BookPage*

"Charming. . . . The archaeological background will lure readers who like to dig for their clues." —*Publishers Weekly*

"If you like an intelligently written historical mystery with just a touch of romance, this will fill the bill nicely."
—*Deadly Pleasures* magazine

"Sophisticated, intelligent, and above all, fun, *And Only to Deceive* will appeal to fans of Anne Perry, Elizabeth Peters, and anyone who can't get enough of Victorian England. . . . Not to be missed."
—Elizabeth Letts, author of *Quality of Care*

"An entertaining debut. . . . Emily Ashton is such an appealing character that readers will want to follow her to new mysteries as she discovers new loves, and herself." —*Nashville Scene*

"Alexander's writing made me remember why I became an English major in the first place. It's for the books. *And Only to Deceive* could easily become one of the classics." —ReviewingtheEvidence.com

"Captivating, enchanting, and delightful! With *And Only to Deceive*, Alexander has created a compelling mélange of murder, intrigue, romance, and sleuthing in nineteenth-century British society."
—J. A. Konrath, author of *Bloody Mary*

Jerry Bauer

About the Author

TASHA ALEXANDER is a graduate of Notre Dame, where she signed on as an English major in order to have a legitimate excuse for spending all her time reading. Following graduation, she played nomad for several years, eventually settling with her family in Tennessee. When not reading, she can be found hard at work on her next book featuring Lady Emily Ashton.

And Only to Deceive

TASHA ALEXANDER

HARPER

NEW YORK • LONDON • TORONTO • SYDNEY

HARPER

FIRST HARPER PAPERBACK PUBLISHED 2006.

Designed by Deborah Kerner

The Library of Congress has catalogued the hardcover edition of this book as follows:

Alexander, Tasha.
  And only to deceive / Tasha Alexander—1st ed.
    p. cm.
  ISBN-10: 0-06-075671-3 (acid-free paper)
  ISBN-13: 978-0-06-075671-0
    1. Great Britain—History—Victoria, 1837–1901—Fiction.   2. Archaeological thefts—Fiction.   I. Title.

PS3601.L3565A84   2005
813'.6—dc22   2004065410

ISBN-10: 0-06-114844-X (pbk.)
ISBN-13: 978-0-06-114844-6 (pbk.)

14 15 16 ❖/RRD 30 29 28 27 26 25 24 23

FOR MATT

·

"my soul's far better part…"

On first looking into
Chapman's Homer

Much have I travell'd in the realms of gold,

And many goodly states and kingdoms seen;

Round many western islands have I been

Which bards in fealty to Apollo hold.

Oft of one wide expanse had I been told

That deep-brow'd Homer ruled as his demesne;

Yet did I never breathe its pure serene

Till I heard Chapman speak out loud and bold:

Then felt I like some watcher of the skies

When a new planet swims into his ken;

Or like stout Cortez, when with eagle eyes

He star'd at the Pacific – and all his men

Look'd at each other with a wild surmise –

Silent, upon a peak in Darien.

— JOHN KEATS

ACKNOWLEDGMENTS

This book could never have been started, let alone completed, without the enduring support of my parents, Gary and Anastasia Gutting, who have encouraged me to write for as long as I can remember. They were also kind enough to provide me with two brothers whose assistance was invaluable: Edward, for his expertise in classics, and Tom, who is an excellent writing partner and novelist in his own right.

I am grateful for my friends in New Haven, Connecticut: Kristen Fairey, who discussed Emily over more pots of tea than I can count (when will Fortnum & Mason start supplying us directly?), and Rebecca Weiner, whose skills as both an editor and a writer helped this book beyond measure.

Myriad thanks to my agent, Anne Hawkins, who is simply fabulous and loads of fun, and to my wonderful team at HarperCollins. I can't imagine a better editor than Carolyn Marino. Jennifer Civiletto provided insightful suggestions and was always available to help me. Thanks also to Maureen Sugden for her careful copyediting of my manuscript.

My husband and son, Matt and Alexander, are the best family anyone could hope for. They made it possible for me to do what I love, and I couldn't be more appreciative. I am also indebted to my grandmother, Anastasia Sertl, for her constant inspiration and support.

Finally, special thanks to Kristy Kiernan, a brilliant writer without whom this book would still be untitled.

FEW PEOPLE WOULD LOOK KINDLY ON MY REASONS FOR marrying Philip; neither love nor money nor his title induced me to accept his proposal. Yet, as I look across the spans of Aegean Sea filling the view from my villa's balcony, I cannot doubt that it was a surprisingly good decision.

The Viscount Ashton seemed an unlikely candidate to bring anyone much happiness, at least according to my standards. His fortune, moderate good looks, and impeccable manners guaranteed that hapless females would constantly fling themselves at him in the hope of winning his affection. They missed his defining characteristic, ensuring that he would never pay them more than the slightest polite attention: Philip was a hunter.

I mean this, of course, literally. Hunting possessed him. He spent as much time as his fortune would permit pursuing wild beasts. The dignified (although I would not choose to describe it as so) English hunt amused him, but he preferred big game and passed much of his time stalking his quarry on the plains of Africa. He could be found in London only briefly, at the height of the Season, when he limited his prey to potential brides. The image he presented could be described as striking, I suppose. He played the part of daring adventurer well.

My encounter with the dashing viscount began as such things typically do, at a soirée. I found the conversation lacking and longed to return home to the novel that had engrossed me all morning. Philip differed little from other men I met, and I had no interest in continuing the acquaintance. No interest, that is, until I decided to accept the inevitable and agree to marry.

My mother and I do not particularly enjoy each other's company. From the day the queen kissed me during my presentation at court in Buckingham Palace, I heard from Mother constant reminders that my looks would soon fade, and she admonished me to do my best to catch a husband immediately. That I had refused several good offers continued to vex her, and I will not bore the reader with the details of these trivial events. Suffice it to say that I had little interest in marriage. I cannot claim that this was due to lofty ideals of love or outrage at the submission demanded by many husbands of their wives. Frankly, I considered the proposition of matrimony immensely boring. Married women I knew did scarcely more than bear children and order around their servants. Their time consumed by mundane details, the most excitement for which they could hope was some social event at which they could meet one another and complain about said children and servants. I preferred my life at home. At least as a single woman, I had time to pursue my own interests, read voraciously, and travel when opportunity presented.

Did I marry Philip, then, because of his keen sense of adventure? Did I long to travel to darkest Africa with him? Hardly. I married him because he happened to propose at a moment when accepting him seemed a simple way out of an increasingly unbearable situation.

As the months following my debut progressed, my mother became more and more desperate, her dearest wish having always been to see me make a brilliant match before the end of my first Season. She lamented continually; it was nearly impossible to converse with her on any other topic. Any topic, that is, other than the proposals being accepted by the daughters of her friends. She began to point out the slightest wrinkles and imperfections on my face, bemoaning what she considered to be the beginning of the end of my wasted beauty. She cut my allowance, telling me I must learn to live on a pittance if I were determined to be a spinster. The final affront came one morning when she entered my room with a dressmaker's tape. She wanted to measure my waist to see how quickly I was becoming old and fat. I could bear it no longer.

That same afternoon Philip called and asked me to do him the honor of becoming his wife. This came as a complete surprise; I had rarely conversed with him, though we saw each other frequently at social gatherings. Having no interest in hunting or in his superficial charm, I tended to avoid him. I did not realize that the hunter always prefers the quarry that is difficult to catch. He claimed to love me endlessly and said all the pretty words we expect to hear on such an occasion. They meant nothing to me. Living with him could not be worse than continued subjection to my mother's ranting. I accepted his proposal immediately.

The wedding took place as soon as my trousseau could be assembled. Six months later I found myself a widow. I had known my husband barely long enough for his name to stop sounding foreign on my lips. When I read the telegram, a feeling of relief and freedom swept through my body, causing me to tremble. The butler reached toward me, assuming I would faint. I never faint. Fainting is a result of affectation or too-tight stays; I will succumb to neither.

I felt no grief for the loss of Philip. I hardly knew him. As the astute reader will already have guessed, the hunter rarely has much interest in his quarry once it is caught, except as a trophy. After a brief wedding trip, my new husband returned to Africa, where he spent the months prior to his death hunting with his friends. We exchanged civil, impersonal letters. Then the prescribed period of mourning began. For twelve months I would have to wear nothing but black crepe and avoid nearly all social events. After that I would be allowed silk, but in dull grays and black stripes. Not until two years had passed would I be able to return to an ordinary existence.

Philip settled irrevocably upon me a large fortune, and, much to my surprise, I now had at my disposal not only the London town house but also my husband's country manor, a place I had yet to see. Although the property was, of course, entailed, Philip's family insisted that I did not need to find a new home. Because we had no children, Philip's heir was his sister's son. The boy, called Alexander, was three years old and quite comfortably ensconced in his parents' house. He did not yet need to relocate to the family seat.

For more than a year, I stayed in London, left for dead as all good widows are. Relief came unexpectedly in the form of my husband's friend, Colin Hargreaves.

I spent my afternoons in Philip's walnut-paneled library, loving the feeling of being surrounded by books. Like the rest of the house, it was elegantly decorated, with a spectacular curved ceiling and the finest English Axminster carpets. Some previous viscount had selected the furniture with as much of an eye for comfort as for appearance, making the room a place where one could relax with ease in the most luxurious surroundings. It was here that Mr. Hargreaves interrupted my reading on a warm summer day. He strode across the room and nodded at me as he reached for my hand, raising it gently to his lips.

"Odd to be in this room without him," he said, glancing about. "Your husband and I planned all of our trips from here." He sat on a large leather chair. "I'm dreadfully sorry, Lady Ashton. I shouldn't speak of such painful things." Devoid of sentimental attachment to my deceased mate, I felt distinctly uncomfortable in the company of his closest friend.

"Never mind. Would you like some tea?" I reached for the bell.

"No, don't trouble yourself. I am here on business."

"Then perhaps you should see my solicitor."

"I've just come from his office. You are aware, of course, of your husband's love of Greece and the Aegean?" he asked, looking directly into my eyes.

"Greece?" I asked, not wanting to reveal more ignorance of my husband's interests than absolutely necessary.

"As I'm sure you know, he spent months there every year. While he was ill in Africa . . ." Mr. Hargreaves paused, looking at me questioningly.

"Please go on."

"He so looked forward to taking you to Greece and showing you the villa."

"The villa?" I had vague memories of my solicitor's mentioning such a place, but he had not given me any details, assuming I was too overcome by grief to concern myself with such things.

"It was not part of the family property. He owned it himself and wanted you to have it. It's a magnificent place, sweeping views of the Aegean. You'll love it. I think he intended to surprise you by taking you there." He paused again. "When he was sick, it was a subject to which he continually returned: 'Kallista must go to the villa.' I promised to arrange the trip for you."

"You must pardon my confusion," I said, shaking my head. "Who is Kallista?"

Mr. Hargreaves smiled. "I believe that is what he called you in"—again the pause—"private."

My eyebrows lifted in amazement. "He never called me Kallista." I didn't mention that the form of address he used most frequently was, in fact, Lady Ashton, albeit in a somewhat ironic tone.

"It is how he always referred to you," Mr. Hargreaves said quietly. "I assumed it was a pet name. Excuse my impertinence, but I believe he preferred it to Emily."

"I see. And the villa?"

"It's on Santorini, one of the islands in the Aegean. I suggest you go in the spring, when the weather is fine, although Ashton always considered winter there a vast improvement over England." He stood up and walked toward me. "I must apologize again. I can only imagine how difficult it is for you to be reminded of him. Using his familiar name for you was thoughtless of me."

"On the contrary, it doesn't bother me at all," I said, still not sure what to make of this habit of my husband's. "For all I care, you may call me Kallista if you prefer it to Emily." I looked directly at Mr. Hargreaves and smiled. He was quite handsome, his dark, wavy hair tousled, contrasting with the perfect elegance of both his clothing and manner. "That is, of course, should our acquaintance become familiar enough to merit the use of Christian names."

"You are as spirited as Ashton described you," he said, flashing a smile. "I shall leave now. Your solicitor has all the papers concerning the villa. As I said, I promised your husband I would ensure that you see it. When you are ready to make the trip, I shall take care of all your arrangements."

I gave him my hand, which he kissed quickly. I watched from the window seat as he sauntered down the steps to the street and across Berkeley Square.

As always after meeting any of Philip's family or friends, I felt overwhelmed. I could not share their grief; I did not know the man. Yet here Colin Hargreaves stood and suggested that Philip actually talked about me. What on earth could he possibly have had to say? My mind reeled. Kallista? Greece? As far as I knew, Philip had few, if any, interests beyond hunting. I had little reason to doubt Mr. Hargreaves, who had stood as best man at my wedding. He and Philip were friends from their early days at school, and Philip always spoke highly of his integrity. Before I could think further on the subject, the butler interrupted me again. My parents awaited me in the drawing room.

"My dear, you really must keep the curtains drawn in the front of the house," my mother scolded, true to her new mission of attempting to reestablish dominance over me.

"Philip has been dead for more than a year and a half, Mother. I can hardly live without natural light indefinitely."

"Prince Albert left this life nearly thirty years ago, and our queen still respects his memory. You would do well to follow her example." My mother, quite possibly Queen Victoria's staunchest supporter, looked critically around the room. "I know Philip was a bit eccentric, but now that he's gone, you surely could update this room. It is as if it is only partially furnished."

Philip had no taste for the cluttered excess currently in favor and had furnished his house accordingly. After our wedding he was delighted to learn that I shared his opinion on the subject. He obligingly removed several of the larger mounted animal heads from the public rooms, and I agreed to leave the remainder of the house untouched.

"In one breath you tell her to mourn the man, in the next to change his house. Really, Catherine, I think you should leave the child alone." My father, whom I had always considered a silent ally, smiled at me reassuringly. "I don't like to be unpleasant, but it is insupportable to me that she should have to be in mourning longer than she knew Ashton."

My mother gasped. "I will pretend that I never heard you say that. You must think of her future. She's young and very rich, not to mention the daughter of an earl. After a suitable period of mourning, she will be able to make an excellent marriage." My mother looked at me. "I have already heard your name mentioned by the mothers of some of the most eligible peers."

"I'd rather not lose my money to the upkeep of someone else's family estate," I said with a sigh. "Besides, why should I marry again? I rather like widowhood." My father laughed until he caught my mother's withering glare.

"Don't be ridiculous. Of course it's much too soon to think of such things. Your heart is still breaking." My mother rang the bell. "You need some tea." I suffered through a cup of the oversweetened beverage she forced on me and avoided any conversation that might prolong their stay. At last I bade my parents farewell, cringing as my mother ordered the butler to have the drapes on the front windows closed. Davis, a consummate professional, gave her a reassuring nod but did nothing without first consulting his mistress. I instructed him to leave them open.

"Very good, madam. If I may?" He continued as soon as I nodded permission. "I must inform you that I've had to let one of the footmen go. A parlormaid, entering the library to dust, saw him rifling through the viscount's desk."

"When did this happen?"

"Yesterday afternoon, madam. The maid was reluctant to come forward. Apparently the man was looking for something he could sell to repay gaming debts. I have searched his room and found nothing. Perhaps you could check to see if anything is missing?"

"Thank you, Davis. I shall check the contents of the desk right away," I said, knowing full well that I had no idea what ought to be in it.

I returned to the library, where, after a cursory glance through the unremarkable contents of the desk, I started searching the shelves for books about Greece and found volume upon volume: histories and classical literature in both the ancient language and translation. Until now I had assumed that these were vestiges of Philip's studies at Eton and Cambridge. I flipped through several of them, not knowing what I wanted to find. Frustrated with my complete lack of direction, I picked up a guide to the British Museum. The book fell open to a page that held a carefully folded note written in a hand I did not recognize. "Your present course of action has placed you in grave danger." The page it marked described a vase on which there was a painting of the great hero Achilles killing the queen of the Amazons. Grave danger indeed.

I examined the note closely. The paper was heavy, the type that an artist might use in his sketchbook, but it bore no indication of the identity of either sender or recipient. Very odd. I sighed, unsure of what to do. After rereading it I placed it in Philip's desk, where I sat, suddenly overcome by a feeling of ominous unease. I rang for tea, hoping the genial beverage (without my mother's too-liberal use of sugar) would soothe my nerves. It was some time before I was able to turn my attention back to the book from which the note had fallen, but eventually I found myself engrossed in its descriptions of the museum's magnificent artifacts. Suddenly, on a whim, I summoned my carriage. I wanted to see them myself.

Naturally I had not mentioned Greece or the villa to my parents, and I smiled as I approached Great Russell Street, wondering what my mother would think if I were to set up house in Santorini for the rest of my years. How long would I have to wear half mourning there? I fluffed my black striped skirts and entered the museum, immediately asking if someone could show me the Greek antiquities. A wealthy widow quickly learns that great institutions long for her money; knowing this, I anticipated a thorough and enjoyable tour.

As I waited for what I hoped would be a knowledgeable guide, I looked around the hall, wondering why I hadn't visited the museum in so long. My father had taken me periodically when I was a girl, but once my education transferred to the hands of my mother and a legion of governesses, I was limited to pursuing those things considered essential by society matrons. Consequently I became fluent in French and Italian and able to speak passably in German. I could sing and play the pianoforte, though not well. In the visual arts, I excelled at drawing, though I never moved to watercolors, preferring the feel of pencils to that of the artist's brushes. Embroidery, etiquette, and household management became second nature, but my mother did not want me to receive anything that could be construed as a classical education. A good wife, she believed, should not think too much for herself. Before I could mull further on the shortcomings of my schooling, a distinguished-looking middle-aged gentleman interrupted my reverie.

"Lady Ashton, it is a pleasure to make your acquaintance. I am Alexander Murray, Keeper of Greek and Roman Antiquities. My colleagues inform me that you are interested in viewing our collection." I gave him my hand and murmured something appropriate.

"Please allow me to express my condolences on the death of your excellent husband," he continued. "He visited us frequently; the entire department was shocked to learn of his demise. We are immeasurably grateful for the artifacts he donated to us during his lifetime. I presume you would like to see those pieces first?"

I hardly knew what to say. I had never known Philip to set foot in the museum, but I realized that fact in itself to be meaningless. Clearly I knew even less about the man than I suspected. As Mr. Murray led me through gallery after gallery, my thoughts divided between my husband and the wondrous objects I viewed. Philip had given the museum several stunning Greek vases. One in particular struck me: a large vase showing three women standing before a young man who held an apple.

"That is a calyx-krater, so called because the shape of the handles brings to mind a flower's calyx," Mr. Murray told me. "It would have been used in antiquity as a vessel in which one would mix water with wine. I believe it was Lord Ashton's favorite. He had a difficult time parting with it but felt strongly that it belonged where others could study it. It is a fine example of red-figure vase painting."

"The detail is exquisite," I exclaimed, leaning closer to the object. "Even the eyelashes are visible on the man's profile."

"The red-figure technique allows for more realism than black-figure because the details are painted onto the unglazed figures. This artist is known for his attention to such things. Note how he shows individual strands of hair and the way he has shaded the folds of fabric on each cloak."

"There is something in it that brings to mind the Parthenon friezes."

"A keen observation, Lady Ashton. The style is very similar to those figures found at the Parthenon. This vase painter is credited with being the most classical of all his colleagues."

"Who was he?"

"I'm afraid we do not know his name, but his work is recognized on hundreds of vases."

"All red-figure?"

"No. Black-figure and white-ground lekythoi, too. If you'll come this way, I'll show you one of the lekythoi. They are the ones for which he is best known."

I did not respond immediately to Mr. Murray but continued to examine the piece before me. "Look how graceful his hand is holding the apple. Whom do the figures represent?" I asked.

Mr. Murray moved closer to the case. "Those are the goddesses Athena, Hera, and Aphrodite. They have just attended a wedding ruined by Eris, or Discord. Furious not to have been invited to the celebration, she determined to cause a scene and dropped a golden apple among the guests."

"They argued over who would keep the gold?"

"In a sense, yes. *Tê kallistê*—'To the fairest' was engraved on the apple. The goddesses each argued that she was the most beautiful and should have the apple. Zeus realized that no judgment would be acceptable to all three and decided it would be best to stay out of the mix."

"Wise," I said, smiling.

"He gave the task of choosing who would receive the apple to Paris, an unfortunate shepherd." He pointed to one of the figures on the vase.

"Whom did he choose?"

"I'm afraid he found Aphrodite most irresistible, especially when she promised that he would have for a wife the most beautiful of all mortal women."

"Hera and Athena were not pleased, I imagine."

"Far from it. They were his sworn enemies from that day forward."

"And Paris's wife?"

"A lovely girl called Helen, unfortunately already married to the king of Sparta, Menelaus. With Aphrodite's help, Paris convinced Helen to leave Menelaus and come with him to Troy, giving rise, of course, to the great Trojan War."

I remained silent for a moment, certain that I should know more of this story than I did, and resolved to read about it that very evening. Something Mr. Murray said had caught my attention, and I had to inquire further.

"Could you tell me again what was written on the apple?"

"*Tê kallistê*. Kallista in Greek means 'most beautiful.'"

And thus I learned that Philip had considered me beautiful. I blushed uncontrollably and allowed Mr. Murray to continue his tour, although I must confess that my attention to his thoughtful commentary was less than it ought to have been.

———

Another day marred by the infinite stupidity of one of our party. To hunt is to bask in the glory of the wild beasts, track them, and spar with them on their own terms. In doing so, the hunter honours the magnificence of his prey. Fitzroy's actions today fit into no gentleman's code. He left camp early, before breakfast, with one of our guides, Lusala, and returned filthy and terrified less than an hour later. The bastard convinced Lusala to bait a rhinoceros rather than track it—then waited in a blind until an unlucky beast stumbled upon their trap. When Fitzroy prepared for his shot, he tripped, startling the animal. Then he took the shot he ought to have refused— firing without aiming properly—wounding the rhino but not killing it. Thinking it was about to charge at them, he and Lusala ran back to camp like the cowards they are. It took me hours to track the poor animal and finish what my friend should have done. We are not here to leave a trail of wounded animals.

Thrashed Fitzroy when I returned. The man has no understanding of the morality of the hunt. It is while tracking that the hunter exhibits his true skill. Will not tolerate this practice of baiting on my expedition. Hargreaves suggests we abandon the whole business and explore Mount Kenya. If he meant to amuse me, he succeeded.

"So, you see, I am actually quite important," I said in mock seriousness to my dear friend Ivy as we took tea in my well-appointed drawing room the next afternoon. "They sent the head of the entire department to speak to me. Obviously word of my fortune has spread even to the hallowed halls of the British Museum."

"You give yourself too much credit," she retorted with a smile. "Clearly they decided to extend their good opinion of Philip to your humble self. But really, aren't you a bit shocked to learn about Philip's passion for Greece? It's rather interesting of him, I think."

"I hardly know what to make of it," I said, pouring more tea. "He never mentioned anything about it to me."

"I suppose the conversation on your wedding trip focused on very different topics," Ivy said.

"I can't remember that we talked about anything in particular. He wrote in his journal, I suppose cataloging where we were each day, and I read a lot. He was very nice about buying me books."

"Beastly of him to die before you realized he might be fascinating."

"Yes, and terrible of him to settle such a large amount of money on me." I laughed. "Of course, I won't be able to enjoy it at all until I get out of this ghastly mourning." Even as the words came out of my mouth, the color drained from my face. "I don't mean that."

Ivy took my hand. "I know you don't, dear."

"I certainly never thought things would turn out like this. Barely in society and already a widow."

"Mourning won't last forever."

"I'm not sure that I even mind, Ivy. Consider my life: I live on my own, with my own servants, and have control over my own money. I can do virtually whatever I want."

"Except move about in society just yet."

"No, of course not, but I'm not certain that I really miss any of that. It was vastly diverting for a while, of course, and I had a lovely time making as many men as possible fall in love with me, but think where I would be if I hadn't married Philip."

"You would still be living with your mother and having your waist measured daily."

"Precisely. A fate not to be borne. But now I have a freedom unprecedented in my life. If Philip were still alive, would my life be much different than it was when I lived with my parents?"

"As an unmarried woman, I would hardly dare to comment on married life," Ivy said wickedly.

"Yes, but you'll know soon enough. Two more weeks and we'll be at your own wedding."

"Yes," Ivy said with a sigh. "I don't know what to think."

Davis came into the room and announced two more callers.

"My dear, I am delighted to see you again," Emma Callum said as she crossed toward me, reaching out with both her hands. "It hardly seems that a year has passed since your dear husband's passing. But here we are."

"Yes, here we are," I said, answering her simpering smile with one of my own as I took her hands. "It's kind of you to come. How are you, Arabella?"

"Very well, thank you." The newcomers sat, and Arabella Dunleigh accepted the muffin I offered her.

"I am desperately excited for your wedding," Emma said to Ivy. "Mother tells me Worth made your dress."

"Yes, it's lovely. I'm looking forward to wearing it," Ivy answered, considerably less lively now than she had been before we'd been interrupted.

"I don't know what I shall wear," Emma continued. I didn't believe her; she spent a large portion of her waking hours thinking and talking about her extensive wardrobe. Unfortunately, despite the large expense her father went to in order to dress his only daughter well, her clothing perfectly reflected Emma's own tastes and whims; the result was not attractive. Without fail, she chose garish colors and unflattering styles. Her face, I admit, was lovely, but it was easy to overlook when blinded by the bright yellow of the gown she was wearing. The brown parasol she carried added to the total effect by making her look something like a spindly sunflower. "I'm certain that it won't be long until we're planning my own wedding, and I do want to enjoy myself in the meantime."

"I'm afraid I don't understand," I said, knowing full well Emma was beginning another of her assaults on me.

"You know better than the rest of us the perils of married life, Emily. The role of matron is not nearly as enjoyable as that of belle of the ball. Although I suppose you never really had a chance to settle into being a married woman, did you?"

"No. Philip was kind enough to die before I got really bored," I snapped back. Arabella gasped. "I'm joking, of course, Arabella. Try not to choke on your muffin."

"I'm horrified to hear you speak of your husband that way," Emma said coldly. "Lord Ashton was one of the best men with whom I've been acquainted."

"The noblest man I ever met," Arabella agreed.

"I should think you would take more care to honor his memory," Emma continued, fingering her hideous brown gloves as she spoke.

"I must confess that I am a trifle nervous about my wedding," Ivy interrupted, valiantly changing the subject. "I don't know what to expect as a wife. Robert has always been very kind to me, and my parents are delighted with the match. I'm sure we'll be happy, but I cannot imagine what my life will be like."

"He has a wonderful house," Arabella said, taking another cake off the tea table. "And you're sure to have a generous allowance."

"Ivy's father will ensure that," I said.

"You must listen carefully to everything your mother tells you before the wedding, my dear," Emma said, her tone all seriousness. "There are things about marriage you will find immensely shocking. She will be able to tell you what you need in order to cope and to bear what you must."

"I'm certain it's terrible," Arabella said, her cowlike eyes wide open. "My sister locked herself in her room and refused to come out for three days after her wedding."

"You should never speak of it, Arabella," Emma said, looking at her friend sharply. "It is enough that she be alerted to the situation so that her mother can prepare her."

"Don't be ridiculous," I snapped. I knew Emma well enough to expect that she would try to insult me whenever the opportunity presented itself; it did not bother me in the least. Ivy, however, being much more sensitive than I am, would not be able to hold her own against Emma's malicious talk.

"We are only trying to help our friend on her way to becoming a good wife," Emma said, her voice sickeningly sweet. "I expect it's difficult for you to think of happy things like love and weddings when you know there will never be joy in your own life again."

"Quite the contrary, I assure you. And, Ivy, I will share with you a piece of advice Philip gave me on our wedding night: Relax. If you manage to, you'll find the entire experience not at all unpleasant." I watched my audience and savored the horrified looks on their faces. Arabella dropped her cake, and Emma rose from her seat.

"I never thought I would hear you speak so crudely, Emily. You are fortunate that Philip is not here to see your disgrace."

"Lord Ashton to you, Emma. I don't believe your acquaintance with the viscount ever reached the point of familiarity."

"I see that despite your wearing half mourning, you really are not ready to receive visitors," Emma said, trying in vain to regain her composure. "We will not trespass any longer on your time." She led Arabella, who was still unable to speak, out of the room. I noticed that she took the last tea cake with her.

Ivy stared at me, shocked. "What have you done?"

"I don't know that I've ever had such fun in my life. I never could stand either of those beasts. Emma always threw herself at Philip before we were married and couldn't bear the fact that he never noticed her. She tormented me in every way she could once our engagement was announced."

"But, darling, you never cared for Philip. Surely you weren't jealous?"

"Of course not. But now that he is gone, I am gaining a better appreciation for the man and his tastes. And as for those two, they came here to congratulate themselves on their own good luck at not being widowed at such a young age and to terrify you at the prospect of your wedding."

"I don't think they meant to be cruel."

"Believe what you will, but I know Emma well enough to see her game. She doesn't like being one of the last of us to marry. But she'll be engaged before long, and woe to the poor man she accepts. He'll find no happiness in his bride."

"You really aren't yourself, Emily. Do you need more tea?"

"No, Ivy, I'm fine. I have just realized that I am now in a position to voice opinions that would have been outrageous for an unmarried woman. Don't worry, I'll send perfect notes apologizing for my behavior and beg them both to forgive me. No one can resist a grief-stricken widow."

"You are awful."

"I think I'm going to rather enjoy sitting with the other widows at balls, machinating the futures of young ladies and gossiping excessively."

"When you return fully to society, I don't imagine you'll stay with the other widows."

"Perhaps you are right, but I do not intend to relinquish my newfound freedom in the foreseeable future. What were we discussing before those harpies interrupted us? I'm sure it was much more pleasant than our present topic of conversation. Did I tell you that I've started to read the *Iliad*?"

"No, you hadn't. How terribly clever you're becoming," Ivy said, laughing. "But in all seriousness, Em, is what you said true?"

"Everything I say is true."

"I mean about what Philip told you," she pressed, unable to meet my eyes.

"It is true, Ivy. Now that I think about it, I should perhaps have listened better when Philip talked to me. He gave very good advice."

THAT NIGHT I DREAMED about Philip for the first time. He looked very lovely, right off a Greek vase. He was storming the walls of Troy, his sandy hair blowing in the wind as he called out, "Kallista! Kallista!"

The next morning I decided that I would definitely continue reading Homer.

25 March 1887
Shepherd's Hotel, Cairo

———

Have spent past week playing tourist in Egypt; sights are spectacular, but seeing anything ancient makes me long for Greece. Hargreaves is back exploring pyramids today—I declined the invitation to join him and instead combed the shops in search of Ptolemaic pieces. Most I found were singularly uninteresting, caught somewhere between the Greek and Egyptian styles, doing justice to neither. Had hoped to locate a nice image of the great Alexander, but all I found were hoards of unremarkable coins being offered at outrageous prices.

After less thought than the topic likely deserved, I have decided to acquiesce to my family's wish that I marry. I recognize that doing so is inevitable and see little point in arguing the timing of the event, although embarking on serious courtship will ensure a bloody tiresome Season.

3

I WAS SURPRISED TO FIND HOW GREATLY I ENJOYED MY readings in classical literature and soon began spending a considerable amount of time visiting the British Museum. Not entirely certain how to approach these new interests of mine, I decided to let my husband be my guide and set myself to the task of studying the objects he had donated to the museum. Mr. Murray was pleased to see me in the galleries so often, and I was delighted to show him that I now had the beginnings of at least an elementary knowledge of Homer.

"Hard at work again, Lady Ashton?" he asked, coming upon me as I sat sketching the Judgment of Paris vase.

"I don't know that something described as work could bring such pleasure."

"How are you finding Homer?"

"'Achilles' banefull wrath resound, O Goddesse, that imposd / Infinite sorrowes on the Greekes . . . , '" I quoted, smiling at him.

"Chapman, eh?" In his library Philip had a multitude of copies of Homer's great work: four different English translations and one in the original Greek. The latter, obviously, was far out of my realm, so I chose Chapman's, the most familiar of the rest, which I knew only from Keats's poem. The bold lines inspired me immediately and vigorously; I pored over it daily.

"Seemed as good a place to start as any, and it certainly has not disappointed."

"No, it wouldn't. A bit fanciful for my taste, though."

"Too Elizabethan perhaps?"

"Quite. Pope suits me better. 'Achilles' wrath, to Greece the direful spring / Of woes unnumber'd, heav'nly Goddess, sing!'"

"Wonderfully direct," I agreed. "But for the moment I shall stay with Chapman."

"No reason not to, Lady Ashton. I shall leave you to your drawing."

I returned my attention to the vase in front of me, keen to accurately capture Aphrodite's graceful pose. Some minutes later, while pausing to compare my work to the original, I had the sensation of being watched and turned to look behind me, half expecting to find Mr. Murray. Instead I saw an unfamiliar man. His position suggested he was studying the frieze that occupied the wall beyond the Judgment of Paris vase, but his eyes were fixed on me. I was not accustomed to encountering the sort of individual who would stare in such a way, and I must admit to having been somewhat unnerved. He did not look away when our eyes met but moved his face slightly, revealing a long dueling scar on his right cheek. I tried to return my focus to my sketchbook but found my gaze periodically drawn to the stranger, who continued to lurk in the back of the gallery. When I heard footsteps approaching me, I nearly jumped.

"I hope I didn't startle you, Lady Ashton," Mr. Murray said, smiling broadly as he walked toward me.

"Not at all, I—" I glanced behind me. The man was gone. "I'm pleased to see you again so soon."

"I've no intention of pulling you away from your work, but I would like to present you with this." He handed me a copy of a book he had written, *Manual of Mythology*. I smiled and thanked him, happily distracted from the unwanted observer.

Time passed quickly while I was engrossed in my intellectual pursuits. Ivy's wedding came and went with little incident. I attended, of course, suitably attired in a dreary gray gown. It was the happiest of occasions, but I must confess to feeling a slight melancholy when I realized how vaguely I remembered my own wedding day. At the time I had merely gone through the motions and done what was expected of me, all the while giving scant thought to what I was doing. Robert's eyes had shone when he saw Ivy approach him at the altar; I don't think I even looked at Philip as I walked toward him. Had *his* eyes brightened at the sight of his bride?

Within a week of Ivy's nuptials, Emma's engagement to the son of Lord Haverill was announced—the *younger* son of Lord Haverill. Hoping for something better, she had refused him until her parents insisted upon the engagement. I was immensely happy to see her get what she deserved.

Ivy and her new husband were spending their honeymoon on a grand European tour, with Paris as one of their stops. I was in the midst of reading a delightful letter from her when, once again, my mother descended upon me.

"Emily, Mrs. Callum tells me in the strictest confidence that you said some very pointed things to Emma about marriage. The poor girl is terrified now and is begging to be released from her engagement."

"I can assure you that I told her nothing that would bring her anything but comfort, Mother. She is disappointed at only catching a younger son."

"I think you are right. Luckily, she comes to the match with a fortune of her own, so they will live well."

"As long as her husband doesn't spend all her money," I said.

"You shouldn't be so cynical, my dear. It's most unbecoming. I don't know what has happened to you lately." She sniffed in the direction of my windows, curtains thrown open to let in the sun. "At any rate, I have just come from Lady Elliott's. She is hosting a small dinner Wednesday next and would like to include you in the party. It will be a suitable occasion for you to begin your gradual return to society."

The thought of Lady Elliott's party was only slightly less hideous to me than crossing the Channel on a stormy day. Lady Elliott, my mother's closest friend, would be certain to join in hounding me the entire time, criticizing my clothing (too light-colored), my house (too much light), and my new reading habits (not light enough). I checked to see that I had covered Philip's beautifully bound copy of the *Iliad* with Ivy's letter and sighed.

"I don't think I'm ready, Mother."

"You cannot hide in your grief forever."

"I thought you wanted me to emulate our queen."

"Not literally, child. Your idea of mourning is very odd to me. Liberal with your clothing, conservative with social engagements. I'm not sure what to make of it."

"You needn't make anything of it. My clothing is perfectly appropriate. Mr. Worth handled the details himself, and I wore nothing but bombazine for an entire year. As for society . . ." I hesitated, not sure what I wanted to say. I certainly didn't want to imprison myself but also did not want to be cornered into accepting invitations from all of my mother's ghastly friends. "I'm afraid it is too painful for me to return to society in London. It only reminds me of Philip."

"I'm sure you feel it keenly," my mother answered, giving me more sympathy than she ever had before in her life. "It puts me in mind of the depth of emotion our queen still shows to her dear, departed husband." I thought it best to ignore this sentiment.

"Therefore, I have decided to go to Paris," I said, surprising even myself.

"Paris?"

"Yes. Philip and I did not stop there on our wedding trip, so there will be no bittersweet memories." I paused for effect. "I have had a letter from Ivy today. She and Robert will be there for the next few weeks, and I mean to visit them. I shall also see Mr. Worth about some new dresses and perhaps go to the Louvre. Philip wanted to take me there." I watched my mother's face.

"You cannot think of traveling alone," she began, and then stopped suddenly. "I do not like this, Emily. It doesn't seem appropriate in the least."

"Why not?" I countered, feeling slightly guilty for inventing stories about my deceased spouse. "It would make Philip happy."

"Philip would be happy to know that you are being cared for by family. If you are not comfortable in London, which I admit is somewhat understandable, why don't you go see his sister? She would be delighted to have you."

The thought of a prolonged stay with any of Philip's family was insupportable. They, who really grieved his loss, and I, who would have to pretend that I knew him: a disastrous combination.

"No. I am going to Paris. It's already decided. I shall have you and Father to dinner before I leave."

"Who will be your chaperone? I cannot make the trip on such short notice."

I breathed a sigh of relief, not having had time to even consider a response to the possibility of her wanting to join me. "I shall bring my maid. I am no longer an unmarried woman, Mother, and am quite capable of traveling on my own. Besides, Ivy will be there, and loads of people go after the Season. I'm sure I won't be lonely."

"I didn't imagine you would be gone so long. Surely you will return to England before Christmas?" She shook her head. "I don't think I should allow it."

"Happily, the decision is mine, Mother. I am a widow and in sole control of my actions." Not sure of how to respond to such a statement from her daughter, my mother retreated into the safe world of society gossip. I had left cards for several people that week and hoped violently that one, if not all, of them would interrupt us before I went mad listening to the usual litany of wedding plans, broken engagements, and suggestions for improving my home's décor. Fortunately, the butler announced a visitor.

"Lord Palmer to see you, madam," Davis stated regally. I told him to send the gentleman in, and soon we were laughing in the company of a truly delightful old man. He was one of the few people my husband and

I had entertained in the days we spent together in London before his final trip to Africa. Eventually, as I knew it must, the conversation turned to Philip.

"Such a tragic loss," Lord Palmer said. "But we shall move on, and you, young lady, have a bright future before you." I began to wonder if I should reconsider my opinion of my guest.

"This is exactly what I've been telling her," my mother said. "She cannot sit in this house forever. We must get her back into society."

"Philip was as dear to me as my own sons," Lord Palmer continued, as I silently thanked him for ignoring my mother's comment. "We spent many pleasant afternoons in the British Museum."

"Are you interested in Greece, Lord Palmer?"

"More so even than Philip, my dear. I dabbled in archaeology in my younger years, but that story shall have to wait until another day."

"I've been reading the *Iliad*. It's marvelous."

"Capital. Whose side do you take? Achilles or Hector?"

"Hector, without question. Achilles is far too arrogant."

"It is so difficult to occupy oneself while in mourning," my mother said, glaring at me.

"I must admit to being surprised by the poem. I would not have thought the tale of a war would so engross me. Yet I cannot help but wonder if I should have read an overview of Greek mythology before jumping straight into Homer?"

"I'm sure Philip has *The Age of Fable* in the library. You may find it helpful to familiarize yourself with it."

"Is that Thomas Bulfinch? Yes, I've seen it on a shelf."

"Emily is a great reader," my mother said.

"He discusses the *Iliad*. Having a rudimentary knowledge of the story will allow you to focus more on the poetry."

"An excellent point, Lord Palmer. I shall take your advice and look at Bulfinch this afternoon."

"Do your sons enjoy classics, too?" my mother asked. As always, she amazed me with her ability to stay focused on her never-wavering goal of marrying me off to whatever eligible person she could. I knew what stirred her interest in Lord Palmer's sons. I could see her counting the months until I would be out of mourning.

"Unfortunately, not."

"Are they married now, Lord Palmer?" My mother looked directly at me as she spoke; we both knew she was fully cognizant of the marital status of every English nobleman over the age of twenty-five.

"Not yet," he replied. "This talk of antiquities reminds me of a question I wanted to ask you, Lady Ashton. Before his death Philip showed me a monograph he was writing."

"I must say, Lord Palmer," my mother began, "I never knew that Philip was such an intellectual man."

"He was much deeper than many people knew, Lady Bromley." Lord Palmer turned to me again. "I returned the manuscript to him with some comments. Do you think I could have it back? I should so much like to have it published. Make it a bit of a memorial to him."

"That would be lovely." My mother smiled. I wasn't sure what to think. "Emily would be so grateful for your assistance. She would never be capable of putting such a thing together herself."

"I'm afraid I wouldn't know where to begin to find any of his papers."

"I'd be happy to take a quick look through his library. They're certain to be there. Not now, of course. Think about it and send me a note. I don't wish to inconvenience you in the slightest." Lord Palmer rubbed his bald head as he spoke.

The conversation turned general again, and I listened halfheartedly, preferring to consider instead what I was going to do in Paris. By the time I found myself alone, I realized I would need a considerable amount of assistance in arranging the details and promptly wrote a note to the only man I knew who had suggested to me that he was adept at making travel arrangements. After putting it in the hands of one of my footmen,

I found a copy of Baedeker's guide to Paris and retired with it to the window seat in the library, quite pleased with myself. Glancing up from the book, I looked outside. Directly across from the window, staring at the façade of my house from a bench in Berkeley Square, sat the man who had watched me in the British Museum.

"I BELIEVE THAT TAKES care of everything. I've given you your tickets, and your suite at the Hôtel Meurice will be ready when you arrive in Paris. It is not so large an establishment as the Continental, but I think you will find it much more elegant. Monsieur Beaulieu, the manager, will meet you at the station himself." Four days had passed, and I found myself once again in the library with Colin Hargreaves, who had responded immediately to my plea for help.

"I cannot thank you enough, Mr. Hargreaves," I said, smiling at him.

"I confess your note surprised me. I didn't think you would want to leave London so soon." He had a way of maintaining eye contact during conversation that was almost unnerving.

"Neither did I." I watched him brush his hand through his tousled hair. "To be quite honest, I decided to go purely out of desire to avoid social obligations." He laughed. "Please don't misunderstand," I continued. "There are many excellent diversions to be found in society, but at the moment I find myself unequal to— I'm not ready to—" I stammered on in this incoherent manner for several moments, until his laughter became too loud to ignore.

"Do I amuse you, Mr. Hargreaves?" I asked severely.

"Yes, you do, Lady Ashton. You are trying too hard to be polite. Why would you want to spend the rest of the year attending the somber, boring dinners and teas acceptable for a widow newly out of deep mourning? I believe I share your view of society."

"Of course one couldn't do without it," I said.

"No, I suppose not. It does provide us with a set of arcane rules of behavior and, as Trollope so aptly called it, a marriage market. And I will admit to finding great pleasure in a ball, so I imagine we shouldn't abolish the entire system."

"Quite right. What would you men do if there were no ladies to watch riding on Rotten Row in the morning?"

"I am certain it could lead to nothing good," he replied, leaning toward me conspiratorially. I offered him a drink, which he accepted gratefully, crossing the room to pour it himself rather than making me get up from my comfortable seat.

"I think that I shall have to give you an open invitation to drink my whiskey whenever you are here; I've no idea what I shall do with it otherwise."

"You could drink it yourself."

"An excellent suggestion certain to terrorize my mother," I said enthusiastically. "Ladies should drink only sherry, you know, and I've always detested it." He smiled and handed me a glass. I took one sip and cringed. "Foul stuff."

He laughed. "I think you shall have to rely on other methods of tormenting her."

"Perhaps I shall try port next. Davis tells me there are cases and cases of it in the cellar." I twirled the undrinkable golden liquid in my glass, and we sat quietly for a moment. "I imagine you and Philip spent many pleasant evenings in this room."

"We did, Lady Ashton." He looked at me rather pointedly. "It was in this room after a ball at Lady Elliott's that he first told me he had fallen in love with you. He watched you avoid the attentions of a baron, two viscounts, and an extremely elderly duke."

"Philip wanted to succeed where other viscounts had failed."

"Hardly. He told me he had seen a lady spurn several very eligible men and that this clearly indicated she wanted something more than a title and a comfortable allowance."

I didn't know what to say; I had never considered the matter. A good marriage was my parents' goal for me, though not one in which I had any particular interest. As I have already said, I felt no inclination toward the institution other than as a means of escaping my mother's house, but could hardly admit this to Mr. Hargreaves.

"A young lady rarely knows what she wants. At any rate, her wishes are largely irrelevant, so it is best that she not form too many opinions about any of her suitors," I quipped, trying to sound lighthearted.

"But you obviously formed an opinion of Ashton. You accepted his proposal immediately and after very little courtship."

My heart sank in my chest. "Yes, I did." There was nothing else to say, so I sat in silence for some time.

"I must beg your forgiveness, Lady Ashton. This conversation is inappropriate on every level. I should not force you to think about painful topics. Please do not imagine that your husband ever spoke of you in an indelicate fashion. It is only natural that he would confide in his best friend."

"Of course. You are forgiven, Mr. Hargreaves. How could I find offense in anything you say after you have so kindly arranged my trip to Paris?" I refilled his glass and changed the subject. "Will you leave London for the country soon?"

"Probably not. Like you, I prefer to travel abroad."

"Then perhaps our paths will cross again in Paris," I suggested.

"I would enjoy that very much."

We conversed for another quarter of an hour, until it was time to dress for dinner, at which point he rose to leave.

"Mr. Hargreaves," I said as he headed toward the door. He turned to me. "I think we may dispense with formality. Please call me by my Christian name."

"Thank you, Emily. I'm honored." His smile was excessively charming and brightened his dark eyes most attractively.

5 April 1887
Berkeley Square, London

Much though I love the African plains, it is impossible to deny the superior comfort of a house in London.

Have taken a desk in the Reading Room at the British Library in what I hope will not end up a vain effort at making progress on my research during the summer. My friends are less likely to disturb me there than at home, and close proximity to the museum's artifacts is apt to bring inspiration. As I seem to spend more and more time in town every year, I am considering a significant expansion of my collection of antiquities—could then have a gallery here as well as at Ashton Hall.

WITHIN ANOTHER WEEK I FOUND MYSELF COMFORTABLY settled into a sumptuous suite of rooms overlooking the Jardin des Tuileries in the Hôtel Meurice on the rue de Rivoli. I saw Ivy soon after my arrival and was delighted to find my friend enjoying her honeymoon. Although she and Robert were pleased to see me, I couldn't help but notice that they seemed concerned that I had no immediate plan to return to England. I confess that after they left for Switzerland, I felt quite lonely, almost regretting my decision not to bring a companion with me. Walks in the Tuileries filled my mornings, and I took tea with other English guests at the hotel, and before many days had passed, I grew accustomed to the rhythm of the city.

Being alone in Paris was quite different from being alone in the house in London, although I suppose this was largely due to my own state of mind. Having entered the period of half mourning, I could now go about as I pleased, and people in Paris seemed less concerned with the demise of my husband than those in London did. In London I felt self-conscious when I began leaving my house after my husband's death, as if everyone who saw me knew that I hadn't really mourned him. In Paris I knew that no one would give me a second thought. I rarely encountered anyone who knew Philip personally, and therefore I avoided those uncomfortable encounters with people who wanted to talk about him. My social standing did cause me to be invited to a number of soirées, dinners, and parties, but I felt no need to attend any that did not interest me, confident that my mother would not appear from behind a bush in the Tuileries to scold me for refusing an invitation.

During this time I finished reading Chapman's *Iliad* as well as *The Age of Fable*. Rather than turning my attention to the *Odyssey*, as I had originally planned, I delved into Pope's translation of the *Iliad*. The Meurice was only a short walk from the Louvre, and I spent many afternoons there mesmerized by the exquisite collection of antiquities. After touring all the Salles Grecques, I returned to my sketchbook, starting with a fragment of the Parthenon friezes that depicted an Athenian girl and two priests. I could not reproduce the scene as accurately as I would have liked, and wished that I had paid better attention to the drawing master who had taught me at my mother's house. But, my lack of skill notwithstanding, what better way to spend an afternoon than in a noble attempt to capture some of the Parthenon's exquisite beauty? Every moment that I spent reading, sketching, or wandering through the museum brought me closer to the man I had married, a feeling I welcomed, although I was not quite sure why.

"There is a man waiting to see you, Lady Ashton," my maid informed me as I returned to my rooms following one such excursion to the Louvre. "A Frenchman, madam," she said, wrinkling her nose to show dissatisfaction. "I only agreed to let him wait because he said he was delivering something of Lord Ashton's."

"Meg, we are bound to see Frenchmen occasionally, given that we are in their country. Bring him to me. I'd like to see what he has." A few moments later, she announced a Monsieur Renoir, who carried under his arm a good-size flat package wrapped in brown paper.

"Madame, I was devastated to learn of your husband's death. It was a tragedy indeed." His dark eyes burned intensely. "It pleases me more than you know to be able to deliver to you this picture." He placed the package on a table away from the window. I opened it immediately and was shocked to see my own face.

I couldn't speak. I had heard of the work of the impressionists but had seen few of their paintings. Renoir had captured the essence of my face while bringing to it a beauty I had never seen, colors and light dancing across the canvas.

"How did you paint this?" I sat down. "Please pardon me, but I am rather confused. Obviously, I did not sit for this portrait."

"I hope you do not find it displeasing."

"No. No. It's lovely, Monsieur Renoir."

"Lord Ashton stopped in Paris en route to Africa before his death. He showed me a photograph taken on your wedding day and asked that I paint a portrait of his bride. I had to rely on his descriptions of your coloring. Now that I see the original, I think he did you justice."

"I hardly know what to say. Did you know my husband well?"

"*Oui*, madame. He did not buy his paintings from dealers but directly from the artists. He had an appreciation of impressionism not shared by many, which I like to think shows a greatness of mind. He dined with us whenever he came to Paris."

"I had no idea." I paused. "Did he pay you already?"

"My child, this is my wedding gift to the two of you. I only wish he could have seen it."

"Thank you, sir. I shall treasure it." Monsieur Renoir cocked his head and looked at his painting.

"*Portrait of Kallista*. I think it is one of my finest efforts."

SOON THEREAFTER I ACCEPTED an invitation to tea at the apartment of Cécile du Lac, an older woman to whom I had been introduced at a dinner party. The note she sent struck me as surprisingly charming, and, having passed several rather uneventful days, I agreed to attend. Meg helped me into yet another gray dress and arranged my hair beautifully, all the time lamenting that I was not going to tea with, in her words, "a nice English lady."

I have had the good fortune always to have lived in lovely homes. Large rooms, beautifully furnished, with fine collections of art adorning their walls. Madame du Lac's house, however, was opulent beyond anything I had seen in a private residence. Her quarters surpassed even Buckingham Palace, although that may be more of a comment on the queen's taste than on Madame du Lac's. She received me in a sitting room whose white-paneled walls and ornate ceiling were embellished with gilt flowers, cupids, and caryatids. A large mirror hung above a marble fireplace on which an enormous golden clock rested between two towering golden candlesticks. The parquet floor shone brightly, and the chairs placed around the room were upholstered in a pale, icy blue, all their wood gilded. Curtains in the same blue silk were tied back to reveal long windows. Madame du Lac seemed to belong in another time. Dressed in a flowing tea gown, she ushered me into this pleasantly bright room herself, motioning me toward one of the delicate chairs.

"Sit if you can, child, though how you can manage anything in that corset is a mystery to me." I smiled politely, not having the nerve to say anything. "I'm afraid you shall find my manners somewhat lacking. I am old enough to disregard them. If that makes you uncomfortable, I am sorry for you." She clapped her hands, and two tiny dogs appeared and jumped into her lap.

"I am perfectly comfortable, thank you," I lied, still smiling. One of the dogs began nipping at the lace on her gown, and the other followed his lead.

"Caesar! Brutus! Down!" she cried, removing them both from her dress and putting them on the floor, where they sat nearly motionless, staring up at her. "Do you have dogs?"

"I believe there are some hunting dogs on my husband's estate. I have not been there."

She did not pursue the subject. "I have been interested in speaking to you since seeing the lovely portrait Renoir painted for your husband. Very romantic, I thought."

Had I not been so tightly laced, I would have squirmed in my seat, believing that I was once again caught having to pretend to have had a deep attachment to my poor husband. "He was a kind man," I said noncommittally, wondering how soon I could leave without insulting her.

"You must have to suffer through conversations like this too often.

He was a man whom everyone admired. How terrible for you. You didn't know him long, I believe?"

"No."

"Did you know him at all?"

I froze, unsure what to say.

"Don't be alarmed, *chérie*. I am not judging you. Like yours, my husband died soon after our marriage, and I was plagued by his friends. They all assumed I knew him as well as they did, when in fact I rarely conversed with him. The marriage had been arranged by our parents. We had nothing to do with the decision. After he died, it was quite embarrassing and very difficult to keep up the appearance of having been close to him." Before I could begin to formulate a response to this, Madame du Lac pulled a tasseled bell cord; almost instantly, a servant in full livery that must have been designed to match the room appeared. "I drink only champagne. You do not mind?"

"Of course not." I accepted a glass from her man and started to drink it slowly. Feeling a bit braver, I added that I had never before been served champagne for tea. This comment earned a hearty laugh from my hostess, and I joined in her merriment. The wine loosened my tongue, and soon the whole story of my marriage poured out. Madame proved to be a refreshingly sympathetic listener.

"My greatest difficulty has been just what you said, pretending to know him better than I did. I know that as time passes, people will stop mentioning him, and therein comes my problem. The more I learn about Philip, the more interesting he becomes to me. I made no effort to know him before his death, and I fear that is something I shall grow to regret deeply."

"You had very little time to know the man, Kallista. I shall call you Kallista. It is vastly superior to Emily."

"I assumed him to be transparent, like most people I meet in society. Now instead I find that he was a scholar of sorts, a patron of museums, and a friend to artists. I thought he was a stupid hunter."

"Would you have behaved differently had you known any of these things before your marriage?"

I paused to consider her question. "I don't think so," I said at last. "I don't think I should have had much interest in Greek antiquities or Homer or the impressionists then. My only real concern was avoiding my mother."

"Then the fact that you were not interested in Philip is irrelevant. Had you known about his passions before his death, you most likely would have decided they were boring and wouldn't be able to enjoy them so thoroughly now. They would mean as little to you as his hunting trophies do."

"Perhaps you are right, but now I am filled with an overwhelming urge to learn everything about him that I can. When Mr. Hargreaves told me about the night Philip fell in love with me, I felt something inexplicable."

"Don't fall in love with your dead husband, Kallista. It can bring you no joy." Madame du Lac motioned for the footman to refill our glasses.

"Oh! I would do nothing of the kind. But how can I help wanting to know more about him? Monsieur Renoir said he bought paintings, but there aren't any impressionist works in our house. Perhaps they are in the country, although it seems unlikely. Where could they be?"

"I couldn't begin to guess. Try not to spend too much time worrying about such things. You must enjoy Paris. What are your plans while you are here?"

"I have already achieved my primary goal of escaping London and can now think about what I should like to do next. Mr. Worth is coming to me Tuesday, so I can order some dresses, but other than that I don't really have any plans." Madame du Lac picked up an embroidery scissors out of her workbasket, rose from her chair, and snipped some material from the hem of her curtains. She handed me the swatch.

"Have him design you a dress in this color. I have never before seen anyone so flattered by a color as you are by this shade of blue."

"Madame, I am still in mourning. . . ."

"I insist that you call me Cécile. Otherwise you will make me feel old enough to be your grandmother, which I probably am. Silly custom, mourning clothes. Men wouldn't stand for it. That's why you rarely see them with more than a black armband. But it is different for us, and I surely don't want to see you cut from society. The time will pass quickly, and before you know it, you will be able to wear what you wish."

"Men don't need mourning clothes because their suits are already dreary enough, don't you think?"

"Quite right, Kallista," Cécile said, laughing. "Make sure Worth has the dress ready for you."

I thanked her and slipped the fabric into my bag. All the way back to the Meurice, I felt as if I were floating. As I stepped out of my carriage in front of the hotel, I once again had the unsettling sensation of being watched and was suddenly terrified that I would turn around and see the man with the dueling scar. I glanced furtively over both shoulders but saw no one suspicious; I quickly placed blame on my consumption of champagne too early in the afternoon. The next time I spent an afternoon with Cécile, I would have to insist upon tea.

11 April 1887
Berkeley Square, London

———

Terrible ball tonight. Hargreaves and I managed to leave almost immediately after arriving and spent the rest of the evening at the Reform Club (he steadfastly refused to go to the Carlton, insisting that conversing with the Tory establishment would be even less desirable than dancing in the Duchess of Middleton's too-hot ballroom). He's too bloody political, but as the food is much better at the Reform Club, I readily agreed to his plan.

Anne insists that she must introduce me to her friend, Miss Huxley, who apparently is quite keen to become Lady Ashton. This fact in itself is enough to make my interest in the young lady negligible, despite Anne's assurances of her fine qualities. Perhaps I ought to remind my sister that so long as I am a bachelor, her son remains my heir.

5

MY SOCIAL LIFE IMPROVED CONSIDERABLY AS MY ACQUAIN-
tance with Cécile grew. She included me in her salons and frequently invited me to dine with her on evenings she spent at home. I still chose not
to attend balls or large parties. I suppose that I could have but didn't
imagine I would get much pleasure from watching my peers dance in
lovely, colorful gowns while I sat with the other widows. I would wait
until I, too, could dance.

I soon received a letter from my mother, who was somehow under
the impression that Cécile was related to aristocrats who had narrowly
escaped the Reign of Terror. She encouraged the friendship, implor-
ing me to overlook any eccentricities in view of the connections
I might make. Had she known the sort of connections I made through
Cécile, I am certain that her opinion would have been quite the
opposite.

Before long, Ivy and Robert returned to Paris; I was delighted to see
them again. Ivy left her husband answering correspondence, and we escaped to the Tuileries, where we could converse in private. Walking
along the wide, central path through the park afforded us the best possible views of the garden and its backdrop of the Arc de l'Étoile and Ram-
ses II's obelisk in the place de la Concorde. Although the Bois de
Boulogne was perhaps a more fashionable place to walk, I preferred the
Tuileries, which I could see from my rooms at the Meurice.

"You'll never guess what I did last night," I said. "Cécile took me to
the most wonderful dinner party. It was all artists, celebrating Monsieur
Renoir's recent marriage. Cécile goaded me into drawing a portrait of him

as a wedding gift. I did it in the style of a Greek vase, showing him as Paris carrying off Helen."

"Oh, Emily! You didn't really draw for them? Weren't you terrified?"

"It was all a joke, you see. No one expected me to draw well, and of course I didn't."

"But do you really think you ought to associate with them?" Ivy paused and blushed. "Emily, those women lived with men for years and years without marrying them. I have heard that Alice Hoschedé has a husband but that she and her children live with Mr. Monet. You do need to consider your social standing." Robert's influence clearly had lessened any liberal leanings my friend had before her marriage.

"Cécile moves in the highest circles in Paris. Her association with artists is well known, and no one appears to hold it against her."

"Her situation is somewhat different."

"Yes, her husband has been dead longer."

"That's not what I mean," Ivy continued. "Madame du Lac clearly isn't going to marry again, while you have your whole life ahead of you."

"Ivy, darling, has marriage so altered your mind? I cannot believe you are reprimanding me. Has my mother sent you?" I smiled.

"Perish the thought!" Ivy's chestnut curls bounced as we both laughed. "I admit that being married has changed my opinion on a number of subjects, however. I would so like to see you happy again, Emily."

"I'm quite happy now, Ivy. I do not know when my mind has been more pleasantly occupied. But I will confess to thinking of Philip more than I ever thought I would. It's quite extraordinary. We hardly knew each other, yet he went traipsing about telling his friends he loved me, ordering portraits, bestowing a Greek name on me. I do wish I knew what inspired him."

"Your lovely self, I am sure." Ivy laughed, the dimples on either side of her mouth deepening. "Perhaps he was a hopeless romantic disguised as an adventurous hunter."

"Laugh if you will," I said, my tone growing serious. "But I feel as if there must be some flaw in me. How else did I manage to see nothing in him during the short time we were together? Clearly, he was more perceptive than I."

"I don't think you tried to look, dear. But does it really matter? The material point is that now you know to pay better attention to those around you, particularly to eligible men who fall madly in love with you. Philip certainly didn't lack for female admirers. He chose you from a large number of readily available brides, each backed by mothers nearly as ferocious as your own."

I started to laugh, then stopped abruptly, taking Ivy's arm and pulling her toward me.

"Do you see that man?" I tilted my head slightly to indicate a person who was walking slowly on the opposite side of the wide promenade, not quite behind us.

Ivy nodded.

"I think he is following me."

"Whatever can you mean?"

"I caught him watching me twice in London."

"Are you certain it was the same man?"

"It would be impossible to mistake that scar." His slow pace matched ours perfectly. "Very strange that he would choose to come to Paris at the same time as I, don't you think?"

"Surely it's nothing more than coincidence, Emily. Why on earth would he be following you?"

Before I could respond, my gaze rested on a particularly dashing tall figure striding toward us. I waved when I recognized him, pleased at the opportunity to add a gentleman to our party. The presence of the unknown man had shaken me.

"Lady Ashton, Mrs. Brandon. What a surprise to find you here." Colin Hargreaves bowed smartly as he spoke. "I have only just arrived in Paris myself."

"It's delightful to see you," Ivy replied. "Have you come from London?"

"I had business in Berlin." I accepted the arm he offered, and we continued to walk. "Congratulations on your marriage, Mrs. Brandon. I hope you have found much happiness."

"I have. Thank you." Ivy's china-doll complexion glowed. "Perhaps now that you are here, you can rescue Lady Ashton from the unwanted admirer who she seems to think has followed her from London."

"Who is the unfortunate man?" he asked, looking at me. I searched the path around us but saw no sign of the man with the scar.

"I don't know his name, but it appears that you have scared him off," I said, forcing a smile and trying to appear completely at ease.

"You have no idea who he is?"

"None at all."

"And you have seen him both here and in London?"

"Yes. Once in the British Museum. It was very odd, but I didn't think much of it until I saw him later in Berkeley Square staring at the front of my house. I asked Davis to keep an eye on him. He was there for the entire afternoon."

"Did you report either incident to the authorities?"

"No. It didn't seem that serious. He didn't actually do anything to me," I replied, suddenly feeling rather silly. "Ivy is right. It's merely a coincidence," I said dismissively.

Mr. Hargreaves paused, surveying the scene around us, seemingly satisfied that there were no unsavory characters in the vicinity. "I trust that you are both taking precautions against the cat burglar who has been plaguing the city?"

This mysterious thief had been at the center of Parisian gossip for several weeks. He slipped into houses unseen, stole nothing but the most exquisite pieces of jewelry, and seemed to leave no clues. Often his victims were not even certain when they had been burgled, not noticing that anything was amiss until they looked for a particular necklace or pair of earrings.

"I have nothing with me that would appeal to him," I said. "His taste, from what the newspapers report, runs to things rather more splendid than the jet I'm allowed while in mourning."

"Robert puts my jewels in the hotel safe every night," Ivy said.

"Very good," Hargreaves said, as we continued to walk. "So, Lady Ashton, unwanted admirers aside, has Paris proven the respite you hoped?"

"More than you can imagine, Mr. Hargreaves. I wonder if I shall ever go back to London."

"Understandable, but do remember that you cannot stay here forever. Your villa on Santorini beckons," he said, his deep voice teasingly melodramatic. "How have you been occupying yourself other than strolling in the Tuileries?"

"Emily knows every inch of the Louvre. She spends more time there than you can imagine." Ivy clearly felt pride in my newfound intellectual interests.

"Ivy is too generous," I said. "After all the time I have given to the great museum, I can say with confidence that I know approximately six square feet of its contents. It's overwhelming. One could spend a lifetime in its halls and never see everything. And now my time there shall be limited, because I've decided to begin drawing lessons after having mortified myself in front of Monsieur Renoir." I related the story to Mr. Hargreaves, who was rather amused.

"I am glad to see that you have lost much of your sense of decorum. Excellent. Your mother would be pleased."

"Especially if she knew I was wasting a perfectly good opportunity by talking to one of the empire's most eligible bachelors about such things instead of flirting with him."

"I don't know whether to be flattered at being privy to your academic pursuits or mortified that you do not consider me worthy of flirtation."

"Mr. Hargreaves, if you are free Thursday evening, I should love to have you dine with us at Café Anglais," Ivy said. "Emily will be there, and several of our other friends."

"It sounds delightful, Mrs. Brandon," Mr. Hargreaves said, smiling agreeably.

"He is lovely, Emily," Ivy said with a sigh after he had excused himself to meet the gentlemen with whom he planned to go riding. "I don't know when I've seen someone so striking in appearance. Can't we find someone among our acquaintances to marry him off to? I'd so like to keep him in our circle."

"I believe he has no immediate plans to marry," I replied, finding the prospect of a married Colin Hargreaves utterly loathsome. "He travels a lot and probably prefers his freedom."

"That's what everyone said about Philip before he proposed to you."

"We have already established that Philip was a gentleman of unique character, my dear. To find two such men in so short a time would be more than one could reasonably hope for."

———

Marriage market becoming more and more difficult to ignore. Would prefer to get the boring business of dealing with it over with as soon as possible. Prospect of finding an acceptable wife from the throngs of ladies who present themselves to me on a daily basis does not seem promising—I would like a spouse who is not abjectly stupid. Truth be told, I really want a wife who captivates me, but as producing an heir is my paramount concern, I shan't have the luxury of gallivanting about in search of my Helen. It would take too long and almost certainly be a futile endeavour.

Debated with Lord Palmer for nearly two hours this evening after dinner (terrible food). Have not yet persuaded him to give serious consideration to my theory that Achilles is a noble man who is in impossible circumstances. His tantrums, seemingly narcissistic behaviour, and antisocial tendencies are the result of what has happened to him, not a flaw in character. Could we expect any man, even Achilles, to have behaved differently?

6

DINNER AT CAFÉ ANGLAIS NEVER FAILED TO DELIGHT ME, and on the evening of Ivy's party, the esteemed chef outdid himself. Ivy spared no expense on the menu, and I am convinced that we had a meal nearly as extravagant as "Le Dîner des Trois Empereurs" hosted years ago by the restaurant. If anything, ours was better. Czar Alexander II had complained that he did not have foie gras; the chef told him it was out of season. Not so for us on that evening. I have no idea how, but the staff managed to find foie gras in the summer. Every course was exquisite, but it was the simple preparation of the delicacy for which the czar had longed that brought me unprecedented bliss. It was smoother than butter in my mouth.

The party broke up quickly after dessert. Colin offered to escort me home and asked the waiter to get us a cab, but when we stepped out of the restaurant, I asked if we could walk instead. The evening was cool, and the air felt marvelous, especially after I had so thoroughly stuffed myself. The atmosphere of the city bore little similarity to that of London. In Paris one felt buoyed by a sweeping energy that intensified emotions, made colors softer, and seemed to make even the act of drawing breath a tactile pleasure.

"I mean it when I say I have no desire to return to London," I said, looking up at the clear sky.

"I am quite in sympathy with you, although I would not discount the pleasures of London so completely. I do not think you have had the opportunity to thoroughly investigate them."

"I know you are correct, but I cannot separate London from my mother, and until that is possible, I shall never be comfortable there."

"I think if you agreed to marry an old, crusty duke with a large fortune, produced several dozen children, and asked for her advice on every possible occasion, you would get along with her famously."

I laughed. "You appear to spend little time in England. What do you do?"

"Nothing too different from your husband."

"You'll forgive me, Mr. Hargreaves, but we weren't married long. I can't say that I really know what Philip did, other than hunt in Africa."

"That certainly encompassed a lot of our time, although recently more of Ashton's than my own." His voice grew quiet as he spoke of his friend. "We determined, while at Cambridge, that we would visit every famous site from classical antiquity. Caused quite a scene in the harbor at Rhodes looking for the remains of the Colossus, which, I may point out, don't appear to be there."

"Misguided youth," I said with a smile.

"Quite. I met that fellow Schliemann in Berlin, and he gave me excellent directions to the site he believes is ancient Troy."

"Did you go there?"

"No. We started with the Colossus because we knew a chap at university who was headed for Cyprus and figured we could travel with him as far as Rhodes. After the next term, we went to Rome but soon became distracted from the project as we both took on more responsibilities."

"I should love to see it."

"Rome?"

"No, I quite prefer the Greeks. I'd like to go to Troy."

Colin laughed. "I cannot picture you trudging through the Turkish countryside."

"I thought you had liberal views on what women should be allowed to do. It's not as if I were suggesting joining one of your hideous hunts. I imagine that there aren't wild animals behind every rock in Turkey waiting to charge at helpless humans."

"I wouldn't object in principle to your going to Troy, but I will admit that I don't view you as an adventurous type." His eyes searched my own.

"Beast! You don't know me at all."

"Would you have the wardrobe?" He was laughing, and I realized he was teasing me.

"Isn't Ephesus in Turkey? Perhaps I could visit there on the same trip. I'll send you a note from the Temple of Artemis, where I assure you I will not appear in evening clothes."

"I didn't realize you had an interest in antiquity."

"Philip inspired me."

We had reached the rue de Rivoli and were nearly at the Meurice. "Let's keep walking; I would like to see the river at night." We turned away from the hotel and walked until we reached the Pont-Neuf. The air had grown chilly, and I had not worn even a light wrap; Colin stood near me to shield me from the wind blowing over the bridge.

"Can you imagine how many people have crossed this bridge?" I asked. "It must be three hundred years old. Do you think that Marie Antoinette ever stood here and looked across the Seine at the city?"

"Hardly. I think she would have had a greater appreciation for the views at Versailles."

"We consider this bridge old, but if it were in Athens, would anyone even comment on it? I shouldn't be impressed with anything less than two thousand years old if I were in Greece."

"Then you would miss some particularly fine Roman ruins, my dear. Why don't you plan a nice, civilized trip to Athens on your way to Santorini when you go?"

"I shall have to see how it fits with my plan to visit Troy."

Colin shook his head and took my arm. I let him guide me back to the hotel, but not before contemplating at some length the pleasure I derived from his standing so close to me.

COLIN CALLED ON ME the next afternoon, and I confess I was delighted to see him. I planned to dine in my rooms that evening and invited him to join me. He readily accepted.

"What time shall I return?" he asked. "I'll only need to dress."

"Don't be silly," I replied. "We shan't dress. I ordered a light supper and asked to have it early. It's only the two of us, and I don't think there are society spies lurking to reveal the fact that we intend to dine in afternoon clothes. I imagine that Meg will be suitably shocked, but she'll most likely recover."

"I thought ladies enjoy dressing for dinner."

"I'd enjoy it more if I could wear something other than mourning clothes."

"Yes, I can see that. Nonetheless it does you credit to honor your husband."

"I mean no disrespect to Philip," I said, hesitating.

"Of course not. I know you loved him."

I closed my eyes and sighed.

"I'm so sorry."

"Please do not apologize, Colin. But I cannot live the rest of my life being constantly reminded of my dead husband." I stopped. "I don't mean to sound cold. Do you understand?"

"I think I do," he said, and paused. "I should very much like to have a conversation with you during which I do not feel the memory of Philip looming over us." He looked in my eyes. "Do I offend you?"

"Not at all," I assured him, feeling a strange sort of thrill at being unable to remove my gaze from his. "I did not know Philip as well as perhaps I ought to have. Our marriage was very short."

"It takes considerable time for true companionship to develop," he said. "You need say nothing more on the subject. Tell me your plans instead. When do you intend to travel to Santorini?"

"I'm not sure. Paris has been remarkable, and I have no intention of leaving anytime soon."

"How long do you think you will stay?"

"I don't know. I won't be out of mourning until nearly Christmas, so I can't really do anything until then. I may as well be here as anywhere."

"You're only in half mourning," he said, running his hand through his thick hair, something he seemed to do rather frequently. I wondered if it was this habit that kept him from adopting the style of wearing it slicked back as Philip had.

"Yes, but that's really nothing spectacular. You can go wherever you want, just as long as you make certain not to have too good a time. And no dancing, of course."

"Do you like to dance?"

"I adore it."

"I admit that I've never given much thought to the practices of mourning. Do you think they have helped you manage your grief?"

"Not particularly." I smiled, liking his direct manner. "Tread lightly, my friend, lest our conversation return again to Philip."

"Men do not have to abide by such rigorous rules, yet I cannot believe they mourn their wives less than women do their husbands. Perhaps we ask too much of you ladies."

"A very enlightened comment. I'm most impressed," I said, smiling. "But in all seriousness, I think it's terribly unfair."

Colin leaned back in his chair and stared at me. After some time I wondered if I should speak but found myself mesmerized by his dark eyes.

"Dance with me, Emily," he said quietly.

"What?"

"Dance with me."

"There's no music."

"I'll hum."

"I shouldn't. I'm in mourning."

"You're not dead," he said, standing, never taking his eyes off me. I gave him my hand, and we began to waltz in what little open space my sitting room offered. His grace surprised me, but not as much as the way my skin responded to his touch. The feeling of his hand on my waist caused me to breathe deeply, and when at last he released me, my hands trembled as I stumbled back to my seat.

"I think I should go," he said quietly.

"Yes, you're probably right," I agreed, not sure what to think. "But we haven't had dinner."

"I find that I am no longer hungry." His eyes shone with an intensity I had not seen before in anyone. He kissed my hand, his lips lingering longer than strictly necessary, and rushed from my rooms.

21 APRIL 1887
BERKELEY SQUARE, LONDON

———

Met a stunning girl at the Brandons' last night—Earl Bromley's daughter. Could not dance with her, as her card was already full. Dreaded encounter with Miss Huxley worse than expected. Will have words with Anne for having introduced me to her. Not only is she capable of speaking for fully a quarter of an hour without drawing breath (and on topics so boring that a mere three hours later I can't recall a single one), she has a way of clinging to a chap's arm that suggests she has no intention of ever letting go. Managed to eventually pry her away and sicced her on Hargreaves, who was unable to escape with as much ease as I did, not having the option of handing her off to a more handsome friend.

Have given thought to Lord Palmer's views on Hector v. Achilles and cannot agree. Hector is what man can strive to become; Achilles is that of which he can only dream. Who would not prefer the latter?

7

Soon thereafter I hired, on Renoir's recommenda-
tion, a drawing master called Jean Pontiero to instruct me twice a week.
His mother was French, his father Italian, and the two countries seemed
engaged in an endless battle for his soul. He preferred Italian food,
French wine, Italian music, and French women. Once I learned to decipher his speech, an odd combination of the two languages, we got along
famously. He did not judge my limited skills too harshly; in return, I included a pasta course at luncheon on the days he came to me.

"The view from your rooms is too French. We cannot work here any
longer," he told me one day.

"I'm afraid we shall not be able to escape the French landscape, so we
shall have to make do. Why don't we go sit in the park? It's quite warm
today. A breeze would provide welcome relief." Monsieur Pontiero
sniffed, packed up my drawing materials, and led me to the Louvre,
where he set me to the task of sketching the first of ten paintings by
Francisco Guardi showing Venice during a festival in the eighteenth
century.

"I do have quite a keen interest in antiquities, Monsieur Pontiero.
Perhaps I could draw something Roman instead? The sarcophagus re-
liefs in the Salle de Mécène?" He ignored me and began to lecture on
the use of light in the painting before me. I sighed and began to sketch.
Before long we were interrupted by a short, rather pale Englishman,
whom my teacher quickly introduced as Aldwin Attewater.

"You would be interested in his work, Lady Ashton," Monsieur Pontiero said, smiling. "He copies antiquities."

"Do you really?" I asked. "I should love to see your work. Monsieur Pontiero won't let me draw anything but these landscapes, but I'd much rather sketch Greek vases."

"Black- or red-figure? Which do you prefer?" Mr. Attewater continued without waiting for me to answer. "I'm partial to the black myself. Of course, a mere sketch cannot do such a piece justice, which is why I prefer to reproduce it entirely."

"It also brings a much higher price that way," Monsieur Pontiero added. "Aldwin does a great deal of work for you English aristocrats who are willing to pay exorbitant prices for obvious fakes."

"My work is never obvious," Mr. Attewater replied. "It can be found in some of the world's best museums."

"Perhaps in your imagination, Aldwin. But look at my pupil's work. It is good, no?" Mr. Attewater looked over my shoulder at my uninspired rendition of poor Mr. Guardi's landscape and shrugged.

"Decent form, little passion. Move her to another gallery, Pontiero. If it's antiquities she likes, she should draw them. She is paying you, after all."

"Money, money, that's all you think about," Monsieur Pontiero jibed good-naturedly. "It is the art that matters, and she should start here."

"Your husband was the Viscount Ashton?" Mr. Attewater inquired.

"Yes, he died in Africa more than a year ago."

"I remember hearing that. Please accept my most sincere condolences. I'm certain that he is greatly missed in the art world. He was an excellent patron."

"Thank you, Mr. Attewater," I answered, and proceeded to change the subject. "Do you have a studio in Paris?"

"No, I prefer to work in London."

"The soot in the air helps to give his sculpture an ancient look," Monsieur Pontiero joked as his sharp eyes evaluated my sketch. "That's enough for today, Lady Ashton. I can see that you are too distracted to work." He sighed. "I imagine that Aldwin would be happy to lead us through the Ancient Sculpture collection. Perhaps he will allow you to choose the next work he plans to imitate."

"Maybe I will commission the work myself," I said, smiling. Monsieur Pontiero frowned.

"Your money would be better spent on Renoir or Sisley. At least their works are original."

"True," I began, "but if Mr. Attewater can produce an object of exquisite beauty, I'm not sure that his source of inspiration is of much consequence."

"Copying requires nothing more than mechanical skill," Monsieur Pontiero said. "The genius of the artist can never be duplicated. A work done by someone else's hand will always lack the spark of brilliance."

Mr. Attewater grinned. "I don't think you could tell the difference, my friend." They bickered back and forth well into the Greek collection, stopping only when I gasped at the sight of a particularly lovely sculpture of the goddess Artemis.

"You like this?" Mr. Attewater asked. I nodded. "What do you think, Pontiero?"

"It is exquisite."

"Does it contain a spark of brilliance?"

"Yes, it does," Monsieur Pontiero answered quickly. "Don't try to claim that it's one of yours. No one would believe you."

"I could reproduce it well, but it is not mine. Nonetheless, it is a copy, done by a Roman in the style of one done in bronze during the fourth century B.C. by a Greek called Leochares. Would you consider it a fake?"

"Hardly. It's an ancient piece."

"Ancient yes, but a copy of a sculpture more ancient." Mr. Attewater turned to me. "The Romans loved to copy Greek sculpture. Have you been to the National Archaeological Museum in Athens? There you will find *real* Greek statues."

"I shall have to go," I said, still looking at the beautifully carved Artemis.

"You'd prefer Rome," Monsieur Pontiero insisted.

Realizing he was about to embark on another of his monologues on the virtues of things Italian, I quickly interrupted. "Mr. Attewater, do you think our descendants will look at your copies in museums thousands of years from now, appreciating them as art in their own right, the way we do this statue?"

"Don't encourage him," Monsieur Pontiero scoffed. As we turned the corner, I was pleasantly surprised to see Colin Hargreaves seated on a bench at the far end of the gallery. He rose immediately when he saw me, and I introduced him to my companions. As always, he was exceedingly polite, and he asked to accompany us on our tour. Mr. Attewater, however, excused himself.

"I shall have to leave you now," he said. "I have an appointment I must keep. It has been most pleasant making your acquaintance, Lady Ashton."

Soon thereafter Monsieur Pontiero begged our leave to call on his next pupil. Colin took my drawing material from him, and we continued to walk through the museum.

"Please forgive me, Emily, but you should perhaps be a bit more discerning about the company you keep. Aldwin Attewater is not the sort of man with whom you ought to consort," he said in a soft but forceful voice.

"He seemed pleasant enough to me," I retorted, feeling my face grow red.

"Don't be naïve."

"I can't see why you should object to the acquaintance." It astonished me how quickly he was willing to attempt control over this small part of my life. Was this what came from dancing with him in such inappropriate circumstances?

"His profession precludes him from any position of honor."

"I did not think you were the type of man who would consider an artist dishonorable."

"My dear, he is not an artist. He is a forger."

"I don't see that he does anything wrong. Not everyone can afford originals, and I myself would enjoy having reproductions of some of the objects from museums."

"Then make use of the British Museum's casting services, Emily. There is a significant difference between a man who openly copies objects and one who produces forgeries. Mr. Attewater falls into the latter category, and you should not associate with such a man."

"I disagree with you. Mr. Attewater was completely candid about his work. He has no intention to deceive. Furthermore, I would not have expected someone with your liberal views to lecture me on the company I keep. It's not as if I intend to dance with him." I glared at him. He met my stare with one of his own.

"I'm only trying to help you, Emily. I admit I did not expect to receive such an immature response."

"Happily, as you are not my husband, I do not have to give your opinion more attention than I choose," I snapped. "Good day, Mr. Hargreaves." I grabbed my sketchbook from his hand and marched out of the museum, pleased beyond imagining that there was no man to whom I had to answer for my actions.

"HE IS ABSOLUTELY INFURIATING!" I exclaimed to Cécile as we rode in her carriage to a party at Gordon Bennett's house that evening. "Can you believe he had the gall to speak to me like that?"

"I admit it is somewhat surprising, given what little I've heard about him."

"His character is full of hypocrisy, and I shan't waste another moment thinking about him."

"I imagine you won't," Cécile replied sarcastically, not even having the courtesy to pretend to believe me. "I think he's a very interesting man."

"Who cares? Did I tell you the story of Philip's triumphant elephant hunt?"

"Yes, *chérie*, you did. I thought you disliked hunting."

"I do. But it seems that Philip was able to commune with the animals in a way that was truly noble."

"If he really communed with the animals, I would think he wouldn't have wanted to shoot them. I must say that your renewed interest in Philip is somewhere between distressing and morbid. It is time that you move on, Kallista. Philip was a good man, but he is dead. You can get nothing more from him, especially love."

"You're right, of course, but I cannot help regretting that I did not know the man better. He grows more fascinating with every account of him that I hear. Arthur Palmer called on me yesterday and told me that Philip actually arranged to have the son of one of their African guides schooled in England. Apparently the boy speaks quite good English."

"No one questions Philip's excellent character. I only ask that you remember he is dead."

"I know that quite well," I said sharply.

"I think it's what makes him so appealing to you. After all, he's not here to tell you to keep within the confines of good society."

"Well, that certainly doesn't hurt," I admitted, my good temper slowly returning.

"Who is this Arthur Palmer? Is he as handsome as Colin Hargreaves?"

"Not at all! The elder brother, Andrew, got all the good looks the family has to offer. I don't really know him, so I can't comment on his personality. Their father was a friend of Philip's and is marvelous. They studied Greek antiquities together. I quite forgot I promised to locate some of Philip's papers for him. As for Arthur, being Lord Palmer's younger son, he has few prospects. Worse, he doesn't seem particularly bright."

"He'd do well to marry a wealthy heiress."

"He'll have to look elsewhere, I'm afraid. I would never be able to think of him in that way. Besides, I shall never marry again."

"A wise decision, Kallista. Keep control of what is yours. Why does this Palmer's father need Philip's papers?"

"It concerns some work Philip was doing before he died. Lord Palmer would like to complete it and publish it as a memorial."

"Sounds like a fitting tribute," she said with a sigh. The carriage slowed as we approached our destination. "I fear this will be another tedious night."

Happily, her prediction proved to be incorrect; the evening was quite entertaining. Mr. Bennett's house was an exercise in excess, filled nearly to bursting with flamboyant works of art and eclectic objects he had collected on his travels around the world. I do not know that one could say it was a tastefully decorated home, but it did an excellent job of capturing its owner's character.

"Lady Ashton!" I heard a bright voice calling to me.

"Miss Seward, I am so pleased to see you." Miss Seward had caused no small measure of controversy when I first met her at Ivy's dinner party. Her modern ideas had clashed horribly with the more conservative ones of Sir John Harris, a friend of Ivy's parents. Sir John was particularly outraged when Miss Seward, an American who had recently graduated from Bryn Mawr, suggested that I ought to learn read ancient Greek.

"I meant to call on you but have not had a moment to spare. Who is your friend?"

"Madame Cécile du Lac, Miss Margaret Seward," I said, making the introduction. As always when she met a new acquaintance, Cécile quickly evaluated Miss Seward; this time she looked as if she approved.

"*Enchantée*, Margaret," Cécile said. "Kallista has told me about you. Your dress is most interesting. I shall speak to you about it later." She left without another word before Miss Seward could reply.

"Does she disapprove of my gown?" she asked, looking down at what I found to be an oddly attractive dress. Miss Seward had strayed from the constraints of fashion, appearing in a high-waisted Empire gown that clearly required no corset. It was much more flattering and elegant than the aesthetic dresses I had seen in Liberty's, which I always thought gave one the appearance of a rather burdened medieval matron yet must have given the wearer a similar ease of movement.

"Quite the contrary. I imagine she wants to order one, if not several, for herself."

"Clearly she has excellent taste," Miss Seward replied, smiling. "We must get some champagne. It's the only thing capable of making this party worthwhile." She beckoned to a footman, who quickly supplied us with full glasses. "How is your study of Homer coming along?"

"Quite well, Miss Seward. I have considered your suggestion to attempt to learn Greek so that I can read the original, and I intend to hire a tutor when I return to England."

"You will not regret it."

"In the meantime I would very much like to learn your thoughts on the various English translations. Are you free for tea tomorrow afternoon?" We arranged to meet, and Margaret was quickly swept up in a group of Americans. I excused myself and went in search of Ivy and Robert, whom I found talking to Andrew Palmer.

"We have met before," Mr. Palmer said as he kissed my hand. "At your wedding."

"Of course," I replied. "Thank you for the kind note you sent after Philip's death. I appreciated your condolences."

"He was an excellent man and an even better friend. I only regret that we couldn't do more for him in Africa."

"All of you on the hunt provided him with fine companionship and the adventure he loved in his final days. For that I am grateful." As I spoke, I realized that for the first time I was actually comfortable talking about Philip. "He told me numerous times how he enjoyed your company."

"Did he tell you much about our friendship?"

"I must confess that, given the brevity of our marriage, much of what I know about Philip comes from his letters to me. We had hardly been married a few months when he left for Africa."

"Yes, I remember that," he replied with a winning grin. "And now it is my turn to confess. I was quite surprised that he left such a lovely bride so soon after the wedding."

"Don't be a beast, Palmer," Robert interrupted.

"My apologies, Lady Ashton."

"There is no need, Mr. Palmer. I knew the safari had been planned before our wedding date was set. I had no intention of asking him to change his arrangements. Regardless, he was quite adamant that he go."

"Yes." He paused. "I wonder why that was?"

"I believe," Ivy interjected, "that there was something about an elephant, isn't that right, Emily? He'd always wanted to hunt an elephant."

"Yes, something like that, Ivy." I looked back at Mr. Palmer. "I admit to not remembering the particulars, but it did have something to do with elephants."

He laughed. "You are charming! I wonder that he left at all. Don't worry your pretty head with details, Lady Ashton. Suffice it to say that, as always, your husband fulfilled his commitment to his friends, proving himself to be the most admirable of all of us. None of the rest of the bunch could communicate particularly well with the guides. We would have been lost without him."

"He was very dependable," I said, hoping to sound authoritative.

"Do you like Paris?" Mr. Palmer asked.

"I adore it."

"Nothing like London, is it? Much more fun to be had here. Have you been to the theater?"

"No, it doesn't seem appropriate. I'm still in mourning."

"Yes, I noticed your hideous dress," he said, with such a pleasant smile that I could take no offense. "My brother and I are planning to attend a play Thursday night with a merry group of friends. You must join us."

"Don't insist on ruining the girl," Robert interjected with the slightest touch of humor.

"I don't think there's any reason she cannot attend a respectable performance," Ivy said. "It might be fun, Emily. You should go." Robert looked at his wife severely but said nothing.

"I shall consider your invitation, Mr. Palmer."

"I can ask for nothing more," he replied, giving me an exaggerated bow.

"Look, Emily, there is Colin Hargreaves. He looks fine tonight," Ivy confided to me in a low whisper. I had not had the opportunity to tell her of my recent exchange with Colin.

"I'd rather not speak to him," I whispered back. I spotted an acquaintance on the other side of the room and excused myself from the group, but not before Colin reached us.

"Good evening, Lady Ashton."

"Mr. Hargreaves." I could not bring myself to meet his eyes. "Please excuse me." I saw Mr. Palmer grin and raise his eyebrows as I walked away.

When dinner was announced, I, by some misfortune, found myself near Colin, who took my arm and guided me to the dining room.

"Please forgive me," he said in a low voice.

"I have nothing to say on the matter," I replied, trying to ignore the feeling of his arm on mine.

"May I call on you tomorrow?"

"I'd rather you didn't."

"Was I so awful?"

"I already have one father, Mr. Hargreaves. I would prefer not to have a surrogate looking over my shoulder and judging my every move."

"Be fair. I've done nothing of the sort. I only suggested—"

"Yes, suggested that you know better than I whom I should consider an acquaintance."

"You completely misunderstand me."

"Can you explain yourself?"

"Suffice it to say that not everyone you meet here is what he seems to be."

"Should that mean something to me?" I let my eyes meet his.

"Perhaps you could just consider it the advice of a friend."

"I think I can take care of myself."

"I think you are overreacting." We reached the table, and I removed my hand from his arm without speaking, hoping I would not find that he was my dinner partner. I was pleased to see Mr. Palmer appear beside me.

"Hargreaves! Looks like you still don't know how to handle a lady. Has he been torturing you, Lady Ashton?"

"Yes, he has," I replied, enjoying my newfound compatriot's allegiance.

"I assure you my intentions are the best," Colin said. He bowed smartly and went to find his own place at the large table.

"Hargreaves is so handsome that he can get away with any sort of behavior," Mr. Palmer said. "Many have been fooled by his initial show of good manners."

"Fear not that I shall succumb to his wiles." I sat as the footman behind me pushed my chair toward the table. "How lucky that you are seated next to me."

"I've been a bit devious, Lady Ashton, and switched place cards. Will you forgive my blatant dishonesty? I hoped to have the opportunity to speak with you again in order to plead my case concerning young widows attending the theater."

We chatted effortlessly for the entire first part of dinner. Then, not wanting to be rude, I turned my attention to the elderly gentleman seated on my other side.

"I could not help but notice your ring, Monsieur Fournier," I said. "Is it Greek?"

"It is a Mycenaean seal, Lady Ashton," he replied, fingering its gold surface as he spoke. "Found in one of the shaft graves Schliemann excavated. I like to think it belonged to Agamemnon."

"I understand that you have a considerable collection of antiquities?"

"You are correct. Your late husband and I shared a passion for things ancient."

"Did you know him well?"

"No, not particularly, but we met with some frequency, usually when trying to outbid each other for a Greek vase."

"They are exquisite, aren't they?"

"Yes. Do you have a favorite?"

"I do," I replied, smiling broadly. "It's in the British Museum and shows the Judgment of Paris."

"I believe I know the one to which you refer. It's by a very famous painter."

"Yes. It astounds me that we are able to so well identify the works of artists who left no signatures."

"An artist's style is often as recognizable as his signature."

"I know you are correct, but I would never have thought such a thing could be said about Greek vases before I began to study them. To the untrained eye, the painting on them appears rather formulaic."

"Until you begin to notice the details."

"Precisely. And it is just those details that make the Judgment of Paris vase so spectacular. I almost wish Philip hadn't donated it."

"I understand he felt very strongly that the best pieces should be in museums, a sentiment with which I do not entirely agree."

"Why is that?"

"I spend much of my fortune funding archaeological digs. Museums cannot afford the patronage I give. I see nothing wrong with reaping the benefits of my investment." He pulled the ring from his finger and held it in front of me. "Which do you prefer? Looking at it or feeling it on your hand?"

"It is magnificent," I murmured, gently touching its decorated bezel. The scene depicted was one of a group of Greek soldiers pulling the Trojan horse. "But shouldn't scholars have access to pieces like this?"

"I'm happy to allow them to visit my private collection."

"I think that having them in museums ensures that we shall have an-other generation of scholars. People are inspired by seeing them. I know

I am. How is one to develop a significant interest in an ancient civilization without viewing artifacts?"

"That's what books are for. And I do not say that museums should have nothing—just that I should have my pick of the lot. They'd have nothing without my kind, after all."

"Of course you should have something, but perhaps the most significant finds should belong to the museum."

"Your enthusiasm is invigorating, my child."

"Please do not think me impertinent."

"Not at all. Tell me, did Lord Ashton ever locate that bust of Apollo?"

"I'm not sure that I'm familiar with it."

"Fantastic thing, to judge from his description. Said it was attributed to Praxiteles, one of the finest masters of Greek sculpture. You know of Praxiteles?"

"It is impossible to have even a moderate interest in Greek art without becoming immediately familiar with him."

"It would be quite a coup to have anything by such a master in any collection. Lord Ashton was searching for that Apollo everywhere when I last saw him in Paris. Must have been well over a year ago now. Well, if he found it, you've got quite an excellent piece; and if you ever want to sell it, please let me know immediately."

Mr. Palmer leaned toward me. "Tell me you're not interested in those crusty old pots, too."

"I think they're lovely."

"You are too sweet," he murmured. "You simply must come to the theater with me."

———

Regret to say that today marked only the second visit to my desk in the Reading Room. Impossible to accomplish anything during the Season, even after adopting a firm policy of accepting only every fifth invitation. Did read the Duke of Buckinghamshire Sheffield's "Essay on Poetry," so all is not lost: "Read Homer once, and you can read no more; / For all books else appear so mean, so poor, / Verse will seem prose; but still persist to read, / And Homer will be all the books you need." Brilliant thought.

Saw Lady Emily Bromley on Rotten Row this morning. She is a fine horsewoman—anyone who rides so well must enjoy the hunt.

8

"YOU'RE MORE FOND OF HIM THAN I WOULD HAVE EX-pected!" Ivy exclaimed.

"He's loads of fun, Ivy. It's refreshing," I said, refilling our teacups.

"I admit that I liked his idea of going to the theater, but he was terribly blunt about Philip, didn't you think?"

"He meant no harm. He's the first person I've met in years who simply wants to see me enjoy myself. Imagine that!"

"We all want that, Emily. You know that I agree with you completely when it comes to society and its rules, but I'm afraid that Mr. Palmer flouts them rather too much."

"He's high-spirited and says what he thinks. I see nothing wrong with that."

"You don't extend the same courtesy to Mr. Hargreaves when he speaks his mind."

"That is unfair, Ivy. The situations are completely different. Mr. Palmer is trying to expand my horizons, not constrict them."

"Robert says he's a decent man."

"He is amusing and doesn't expect me to play the part of grieving widow."

"I can understand that he has a certain appeal."

"How generous you are," I said, smiling. "He's taking me for a drive in the Bois de Boulogne this afternoon."

"Perhaps I should join you as a chaperone," Ivy teased.

"Widows don't need chaperones, my dear. What a pity it's Meg's afternoon off. She'd be pleased to see me with the son of an English peer.

She's frightfully biased against the French." A sharp knock on the door announced Margaret Seward's arrival; she entered, her arms filled with books.

"I'm sorry I'm so late," she said, depositing the books on a table. "You will forgive me when you see what I've brought."

"It's lovely to see you, Miss Seward," Ivy said.

"You must call me Margaret, as I have no intention of calling you Mrs. Brandon."

"I'd be delighted," Ivy said, and joined me at the table to examine the newly arrived books.

"Greek grammar, history, and philosophy," Margaret announced, holding up individual volumes. "My own notes on lectures I've attended and, should your interests take you even further, an introductory Latin grammar. Greek is magnificent, of course, but you should not overlook Latin."

"This is wonderful, Margaret. Thank you," I said.

"I'm sure you have much of this in your library at home, but I have a terrible habit of making notes in my books and thought you might appreciate the marginalia."

"This makes me wish I hadn't agreed to go out with Mr. Palmer. I'd much rather stay here and read."

"Then stay," Margaret said, slouching into a comfortable chair. "I'd be happy to tell him you're unavailable."

"No, I couldn't," I sighed.

"Is this Andrew Palmer?" Margaret asked. I nodded; she wrinkled her nose and turned to Ivy. "Do you like him?"

"He's from a very good family."

"He doesn't seem particularly interesting."

"Mr. Palmer is the rare sort of man who does not expect a lady to be completely at the mercy of society. I like him very much."

"I will bow to your superior judgment, Emily," Margaret said, grinning. "I suppose there are many stupider men."

"I must be off," Ivy said, glancing at her watch. "If we are to leave Paris tomorrow morning, I must oversee my packing. I'm so sorry not to have the chance to visit with you, Margaret, but I know that you and Emily want to discuss Homer, and that is a subject on which I would have very little to say."

"You should read him, Ivy," Margaret said.

"He's marvelous," I added.

"I shall leave him to the two of you with little regret."

"She is a sweet, simple thing, isn't she?" Margaret observed after Ivy's departure.

"The dearest person I've ever met."

"Well—on to the task at hand. I think you should start by reading this series of lectures given by Matthew Arnold, the first professor at Oxford to lecture in English instead of Latin." She handed a monograph to me as she spoke. "He discusses the merits and shortcomings of various translations of Homer. How long are you going to be in Paris?"

"I have no fixed plan."

"I'm leaving for London at the end of the week to attend a series of lectures at University College. You should consider coming with me."

"I do not want to return to London yet."

"As you wish. If only I knew someone in Paris who could begin to teach you Greek."

"There is no urgency. For the moment I am content with Homer in translation, despite its deficiencies. The poetry captivates me absolutely."

"Understandable."

"I am so grateful for your guidance. We have a little time before Mr. Palmer will call for me, and I fully intend to keep you occupied for every moment I can."

" 'The beauteous warrior now arrays for fight, / In gilded arms magnificently bright,' " Margaret quoted. "Let us begin."

Because our time was so limited, she suggested that we read aloud from Pope's translation of the *Iliad*. Although of the two of us she alone possessed any academic knowledge of Homer's great work, I surprised us both by being able to read it with a remarkably dramatic flair. Margaret was delighted and urged me to stand on a chair, book in hand. I quickly warmed to my subject and found myself speaking in as noble a voice as I could muster:

> *Declare, O Muse! in what ill-fated hour*
> *Sprung the fierce strife, from what offended power?*
> *Latona's son a dire contagion spread,*
> *And heap'd the camp with mountains of the dead;*
> *The King of Men his rev'rend priest defied,*
> *And for the King's offence, the people died.*

So engrossed was I in the poem that I did not notice Mr. Palmer enter the room until he was directly in front of me. The look of amazement on his face made me start to laugh; I lost my balance and tripped off the chair but managed not to fall completely, no small accomplishment in a corset.

"We will have to continue this tomorrow, Emily," Margaret said, laughing.

"I shall have read Mr. Arnold's lectures by then," I replied.

As she departed, Mr. Palmer turned to me. "Dare I ask what was going on here?"

"Best not to." I smiled, taking the arm he offered me.

We went downstairs and set off in his hired carriage. The late-afternoon light is lovely in Paris; I was contemplating its soft tone against the old stone of the city's buildings when my companion interrupted my thoughts.

"You'll excuse my forthrightness, Lady Ashton, but I am struck by your beauty."

"Thank you," I murmured.

"I am pleased that you agreed to accompany me today, even though I suspect you did so primarily to soften the blow of turning down my invitation to the theater."

"Imagine no such thing, Mr. Palmer. I accept and decline invitations as I choose, neither to soothe ruffled feathers nor out of a sense of obligation."

"Excellent. That must be the luxury of being a widow."

"I would hardly consider it a luxury. Had I better sense, I would have adopted the policy while I still lived in my mother's house."

"I see I have found a kindred spirit of rebellion in you."

"I am not a rebel."

"Believe what you want; I will hold my own opinions." We arrived at the Bois and joined the parade of carriages traveling through the park next to footpaths filled with fashionable ladies and gentlemen. Many acquaintances passed us; we waved to all and paused to speak to a few of them.

"There's Lady Elliott. Please don't stop for her," I begged. "She's a great friend of my mother's who has recently arrived in Paris. I haven't responded to her note and would prefer not to see her."

"Are you a poor correspondent?"

"I should say not. Generally I am quite good at replying to letters."

"You mentioned that you and Ashton exchanged letters when he was in Africa."

"Well, as much as was possible. I heard from him more frequently before he actually reached the Dark Continent. I imagine mail service is somewhat lacking in the bush."

"Yes, it is."

"He sent me letters almost daily on the journey from London to Cairo. After that I did not hear from him again."

"Those letters must have brought you great comfort."

"I suppose they did. I've often thought of reading them again. Maybe I shall when I return to London."

"You did not bring them to Paris?"

"No, why would I?"

"No reason. I just thought you might like to have them with you." He was quiet for a while and then laughed.

I looked at him quizzically. "What?"

"I am laughing at myself for being jealous of your dead husband. It pleases me to know that you don't read his letters and journal nightly to console yourself."

"It never occurred to me to consider reading his journal. Really, Mr. Palmer, this is a strange conversation. I'd rather not speak of Philip."

"Of course, Lady Ashton. My apologies. Shall we hunt down Lady Elliott and invite her to join us?"

"Ivy's right—you are a beast."

"Brandon should keep better control of her; I cannot have my reputation so tarnished."

"I think you are tarnishing it yourself," I said.

"And now you laugh at me."

"No, not at you. But it is delightful to laugh again, even with someone who has such bizarre manners."

"I do hope you can overlook my eccentricities. I know I speak too frankly and meddle where I shouldn't. I have no tolerance for superficialities and like to find the honest truth about those I befriend. I should, perhaps, be more delicate when it comes to a subject like you and Ashton. You are too lovely to suffer any discomfort."

"I shall reserve the right to be direct and inappropriate when questioning you at some future time. In the meantime, however, do you see Emma Callum over there?" I had spotted her walking not far from our carriage.

"Isn't she recently engaged?"

"Yes. She's in Paris to select her trousseau."

"Well, I hope she exhibits better taste in choosing it than she did that dress."

"You are terrible, Mr. Palmer."

"Please call me Andrew. I don't like to be reminded of my station in life."

"Very well, Andrew. You may continue to call me Lady Ashton, as I very much enjoy being reminded of mine." He looked shocked. "Surely you know I am joking."

"I do like you very much, Emily."

We drove on, speaking freely to each other and laughing often. The afternoon passed quickly and happily, although the air turned chilly as the sun sank low in the sky. When at last I returned to the Meurice, I was quite cold. I paused at the desk to ask the maître d'hôtel to have someone sent up to tend to my fire, knowing that Meg would not return from her afternoon out for some time. He handed me several letters from England and a note from Colin, which I opened and read as I walked to my rooms. He was leaving Paris and wrote to say good-bye. I forced the paper back into its envelope and fumbled with my key, suddenly realizing that my door was already unlocked. Unlocked and partially open.

Never thought I could be grateful to a dragon like Lady Bromley for anything but am forever in her debt for seating me next to her daughter at dinner tonight. Lady Emily's sharp wit took me completely by surprise—I expected nothing more than the usual trite commentary on the Season. Not sure I managed to say two words of sense to her all evening. Must call tomorrow.

Have found most extraordinary calyx-krater at Leighton's shop; 5th c., probably from Rhodes, depicting an athletic contest. Fournier was there, too; needless to say, bidding war ensued, but his fortune is no match for mine. Sanctimonious bastard. I won and told Leighton to send it directly to Murray at the Museum, knowing this would incense my rival, who hates to see anything go off the market in such a (relatively) permanent fashion. Am regretting this somewhat, as would have liked to keep the vase with my collection, at least temporarily, but could not help myself.

9

I SHALL NEVER FORGET THE SCENE THAT GREETED ME WHEN I opened the door to my suite. Everything was in a state of complete disarray: books strewn about the floor, their pages crumpled and torn; the contents of drawers dumped; my drawing supplies scattered about the room. The magnificent portrait Renoir painted of me had been ripped from its frame. Happily, the canvas itself was not damaged, the only bright spot in a hideous mess. As I stood looking at the painting, the man sent to attend to my fire walked through the open door and rushed to my side.

"Please sit down, Lady Ashton. I will get help immediately." Within a few moments, Monsieur Beaulieu, the manager of the hotel, arrived with a bottle of smelling salts that I quickly refused; I do not faint. I did, however, accept the glass of Armagnac he offered, and before long the police had arrived. Never had I been more grateful for the perfect English spoken by the staff of the Meurice. I speak French fluently, but, upset as I was, it was much easier to answer their questions in my native tongue while Monsieur Beaulieu translated.

"What on earth has happened here?" Andrew burst into the room. "I was in the lobby and heard of the commotion. Are you hurt, Emily?"

"No, I'm fine. It was like this when I entered the room."

"Is anything missing?"

"I really haven't had the opportunity to determine that, Andrew."

"How can I assist you?"

"I'm all right. Monsieur Beaulieu has been remarkably helpful."

"I should hope so, after the security of his hotel has been this lacking. How did the thief open the door?"

"It appears that the lock was forced," Monsieur Beaulieu replied. "I assure you, Mr. Palmer, that the lobby has been fully staffed all day. I am as shocked as you that someone could enter the hotel and do such a thing."

"It's not your fault, Monsieur Beaulieu," I said, looking at Andrew. "Andrew, could you please fetch Robert and Ivy for me?"

"Are they still in town?"

"They leave for Italy tomorrow."

"I wish they were going to London. I could arrange for you to travel with them. You should not stay here any longer." He left the room before I could reply, and soon returned with my friends, who agreed that I should make plans to go home. Nothing had been stolen from my rooms, leading the police to suspect that the burglar had been interrupted mid-task.

"What if he had still been here when you returned, Emily? What then? You really must go home," Robert said.

"There's no reason that I should leave."

"What if he comes back?" Ivy asked.

"Your burglar obviously did not get what he came for," Andrew said. "I believe it's likely that he would come back. Were he simply a sneak thief, he would have taken anything of value, and even if interrupted, would not have left empty-handed. Something would be missing. The fact that nothing is gone indicates to me that this man thinks you have something of great value. Perhaps he did not have time to complete his search of your belongings. At any rate, he'll certainly return."

"If you decide to stay, Lady Ashton, I can have your rooms changed to another location in the hotel," Monsieur Beaulieu said.

"You cannot think of staying!" Ivy interjected. "What if he returns when you are in your room? I cannot bear the thought of it."

I was not wholly convinced but will admit freely that I no longer felt entirely comfortable.

"It does seem odd, doesn't it, that a burglar would have taken the time to remove Renoir's painting from the frame and then left it?" I said.

The most senior police officer looked down at me and winced slightly. "Madame, perhaps his taste in art precluded him from taking such a work."

Two of the hotel staff restored my rooms to their original condition while Meg hovered over them, shooting menacing glances whenever she could. The episode had done nothing to improve her opinion of the French in general, and, unfortunately, she did little to hide her attitude. Robert and Ivy offered to stay in so that I wouldn't be alone, but I refused to let them cancel their plans for their final evening in Paris. Instead I sent a note to Cécile asking if I could spend the night with her. She replied immediately, saying that her carriage was waiting for me outside the Meurice. She had planned to dine in that evening with Margaret, whom she had befriended immediately after seeing her lovely dress at Mr. Bennett's, and assured me that they were both eager to see me.

"*Mon Dieu!*" Cécile exclaimed when I arrived at her house. "My poor girl! Thank goodness you kept your jewelry in the hotel safe."

"Nothing was stolen. It's very odd, don't you think?" I asked after recounting all the details of the incident.

"An inefficient crook, I imagine. I, too, am surprised he did not take the Renoir, but impressionist paintings don't command high prices. Our friends do not receive the level of recognition they deserve."

"I suppose you're right. My sketchbook is destroyed—all the pages torn out and scattered about the floor. Your books, Margaret, are damaged but not unreadable. I'm so sorry."

"Don't think about it. It's nothing," she replied, sitting next to me.

"I am convinced that the man I've seen following me is involved in this," I said. "The police assured me they would search for him but thought it was unlikely that they would meet with any success. But why would he follow me all the way to Paris to break into my hotel? Other than the Renoir, which clearly was not his object, I've nothing of consequence here that I didn't have in London."

"It would have been more difficult for him to rob your house in town. Your servants would have raised an alarm," Cécile replied. "He is not so inconspicuous as our cat burglar."

"Yes, but what if one of my servants was his accomplice? Before I came to Paris, my butler informed me that he had fired one of the footmen for rifling through Philip's desk. I wonder what I possess that is so interesting." I told them about the note I had found in Philip's guide to the British Museum.

"The footman was probably looking for some small trinket to sell. It's not such an uncommon situation," Margaret said. "I doubt he had more nefarious plans. As for the note, it's most likely been sitting in that book for years and years, probably put there by Philip. I don't see how it could possibly be related to what is happening to you now."

"I suppose you are right," I said, not entirely satisfied. "But I would very much like to know the story behind it."

"Are you going to stay in Paris?" Margaret asked.

"I have not decided."

"It would be terrible if you felt you must flee to London after such an occurrence," Cécile said.

"I have mixed feelings about leaving but must admit that I'm quite interested to see if my mysterious friend will turn up again in London. Meg would be delighted to go home, of course. She insists she knew that something dreadful would happen if we stayed in France for any length of time."

"I have my maid looking after her. Odette is charming and very clever; I think they will get along well. Perhaps a small step toward changing her perceptions?"

"It would be nice." I laughed. "But I fear there is little hope of that."

"I think you should return to London," Margaret said matter-of-factly. "But not because I'm afraid the thief will return."

"Why then?" I asked.

"Because I think you would benefit from attending the lecture series

I told you about this afternoon." She turned to Cécile. "Don't you agree?"

"I suppose so, although I'm certain you could find many equally interesting opportunities in Paris, Kallista." She looked at me. "But I think you have already decided that Margaret would make an excellent traveling companion."

"I admit that the idea of the lectures appeals to me greatly."

"Then it's settled," Margaret said in her firm, bright voice. "You will leave with me, and I will depend on you to offer me asylum at regular intervals. I'm staying with a friend of my mother's who may well bore me to death."

"We must have some champagne. It is, after all, almost your last night in Paris. We are not going out, but we must make something of the occasion." Cécile rang for the footman, who returned with a bottle and three tall glasses. "Has Worth finished your dresses?" she asked as the footman filled the glasses.

"No, but he will send them to his London shop for the final fittings."

"Excellent. I look forward to seeing you in the blue gown."

"Yes, I shall have to return to Paris at once when I'm out of mourning," I said with a smile.

I retired early that evening, more tired than I realized. Margaret and I departed on the first train Thursday morning, and before long we were welcomed to London by a particularly dreary day.

20 MAY 1887
BERKELEY SQUARE, LONDON

———

Dined with Fournier, who is wonderfully furious over losing vase to me. I suggested we view it together in the museum; he was not amused. He is in the process of acquiring several pieces of gold jewellery found at Mycenae. I wonder at the channels through which such things become available—though he assured me the provenance is beyond reproach.

Rest of the day spent on mundane errands. Palmer has goaded me into buying a new horse, which I shall call Bucephalus, and I placed an obscenely large order with Berry Bros. & Rudd. Must keep the wine cellar up to snuff. Was forced to converse with Miss Huxley in the park on my way home. New—faster—horse shall keep me safe from suffering such a fate in the future.

10

I HAD ALWAYS CONSIDERED THE HOUSE IN BERKELEY Square as Philip's and, even after living in it for more than two years, thought of myself as a visitor. Upon returning from Paris, however, I felt the pleasant sensation of homecoming as I looked up at the elegant Georgian edifice, with its classical lines and tall windows. The entire upstairs staff queued up next to the baroque staircase in the entrance hall to welcome me back, and Davis seemed genuinely pleased to see me return. He assured me that everyone on staff would be on the alert for any sign of the man who had followed me and that it would not be possible for the thief, whoever he was, to break into my house. Cook outdid herself at dinner. According to the lower footman, who had a tendency to speak to me while he served, she wanted to make sure that I felt no culinary loss at my return to England, where she was certain the beef was superior to any that could be found in France.

After dinner I retired to the library and looked for something to read. The book I had carried on my honeymoon caught my eye, and I picked it up as I rang the bell for Davis.

"Would you bring me some port?" I tried to sound nonchalant and a bit sophisticated as I spoke.

"Port? Perhaps your ladyship would prefer sherry, if I may be so bold as to make a suggestion."

"I believe that my husband had a fine cellar, did he not?"

"Yes, madam."

"I see no reason that it should go to waste so long as I am in the house, and I've never cared for sherry."

"Which port would you like, madam?"

I looked at him searchingly. "I have no idea, Davis. Could you make a professional recommendation?"

"The '47 would be an excellent choice."

"That will be fine," I said, noticing that my solemn butler nearly smiled as he disappeared in search of the port. I looked at the book in my hand and wrinkled my nose. *Lady Audley's Secret* was not the book a young bride ought to have taken on her wedding trip, and my mother had forbidden me to pack it. I, of course, had not listened to her and began reading the story of the gorgeous Lucy almost as soon as our train pulled out of Victoria Station. If Philip disapproved, he did not show it, laughing instead when he saw what I was doing. He asked that I promise never to push him down a well, as Lucy did her husband to avoid being exposed as a bigamist. I remember assuring him that, as I had no intention of being married to more than one man, he had little to worry about, but that one never could be too careful around wells. I also noted with some satisfaction that he knew the plot and so must have read the book himself.

Davis returned with my port as I was lost in this memory, and I jumped a bit when I realized he was standing next to my chair.

"Thank you," I said, taking the glass he presented to me. I looked up at him and raised an eyebrow. "Do you think I shall like it?"

"The 1847 was the best vintage of the century, madam. It does not disappoint."

I took a small sip and sat for a moment. "Delicious." Now my butler did smile. "I saw that, Davis. You shall never be able to intimidate me again now that I know you smile." He clearly did not know how to respond. "I've been sitting here thinking about Lord Ashton. You worked for him for many years, didn't you?"

"I was in his father's household when Lord Ashton was a boy."

"I never considered Philip as having a childhood. Silly, isn't it?" No response from the proper Davis. "What was he like?"

"Always getting into trouble, Lady Ashton. Climbing the roof, scaling garden walls, digging huge, muddy holes. Used to mount what seemed to him at the time grand expeditions through the grounds of the estate."

"Then I am pleased to know that he was able to go on real expeditions as an adult."

"Yes, Lady Ashton." He stood silently for a moment. "Will that be all?"

I nodded, and he left me alone. I took another sip of the port, which really was good, and thought how enjoyable it was to behave in a way no one expected. I was trying to picture a smaller version of Philip tromping through the forests of his manor pretending to hunt for elephants when, for no apparent reason, I remembered the Praxiteles bust of Apollo that Monsieur Fournier had mentioned in Paris. Certain that it was not in the house, I went to Philip's desk and took out his journal, which I had put in one of the drawers shortly after it was sent to me from Africa. During our wedding trip, he had written in the book almost constantly and seemed to record many purchases that we made; I hoped to find such an entry for the bust.

Flipping through the leather-bound book, I came across sketch after sketch of various antiquities, but nothing that could be Apollo. Philip's technique was careless at best, but he managed to create a decent impression of the pieces he drew. Finally, toward the end of the volume, I found it: Apollo, hastily drawn, with *"Paris?"* written under him, with no indication that my husband had located, let alone purchased, the bust. I was about to return the journal to its drawer when I noticed a sentence written farther up on the page.

> *K lovelier than ever tonight. She still rarely looks at me when we speak, but am confident this will change. Paris had to convince Helen, after all, and I've no assistance from Aphrodite.*

I decided to read more, going back to the beginning of the volume. Here I found Philip's version of our courtship and marriage, the plans for his safaris, comments on Homer, and general musings about the state of the British Empire. I laughed as I read his account of a dreadful evening spent with the Callums, none of the family attempting to hide their desire that he marry Emma, whose flirting had been particularly disgraceful that night. His lament on the pains of being a gentleman was particularly witty.

Soon came the story Colin had told me of the night Philip fell in love with me. Seeing on paper, in his own handwriting, the description of this event that meant so much to him and went largely unnoticed by me, I felt tears well in my eyes. He considered me his Helen. Of course I had to read more.

That he despised my mother surprised me; that this feeling began because she never left us alone in the drawing room before our marriage thrilled me. What would he have done had we been left alone? I loved the five pages he wrote planning what to say to my father when he asked for my hand, but not as much as those written in joyous rapture after I accepted his proposal.

I closed my eyes and tried with all my might to remember the details of that day. I know I had been arguing with my mother when he arrived and that she'd sat in a corner of the room embroidering, shooting menacing glances at me whenever she thought Philip wasn't looking. I realize now that she must have known he was going to propose; my father would have told her. She was probably terrified I would refuse him.

Distracted from my social duties by anger, I had wandered over to the window and stood in front of it looking into the street. Philip had walked up beside me.

"Emily, it cannot have escaped your notice that my feelings for you have grown daily at an astounding rate." I did not reply. "Never before have I known a woman with such spirit, such grace, and such beauty. When I think of the life I have before me, I cannot bear to imagine it without you." He took my hand and looked intently into my eyes. "Emily, will you do me the honor of being my wife?"

I was utterly shocked. Certainly he had called more often than other gentlemen of my acquaintance, but I had never noticed any particular attachment on his part; I obviously had none. Looking back, I realize that, my primary concern being avoiding marriage, I had never given much consideration to any of my suitors. As I looked at him, and at my mother peering anxiously toward us, I decided I would rather have him than her.

"Yes, Philip. I will marry you."

A bright smile spread across his face, and his light eyes sparkled. "You make me the happiest of men." He squeezed my hand. "May I kiss you?" I nodded and turned my cheek toward him; sitting in the library now, I remembered the feel of his lips against it and the warmth of his breath as he whispered, "I love you, Emily."

> *I thought I would go mad with desire when she presented that perfect ivory cheek for me to kiss. Had her blasted mother the courtesy to leave us alone for even a moment, I would have taken the opportunity to fully explore every inch of her rosebud lips. For that, I am afraid, I shall have to wait.*

I closed the book and placed it on the table beside me. For a moment it felt as if I had been reading a particularly satisfactory novel in which the heroine had won the love of her hero. But I was the heroine, and the hero was dead, dead before I had even the remotest interest in him. I started to cry, softly at first, then with all-consuming sobs that I could hardly control. I went back to Philip's desk and opened the drawer from which I had taken his journal. In it I had also placed a photograph he had given to me shortly after our engagement. I pried it out of its elaborate frame, clutched it to my chest, and ran from the library, up the stairs to my bedroom. Meg rushed in from the dressing room, but I waved her away, falling asleep sometime later, still dressed and holding Philip's picture.

I SHOULD HAVE SPENT the next morning leaving cards for my friends to alert them to my return to town, but I found the idea of doing so completely unappealing. Instead I took both breakfast and lunch in my room and did not ring for Meg to help me dress until nearly one o'clock in the afternoon. My head ached, and my eyes were red and swollen from crying. By two o'clock I had returned to my place in the library to resume reading Philip's journal. While I was in the midst of an admittedly tedious account of a grouse hunt, Davis entered the room.

"Mr. Colin Hargreaves to see you, madam. Shall I show him into the drawing room?"

I felt myself flush. "Tell him I'm not at home."

"Yes, madam." Davis turned to exit the room, and I called to stop him.

"Wait! I may as well see him. Bring him here, Davis. I prefer it to the drawing room."

I did not rise when Colin entered the library, and I barely glanced up to acknowledge his presence. "What a surprise, Mr. Hargreaves," I said coolly.

"I know I'm calling at a beastly hour, but I just saw Arthur Palmer at his club, and he told me what happened in Paris. Are you all right?"

"I'm fine. Thank you for your concern."

"You look truly unwell. Shall I ask Davis to fetch you some tea?"

"No, please. I want nothing."

"This is about more than the break-in, isn't it, Emily? Palmer said you were utterly composed through all of it, yet—forgive me—you look dreadful now."

I gazed at his handsome face and sympathetic eyes and started to cry again.

He knelt in front of me and took my hands in his. "What is it?"

"I . . . I miss Philip, Colin. I really miss him."

"Of course you do, especially after going through such a ghastly experience. Had he been with you, you wouldn't have had to deal with the police yourself or worry about how you would get home."

"No, that's not what I mean." I stood up and walked away from him. "I don't know why I'm telling you any of this."

"I hope you consider me a friend, Emily, in spite of the things I said to you in the Louvre. Please believe me when I say that I never meant to offend you."

"It all seems rather irrelevant now at any rate," I said with a sigh. "You should be the last person I would trust with this information."

"You can depend on me, Emily. I would never deceive you."

"But you were my husband's best friend."

"Whatever he did, Emily, I can help you."

"Whatever he did? I would say that he never did anything; I was the one entirely at fault."

"You? How are you involved? Did it begin on your wedding trip?"

"No, it started as soon as I met him." His dark eyes fixed on my own, and I felt rather confused. "I don't think we are discussing the same subject. To what are you referring?"

"No—please, go ahead. I must be confused. What is troubling you?"

"I never loved Philip. I never even tried to get to know him; I only married him to get away from my mother." I paused and looked at Colin, who stood immobile, his mouth slightly open, as if he were unable to speak. "I see that you are shocked."

"Yes, I am," he said quietly.

"But now, now that he is dead, I have spent more than a year hearing from every person I meet how wonderful he was. I have read his journal, learned of his interests, his passions, and I find myself quite desperately in love with him." Having said it out loud, the statement seemed ridiculous even to me.

Colin moved closer to me, his eyes locked on mine. "I don't know what to say."

"Please don't think me coldhearted. I don't believe I knew myself well enough when he courted me to love anyone. I would give anything to go back and begin again."

"Thank God he never knew. He loved you completely and thought you kept a distance from him because you were innocent."

"I can tell from your tone that you are angry with me."

"Not angry. Maybe disappointed."

"Then you are unfair. My mother raised me, with the express purpose of marrying me off to the richest, highest-ranking peer possible. I never had any say in the matter. I could not study what I wished, could not pursue any interests other than those she thought I should have, and learned years and years ago that romantic feelings would have nothing to do with my marriage. Can you blame me for distancing myself from my suitors?"

"Perhaps not, but one might hope that the woman who has accepted one's proposal would at least try to make the marriage a happy one."

"I never said we were not happy. Quite the contrary. I should never have told you any of this." I stormed across the room.

"I have always thought the upbringing of young ladies to be significantly lacking. Now I have my proof."

"Can you not at least give me credit for recognizing the man he was, even if I have done so belatedly? It is not as if I married him and loved someone else. And believe me, realizing that I love him now, after his death, is punishment enough for anything I have done." Colin stared at the floor and said nothing. "I know I made him happy, Colin." I picked up the journal and shoved it toward him. "Read this if you don't believe me. He was utterly satisfied; pity *me* for missing my chance to share in his bliss."

"I know better than anyone how happy you made him. He told me daily." His eyes met mine again. "I suppose I am disappointed that you have shattered the myth of the perfect marriage for me."

"Really, Colin," I said.

"I am truly sorry for you that you could fail to see such love when it was in front of you." I found the intensity with which he looked at me irritating.

"Thank you. You're an excellent confidant, Colin," I snapped. "I feel much better now."

"You were right. You never should have told me any of this. I am at a loss for what to say."

"Perhaps you could change the subject. When you came in, you thought I wanted to talk about something else. What was it?"

"Nothing, really. I thought it concerned business Ashton conducted on your wedding trip. Clearly I was mistaken."

"Clearly." Evidently I would have to change the subject. "I do have a matter of business of my own with which I could use your assistance. I would like to set up some sort of memorial to Philip, maybe something at the British Museum, I'm not really certain."

"I believe it would be best if you took it up with your solicitor, Emily." I opened my mouth to speak, but he raised his hand and continued before I could form a single word. "Do not imagine I am angry with you. I think, though, that I should like the remainder of my involvement with you to be completely severed from your involvement with Ashton."

"What precisely should I take that to mean?"

"I have a difficult time reconciling the woman before me with the naïve girl my best friend married, and I fancy I should like to keep the two images separate."

"You have completely confused me."

"Then perhaps the two are not as different as I had hoped." I said nothing in response. "Please do not imagine I think less of you after hearing your confession. On the contrary, I admire your honesty." He put his hand lightly on my cheek and left.

I remained standing for a moment after he departed, and placed my hand where his had rested on my cheek; it was as if I could still feel his touch. I dropped onto the nearest chair, wondering why I had spoken to him about such things. Why had I not written a tearful letter to Cécile instead? She would chastise me for falling in love with Philip. If only Ivy weren't so newly married, she might have been a good audience for my grievances. Funny that before her wedding I never minded telling her that I didn't love Philip. Now that she was happily settled, I must have feared she would judge me more harshly than she had as a single woman. I sighed. What Colin Hargreaves thought of me really did not matter in the least, and I did feel better for having told someone the truth.

Soon after Colin's departure, I went to the British Museum; I wanted to look at the Judgment of Paris vase. On my way through the Greco-Roman collection, I saw something that seemed familiar. When I stood before the case, I recognized it as the Praxiteles bust of Apollo. Philip must have succeeded in finding it, a realization that brought me no small measure of satisfaction. I looked at the card next to the object, expecting to see my husband's name listed as the donor. Instead a Thomas Barrett was given credit for the gift. Obviously this was not the bust to which Monsieur Fournier had referred; I must have been confused by the Frenchman's description.

I continued on to my favorite vase and stared at it for a considerable length of time, wishing that my husband were at my side. How I longed to hear his expert opinions on the artifacts surrounding me in the gallery. I vacillated between sorrow and a bittersweet joy at the thought that studying the things he loved could make me know him better than I did before his death. At the same time, I felt a terrible guilt for never having opened my heart to a man so deserving of my love. As I was contemplating my morose situation, Mr. Murray approached me.

"Lady Ashton! I am delighted to see that you have returned from France. Did you enjoy the City of Light?"

"Immensely, thank you. I'm so glad to see you, Mr. Murray."

"You look melancholy today," he said, hesitating slightly.

"I'm feeling rather sorry for poor Paris. I don't think that marrying Helen turned out to be much of a reward."

"I don't think he would have agreed. 'But let the business of our life be love: / These softer moments let delights employ, / And kind embraces snatch the hasty joy.'"

I continued for him. " 'Not thus I loved thee, when from Sparta's shore / My forced, my willing heavenly prize I bore, / When first entranced in Cranae's isle I lay, Mix'd with thy soul, and all dissolved away!' " I smiled.

"Most impressive, Lady Ashton. You have embraced Pope."

"I have begun a study of several translations of Homer. Are you familiar with Matthew Arnold's lectures on the topic?"

"I was there when he delivered them at Oxford. Brilliant man."

"While I think it must be true that Homer can never be completely captured in translation, I am quite interested in whether an English poet can bring to us an experience—emotionally, that is—similar to that felt by the ancient Greeks upon hearing the poem in their native tongue."

"A question that, unfortunately, can never be adequately answered."

"Perhaps, but marvelous to contemplate, don't you think?" I stood silently for a moment, imagining an evening at home with Philip, discussing the topic. Could he have recited some of the poem for me in Greek? That would have been spectacular, although I would not have understood what he was saying. The thought of him doing so, particularly some of the more touching scenes between Hector and Andromache, was surprisingly titillating, and I had to willfully force my attention back to the present.

"Mr. Murray, I have been considering for some time making a significant donation to the museum in memory of my husband. How would I go about arranging the details?"

"I would be honored to assist you in any way I could. Perhaps I could set up a meeting with the director of the museum? You could share with us your ideas and let the solicitors handle the rest."

"Excellent. I shall look at my calendar and send you a note."

"And, Lady Ashton, if you are as interested in Homer as you appear to be, you might want to attend a lecture being given at University College next week by a young scholar, Mr. Jeremy Pratt. I believe he plans to address the differences in translations of the *Iliad*."

"Thank you, Mr. Murray. In fact, I am planning to go with a friend of mine. Perhaps I will see you there."

Back at home that evening, I found that a decanter filled with port had replaced the sherry in the library. Davis, it seemed, had decided to accept my new eccentricities. I rang the bell, and he entered the room almost immediately.

"Thank you, Davis. I appreciate your consideration."

He smiled at me. "I draw the line at the viscount's cigars, madam. Ask for them and I shall give my notice."

31 May 1887
Berkeley Square, London

"What winning graces! what majestic mien! / She moves a goddess, and she looks a queen!"

The future Lady Ashton is found, although I am afraid she is, as yet, not much impressed with me. Expect to have a capital time changing this. I watched her at the ball tonight, every eligible peer in Britain vying for her attention. She danced all night—and how she moves!—but took little notice of her partners, regardless of their titles or fortunes. Had the sublime pleasure of waltzing with her and am convinced that somewhere beneath her demure smile is the only woman I shall ever love. Aphrodite be damned! Paris should have given the apple to Lady Emily Bromley, who forevermore shall be known to me as Kallista.

11

I ALLOWED MYSELF THE LUXURY OF BEING THE DIS-
traught widow for several more days before returning to the realities of
life. As I made the requisite round of calls, I realized that I had begun to
look forward to my friends' mentioning Philip; talking about him brought
me great pleasure now that I genuinely mourned him. I went so far as to
invite his sister, Anne, to stay with me for a few days, and I found her a
great comfort. She regaled me with stories of their childhood and his
years at university, uncovering another facet of him to me. Philip had confided in her and wrote to her frequently when he was not at home. After
hearing her stories and continuing to read his journal, I felt that I had a
nearly complete knowledge of my late husband's character.

Eventually I decided the time had come to go through the rest of
Philip's possessions. Soon after his death, my mother, in a rare moment
of helpfulness, had assisted me in selecting those things he possessed of
sentimental value and setting them aside. Now I needed to remove his
clothing and toiletries from his dressing room. I asked Davis to coordi-
nate this, telling him to dispose of the items in any way he felt appropriate. Before he set Baines and one of the other footmen to their task, I
went into the dressing room myself.

I don't think I had ever gone into that room before. On our wedding
night, Philip and I had entered the bedroom together, and Meg had immediately ushered me into my own dressing room. As she had shut the
door behind me, Philip had pulled it open.

"Take your time, Lady Ashton. I shall be in my dressing room and
will not leave it until you call for me. I only ask that you don't keep me

waiting all night." He smiled. "Please make yourself as comfortable as you can in our room and try to relax." I remember that his use of the phrase "our room" had horrified me, not because of what I knew must transpire between husband and wife but because I realized that I would have no privacy, even when sleeping. I had always loved lounging in my bed, reading the morning post, having breakfast sent up to me; it was one of the rare places I could escape my mother and enjoy solitude. Now was I to have no escape?

Meg had misunderstood my look of panic and offered me a glass of sherry, which I'd blindly accepted and drunk despite my dislike for the stuff. It took her a considerable length of time to undo the nearly endless row of tiny pearl buttons that fastened my dress, and I was thankful for the respite. She unlaced my corset and removed the pins from my hair. Once the lace-covered nightgown was over my head, she left me alone. I sat for a while longer brushing my hair and then went back to the bedroom, where I leapt into the large bed. I tried the pillows on each side before deciding where I would sleep, then sat bolt upright, my skirt billowing around me, put a pillow on my lap, and called for my husband.

I can still recall the sight of Philip in his nightshirt, his hair slightly disheveled, climbing into the bed. He sat next to me and took my face in his hands.

"I am the happiest man in the world." He brushed the hair away from my face and began gently kissing my lips. "You taste like sherry," he murmured.

I remembered my response. "I don't know what you taste like."

"Port" was his reply. I smiled as I thought of this, wondering if it had something to do with my opinion of the drink itself.

Now, standing in his dressing room, surrounded by his clothes, I imagined that I could almost smell him. I closed my eyes as I remembered his soft touch on my body, then took a last look around and went back downstairs, passing Davis in the hall.

"Please try to have them finish quickly," I admonished him, heading for the library; I wanted to read Philip's account of our wedding night and hoped that he had been indelicate enough to write about such a thing. Before my curiosity could be satisfied, the parlormaid interrupted me, informing me that my parents awaited me in the drawing room.

"Good morning, Mother," I said, and kissed my father. "I'm surprised to see you out this early in the day."

"I was so pleased to receive your invitation to dine that I asked your father to bring me here immediately to accept. Besides, we haven't seen much of you since your return from Paris, and I do so want to hear more about your trip."

"Yes, I'm sure you do," I replied skeptically. "We shall have a lively party Wednesday. I've invited Lord Palmer and his younger son, Arthur. Robert and Ivy will be there, as well as Arabella Dunleigh and her mother."

"How thoughtful of you to invite the Dunleighs."

"I never really liked Arabella, but I think that was perhaps due to her close connection with Emma Callum. Now that Emma is getting married, it seems that she has quite thrown over poor Arabella."

"Arabella has been out two seasons without receiving a single proposal."

"Yes, and Emma is marrying a younger son. At any rate, I think Arabella could be rescued from the influence of Emma."

"She might do nicely for Arthur Palmer. But what about the older brother?"

"Andrew is still in Paris."

"I understand you saw quite a bit of him while you were there." Now I understood the reason for her kindness; she had already decided that I should marry Andrew. The rank of his family ensured she would overlook his lack of money.

"Yes, he's quite charming."

"I saw Lord Palmer yesterday, and he informed me that Andrew is besotted with you."

"Be that as it may, Mother, I have no intention of entering into any sort of understanding at this time."

"No, of course not." She beamed. "You would want to wait until you're out of mourning."

"Catherine, stop meddling," my father interrupted. "Leave the girl alone."

"I count only nine guests, child. You need one more gentleman," my mother continued. "I think you are wise not to limit your options. Have you considered Lady Easton's son, Charles? His prospects are spectacular. He's already made quite a name for himself in the House. There's talk he may get a cabinet position in the next government. Perhaps you should include him in the party."

"I've already asked Colin Hargreaves."

"Excellent man, Hargreaves," my father said. "Best man at your wedding, wasn't he?"

"Yes. He was Philip's dearest friend."

"Well, I don't see the point in inviting him." My mother paused. "Unless you were thinking of him for Arabella. What is his income? His family is very well off, I believe. Have you seen his house on Park Lane?"

"Mother! This dinner party is not meant to be an exercise in matchmaking. I am trying to provide an evening of good conversation for my friends. Behave, or I shall drop you from the guest list and have Davis turn you away at the door."

"I never thought I should live to hear my own daughter speak to me in such a manner. Samuel, where are my smelling salts? I think I'm ill." My father, humoring her, put the smelling salts under her nose.

"Go easy on your mother, my dear. She's not as young as she once was," he said. "Why don't we get her some tea?"

I rang the bell. Davis brought the tea quickly.

"How are things progressing upstairs, Davis?"

"We are nearly finished, madam."

"Good work."

"Thank you."

"Find anything interesting?" I asked.

"Yes, in fact, we did. One of Lord Ashton's antiquities."

"Is it a good piece?"

"In my untutored estimation, I would have to say that it is one of his finest. Would you like to see it, madam?"

"Please. Bring it at once."

When he left the room my mother reprimanded me. "You really must keep interactions with your servants to a minimum. It will not do to converse with them, especially in front of guests."

"Really, Mother, Davis's opinions are invaluable to me. Not long ago he recommended an excellent port to me, for which I shall be eternally grateful to him."

"Samuel! We are leaving. I will not sit here listening to this kind of talk."

"It probably is best that you go now, Mother. I'm attending a lecture at University College today and will need to leave soon."

"I don't know what has happened to you, Emily, but I hope you regain your manners before the Palmers dine in this house." She rushed out of the room. My father paused before he followed her.

"I'd like to try that port Wednesday, if you don't mind."

I kissed him and told him I would send him a whole bottle before then. I heard Davis coming down the stairs and went to the door, where I gasped with delight when I saw what he was carrying.

"Apollo!" I cried. "Excellent, excellent. I love this statue. Bring it into the drawing room so I shall have something interesting to look at when I receive boring callers, Davis."

He placed it on a pedestal near one of the windows, and I stood there admiring it. It was a perfect copy of the Praxiteles in the British Museum. The features were so exquisite that I could understand why Philip had searched until he found it and why I could locate no record of the purchase. Its being a reproduction, he most likely spent very little money to acquire it, certainly not enough to merit recording the transaction.

I had no time to give the subject further consideration; if I did not want to miss the beginning of Mr. Pratt's lecture, I needed to leave the house immediately.

Thrilled though I was at attending my first academic address, I am forced to admit that much of what our esteemed speaker said was beyond my comprehension. This did not frustrate me in the least; I had not expected that the experience would be much different. Familiarizing myself with Mr. Arnold's views on various translations of Homer had enabled me to adequately follow Mr. Pratt's lecture, even if I missed some of his finer points. Margaret ably filled in many of the gaps, and I found the entire experience most beneficial. If anything, it inspired me to delve deeper into Homer. Afterward Margaret, who looked a model of sophistication in a smartly tailored suit, introduced me to several members of the Department of Greek and Latin. Those who knew my husband all expressed surprise at seeing his wife attending a lecture, making me wonder what Philip's own thoughts on the matter would have been. I had scant opportunity to contemplate the subject, however, as Margaret was bent on a mission of her own.

"We need to find you a tutor so that you can learn Greek," she said, taking me by the arm and walking me across the hall. "I see several promising candidates." Within half an hour, my friend had bullied an unsuspecting postgraduate student into agreeing to instruct me.

"I'm surprised there were so many ladies at the lecture," I said as we left. "Although I need not tell you that none of my current acquaintances could be counted among them."

"University College is remarkably enlightened. They admitted women to degree courses more than a decade ago. You should consider enrolling."

"I don't know that a university education is what I want," I said. "I think I would rather work on my own than follow someone else's program."

"That's fine, too, I suppose. Just be careful not to lose focus."

"I don't think there's any danger of that happening." We stood outside the lecture hall watching the crowd dissipate. I couldn't help but take note of the fact that no one stood in the shadows watching me. The man with the scar seemed to have abandoned me in Paris.

Called on Kallista today but had the misfortune to do so at the same time as Emma Callum. Instead of being able to forward my suit, I was trapped into escorting Miss Callum home. Such are the perils of the Season.

Have had very smug letter from Fournier—I am certain he is about to purchase something that he knows I would want, but have not been able to ascertain what it is. Cannot find any information from my usual sources. I did, however, get a lekythos—Athenian, mid-5th c.—and a pleasant, though small, statue of Mars. Both would be splendid additions to what I've already got at Ashton Hall. I think I may delay beginning a new gallery in town.

MY DINNER PARTY COULD NOT BE CONSIDERED AN UN-
qualified success despite the flawless food and service provided by my
faithful staff. The turbot in wine sauce, which my mother declared as
fine as that she had enjoyed at Balmoral when dining with the queen,
did not make up for the fact that at the last minute I had decided to invite Margaret, leaving me with an uneven number of guests. This
vexed my mother; she could not tolerate a social function that fell
short of her idea of perfection, no matter how good the food, and she
kept referring to the problems resulting from what she viewed as my
poor planning.

"If only I had known you were coming, Miss Seward, I would have
insisted that my daughter invite another gentleman. How awkward this
is! How are we to know to whom we should speak at dinner? Someone
will always be left out."

"I think the practice of speaking only to one's dinner partner completely dated, Lady Bromley. I prefer conversation with whoever has
something interesting to say." Clearly my mother and Margaret would
not get on well.

Other than the turbot, the only thing my mother seemed to approve
of was my dress. Feeling the loss of my husband keenly, I had decided to
wear unrelenting black that night. The dress, cut beautifully in Mr.
Worth's most elegant lines, showed off my figure to great advantage, a
fact not lost on my mother. It seemed to her that at last I had found a
way to properly mourn Philip while at the same time attempting to attract a new husband.

As for my other guests, if Arabella were to be rescued, it would take far more than a single evening. The number of silly, insensitive remarks she'd made by the time dessert was served had me wondering if she were beyond rehabilitation. Arthur Palmer did not appear to notice her shortcomings and showered her with his own brand of inept attention, which pleased my mother greatly.

"You must be so happy to be back from Paris," Arabella mused as the footmen began to remove the dessert dishes from the table. "I cannot imagine why anyone goes abroad."

"You are not a great traveler?" Arthur asked.

"Not at all. Horrid food, horrid people, and I despise sleeping in hotels."

"I think you would feel differently if you stayed at the Meurice in Paris. The food is delicious, and the kitchen is stocked with every English delicacy you could want," I said.

"Yes, but one still must deal with the French."

"It is perhaps difficult if one does not speak the language," Colin suggested.

"I assure you, Mr. Hargreaves, that I speak French flawlessly. But to deal with the Parisians is nearly impossible in any language."

"I think Lady Ashton will again refer you to the Meurice. The entire staff is fluent in both the language and customs of the English."

"Paris really is lovely, Arabella," Ivy said, her pretty face glowing as she glanced at Robert while she spoke. "I hope you shall have the opportunity to see it."

"Travel provides an incomparable opportunity to improve one's mind," Margaret said.

"But why should I go to Paris to find what I already have in London?"

"Unless, of course, you need to buy clothes," Mrs. Dunleigh said.

"Mr. Worth has a shop in London now, so there's no need even for that," her daughter said, stopping the footman from removing the plate piled with gooseberry tart and meringue cookies in front of her.

"I prefer Mr. Worth to see to my dresses personally, and he, of course, works in his Paris establishment," I replied.

"Really, Emily, I don't know why you are giving Arabella such a difficult time," my mother said.

"I'm sorry, Arabella." I sighed. "I just think there is much in the world you would enjoy if you would only give yourself the chance."

"Lady Ashton has broadened her mind remarkably in the past year," Colin said.

"Don't turn into one of these radical women, Lady Ashton," Lord Palmer admonished me. "The viscount would never have approved."

"How can we ever know that, Lord Palmer? I think a husband would be thrilled to have a wife with such a lively mind," Margaret said.

"I must say that I find Arabella's position charming," Arthur remarked. "I am pleased to find such respect in a woman for the empire."

"Thank you, Mr. Palmer," Arabella said, simpering.

My mother had been trying for some time to catch my eye, indicating that she thought it was time for the ladies to retire to the drawing room. I had no intention of leaving the men alone with my port.

"Are we ready for port?" I asked.

"Splendid, Emily," my father replied. My mother began to stand, tired of waiting for me to take the lead.

"Please sit, Mother. There is no reason that the gentlemen should be deprived of our company in order to have a drink. Besides, I'd like a glass myself."

"That sounds perfect," Margaret agreed. Nine faces stared at us, each of them projecting a varying degree of shock. Colin, to his credit, seemed more amused than anything, but I could see that I had not an ally among the rest of the group.

"I don't think so, Emily," my mother said severely, getting up from her seat. The other ladies, Margaret excepted, followed her. Ivy gave me a pleading look as she left the room, but I stayed in my seat. Davis brought in the port and a box of Philip's cigars. Every glass was filled and drained, but none of the gentlemen would smoke, though I would not have thought the mere presence of ladies would have deterred them. Margaret had no such reservations and puffed away unabashedly. There was almost no conversation, and I felt rather foolish for having chosen such an occasion to go against the conventions of society. Nonetheless, I did not want to admit my mistake; I could hardly go to the drawing room now. Unsure what to do, I sat nervously twirling the port in my glass. Not surprisingly, it was Margaret who broke the silence.

"It amazes me that the other women prefer coffee and the drawing room to this," she said, expertly blowing rings of smoke.

"I don't think they consider it a matter of preference," I said.

"Are we to embark on a tedious discussion of woman suffrage?" Arthur Palmer drawled.

"I wouldn't consider it tedious, but if you prefer to talk about another topic, I would not object," I said, smiling. "Margaret and I attended a wonderful lecture at University College this week. You would have enjoyed it very much, Lord Palmer."

"Was this Pratt's talk about Homer? I'm sorry I missed it."

"Did you agree, Emily, with Mr. Pratt's comment that Chapman's translation of the *Iliad* is so inaccurate as to be useless?" Margaret asked. "I know that you do not read Greek, but I would like to hear thoughts on Chapman's poetry from someone who is not hindered by aggravation with the precise accuracy of the translation."

"As you say, I cannot speak to Chapman's faithfulness to Homer, but it must be agreed that his translation, when considered simply as a poem, presents the reader with a truly noble rendition of the story. The rhythm and sound of his lines is masterful. If the translator's goal was to affect his reader powerfully, he has succeeded."

"I must say in Chapman's defense that, even to someone very familiar with Homer, one is not distracted by inaccuracies in the translation," Lord Palmer said, refilling his glass. "Unless, of course, one is looking for them, which I imagine is what Pratt was doing."

"He was," Margaret replied. "The thing I am most interested in regarding Chapman's translation is his treatment of Achilles as a moral hero. I like to see him get his due."

"Oh, Margaret, really?" I exclaimed. "Achilles possesses not an ounce of humanity; I do not like to see him lauded."

"You deny he is a hero?"

"No, I could hardly do that, but his morality is too black and white, too extreme. Compare him with Hector, who is man at his best, and you will find Achilles completely lacking."

"Except in battle," my friend countered.

"You are, unfortunately, right. I think I could rejoice more in Achilles' victories if his behavior were less—I don't know . . . excessive."

"Not excessive for a battlefield, I think, Lady Ashton," Lord Palmer said, smiling at me. "I do wish Philip were here. I wonder what your reaction would be to his thoughts on Achilles." Before I could ask Lord Palmer what those thoughts had been, his son suggested that we join the ladies. Robert, whose eyes had not left the table since Davis brought in the port, looked exceedingly uncomfortable, while Colin, though silent, appeared content and smiled at me. My father, well pleased with the port, clearly did not care what we did, but, knowing that more than a quarter of an hour had passed, I admitted that the time had come to go to the drawing room. I sighed, dreading the ladies' reaction to my behavior. Colin squeezed my hand reassuringly as I walked past him, but I could not bring myself to look in his eyes.

My entrance into the drawing room was met with icy stares, especially from my mother. Mrs. Dunleigh triumphed openly at my mistake, I imagine thinking it would make her own daughter appear in a better light. Margaret sat down next to her, ignoring the fact that the older woman was trying her best to cut her. My friend would not be so easily rebuffed; she loved a challenge. Robert rushed to Ivy's side as if to keep her from approaching me. At last Lord Palmer spoke, breaking the tension in the room.

"My goodness, Emily," he said, leaning down to look more closely at my bust of Apollo. "You should display this on a sturdier pedestal. This one could fall over if someone were to breathe heavily. What an exquisite piece. I am amazed that Philip kept it for himself. An object of this caliber is the sort of thing he usually donated to the museum."

"You are quite correct, Lord Palmer," I said. "The original of this work is in the British Museum. This is only a reproduction."

"I cannot believe that," Lord Palmer exclaimed. "Philip never purchased reproductions. He felt very strongly about it."

"I assure you that he did in this case. I was in the museum not a week ago and saw the original."

"Don't know that I can trust a woman who drinks port," Lord Palmer said, winking at me. I sighed with relief at this confirmation that he was not completely disenchanted with me. He looked back at the bust and spoke thoughtfully. "It's very strange. I hope he wasn't duped by forgers."

"Forgers?" I asked.

"Yes. There have been rumors for some time of a group making perfect copies of a number of antiquities here in London. It would explain how Philip could have wound up with such a thing."

"The British Museum's casting service makes perfect copies, doesn't it?" I asked.

"Yes, but they are marked as such. Forgers sell their copies as originals."

Before I could inquire further about this fascinating topic, he walked toward my mother, sat down, and was soon engaged in what appeared to be a pleasant conversation. I turned my attention to Robert and Ivy.

"I'm dreadfully sorry, Robert. I don't know what got into me."

"Say no more, Emily. You have been through a stressful time and are not entirely yourself, I fear. Perhaps you should spend some time in Bath."

"Thank you. May I abduct your lovely wife for a moment?" Ivy and I took a brief turn around the room, during which she expressed her abject horror at what I had done.

"I'm afraid you've put your mother back on the marriage path, Emily," she whispered to me. "All she talked about while you and Margaret were in with the gentlemen was how you need the guidance of a husband's firm hand, emphasis on 'firm.'"

"That's why she's in conference with Lord Palmer, I'm afraid."

"I don't know that Andrew would have a particularly firm hand," Ivy said with a wicked smile.

"I have no idea, but I assure you I have no intention of finding out."

"I thought you were fond of him?"

"I am, but I do not plan to marry again. I rather like being the Dowager Viscountess Ashton."

"You are not technically the dowager viscountess, Emily. The new viscount is not Philip's direct heir. And regardless, the role may lose its appeal once Andrew's back in London. I remember how you enjoyed his company in Paris. I think his unconventional nature appeals to you."

"You are right." I smiled. "But that doesn't mean I will marry him."

"We shall see," Ivy said. "But, darling, I am afraid that Margaret is exerting perhaps too much influence on you. I don't think you would have done such a thing if she were not here to encourage you."

"That's wholly unfair, Ivy. I am perfectly capable of being shocking without Margaret's assistance."

"It's wonderful that you have found a friend who shares your intellectual interests. Heaven knows I'm of no use to you in such things. But I worry for you, Emily. Margaret may push you further than you really wish to go." She fell silent as we walked toward the settee where Arabella sat. Arthur Palmer, with whom she had been conversing, excused himself as we approached, and struck up a conversation with Colin about hunting. "Oh, dear, have we offended him, do you think?"

"No," I said, noticing the careful manner in which he had taken leave of Arabella. "I think we have interrupted his courtship."

"I should love to see Arabella happily married," Ivy said quietly as we approached her.

"Arabella, our friend Ivy has become quite an advocate for the married state."

"I am not surprised that Ivy should find happiness as a wife."

"Nor am I. However, I believe her concern now is *your* wedded bliss." After my own mortification over the port, I decided that I had judged Arabella rather too severely and intended to give her another chance. She instantly turned an unattractive shade of the brightest pink.

"I'm afraid I have few prospects, Emily, painful though it is to admit."

"You have clearly won a suitor here tonight," I assured her.

"Mr. Palmer is smitten," Ivy added.

"And you have the force of my mother behind you. When I told her you were coming, she immediately decided that you and the young gentleman should marry. I've yet to meet the man brave enough to defy her." This brought a smile to the girl's face, and even I had to admit that she looked somewhat attractive.

"I expect he will begin visiting you regularly," Ivy said.

Mrs. Dunleigh called to her daughter. Evidently my mother had persuaded her to join my father and herself at a soirée that evening; as far as I knew, the rest of the party planned to attend. No one suggested that I come. At the last moment, Margaret declared it vastly unfair that I would be left home alone, and she stayed with me. We brought the port to the library and took turns reading aloud from the *Iliad* until nearly midnight.

I leaned against the doorway for some time after her carriage pulled away, watching shadows in Berkeley Square. Ever since the break-in, I had watched for the man with the scar, but neither I nor my vigilant staff had caught sight of him. Tonight, however, one of the shadows moved more than it ought. It was he. I stepped down from the doorway and onto the sidewalk, peering into the dark. He was with someone, but the moonlight was not bright enough to reveal the other man's face. Without pausing to think, I rushed across the street and into the park. My long skirts made running difficult, and I nearly tripped as I crossed the square. The men must have heard me coming and had disappeared by the time I reached the spot where they had stood. On the ground I found a single glove made from the finest leather. It had to belong to a gentleman.

21 JUNE 1887
BERKELEY SQUARE, LONDON

Am immensely grateful to the queen for her Golden Jubilee celebra-
tions. Banquet this evening was tedious, as expected, but I managed
to watch the fireworks that followed with Kallista. Between the music
and the explosions, there was too much noise to talk. She did not object
to my holding her hand during the display—I am most encouraged—
now must decide how best to proceed.

Palmer has proven valuable in arranging details of next winter's
safari. Very much looking forward to hunting with him. Fitzroy will
not be one of the party. "Let this example future times reclaim, / And
guard from wrong fair friendship's holy name."

13

I RODE FOR LONGER THAN USUAL THE NEXT MORNING, ALL the while trying to determine how I might find the owner of the glove. There were no markings inside it that might identify either maker or owner. I had little hope of figuring out where it had been purchased. Frustrated, I returned home, where I lingered over a late breakfast looking through a stack of letters that needed to be answered and reading the *Times*. The maid serving me was remarkably attentive. Both tea and toast were perfectly prepared and hot when served, and I complimented Susan on her work.

"All of us belowstairs were rooting for you last night, madam," she replied with a quick curtsy.

"I'm afraid I don't understand," I replied, placing my teacup on its saucer.

"Mr. Davis told us you stayed with the gentlemen, madam. I don't think any of us has ever seen Cook look so pleased. She started planning a special menu for tonight almost at once, said the queen herself would envy it." Susan leapt to attention at the sound of a soft cough behind her back.

"Mr. Andrew Palmer to see you, Lady Ashton," Davis said in his most austere tone. "Are you finished here, Susan?"

"Yes, Mr. Davis, sorry," the maid replied, bobbing another curtsy to me before rushing back downstairs.

"I most humbly apologize, your ladyship. The standard to which I attempt to hold myself was severely compromised by my behavior last night. Please do not think that I encourage gossip among the staff. I—"

"Davis, it's all right. I don't mind. They would have found out somehow, and I'm quite pleased to know that Cook, at least, stands behind me."

"We all do, Lady Ashton."

"Thank you, Davis. Where did you put Mr. Palmer?"

"He's waiting in the drawing room." I finished my tea before going upstairs and paused in front of a large mirror in the hallway to check my appearance. I had not bothered to change after returning from the park; my riding habits had become favorite outfits, as they were the only dresses I owned that would have been black regardless of my being in mourning. I spared no expense on them. The one I donned that day was made from a wool softer than any I had felt before and was cut in a new style, with a vest and jacket over the bodice, all tailored in the most flattering fashion. Pleased with how I looked, I glided into the drawing room.

"Mr. Palmer, how nice to see you. Your father said he expected you soon, but this is quicker than I would have imagined."

"He received my cable late. By the time he read it, I was nearly home."

"And what brings you to me at this ghastly hour? Some urgent business?" I smiled as I sat on a crimson velvet chair.

"Frankly, Emily, I assumed that any woman who dares drink port would never keep to conventions concerning the proper hours to call on a friend."

"Beast." I laughed, but his face turned serious.

"My poor, dear girl. You must have been more upset by the robbery in Paris than I imagined. I shall have to make a point of taking better care of you."

"I don't need taking care of, thank you very much. Furthermore, I don't believe that I have given you permission to do any such thing."

Now *he* laughed. "You are too sweet. But, really, you have shocked society and given me an unexpected thrill. Though you must realize that I wholeheartedly disapprove of what you did." I was not sure if he was teasing me.

"I imagine that by now everyone in London knows what I did, courtesy of the kind efforts of Mrs. Dunleigh."

"Yes, you were the talk of the party last night, but I shouldn't trouble my pretty head about it if I were you. Half the people decided you were crazed with grief over Ashton, the other half that you were out of your wits following the burglary. At any rate, no one will remember nor care in another week. Especially after they hear the news I am about to tell you."

"What?"

"Only the most sensational piece of gossip I've ever heard."

"Tell me!"

"What will you give me in return?"

"Why should I give you anything? You clearly are bursting to share your information."

"I think I deserve something."

"Fine. A glass of my infamous port."

"It's too early in the day for port, naïve girl."

"I didn't mean now." As I looked at him, his appearance appealed to me more and more. He was not strikingly handsome like Colin, whose features reminded me more of the Praxiteles bust than of the typical Englishman. Instead Andrew's face was filled with character that jumped to life when he spoke.

"Will you kiss me?"

"Horrible, horrible man!" I said, laughing. "Of course not."

"Then let me hold your hand in mine when I tell you. It's the least you can do after such a heartless rejection."

I sighed and allowed him to take my hand, enjoying his attentions more than I let him know. "Your story had better be good."

"You do, of course, remember our dear friend Emma Callum?" I nodded. "It appears that her wedding to Lady Haverill's son will not take place as planned."

"Good heavens! Why not?" He held my hand more firmly as I tried to lift it from his.

"Because Emma has eloped to Venice with some Italian count."

"No!"

"Yes. Her father and brother are tracking down the couple even as we speak. She'll never be able to return to England."

"Her father will never cut her off. She'll still have her fortune—and now a title, even if it is Italian."

"You women are dreadfully prejudiced against younger sons. I feel keenly for my poor brother."

"I am sorry for Emma's fiancé. Although there is no doubt that he is out of a bad deal. Perhaps I should be sorry for the count instead."

"You are priceless. May I have my kiss now?"

"Absolutely not," I said, but did bestow on him my most charming smile.

"I'm told you've been seeing a lot of Hargreaves lately. He must be more entertaining than I thought."

"Colin? I don't see him often."

"You know I would never tell you what to do, but you would do well to watch yourself with him. His charm can be deadly."

"I assure you I am not at risk."

"Good. I'm very jealous, you know."

I wondered if I was letting this flirtation go too far but was enjoying myself too much to stop. Andrew could play the game as well as I could, and he was perfectly capable of looking after himself.

"Now, to leave this uncomfortable topic before you persist in breaking my heart further, I do have something serious to ask you." My heart stopped for a moment, as I feared he was about to propose. "My father keeps meaning to get some ridiculous papers from you. Something Ashton was studying? Alexander and Achilles, I think? Are you familiar with this?"

I sighed. "Yes, I am. I have meant to locate them for some time but keep getting distracted." This was the first time I had heard the topic of Philip's work; now I, too, was interested in finding the papers. I wanted very much to know his thoughts on Achilles.

"Why don't you let me help you? Where did Philip keep his papers?"

"In the library. But let's not look for them now," I said, not wanting to search through Philip's papers with Andrew watching me.

"I'm afraid I must press you on the matter. My father is quite set on having the monograph published. Can't imagine that anyone will ever read it. He couldn't invent a more boring topic if he tried."

"That's unfair, Andrew. I find it quite fascinating and would love to read more about it."

"Emily, Emily, I really must insist that you begin your return to society. Clearly you have spent too much time locked up with yourself if you prefer long-gone civilizations to the living one around you now."

"The people in those civilizations were not so different than we are, Andrew, and the art and literature they produced are still meaningful today. Surely even you must be moved when you read Homer." I picked up the *Iliad* and began to read.

Andrew immediately interrupted me. "If you force me to think about prep school, I shall have no choice but to resort to kissing to silence you."

"Then I shall say nothing more. Come with me, and I will try to find what your father needs." We walked to the library, where I sat down at Philip's desk, opened one of the drawers, and pulled out a pile of papers. The manuscript was nowhere to be found. "I'm very sorry, Andrew. Please tell your father that I shall keep looking. It's sure to be filed away somewhere."

"I'd happily do it for you if it weren't such a beautiful day. I want to go riding. Come with me?"

I did not reply.

"Emily? Are you all right?"

I nodded. "Fine, Andrew. Just a bit distracted. What did you say?"

"Want to go riding with me?"

"Not at the moment, thank you." My eyes rested on a small piece of paper, not unlike the one I had found earlier in Philip's guide to the British Museum, that was pushed into the back of the desk drawer. I waited until Andrew left to remove and open it. The handwriting was identical to that on the first note. Its message was brief: *"Grave danger."*

Fournier has had his revenge; purchased a spectacular Roman copy of a Praxiteles discus thrower before I even knew it was on the market. Am devastated. He kindly invited me to view it next time I am in Paris, an opportunity that will come sooner than expected, as I plan to stop there on my way to Santorini in August.

Saw Kallista at Ascot last week; she had little to say to me but at the same time gave no suggestion that my attentions are unwelcome. Her beguiling innocence must explain her actions.

14

I COMPARED THE HANDWRITING ON THE NOTE WITH EVERY document I could find in Philip's desk, carefully analyzing each invoice, receipt, and letter. Nothing matched. Furthermore, my husband's papers could not have been more mundane and gave no indication of what he might have been doing to receive such unsettling correspondence. I locked the note in a desk drawer, next to the other note and the gentleman's glove.

After a quick luncheon, I changed into an afternoon dress and prepared to leave the house.

"Davis? Where is my bust of Apollo?" I asked, adjusting my hat, which, although black, was still rather smart, in the hall mirror before heading to the front door.

"I'm very sorry, madam. The new parlormaid knocked over its pedestal while she was dusting this morning and broke the nose off the statue. I did save the pieces in case you wish to have it fixed," Davis replied as he opened the door for me.

"Thank you, Davis. Don't be too harsh with her; I'm sure it can be repaired adequately," I said, walking out of the house. I had crossed the tree-filled park in the center of Berkeley Square and was heading to Bruton Street when Colin Hargreaves approached me.

"Mr. Hargreaves, where have you been hiding?" I asked.

"I've been meaning to call on you for some time, but business did not allow me the pleasure until this afternoon."

"Well, as you see, I am not at home. In fact, I am on my way to the British Museum."

"Surely you do not plan to walk the entire distance? Your carriage would be much quicker."

"It's a fine day for a walk. I always feel I must take advantage of a sunny day."

"There is something most particular about which I would like to speak with you. May I join you?"

"I don't see why not." I took the arm he offered, and we continued up Conduit Street. As always, his touch made my skin tingle and brought a smile to my face.

"Do you have any record of the antiquities Ashton purchased in the final months of his life?"

"I imagine so; he kept meticulous records. Why?" I thought back to the receipts I had seen that morning. None had been for antiquities.

"No reason in particular. Did he show you the things he bought?"

"No. I had no idea that he owned such things. You know they were not on display in the town house."

"Of course. He had a splendid gallery in Ashton Hall. You haven't seen it?"

"I've never been to the estate."

"That's rather odd, don't you think?"

"I never really thought about it." I looked at him, wondering where this line of questioning would lead. "We returned to London after our wedding trip, and Philip left almost immediately for Africa."

"Did he ever suggest that you go while he was in Africa?"

"No, quite the contrary. He told me that the house was something of a shambles and suggested that I stay in London."

"Surely you could have directed the servants to prepare the house."

"I cannot imagine why you are so concerned about this, Colin." We began walking again. "I passed the fall with Ivy on her parents' estate. Why would I have wanted to sequester myself in Derbyshire, away from all my friends?"

"Do you remember Ashton shopping for antiquities while you were on your wedding trip?"

"No, I don't."

"Did he ever leave you to conduct business during your travels?"

"Yes, he did. Is that so uncommon?"

"No, but it would be of great assistance to me if you could remember what he was doing."

"I never asked him. Why all these questions? Had Philip discovered some new archaeological secret? Some long-forgotten Greek vase?"

"No, I'm not suggesting any such thing. I'm wondering if he left any unfinished business that should be completed."

"It's awfully late to be considering that, isn't it? Lord Palmer has asked me to look for papers on one of Philip's projects. He plans to edit and publish the material. I imagine that any of Philip's nonacademic business has long since been taken care of by his solicitor."

"What sort of papers are they?"

"They're the draft of a monograph. Why are you so interested?"

"I've already said more than I ought." He paused at Tottenham Court Road. "Shall we turn here or continue in Oxford Street?"

"I thought I would go up Bloomsbury Street," I replied. We walked in silence until we reached Great Russell Street, where Colin deposited me at the entrance to the museum.

"Please excuse my questions if they seemed strange. I only want to help." I watched him rush back to the street and hail a cab. I shook my head, curious to know what on earth had prompted him to become so belatedly concerned with my husband's business affairs. Could Colin have written the notes?

Looking at my watch, I realized that I was late for my rendezvous with Lord Palmer, who had promised to give me his own tour of the Greco-Roman collection. Once inside, I found him quickly; I was a bit let down to see that Arthur Palmer, Arabella Dunleigh, and her mother accompanied him, certain that Arthur would have little to contribute to any discussion of classical artifacts.

"Andrew will be disappointed to have missed this party," Arabella said, smiling at me. She wore what had to be her finest afternoon dress, blue and green stripes of gauze and moiré over yellow taffeta, with fine lace cuffs. I don't know that I had ever seen her look so well turned out.

"My brother prefers to spend the afternoon at his club, my dear," Arthur said with a tone of familiarity that surprised me. I would not have guessed that his relationship with Arabella would progress so quickly.

"Then he must not have realized that Lady Ashton planned to join us," Arabella replied. Clearly Arthur's attentions had put her in a generous mood.

"I didn't tell him because I knew that she hoped for a serious discussion today," Lord Palmer said. "Andrew's presence would have detracted from that, I'm afraid."

"Your son's talents lie elsewhere, Lord Palmer," Mrs. Dunleigh said, smiling broadly.

"Yes, I suppose they do," Lord Palmer answered. "Come now, let's begin our tour." I wanted Lord Palmer to show me some simple inscriptions suitable for me to attempt to translate as I studied with my tutor, since I liked very much the idea of working on a text whose original form I could see in the museum. Alas, the rest of our party forced us to move through the exhibits with more speed than I would have wished.

"I'm afraid that I shouldn't have brought the others," Lord Palmer said to me quietly. "I had hoped that the young people would amuse each other and that Mrs. Dunleigh would be too busy playing chaperone to detract from our plans."

"That's all right, Lord Palmer. It's been a wonderful afternoon." I stopped in front of a blue-and-white cameo-glass vase. "This is lovely. Is it Roman?"

"Yes, early first century A.D., I believe. It is one of the more famous pieces in the museum. It must have been nearly fifty years ago now that some . . . ah, intoxicated bloke leaned on the case and smashed the vase. As you see, the museum staff have done a capital job of repairing the thing, although, if I remember correctly, they weren't able to make all the pieces fit."

"That reminds me, Lord Palmer, that my lovely bust of Apollo has lost its nose after a too-zealous dusting by a maid. I wonder if Mr. Murray could suggest a restorer for me?"

"I know several qualified chaps who could help you out. I'll send their names to you. I hope your butler reprimanded the maid."

"Well, it is only a copy, but I'm sure that Davis was as severe as necessary with her."

I turned around at the sound of a shriek from Arabella, who had just spotted the vase.

"I like this!" she cried.

"It is nothing more than a standard Wedgwood, my dear," Mrs. Dunleigh said.

"Not quite," Lord Palmer corrected. "It is the piece that inspired innumerable Wedgwood copies, but they were done in jasperware rather than glass. There was a prize offered to anyone who could duplicate it in glass. The chaps who won were so successful that we are now barraged with cameos in all forms."

"I should love to have something so beautiful for my own," Arabella said.

"You could, my dear, for the right price," Arthur said, his uneven teeth marring his smile.

"Oh, I should never want a copy. I'll follow Lord Ashton's example and stick to originals."

"All originals have a price, Arabella, even those in museums." He laughed, and I looked at him, wondering what he could possibly mean by such a statement. Before I could inquire, he took Arabella's arm and whispered something that made her laugh loudly. Mrs. Dunleigh then asked Lord Palmer if we could see the Rosetta Stone, adding that it was the only thing she considered *really* worthwhile in the museum. I closed my eyes and sighed, realizing that the sooner our excursion ended, the better.

THE NEXT FEW WEEKS found me in Andrew's company more than ever. He took me to the theater, to dinner, and we walked together in the park frequently. At soirées he brazenly monopolized me, something to which I rarely objected. His sarcastic commentary on the scenes before us was always more entertaining than the polite, nonsensical conversation to which I was accustomed. He possessed a seemingly incompatible way of disregarding some rules of society at the same time as he rigorously upheld others. Nonetheless, he grew more charming with closer acquaintance, and I determined that the rules he chose to uphold were the ones he thought would protect me. A foolish effort, of course, but I appreciated it regardless.

My mother did not entirely approve of my spending so much time with Andrew. She liked his family, of course, but felt that I could do better. In her mind, given my own title and fortune, I should be able to attract the most eligible men in the empire. Andrew was heir to a large estate, but one that included very little cash. The property he stood to inherit would make it easy for him to secure generous lines of credit, and I assumed that this was how he, like many gentlemen, supported his flamboyant lifestyle. This, of course, did not impress my mother. The fact that Andrew and I did not observe the social niceties troubled her greatly, and she admonished me to change my behavior lest I ruin my chances of remarriage. Contrary to her intentions, her concerns served only to encourage me.

My becoming more familiar with Andrew did little to fade the specter of Philip's memory; if anything, it intensified it. After spending an evening with Andrew, I would go home to my empty bed keenly missing my husband. How unfair that I had never laughed with Philip, that I had never teased him, that I had never flirted with him. I thought of our wedding trip and how, when I retired before him, I would lie awake anxiously wondering if he would rouse me when he came to bed, always hoping just a bit that he would. Although he did not inspire any passion in me, I did enjoy our physical encounters; if nothing else, they certainly satisfied my curiosity.

The memory of Philip did not trouble Andrew; as far as he was concerned, the dead are dead and it should be left at that. He did speak about Philip periodically and told me many stories about their friendship. As always, I devoured any new information about Philip, and everything Andrew told me confirmed my belief that my husband had been an extraordinary man.

Margaret, though supportive of anything I did in an attempt to reject society, was not overly fond of Andrew. She said he distracted me from my work, an observation that, while not wholly untrue, I considered unfair. I met with Mr. Moore, my tutor, three mornings a week, and he had been both surprised and pleased by my quick progress toward learning ancient Greek. The only point of contention between us was that I wanted to translate Homer; Mr. Moore insisted that I start with the Xenophon, which was written in the standard Attic dialect spoken in Athens. Margaret and I attended numerous lectures, at both the British Museum and University College, and we hoped to descend upon Cambridge in the near future. What, precisely, we would do there, I was not entirely certain, but I had no doubt that Margaret would come up with something marvelous. If Andrew were less than enthusiastic about our plans, he never suggested that I should abandon them.

Though she would not admit it to me, Ivy clearly harbored the hope that I might marry Andrew. My dear friend longed to see me share the happiness the married state had brought her. Nonetheless, although I thoroughly enjoyed the time I spent with him, I still had no intention of marrying; I did not want to relinquish control of my life to anyone.

We lunched together frequently at my house, spending an hour in the library afterward before he left for his club. Ivy felt this to be consummate proof that we were near marriage, despite my protests. I was happy to have someone with whom to dine on a regular basis; being a widow sometimes felt very lonely.

"I don't understand why you spend so much time in the library," Andrew said after one of our lunches. "Why don't we go to the drawing room?"

"I much prefer it here. The wood has such a feeling of warmth, and I find being surrounded by books to be greatly comforting."

"You are a funny girl," he drawled, sliding closer to me on the settee.

"I like thinking of Philip in here. Colin tells me that they spent many happy evenings in this room."

"Spare me Hargreaves's opinion, if you don't mind." He stood up and paced in front of my husband's desk.

"Why do you dislike him so?"

"I don't dislike him; I just have never felt I could trust him."

"Has he done you some grave injustice?" I asked mockingly.

"Not precisely, but he's the sort of man who is very difficult to read. Do you know him well?"

"No, I suppose not, but he's always seemed to be very straightforward. Philip thought his integrity beyond reproach."

"Well, I've always valued Ashton's opinion, but I fear in this case he may have been deceived. Hargreaves spends too much time rushing around on spur-of-the-moment trips to the Continent. If you ask me, he's either up to no good or has a very demanding mistress in Vienna."

"You are too terrible!" I cried. "I rather like Colin."

"And that, my dear, is his biggest flaw." He sat close to me again. "I feel so alive when I am with you."

"I know. I can see it in your face."

"Yet you give me no indication of your own feelings," he said, frowning slightly.

"I am a very respectable widow still in mourning. Please do not try to ruin my character," I reprimanded him, laughing.

"You shall be the death of me," he said, taking my hand.

"Shall I summon help? Or perhaps I should leave you to die so that Arthur inherits. It would be better for Arabella should your brother ever propose," I said, smiling at him.

"I die a thousand deaths in your presence every day," he said, moving even closer to me as he brought my hand to his cheek. "Forgive my impertinence."

"For what?" I asked.

"This," he replied, leaning forward and kissing me fiercely on the lips. I tried to pull back but quickly lost interest in doing so and instead let his mouth explore mine. Eventually I pushed him away.

"You are a beast, and I should insist that you leave immediately."

"But you won't, will you?"

"No. But I will ask my mother to chaperone every time I see you in the future," I said flippantly. I did feel rather uncomfortable and hoped he would leave soon. He stayed another half hour before going to his club. As soon as he was gone, I started to cry, wishing desperately it had been Philip's kisses that I so enjoyed.

———

"Persuasive speech, and more persuasive sighs, / Silence that spoke, and eloquence of eyes."

I am determined to propose to K before the end of the week and must decide what I shall say, to both her and her father. Hargreaves assures me that any reasonable woman would accept me for my wine cellar alone. While I do not doubt that she will agree to marry me, I would like to have an eloquent speech for the occasion. Regardless of my confidence, I cannot help but feel a great deal of anxiety when contemplating such a significant step.

15

SEVERAL DAYS LATER THE RESTORER RECOMMENDED TO me by Lord Palmer delivered my bust of Apollo, beautifully repaired, along with a note. Apparently, because the artisan who completed the work determined that the piece was beyond a doubt a fourth-century-B.C. original, he felt the need to suggest that I take better care of it.

My heart raced as I reread the note. My mind kept going back to the comment Arthur Palmer had made to Arabella in the Roman gallery that any original, including those in museums, could be obtained for a price. Everyone agreed that Philip's integrity was of the highest. Why, then, did he have in his possession a piece that clearly belonged in the museum? I flung myself onto the settee.

Davis, whose entrance I had not noticed, cleared his throat. "Mrs. Brandon, madam." Ivy, stunning as always in a fashionable walking dress, followed him almost immediately, and I embraced her when she came into the room.

"I don't know when I've been so happy to see anyone, Ivy."

"Goodness! I shall have to call more often," my friend exclaimed. "You look a trifle pale, Emily. Are you unwell?"

"I hardly know how to answer that question," I said, my gaze resting on Apollo's perfect face staring at me from a table across the room. I recounted the story to Ivy, still unsure what to make of it.

"So it seems that I am in possession of the original bust, which is supposed to be in the British Museum."

"And the one in the museum is a copy? How could that be?"

"Lord Palmer told me he has heard stories of a ring of forgers rumored to work in London."

"Surely the keepers at the museum would notice the differences between the original and a forgery?"

"I don't think they would have any reason to question a piece after initially acquiring it."

"But how did Philip get the original? He must have believed he was buying a reproduction."

"That, Ivy, is precisely the point that is causing me much anxiety. Lord Palmer insists that Philip would never buy a reproduction. He was adamant in his belief."

"That's not so difficult. The piece came on the market, Philip determined it to be genuine, and bought it. Obviously he did not know it was supposed to be in the British Museum."

"But doesn't that seem odd? It's a striking piece, and, given the amount of time he spent in the Greco-Roman galleries, it seems unlikely that he had never seen it."

"Yes, I agree he most certainly had seen it. But think, Emily, how much there is in the British Museum. A person could never claim complete familiarity with even one collection. Philip probably thought his bust of Apollo similar to the one in the museum but not identical."

"To find two such busts attributable to Praxiteles himself is unthinkable. I've read everything I can about the artist, Ivy. Only one other of his original works has survived. Virtually everything that we know about him comes from Roman copies and ancient texts. An authentic Praxiteles is a treasure. Philip must have known that it belonged in the museum."

"You're not suggesting that he dealt knowingly with these forgers?"

"I hardly know what I'm suggesting." We sat silently for several moments. "I think we must consider the facts before us. I have the original Apollo that Praxiteles made. The one in the British Museum must be a very good forgery."

"Are you absolutely certain that yours is the original? Could the restorer be wrong?"

"I don't think so. He gives his reasoning in his note and says that he showed the piece to several others with whom he works. They unanimously agreed that it is authentic. Lord Palmer would not have recommended them if they were not competent, so I have no reason to doubt their conclusions."

"Is it even possible to copy something so well?"

"It certainly is. Did I ever tell you about a fascinating character Monsieur Pontiero introduced to me in Paris? A Mr. Attewater, whose career is copying antiquities. He was quite confident that his work is virtually indistinguishable from the originals."

"Does Mr. Attewater live in London?"

"He does."

"Perhaps he could go to the museum and look at their Apollo, then let us know if it is in fact a copy? If it is, we could alert the keeper."

"I'm not sure that I want to do that, Ivy."

"Why not?"

"We still do not know Philip's role in this. How did he come to have something that should be in the museum? Given what little we know, it appears that at best he purchased something of dubious provenance, and for a man of his character to have done such a thing would be inconceivable."

"Please forgive me for saying this, Emily. I know that you have grown very fond of Philip over the past few months, but what do we really know of him?"

"That is my concern, Ivy. I know from his diary that he did have strong feelings for me, and the portrait by Renoir confirms his romantic nature. But when it comes to matters of character, what firsthand information do we have?"

"Well . . ." Ivy looked around the room as she thought. "We may have no direct confirmation of excellent character, but I think you would have known if he were really bad, don't you? He treated you well during your marriage."

"He did, but I imagine that many a great criminal mind has the capacity to love a woman."

"Emily! Are you calling him a criminal?"

"No! I'm only saying that his treatment of me cannot be relied on to serve as an ultimate substantiation of his true nature. At any rate, we both know that I did not pay much attention to Philip while we were married. I learned almost nothing about him."

"What has made you believe now that he was a good man?"

"Primarily stories told to me by Lord Palmer and Colin Hargreaves. Andrew, too. However, Colin has been asking me some very strange questions about Philip's business transactions, specifically those concerning purchases of antiquities. I've just been through Philip's papers and found nothing that refers to them."

"Could Colin be collaborating with the forgers?"

"I'd sooner believe that of Colin than of Philip if it weren't for the physical evidence of Apollo. We haven't caught Colin with a stolen artifact."

"But Colin could still be involved. Why else would he be so interested in Philip's purchases? Did your husband have any other antiquities in the house?"

"Not to speak of. There is a vase in the library, but other than that, nothing," I said, shaking my head.

"A bit surprising for someone who was so interested in the subject, isn't it?"

"Apparently he kept his collection at Ashton Hall, where I shall have to visit as soon as possible. Perhaps I can find some documentation there. And I think I shall write to Cécile. Monsieur Fournier told me that Philip was looking for Apollo in Paris. Perhaps Cécile could determine if he did indeed purchase it there and from whom. There must be some simple explanation for the whole thing."

"I hope so, Emily. It would be rather shocking to have to completely reform your opinion of Philip after all the trouble you've gone to falling in love with him."

"You are rather understating things, my dear," I said. "Do you think Robert could spare you in order that you might accompany me to the country?"

"I'm certain he could be convinced." She giggled. "Men can so easily be persuaded."

Much to my surprise, it was Andrew, not Robert, who attempted to undermine our plans. He protested vehemently after receiving a note I sent canceling a trip to the theater.

"I cannot understand why you must rush off to the country, Emily. It makes no sense."

"Why does it have to make sense?" I asked. I felt that telling Andrew of my suspicions would be disloyal to Philip, and I had no intention of explaining my motives. "I haven't seen the house, Ivy will return to her own estate before long, and we have decided to have a bit of an adventure."

"Nonsense." He snorted. "I don't like the two of you traveling unaccompanied."

"We aren't. Miss Seward is coming with us."

"Margaret Seward is hardly the type of woman who is likely to put my mind at ease on any subject."

"Andrew, do not force me to become irritated with you," I said severely, wishing that I had not allowed Meg to lace me so tightly. I could hardly draw breath as I spoke. "Going to visit a house in which I, in a sense, live is hardly dangerous."

"How can you suggest that you live there when you have just admitted to never having seen it?"

"You know very well what I mean. I want to see the estate, and I want to go with my friends. Don't be difficult. We can go the theater when I return."

"I shall miss you," he said, reverting to his usual mode of charm.

"I shall be back in two days." I smiled.

"Before you go," he started. "My father is still waiting for those bloody papers of Philip's. May I come back tomorrow and look for them?"

"I don't see why not. I'll tell Davis to expect you."

5 July 1887
Berkeley Square, London

Can hardly wait to depart for Greece, although things here better than expected.

After days spent agonizing over how best to present my suit, spoke to Lord Bromley at the Turf Club yesterday regarding his daughter. At the end of my rather elegant speech, the old man laughed heartily, got me a drink, and said that it was unlikely I could find a father in England who would not gladly relinquish his daughter to me. Delighted to offer me K's hand and assures me entire family would welcome our marriage. Went to Grosvenor Square today—overjoyed to report that my proposal has been accepted. Paris himself would envy me my bride. . . .

16

"I don't think I truly appreciated how rich Philip really was until now," Ivy said as our carriage approached the entrance to Ashton Hall, Philip's family seat. "How long has it taken us to reach the house from the main road? I feel like I am at Windsor."

"You should never appraise a man's fortune from the outer appearance of his estate, Ivy. Reserve judgment until you have seen the entire inside. Lord Palmer has shut up two of the wings of his country house. Fortunes are not what they used to be."

"That is very true," Margaret agreed. "But these grounds are spectacular, Emily."

"You really ought to spend the holidays here," Ivy suggested.

"I shall have to give the matter serious consideration." I wondered what it would have been like to spend Christmas here with Philip. My family, of course, would have visited, as would his. Did he prefer Ashton Hall or London? I had no idea. I looked at Ivy and smiled, knowing how nervous she was at the prospect of hosting her own holiday celebrations for the first time. Robert's mother had already joined them and evidently had a great many ideas about the renovations the couple were making to her former home. Poor Ivy! Her sweet nature made it difficult for her to stand up to her mother-in-law, but I knew that as time passed, she would find her own mischievous, though harmless, ways of making sure she was the only mistress of her estate.

The carriage stopped in front of the magnificent house, and I looked in wonder for several moments before accepting the footman's assistance in descending to the drive. I wished that Cécile were with us, as the façade reminded me a bit of Versailles, albeit on a slightly smaller scale. Mrs. Henley, the housekeeper, greeted us at the door and began immediately apologizing for the state of the interior.

"I assure you I am not here to judge you, Mrs. Henley. I've only come to take a look at the place; I'm sorry I haven't done so before. I realize that you had very little warning of my arrival."

"His lordship sent so many boxes and asked that they not be disturbed. Emory stacked them in the library." The man standing at her side bowed slightly. "We didn't know what to do with them after we heard of Lord Ashton's death, madam, and didn't want to disturb you."

"Please do not worry yourself, Mrs. Henley. You've done quite well. What are these boxes, Emory?"

"I couldn't say, madam. They arrived quite regularly for several months before your wedding, so I assumed they were items you and his lordship had purchased to redecorate the house." I looked at my friends and raised an eyebrow before replying.

"Would you please take me to the library?"

"Of course, madam."

"Shall I bring you some tea, your ladyship?" Mrs. Henley inquired. "You must be in need of refreshment after your long trip. Those railroads are not as comfortable as they might be."

"That would be lovely, Mrs. Henley." I smiled. Margaret, Ivy, and I followed Emory through a seemingly endless maze of rooms until we reached the largest library I had ever seen in a house. The housekeeper told us it contained more than thirty thousand volumes, a number I would not have believed had I not been standing in their midst when I heard it. Margaret was immediately drawn to them and began investigating the contents of the shelves. Massive fireplaces stood at either end of the room, and the remaining wall space was lined with bookshelves that rose to the ceiling, whose gilded stucco was painted with scenes from Greek mythology. The furniture, although very masculine looking, was made from a light-colored wood, brightening the room. Sunlight poured through tall

French doors that overlooked the gardens behind the house. Altogether it was a very pleasant library. The only fault, as Mrs. Henley had warned us, was an extremely large pile of shipping crates in the middle of the floor.

"What on earth do you think could be in them?" Ivy asked, trying to peer into one.

"Let's find out." I motioned for Emory to open the box nearest to me.

"Shall we try to guess what it is?" Ivy asked. "Hunting trophies?"

"I hope not!" I exclaimed.

"I beg your pardon, your ladyship, but those come in much larger crates," Emory said apologetically.

"Maybe wedding gifts from Philip?" Ivy suggested.

"That hardly seems likely." I smiled. "I'm certain he would have told me of their existence." I thought of the moment on our wedding night when he had presented me with my gift, a delicate ivory brooch set in gold. He gave it to me while we lay in bed under a mountain of down-filled blankets after having, as my mother would say, performed our marital duties. The memory brought a bright smile to my face that quickly disappeared when I saw what Emory held up to me after unwrapping miles of packing material: a lovely statue of the goddess Aphrodite. I looked at my friends knowingly.

"I didn't realize they were antiquities, madam. Would you like to display them with the others?"

"No, Emory. I'd like to open them here and set them up temporarily over there," I said, nodding in the direction of a group of long tables. "I'd like to catalog them before we do anything else."

"Would you like to see the house while I unwrap the rest, madam?"

"That's an excellent idea, Emily," Ivy said. "Shall I ring for Mrs. Henley?" I didn't really want to leave the library but agreed with Ivy nonetheless, knowing that it would take considerable time for Emory to open all the boxes.

"Would you mind if I stay here?" Margaret asked. "It's a spectacular library."

"Not at all. Enjoy the books," I replied. "You may send for someone to help you if you like, Emory," I said as Ivy and I embarked upon our tour.

"Thank you, your ladyship, but Lord Ashton preferred that none of the staff but myself touch his antiquities," Emory replied, standing proudly as he spoke. "Except for Mr. Davis, of course."

Ivy laughed softly as we left the room. "What would Philip say if he knew you allowed a mere parlormaid to dust his bust of Apollo? Especially given the end result?"

"Not amusing," I scolded. The splendor of the house soon captivated me, and for over an hour I forgot about Praxiteles and the forgers. Every room was beautifully furnished in the height of luxury, walls covered in silk, floors carpeted with the finest rugs from the Orient. Not surprisingly, my favorite room was Philip's gallery, which was filled with the most exquisite Greek antiquities I had seen outside of a museum.

"I could definitely live here," Ivy said, sighing.

"It's a magnificent house," Mrs. Henley agreed. "And the family has always been wonderful. The viscount was a bit eccentric, but I imagine you know that as well as anyone, madam. Nothing wrong with poking about in museums, I suppose, but I could do without his hunting trophies. Too many of them, I've always thought."

"The hunting trophies!" I cried. "I had completely removed them from my mind. Take us to them, Mrs. Henley."

When at last we came to the end of a series of long hallways and the housekeeper opened the door, I could barely contain myself.

"Oh, dear, Ivy, this is the most dreadful room I've ever seen!" I cried. "Margaret must see it."

"This is the oldest section of the house, madam, the old medieval hall."

"Yes, that explains the size," I said. The immense room was packed with stuffed and mounted animals of every size and shape; heads of more unfortunate beasts lined the walls.

"There's his elephant, Emily," Ivy said, pointing across the room.

"Mr. Hargreaves was kind enough to arrange for the taxidermy and shipment from Africa," Mrs. Henley said.

"What on earth does one do in a room like this?" I asked.

"If I may, Lady Ashton?" Mrs. Henley said, hesitating.

"Please go ahead."

"The gentlemen liked to come in here with their port and cigars after dinner and exchange hunting stories while they examined the animals."

"There's one occasion on which I would gladly join the ladies in the drawing room," I said, smiling. "I think we shall return to Miss Seward now. Thank you for the tour, Mrs. Henley. The house is spectacular, and you clearly run it well. I'm glad to know that it is in such capable hands." The elderly housekeeper beamed the entire way back to the library.

That evening, after a light dinner, we retired to the library to examine the contents of Philip's crates. My heart sank as I entered the room, the long tables now filled with antiquities. Ivy, who appeared to enjoy playing detective very much, procured paper and pen from a desk and began to record details of each of the pieces. Margaret, equally excited, helped her phrase her descriptions accurately. My mood, however, plummeted quickly. Mixed with the feeling of despair at what my husband might have done was a growing sense of jealousy at Ivy's own happy marriage. I pushed the emotion away, putting myself to work at the task at hand.

There were twenty-seven pieces in all, ranging from small cameos to larger vases and sculptures. The biggest, a marble statue depicting the god Pan, stood nearly as tall as my shoulder. At first glance nothing seemed particularly familiar to me, but then I approached the table farthest from me; on it rested something I would never mistake, the Judgment of Paris vase from the British Museum. I covered my mouth with my hand and sank onto a nearby chair.

1 August 1887
Berkeley Square, London

———

Am packed and ready to depart for Greece tomorrow. Saw K this afternoon—she was very quiet. Dare I flatter myself by thinking that this is because she is sorry to see me go?

Have begun research on a comparative study of Achilles and Alexander the Great (added two more boxes of books to my luggage as a result). Two extraordinary lives—albeit one mythological. I wonder what Alexander might have accomplished had he not died in Babylon? Could he have sustained his blazing success over a longer lifetime?

"Who dies in youth and vigour, dies the best . . ."

17

Now that the sun had set, the room seemed to have grown gloomy, although perhaps the chamber itself was less to fault for my perceptions than was my own humor. Ivy and Margaret, facing the other way, had not noticed my distress, and I didn't have any desire to draw their attention to it. I could no longer avoid the thought that Philip had almost certainly done something illegal; confirmation would come as soon as I could have someone analyze the vase. I remembered Mr. Murray telling me how difficult it had been for Philip to give it up to the museum. I hoped that Philip had commissioned an excellent copy for himself but feared that I would learn only too soon that he had kept the authentic one.

I searched my mind for any memory of my husband that could remotely relate to the matter at hand and returned in thought to a day in Amsterdam. It was the second week of our wedding trip; having finished *Lady Audley's Secret*, I searched to no avail for an English bookstore from which I could purchase another novel. Finally I happened upon a bookstall that had a ragged secondhand copy of *Pride and Prejudice*, which I promptly bought. Philip, engaged in business of some kind, had not accompanied me. Back at the hotel, I showed him my purchase and settled in for a nice read. The next morning at breakfast, he presented me with a beautifully wrapped parcel containing a first edition of the book.

"It is always preferable to have the genuine article, Lady Ashton," he had said with a smile.

The sound of Ivy's voice brought me back to the present.

"What shall I call this, Emily?" she asked. "Perhaps 'Bronze Statue of Man Forgetting Pants'?" She giggled.

"Really, Ivy! I'm shocked," I said, laughing with her. "He's doing the best he can with his cape. He has a rather fine figure, doesn't he? Curly hair like the great Alexander." I looked more closely and moaned. "I've seen this before; it's in the British Museum."

"Are you certain?" Margaret asked.

"Fairly certain. And that vase," I said, pointing toward the Judgment of Paris. "I know without a doubt that Philip donated the original to the museum."

"I don't know that we have any reason to doubt him, Emily," Ivy said, lowering herself onto a settee. "Of course, the presence of Apollo in your house is troubling, but it does not mean that all of these pieces have been illegally obtained. Maybe he did buy copies."

"Or maybe he stole the originals."

Ivy glared at Margaret as she spoke.

"The more I consider the possibility, the more likely I find it," I said, ringing the bell for Emory. "Nonetheless, I will attempt to withhold complete desperation until we can have someone look at these pieces or their counterparts in the museum. I am afraid, however, that when we look, we shall find the twins of each of them there."

"How will you determine which are the originals? Will you take all this back to London?"

"No, I think they should remain here. I'll have Emory box them up and keep them safely out of sight." I looked at Ivy and raised an eyebrow. "Would you like some port?"

"Absolutely," Margaret replied instead. "The situation clearly calls for port."

"Emily! You wouldn't dare! Not after your unfortunate dinner party!"

"No one is here to report our behavior, Ivy." Emory, who responded to my call, showed no sign of shock at my request. Good training enabled him to give the appearance of a man who thought nothing of a young lady's requesting his master's finest vintage port, although when he returned with it, I thought I detected a slight sheen on his brow, as if he were sweating on this cool evening. I watched as Ivy sipped from her glass and exclaimed with delight.

"Why do they force sherry on us instead of this?" she demanded. "It's dreadfully unfair."

"My sentiments exactly, which is why I intend to remove all sherry from my cellar and replace it with whatever port Berry Bros. & Rudd recommends to me. Cécile drinks nothing but champagne. Perhaps port should be my signature."

"Champagne is far less shocking, and I myself have seen Cécile drink wine, tea, and, for that matter, sherry," Ivy retorted.

"Perhaps we should ceremoniously dump out all the sherry from your cellar," Margaret suggested.

"This is dreadful of you, Emily. Robert will never let me drink the stuff. I'd rather that I never knew how much I liked it."

"We shall have to work on social reform slowly, my dear, one husband at a time," I said, smiling.

"Well, don't start with Robert. He'd think me a disgrace."

"I suppose that is what he considers me?" I asked.

"No, like everyone else, he thinks you are lost without Philip."

"I take offense at that, Ivy," Margaret said. "I do not think Emily is in the least lost without her husband."

"I didn't mean us, Margaret," Ivy replied, trying to sound polite. "But the topic brings to mind a conversation I had with Robert this morning, before we left. He saw Andrew at his club yesterday and tells me that the man could speak of nothing but you."

"I find that hard to believe," I said, sipping my port.

"I'm not particularly fond of the image of him sitting around at some men's club talking about you," Margaret said, pulling a book down from its shelf.

"I think he's quite in love with you, Emily. Robert thinks his intentions are serious."

"What makes him say that?"

"Well, he didn't tell me precisely, but it was the overall impression he gave."

"Andrew Palmer is irreverent, funny, knows more gossip than my mother, and as far as I can tell is serious about absolutely nothing. He is loads of fun, and I adore spending time with him, but I could never love him."

"Yet you kissed him," Ivy said.

"Yes, I did, and I'm glad of it. That doesn't mean I'm going to marry him."

"Well, I shouldn't like to be the one to dash his hopes of happiness," Ivy said, settling in with her port and smiling. "Aren't we supposed to smoke cigars with this?"

"Margaret would say yes, but I can't stand the smell of the things, can you?"

"Not really," she said. "Although it does remind me a bit of Robert."

"Are you very happy with him, Ivy?" I asked.

"Married life agrees with me." Her mischievous grin gave way to a demure smile.

"I can see you transformed to matron before my eyes! It's terrifying."

"Robert is very kind to me, and, unlike you, I have no desire to control money and property or any of that sort of thing. I enjoy having him take care of me."

"You are lucky to have found a husband who can be trusted to do that," Margaret said, looking up from the book she was reading.

"It's nice being on a pedestal," Ivy replied. I wondered if she would grow tired of such a relationship, as surely Robert would over time. "Should I swirl this in the glass? It makes me look rather sophisticated, don't you think?"

"You look stunning, as always, but I haven't the slightest idea if it's the thing to do with port. I shall ask Davis when we return to London."

"I think there are few things more comfortable than a good marriage, and I am thankful to have found that with Robert."

"Comfort is certainly important," Margaret agreed, though I could tell from her voice that it would not induce her to settle into such an arrangement.

"Do you love him, Ivy?" I asked. "I mean, really love him? Desperately, passionately? Does he fill your every thought? When you retire to bed at night, do you long for the moment he reaches for you?"

"Well, not exactly. Really, Emily, I think one has to have realistic expectations. I have read all the sordid novels you have, and I remain unconvinced that anyone ever achieves that sort of thing in real life."

"I'm not sure."

"I know you didn't think like this when Philip was alive, but do you feel that way about him now?"

"No, not really. Of course, he is dead, so it's rather frustrating to feel anything for him." I remembered his face as it looked when he kissed me for the first time on our wedding night. "But I will admit that when I look back on things, I feel rather more excited about them than I did as they transpired."

"I'm not entirely sure what you mean. Should I be shocked?" Ivy asked.

"No, not at all. I think that as we experience things, they happen too quickly to be thoroughly analyzed. I am sitting here contemplating the first time Philip kissed me after we were married and realize now how romantic and enrapturing it was. At the time, however, I didn't feel much other than fatigue. Had I been able to step back and observe us, I might have found the scene thrilling."

"But if you had been passionately in love with him, I think you would have felt the thrill. Surely passionate love doesn't require thorough analysis," Margaret said.

"You're right, of course," I replied. I sipped my port and slouched into the chair, but only for a moment. "We must return to the matter at hand. How am I going to determine the status of these things?"

"Will you ask the British Museum to assist you?" Ivy asked.

"No, I would prefer to avoid that for as long as possible. Do you suppose if my husband turns out to have really been a thief, I should be obligated to expose him?"

"I don't see how you could not," Margaret said.

"Perhaps if we determine that to be the case, we can concoct some way to return the original pieces to the museum and no one will be the wiser. Why tarnish his memory now?" Ivy suggested.

"I am going to consult with Mr. Aldwin Attewater. He should be able to tell me what is authentic."

"Can you trust him?" Ivy asked.

"I think I can. He spoke to me quite candidly in Paris. At any rate, I don't have to reveal to him why I suspect the museum is displaying reproductions." I paused. "You know that Colin Hargreaves very strongly warned me off the acquaintance. I do wonder about him. His behavior has been so strange at times. Did I ever tell you that Andrew actually told me to keep away from him? Said his charm could be deadly."

"What on earth could that mean?" Margaret asked.

"At the time I assumed he meant that he would trifle with my emotions; now I question that conclusion. Perhaps Andrew knows that Colin has connections to these forgers. He also told me that he has never felt he could trust Colin. It is almost as if he were warning me," I said, remembering the note I had found. "I wonder if he also warned Philip?"

FOR SEVERAL HOURS after Ivy and Margaret had gone to bed, I sifted through every paper I could find in the library, hoping to locate some documentation of the antiquities. Philip's files were carefully organized, and I quickly found records of those objects displayed in his stunning gallery. There was no mention anywhere of the objects currently in the library, nor any suggestion that he knew of or suspected forgers at work in the museum.

Eventually I retired but still did not sleep. Finding myself alone in

Philip's bed overwhelmed me, and I spent much of the night searching through the contents of the master bedroom. Philip had not been to the house since our marriage, and I felt that the room was a vestige of his bachelor life. His dressing room contained nothing of particular interest; the same could not be said of the bedroom itself. A low shelf standing below the windows across from the heavy four-poster bed held a surprising collection of books, among them *Lady Audley's Secret*, the edition of Beeton's Christmas Annual that contained *A Study in Scarlet*, a catalog of objects from the British Museum, and Shakespeare's *Troilus and Cressida*, as well as a few volumes on the subject of big-game hunting. The selection of books kept in one's bedroom is highly personal and indicative of one's character, and after looking at these, I felt that I knew Philip more intimately than before. I loved the idea that he might have read *Lady Audley* on a blustery evening during which sleep eluded him, and I wished for the chance to nestle beside him with a novel of my own. How delightful it would have been to spend an evening in bed with him, reading and exchanging comments.

Ivy had told me about Conan Doyle's Sherlock Holmes, but I had never read either of the novels. I picked up *A Study in Scarlet* to bring back to London and then noticed a series of leather volumes with unmarked spines identical to Philip's journal. As I suspected, they contained records of previous years of his life. I immediately opened the first book and began to read but stopped before I finished a page. Much though I wanted to know my husband better, I didn't feel entirely right reading his private thoughts, especially those written years before he ever knew me. I opened the book again.

Truly, she is the most beautiful creature I have ever seen and cannot imagine finding more beauty in a single being.

Who was this trollop tempting my future husband? I ground my teeth as I skimmed ahead, jealously hoping that she had died of consumption before the relationship grew serious. No, not consumption; that would take too long and almost certainly ensure the formation of the dreaded attachment. I sighed when I realized I was reading the musings of a fifteen-year-old Philip on the subject of a horse. I replaced the volume on the shelf. It would be naïve to think that Philip had not loved before he met me. The former object or objects of his affection were likely to have had the good sense to return his feelings; reading about it would serve only to remind me of the foolishness of my own behavior toward him.

When Mrs. Henley had unpacked my valise, she put on the night-stand next to the bed the photograph of Philip I now always carried with me. I looked at it and wondered how I could ever doubt his character. No matter what I had found in the library, how could I believe that Philip would knowingly purchase artifacts that belonged to a museum?

Even as I thought this, the seeds of doubt were forming deep in my mind. I never knew him; all I knew now was what others wanted me to believe. I blocked these thoughts, not wanting reality to crush the romantic fantasy I so desperately longed to be true. I tried to imagine Philip dealing in the black market, skulking around with forgers. All this accomplished was to show me that I had a great difficulty imagining him doing much of anything; I didn't know him well enough to improvise his speech, mannerisms, or expressions. Once again the feeling of lost opportunity rushed over me, and I spent the remainder of this restless night crying, clutching the picture of the man over whom I suffered an unbearable feeling of regret.

———

*As always, it is a great relief to escape from the Season in London,
although for the first time, doing so has meant leaving behind someone more dear to me than I could ever have expected. Perhaps next
year will have K join me here.*

*Fournier's discus thrower more exquisite than I imagined.
Retaliated by acquiring two more vases—one depicts the Judgment of
Paris and is perhaps the finest work of its kind. Don't know that I
shall be able to give it up, although there is no question that it belongs
in the British Museum. Also saw Renoir et al. in Paris—bought six
more pictures for the villa. Something in the informality of my
friends' paintings fits beautifully on this unspoiled island. Must convince Monet to come here and paint for me—his views of the caldera
would be incomparable. How I would love to see him attack with bold
brushstrokes the light bouncing on the Aegean.*

18

ASIDE FROM HIS COPY OF *A Study in Scarlet*, THE ONLY thing I took from Philip's bedroom at Ashton Hall was a notebook in which he had recorded information on each of the objects in his collection of antiquities as well as observations on some of his favorite pieces in the British Museum. Back in London, comfortably ensconced in a large chair in the library (no corset for me that evening), I armed myself with the notebook and Philip's journal, resolved that a lively exchange of ideas about ancient Greece could be adequately replaced with reading my dear husband's thoughts on the subject.

Like me, he seemed to prefer red-figure vases to black, finding the detail superior on the former. He mused for several pages about the white lekythoi that Mr. Murray had mentioned to me when he first showed me the Judgment of Paris vase. Philip was struck by the humanity of these pieces, many of which he believed had been made as funerary objects, and wondered about the identity of the figures represented on them. I determined to take a closer look at them the very next day at the museum.

Not surprisingly, he adored any vase that depicted scenes of the hunt. I paused for a moment, considering their appeal, but could not bring myself to reach Philip's level of appreciation and decided to skim through the rest of his thoughts concerning them. Unfortunately, much of the rest of the notebook was filled with notes he had written about hunting in ancient times. I sighed, flipping through pages until I came across a draft of an essay of sorts that he had written about the *Iliad*.

In it I found no mention of the things I loved about the poem: its humanity, its energy, the heroic ideals of its characters. Most unsettling to me was his excessive praise of Achilles.

I had already admitted to Margaret that Achilles' strength on the battlefield was unparalleled. That this impressed Philip did not shock me. However, it overshadowed for him everything else in Homer's great work. He used it to justify Achilles' egotistical fits and could not praise the hero enough for his unwavering sense of morality. While it is true that Achilles' straightforward approach to his world could be considered admirable, I found it immature and overly simplistic. And in all these pages of writing, Philip never once mentioned Hector, except as Achilles' enemy. How could he have so overlooked Homer's most human character? A man who painfully realizes that his best will never be enough, whose heart-wrenching decision to fight Achilles nearly brought me to tears?

Dissatisfied, I put down the book, irritated that Philip was not there. I desperately wanted the chance to argue about these things with him. As I sat there, I slowly began to realize that my own opinions were quite different from those of my husband. Until then I had attributed all my interest in classical antiquity to Philip and had assumed that his own studies would serve as an adequate guide for mine. I no longer felt driven to study as a way to know Philip; I wanted to study because I loved the poetry, because the beauty of Greek sculpture moved me, because I was touched by the sight of tiny details on a vase. Suddenly Philip became one in a series of people whose academic opinions might or might not matter to me.

The culmination of these thoughts did not make me lose any love for my husband, nor did it make me grieve less for his loss. Instead it made me miss him all the more, because it revealed conversations I would never have with him. I could, and would, continue my studies, this time allowing only my own interests to serve as my guide. What I would never have, however, was the chance to end an infuriating argument on the merits of Hector versus Achilles with a series of soft kisses that gradually became more passionate as the topic at hand faded from memory.

As soon as I had returned to town, I sent notes to two gentlemen. The moment their replies arrived, I rushed to compare their handwriting with that in the missives now locked in my desk drawer. I was not surprised in the least that Colin's did not match but found myself mildly disappointed when I realized they were not written in Andrew's hand either. My idea about Andrew and warnings had not proved sound.

Before closing the drawer, I removed the glove and placed it on the table in my entrance hall. I told Davis that someone had dropped it in the library and that he should leave it on the table to be claimed.

Nearly a fortnight passed before I was able to find Mr. Attewater. As usual, Davis proved himself indispensable, taking on the task of tracking him down, locating him at last through one of the rather less exclusive gentlemen's clubs in town. In the meantime I found myself once again spending a considerable amount of time with Andrew, who continued his habit of calling almost every day.

"What shall we do? Are you planning to ride?"

"I'm awfully tired, Andrew, and intend to stay in all day. I have a great deal of work to do before Mr. Moore comes tomorrow."

"Capital. Then now is as good a time as any to present you with this." He held a small parcel out to me; I did not take it.

"Andrew, you know I cannot accept a gift from you."

"Don't be ridiculous, Emily. It's as much from my father as it is from me, to thank you for those terribly boring papers of Ashton's."

"Oh! Did you find them?" I asked, trying to sound surprised. I knew he had spent nearly an hour in the library while I was in the country. At my request, Davis had stood over Andrew's shoulders the entire time, carefully observing what he was doing. I did not want Andrew to know that I had already received a full report on his visit.

"Yes, yes, though I cannot imagine what my father is going to do with them. At any rate, you must take this," he said, handing me the package.

I hesitated, knowing that I should not accept anything from a man to whom I was not engaged. But surely Andrew, who had such a sporadic respect for the rules of society, would not consider my taking his gift to mean more than it did. I opened the paper and gasped. Inside was an ancient bronze coin bearing a portrait of Alexander the Great.

"Where on earth did you get this? It's fascinating," I said, looking at it closely.

"Some dusty old shop in Bloomsbury. I thought you might like it and knew my father would approve."

"It's lovely, Andrew. I shall treasure it."

After accepting the coin, I began to consider more seriously my relationship with Andrew. I did not love him and wondered if I ever could. I thought of the passages in Philip's journal relating to the early days of our engagement. It would be terrible to love someone so much who did not return the feeling. Although I did not believe that Andrew loved me, I did not want to do anything to increase his attachment to me. If I were ever to love a man, I wanted to do so completely; nothing less would satisfy me, and clearly Andrew would not be the man. It would be best if he considered me nothing more than a good friend; I would not allow him to kiss me again.

I started seeing him less frequently, turning down most of his invitations. When I was with him, I tried to make sure it was in a large group of friends or with other members of our families. One evening I invited him and his brother to dine with me, anxious to see if Arthur planned to propose to Arabella anytime soon. Unable to broach the subject during dinner, when the conversation kept to the usual sort of polite nonsense, I brought it up after we retired to the library.

"I saw Arabella yesterday, Arthur. She spoke highly of you."

"She is an excellent lady." I did not like his tone; it suggested that she was a fine piece of livestock.

"Do you see her often?" I asked, not feeling the need to inquire delicately to such a man.

"Yes, quite as often as I can." He was pacing around the perimeter of the room, vaguely looking at the titles of books on the shelves in an attempt to find something to read aloud.

"I wonder if I should encourage her feelings for you?" I continued. "I would not like to see her hurt."

"I assure you my intentions are honorable, Lady Ashton." He opened a volume of Ovid. "Are all his Greek books in this section?"

"Ovid was Roman, Mr. Palmer," I said, disliking the easy manner with which he dismissed the subject of Arabella. "The Greeks are on the next shelf."

"Shall we have port tonight, Arthur? Emily tells me Ashton left quite a stash." Andrew turned to me. "You don't mind, do you?"

"Of course not." I rang for Davis and was shocked that when he arrived, Andrew directed him to bring the port rather than letting me do so. Davis nodded to him politely, as he always did, and turned to me.

"You would like me to bring port to the gentlemen, Lady Ashton? And for you?"

"Port for all of us, please." I waited until the butler had left the room to turn my attention to Andrew. "I don't like you directing my servants."

His blue eyes laughed. "Don't you realize that I will persist in taking whatever liberties I can with you, Emily? You have been very cold to me lately. If I cannot kiss you, I shall have to resort to playing man of the house with your butler."

"Don't do it again," I snapped, shocked that he would say such a thing in front of his brother. I was about to say so when Davis returned.

"How did you like Ashton Hall, Emily? I never inquired after the trip you took there." Andrew laced his long, thin fingers together and laid them in his lap.

"It's a remarkable place. Have you been there?" I asked coldly.

"Now, don't hold me in contempt, Emily. It doesn't suit you, and you shall break my heart if you continue." He looked around the room as he spoke. "What a shame my brother is relentless in his pursuit of literature.

I should like to go to the drawing room so that you could play for us."
Arthur was continuing his tour of the shelves, pulling books down occasionally and leafing through them.

"I have no desire to play the piano," I replied. "Are you looking for
something in particular, Mr. Palmer?"

"No, Lady Ashton, just at a loss to choose something. I apologize if I
seem distracted. My mind is elsewhere this evening."

"My brother has been rather elusive on the subject of Miss Dunleigh,
don't you think? I happen to know, Emily, that there is more to the story
than he has revealed."

"I'm sure that if Mr. Palmer wants me to know, he'll tell me himself."

"You persist in punishing me!" Andrew cried. "Dreadful girl! What
shall I do to return to your good graces?"

Truth be told, Andrew was beginning to tire me, and I doubted that I
should want to remain even his friend for much longer. His disrespectful
attitude, which initially I found amusing and even a bit exhilarating, had
begun to grate on my nerves. Happy though I was to escape from some
of the bonds of society and its elaborate rules of behavior, I did not desire to remove myself completely. I did not want to embark on a lengthy
discussion with Andrew concerning his faults, nor did I want to be subjected to one of his drawn-out apologies. I decided to be charming for
the rest of the evening and subsequently distance myself from him.

"I shall reprimand you no further, Mr. Palmer," I said, bestowing on
him my most attractive smile. "Tell me, have you any further news of
Emma Callum and her Italian count?"

"I'm afraid that I must disappoint you on that subject. Her family has
closed ranks and is revealing very little."

"Too bad. Perhaps I shall call on them the next time I'm in Italy. I
wonder where the count lives."

"Venice, I think. Do you plan to travel there soon?"

"No, not at all. I shall most likely stay in England for the winter and
then go to Greece in the spring."

"Ah—to the villa."

"Yes. Have you been there?" I asked, watching Arthur continue his perusal of my husband's books.

"Of course. I would be happy to arrange for your trip. I'm quite familiar with Santorini."

"Thank you for the kind offer, Andrew, but Mr. Hargreaves promised Philip he would take care of everything."

"Really? I'm stunned to know that Ashton would consider Hargreaves qualified to do such a thing."

"Especially after that screaming argument they had in Africa," Arthur said, wrinkling his nose.

"I didn't know they argued," I said.

"Oh, yes, nasty row the night before Ashton got sick," Arthur continued. "No offense, Lady Ashton, but I can't say I've ever thought much of Hargreaves. Something about him's not quite cricket."

7 SEPTEMBER 1887
IMEROVIGLI, SANTORINI

———

Hargreaves arrived last week, bringing a much-appreciated supply of port. We took the boat across the caldera and spent a capital day exploring the old volcano. Discussed the possibility of funding an excavation of the island—I wonder if beneath the remains of ancient eruptions one could find treasures similar to those at Pompeii?

Have arranged to visit Delphi next week. Villagers there have been selling the most astounding artifacts—all from the remains of Apollo's oracle. Terrible crime that the site is not better protected. I fear that the significance of many of the objects will never be fully understood, as they are mercilessly ripped from their environs, robbing scholars of the opportunity to study them in context.

19

THE NEXT MORNING I RECEIVED CÉCILE'S REPLY TO MY letter asking her to find out what she could of Philip's purchase of the Praxiteles Apollo.

Ma chère Kallista,

I cannot tell you how distressed I felt after reading your letter. I hoped you had abandoned your morbid fascination with Philip, but clearly not. My child, it is always best to leave the dead buried. Nonetheless, I could not resist your plea for help and as a result have spent a fascinating week pretending to be in the market for antiquities. What a collection of characters I have found! Talented artists whose work would deceive any expert, ruthless dealers who reap huge profits, and buyers from the highest circles of society.

As you probably know, it is simple to buy an excellent copy of nearly any museum piece, so I began my adventure by letting it be known that I had seen Philip's Praxiteles bust and wanted to purchase a copy. I was soon approached by Monsieur LeBlanc, a man of dubious character but impeccable manners, who assured me that his artisans could produce a copy of anything I desired. When I told him of my friendship with Lord Ashton's widow, he asked if, like Lord Ashton, I preferred to purchase originals. He made it most clear that he could even obtain items from certain museums, as well as things acquired illegally from archaeological digs.

I am sorry to tell you that Monsieur LeBlanc, as well as several others, confirmed for me that your husband had frequently dealt with black-market dealers in the last year of his life. He purchased Apollo on a trip to Paris the week before your wedding from a private collector who had bought it only six months earlier; the gentleman prefers to remain anonymous. A colleague of Monsieur LeBlanc arranged the sale and gave me this information, believing that it would prove to me that he is equally capable of handling my own black-market purchases. Many underworld doors opened for me when I mentioned the name Lord Ashton. I know this information will bring you pain, but I do not think you should dwell on it. Bury his indiscretions along with the man and close this chapter of your life, chérie.

Please return to Paris soon, Kallista. I think your mood would improve immeasurably.

I am, as always, your most devoted friend,

Cécile du Lac

This confirmation of Philip's illicit activities dealt me a blow like none I had suffered before; I felt utterly betrayed by him and angry at myself for falling in love with such a man. Tomorrow Mr. Attewater and I would visit the British Museum, and I knew he would tell me that the objects in which I was interested were fake. Then what would I do? There could be no question that the originals must be returned to the museum, but how? As I pondered the subject, Davis announced Andrew, who rushed into the room almost before my butler spoke his name.

"Darling, I was a beast to you last night," he said, reaching for my hand as soon as the butler had closed the door. "But I see now why you have been so harsh with me lately. Your pointed questions to Arthur about his imminent engagement clearly indicate that you are afraid my own intentions to you are not honorable. My dear, you could not be more wrong." He continued before I could stop him. "Arthur suggested to me that your concern for Arabella clearly mirrored your own hopes. You know I adore you, Emily, and must admit that you are in dire need of a husband."

"Andrew!" I exclaimed.

"I am only teasing you, dearest. Please marry me, Emily. Think of the fun we would have together."

I drew a deep breath before I replied. "Andrew, you do me the greatest honor asking me to be your wife, but I fear I cannot accept your proposal. My feelings for Philip still overwhelm me. I could not marry another."

"Of course we would not marry before you are out of mourning. We wouldn't even need to announce the engagement."

"Please, Andrew, do not press your suit. I have no desire to hurt you," I said gently.

"I want to marry you, Emily," he said, more firmly than I would have expected. "Would you deny me my greatest wish?"

"I'm afraid I must, as it is incompatible with my own feelings."

"I cannot believe you feel nothing for me."

"I enjoy your company immensely but do not believe that we are well suited for marriage. And as I have already said, I am still deeply in love with Philip." I looked at him directly as I spoke, feeling I owed him at least that. He stood, shifting his weight from one foot to the other for some time, as if he were waiting for me to change my mind. Eventually he spoke.

"I am not accustomed to being so easily dismissed. You'll forgive me if I beg your leave." He left the house without looking at me.

Once again I sat alone in the library, my mind spinning. My concern for Andrew paled next to my feelings concerning Philip and antiquities theft, but I did not enjoy rejecting Lord Palmer's son. His proposal came as a total shock, but when I remembered that Philip fell in love with me while I largely ignored him, I decided that men must prefer women who have little interest in them. The more I pushed Andrew away, the more serious his pursuit became. Perhaps men should not be allowed to hunt; the love of the chase creeps too much into other realms of their lives.

I had no doubt that Andrew would fall in love again quickly, and I wondered if his desire to marry me was inspired more by my fortune in the Bank of England than by my wealth of personal attributes. I knew he needed money, and I pitied him. His title, however, would make him the perfect catch for the daughter of an American railroad baron whose wife kept a copy of *Debrett's* on her bedside table. Yes, an American would suit Andrew well. I wondered if Margaret could think of someone who would make an excellent match for him.

Not many days passed before I found myself receiving another gentleman in the library. This time, however, there was no danger of a proposal.

"You have been immensely difficult to track down lately," Colin said, his long legs stretched out before him as he sat on one of my favorite chairs.

"I cannot agree with you, Colin," I said, meeting his eyes.

"Well, I suppose if I were willing to gallop down Rotten Row at top speed, I should have an easier time of it."

"I don't think I shall be doing that much anymore," I said wryly.

"Dare I hope that Palmer has fallen from grace?" he asked.

"No, of course not," I began, not wanting to tell Colin of the refused proposal.

"How is your study of Greek?"

"I will admit candidly that it is more difficult than I had anticipated. Furthermore, I've been rather distracted lately."

He handed me a parcel wrapped in brown paper. "I've been told more than once that racing about town horrifying society matrons is immensely time-consuming." He smiled. "I found this last weekend when I was in the country and thought it might be of some use to you." Inside was a well-used copy of an elementary Greek grammar. "It was mine at school and served me well."

"Thank you, Colin. That is very kind of you."

"It's delightful to meet a woman who wants to broaden her mind; I consider encouraging you my moral duty."

"I'm not sure that I like being someone's moral duty," I exclaimed.

"I did say it with a touch of irony, Emily, and cannot believe that such a tone would be lost on you."

"Of course it was not, Colin, but I in turn cannot believe that you would think I could pass on an opportunity to tease you." I looked directly at him. "Did you dance with me in Paris out of the same sense of duty?"

"No, I did not," he replied, steadily meeting my gaze, "and I hope to dance with you again."

"I'd rather not shock Davis today. He's been quite understanding about the port."

"You are wonderfully easy to be with," he observed. "You have settled well into this house and now seem to belong in this library. I think Ashton would be surprised."

"Why?"

"I wonder if he knew the depth of the woman he took as his bride."

"The truth is that I was not particularly deep when I married him." I sighed. "And since I have already told you all my horrible secrets, I will confess that I do sometimes imagine that Philip and I would have found ourselves happily engaged in academic discussions, but I wonder if that really could have happened. I do not think I would have ever developed the interests I have now if he had remained alive."

"That is not so surprising. You would have been neatly packaged into the role of wife and, before long, mother, with scant time or opportunity to consider any other path. It is unfortunate that so little is expected of wives from an intellectual point of view."

"I believe most men prefer it that way, Colin," I said.

"I would not. I am confident that most of the women I encounter would bore me to death before the first leg of our wedding trip."

"So you are a confirmed bachelor?" I asked.

"I suppose so."

"You deal a great blow to the mothers of London's unmarried girls."

"My work requires a fair amount of travel that would not be appreciated by most wives," he said.

"I have driven past your lovely estate and would be shocked if there were not plenty of women who would gladly be ensconced there while you are away."

"I am not so desperate for an heir."

"Ah, the pleasures of the common man," I teased. "Thank goodness you have no hereditary title to worry you."

"Yes, I have been spared that burden," he said. "I need only be concerned about the estate and fortune." We both laughed.

"What *is* your work, Colin? I can't remember that Philip ever told me."

"He probably had more interesting stories with which to regale you. He was, after all, trying to impress you."

"I wouldn't have thought that a man of your station would work. What do you do?"

"Nothing of significance," he said, running his hand through his hair. "Merely a bit of politics. Terribly boring."

"Why does politics bring you abroad so often?" I asked.

"You are full of questions today, aren't you? I shall put a stop to them by revealing to you the other present I have for you."

"What is it?" I asked, full of curiosity.

"I've ordered a case of '87 port to be laid down for you—the Queen Victoria's Golden Jubilee vintage. Andrew Palmer is not the only man who can assist in your corruption."

"Thank you, Colin. That will be delightful, even if you have done it only out of a sense of moral obligation. You must come to dinner and have some."

"It will not be ready to drink for another thirty years, Emily."

"Right," I said. "I shall make a note in my diary and be sure to invite you."

"I look forward to it." He rose to leave. "Enjoy your Greek, Emily."

"I shall, Colin, very much. Thank you again."

"Oh—and I must thank you." He pulled an evening glove out of his pocket. "I must have lost this the night of your dinner party. Glad Davis didn't throw it out. It's from my favorite pair."

———

The artifacts I have found here are incomparable—some of the most exquisite stonework I have seen. If ever a site begged for systematic excavation, it was Delphi. Almost wish I were not returning to England next month. Lord Bromley has invited me to Darnley House to shoot—I welcome the opportunity to see my darling K. Wedding cannot come soon enough. Perhaps now that the date has been set, Lady Bromley will allow me some time alone with her daughter.

Headed to Athens tomorrow to visit Lysander Vardakas. Have seen his collection of antiquities before—there are few more impressive in private hands—he tells me he has acquired some new pieces of great significance. They cannot be all that he claims, but I still look forward to seeing them.

20

AT LAST THE DAY OF MY MEETING WITH MR. ATTEWATER
arrived. Our rendezvous, which proved more educational than I could
have imagined, began outside the museum, where we sat on a bench for
nearly half an hour talking before we went inside. As I listed the items I
wanted to look at with him, he immediately recognized each and assured
me that he knew their locations in the gallery.

He seemed completely at ease in the British Museum and knew the
Greco-Roman collection in great detail. He had an unmistakable admiration for his ancient colleagues and clearly considered himself to be
their equal.

"I must admit that you surprised me in Paris, Lady Ashton, when you
said that you could see beauty in copies. It is an opinion so unlike that of
your husband."

"You told me you did not know him well," I replied, trying not to
look down at my companion, who stood several inches shorter than myself.

"No, I did not. Lord Ashton had no interest in my work. As you
surely know, he purchased only originals."

"Yes, Mr. Attewater. I am keenly aware of that."

He led me to the first item on my list, the bronze statue Ivy had
found so amusing. "I do not work with bronze much. There are a huge
number of chemicals one can use to achieve just the right patina on
metal, but I prefer the feel of marble. Nonetheless"—he paused as he
circled the case wherein the statue rested—"I did produce a copy of this
for one of my . . . er, patrons."

"Mr. Attewater, I remember you said in Paris that your work can be found in some of the world's best museums. Is that true?"

"It is, Lady Ashton."

"Did you make this statue?"

He peered closely at the figure, pulling a magnifying glass out of his coat pocket and examining as best he could the cloak hanging over the figure's arm.

"Yes! That is mine!" he exclaimed.

I admonished him to speak more quietly, hoping that no one else in the gallery had noticed his outburst.

"There is no question about it." He polished the magnifying glass on his waistcoat and beamed proudly as he looked at the statue. "I left a mark on the underside of the cloak. Take a look." He handed me the glass, and I peered at the cloak. Although barely visible, they could be seen: two tiny Greek alphas.

"A.A.," he said, smiling. "My initials."

"Yes, I understand." I nodded slightly.

I ushered him away from the statue, not wanting to draw anyone's attention. As we continued from piece to piece, the reaction was the same. Mr. Attewater recognized all of them as his own work and on many was able to show me his hidden double alphas. I grew more and more depressed as I realized that every artifact currently in my country library was something that belonged in the British Museum. Apollo, it appeared, was not an anomaly.

"Don't you worry," I asked my companion as softly as I could, "that someone at the museum will notice your alphas? Surely the penalty for such an offense is great?"

"Lady Ashton, I assure you I have done nothing wrong. I have been commissioned on numerous occasions to copy pieces from the venerable halls of this museum. As you have seen, I produce them to the best of my abilities and collect my payment. What the purchaser chooses to do with them is none of my concern."

"But surely you knew what was going on." I could not believe that Mr. Attewater was entirely innocent in the matter.

"My art, Lady Ashton, has been largely unappreciated by the public from the time I began to sculpt. After years of trying to succeed on my own, I realized that I could earn enough money to keep my studio by copying antiquities. Is that a crime? I have never received outrageous payment for any of my works. Believe me, were I to sell them as originals, they would command far higher prices. Furthermore, if I were going to attempt to deceive a buyer about the origin of a piece, I obviously would not sign it."

I looked at Mr. Attewater's worn but well-cared-for suit, noted his dignified manner, and found myself believing him. Here stood a man who wanted to be great; if he had money, he would spend it and not wear something so decidedly out-of-date.

"Why would a person come to you instead of using the museum's casting service?"

"They do not offer reproductions of every piece in the museum. Furthermore, I work much more quickly than they do."

"Yet if your clients are, as it seems, replacing original antiquities with your copies, don't you worry that someone in the museum will notice your initials and hold you responsible for the crime?"

"These pieces have been here for years. Their provenances were verified and the objects examined thoroughly before the museum purchased them. No one has a reason to doubt them now. The experts did all their work on the true originals."

"How does one go about copying the originals?"

"All I need are the precise dimensions of an object and a good sketch. I can get that in a relatively short period of time. My patrons would get me into the museum after hours. It's not as difficult as you might think."

"It's a very clever scheme," I admitted, and looked at Mr. Attewater. "Doesn't it bother you that others are profiting from your work when you receive so little?"

"I get enough." We passed a bust of Julius Caesar. "That is not mine," he whispered, "but it is clearly a fake. The dark color of the marble is achieved through liberal application of tobacco juice, and the pits over the surface come from banging on the sculpture with a brush with metal spikes. It works beautifully."

"Amazing," I said, looking at poor Caesar. "But how can you tell it is not authentic?"

"The beauty of a forgery, Lady Ashton, is that there typically *is* no definitive proof. But here the artist was not an expert." He motioned to the area between Caesar's eye and his hair. "The surface is perfect wherever there is a contour. Everywhere else is pitted to make the marble look aged. I would not have made such a mistake."

"But you do not make sculptures designed to deceive, Mr. Attewater." I raised my eyebrow and smiled at him.

"Touché, Lady Ashton," he replied, bowing slightly to me.

I decided to ask him directly the question that was plaguing me. "Did my husband hire you to make the copies you have shown me?" He did not answer. "Please, you must tell me. I need to know his involvement in this scheme. Did he plan it?"

"I am afraid that I cannot reveal the names of my patrons. I should never work again."

"But you say you are a legitimate artist."

"I am." He began peering at Caesar through his magnifying glass. "But my customers do not always share my scruples." He stood as straight as possible and looked directly at me. "I can, however, ease your mind on one point. I have never done any work for Lord Ashton."

"Thank you, Mr. Attewater." I sighed. "But that does not mean he did not plan this intrigue. It is possible that he had an underling deal with you."

"I had not thought of that," he replied. "However, my buyer is a respected gentleman whom I would not expect to do someone's bidding, so perhaps all Lord Ashton did was buy the stolen originals."

"One hardly knows what to think, but either way it does not look good for Philip," I said. "Why have you told me all this, Mr. Attewater? Don't you fear exposure?"

"I have nothing to fear, Lady Ashton. I have done nothing wrong." He smiled slyly.

"I like you, Mr. Attewater," I said as we continued our stroll through the museum. "I want to commission a work by you."

"I am immensely honored, Lady Ashton. What would you like me to copy?"

"I don't want a copy, Mr. Attewater. I want you to design me an original of your own in the classical Greek style. I like your work and want to see what you can do when not constrained by having to copy something else."

"Do you want it to look ancient?" he asked, his eyes full of light.

"No, do no deliberate damage. I shall not hide the fact that the piece is modern."

"Thank you, Lady Ashton," he said with great dignity. "I shall not disappoint you."

"You're welcome, Mr. Attewater. Perhaps we can get you a more legitimate following of admirers." As I smiled at him, I saw Arthur Palmer rushing past us. "Good day, Mr. Palmer," I called to him. "What brings you to the museum today?"

"Good day, Lady Ashton, Attewater." He nodded briefly at my companion. "I am to meet Arabella and her mother. If you'll excuse me, I am late." He rushed off almost before I could bid him farewell. He had the nervous look I recognized as one of a man about to propose.

"I shall have to call on Arabella tomorrow," I said to no one in particular. "Perhaps I shall have need for your services again, Mr. Attewater, for a wedding gift."

"Your kindness makes me feel that I must confess one indiscretion in my past."

"There is no need to do so, I assure you," I answered.

"Please, follow me." He led me through gallery after gallery until we stopped before a fragment of an Athenian frieze depicting the head of a young man. "Do you like this?"

"It's lovely."

"Yes, it is, isn't it?" Now he took me to the room that held the Elgin Marbles. "Here." He motioned to an object labeled as Slab IV of the North Frieze of the Parthenon. "Look closely. Is anything familiar?"

"Should the other piece be in this room, too? Is it from the Parthenon? It almost looks as if it belongs with this section," I said.

"You are close to the truth. If you have finished with the museum to-day, I should very much like to tell you something about these two pieces once we step outside."

"You are very mysterious, Mr. Attewater."

I allowed him to lead me out of the building. He looked around in a manner that was meant to appear casual, but I'm afraid he was not particularly successful. Then he stood as near me as he could without being improper and spoke in a low whisper.

"I sold that first fragment you saw to the museum. It is the only time I have misrepresented my work." He removed a handkerchief from his pocket and wiped his brow. "I had been hired to copy all of Slab IV—it was an ambitious plan. Evidently my patron had a client who wished to own the original. Can you imagine the price such a thing would fetch?" He looked around again. "The deal fell through for reasons unknown to me. The order for my copy was canceled."

"This, Mr. Attewater, inspires me to ask a great many questions," I whispered back.

"And I am afraid there are few, if any, I would be willing to answer," he replied nervously. "At any rate, I didn't like my work to go to waste, and I had already nearly finished the head I showed you. I could not bring myself to destroy such a beautiful piece, so I made it appear to be an unrelated fragment of its own. I wish you could have seen it before I damaged it. It was exquisite. But it needed to look old, so I hacked up the nose, cheek, forehead, and shoulders, then restored the nose." He stood up a bit straighter now. "A nice touch, I think, doing the restoration. Gives the thing an air of authenticity."

"Yes, but how did the British Museum come to buy it?"

"Money was very tight for me at the time, and I needed more than the piece would command as a copy. With the assistance of a colleague, I invented a decent provenance for the piece, which I said I acquired in Athens."

"You sold it to the museum yourself?"

"I beg your pardon, Lady Ashton, but could you please try to speak more quietly?"

"Of course," I murmured.

"Yes, I represented myself and completed the transaction with the museum."

"I appreciate your honesty, Mr. Attewater," I said, staring at him closely, pleased that he trusted me enough to share his secret. Of course, he could expose Philip as easily as I could expose him, so I suppose he did not take much of a risk.

"I felt you had the right to know. Do you still wish me to create a new sculpture for you?"

"More than ever." I shook his hand. "I am immensely grateful for all the information you have given me. You have cleared up many questions that were plaguing me."

"I am sorry, Lady Ashton, that the answers can bring you little peace." With a smart bow, the little man took his leave from me. I couldn't help but notice a slight spring in his step as he trotted down Great Russell Street, and I hoped that my patronage might allow him to move away from the sordid business in which he was currently involved.

Do not think, gentle reader, that the treasure trove of information given to me by Mr. Attewater did not leave me deeply unsettled. I hardly knew what to worry about first. The fact that so many pieces in the British Museum were forgeries horrified me. The fact that the originals were sitting in the library at my country estate was even more disturbing. But worst of all, my husband, my darling love, a man whom I had come to admire greatly, was no better than a common sneak thief. If anything, he was worse; greed, not poverty, had driven his actions. I felt tears filling my eyes and decided that walking home would do me more good than sobbing in the back of a cab. As I started toward the street, someone called my name.

"Emily!" Arabella waved at me. I had no desire to speak to anyone but did not want to insult her. I waved back and waited for her, along with Mrs. Dunleigh and Mr. Palmer, to come to me.

"Good day, Mrs. Dunleigh, Arabella. I see you found your party, Mr. Palmer." The usual pleasantries were exchanged, and I hoped for a quick escape.

"Arthur tells us you have already been to the museum," Arabella said. "What a pity! You could have joined us."

"I am on my way home," I replied.

"Where is your carriage?" Mrs. Dunleigh asked.

"Actually, I planned to walk. I'm rather looking forward to the exercise."

"Shocking!" Mrs. Dunleigh cried. "My dear child, you must allow me to send you home in our carriage. Our driver has only just dropped us off and is still at the curb. Berkeley Square must be nearly two miles from here, and it is unseasonably chilly today. One would think we were already in the depths of autumn. I should never forgive myself if you fell ill." I knew she was trying to be polite, and I did not want to insult her, particularly in front of the man she hoped would soon be her son-in-law. Unwillingly I allowed myself to be helped into the carriage for the short ride home.

It started to rain almost immediately, so I was forced to admit that I was lucky not to have walked. Between the cool, damp weather and my troubled state of mind, I was trembling by the time I reached home. Davis met me at the carriage with a large umbrella and led me into the house. Unfortunately, Berkeley Square did not provide the respite for which I longed. As Davis took my hat, he told me that my mother was waiting for me in the drawing room. I did not want to see her and delayed by having Davis tell her I would be in as soon as I finished an urgent letter. I slipped into the library, sat at Philip's desk, and quickly penned the text of a cable to Ivy, begging that she return to London as soon as possible. Before I could ring to have Davis send it for me, my mother burst into the library.

"This, Emily, is unpardonable!" She dropped onto the settee. "I will not be kept waiting while you answer correspondence."

"Mother, please understand that I had no intention of insulting you."

"I have heard quite enough," she said. "Your behavior of late can be described in no way other than extraordinary. I realize that losing your husband so soon after your marriage deeply distressed you, but do not expect to be able to use this indefinitely as an excuse for unsuitable actions."

"I cannot imagine what I have done now that has you so concerned," I said halfheartedly. She had already delivered a particularly scathing lecture after my now infamous dinner party; it was unlikely she would return to a subject to which she had done justice.

"I have been somewhat concerned at the way you and Mr. Andrew Palmer conduct yourselves. But I am a reasonable woman and realize that the standard of behavior to which you young people hold yourselves these days is not as high as one would hope. The Palmers are an excellent family, although, given their lack of fortune, I would have hoped you would set your sights higher. A woman in your position could easily catch a duke."

"Mother, I am in no mood to discuss whatever marriage plans you have in mind for me."

"I assure you, Emily, that your mood is of no consequence whatsoever to me." She continued without drawing breath. "As I was saying, your shocking behavior with Mr. Palmer I can tolerate. I suppose his unorthodox approach to courtship appeals to you."

"Mother," I tried to interrupt.

She silenced me by lifting her hand. "I shall hear nothing from you until I am finished. Now I have learned that Mr. Palmer has, in fact, proposed to you and that you have refused him. Is this true?"

"Yes." I sighed. I had tried to keep my rejection of Andrew as quiet as possible but knew that inevitably my mother would hear of it. In her opinion there are few crimes greater than turning down an offer of marriage, unless, of course, it is done in an attempt to intensify the rejected gentleman's feelings. She knew well that I deplored the very idea of doing such a thing; it was a subject covered thoroughly between us in the early days after my social debut.

"I would like to believe that you refused him because you are expecting a superior offer from another gentleman?" Her eyes narrowed as she looked at me. "No, I thought not."

"Is it so terrible to think that I might never marry again?"

"Yes, it is, Emily. It would be a complete waste of everything. You are beautiful, rich, titled. Our family's history can be traced to the earliest days of England. My dear, had you put your mind to it, you could have married royalty. I will always regret that you showed no interest in Prince George." She dismissed the thought with a wave of her hand. "Well, he certainly would have no interest in a widow."

"I would imagine not," I said flatly. "Could you perhaps come to terms with the idea that I, like our great queen, prefer to remain a widow?"

"The queen has remained in mourning. Your current behavior is proof that you have no such intention."

I would have liked to point out that there were any number of rumors concerning the queen which implied that she was not really in mourning, but I knew that suggesting such a thing would begin an argument that I had no interest in finishing.

"You cannot have it both ways, Emily. Either mourn your husband or find another."

"I do mourn Philip!" I shouted, rather more loudly than I intended. Tears sprang to my eyes. "You have no idea what I suffer. I will not be judged by you or anyone else. My refusal to marry Mr. Palmer should be no one's concern but his and my own."

My mother shook her head slowly and smiled in her most patronizing fashion. "We shall see, Emily. You may enjoy yourself now, but eventually your looks will be gone. If you insist on remaining a widow, you had better think about changing your behavior, or you will find that the only company you attract will be that of the most desperate fortune hunters. No one else in society would be willing to associate with a woman who so openly flaunts her disregard for social customs. Which leads me to another topic: This insistence of yours on pursuing Philip's intellectual work is very odd. There is no role for women in the academic world. I could not imagine where you would get such ideas until I met your friend, Miss Seward."

"Margaret is the daughter of a very respectable family."

"Emily, what Americans consider acceptable is often questionable at best. Miss Seward's influence on you is distressing. She is taking you down a path that can lead to no good. You have been attending lectures, child. Have you lost all sense of decorum?"

"My behavior is not so bad as you suggest, Mother," I snapped. "I have, perhaps, not always done the right thing but in general am above reproach. If you have difficulty understanding my need for an intellectual life, then I am very sorry for you. One would hope that one's own mother might offer support rather than relishing the role of critic."

"Emily, if I am more critical of you than others, it is only to protect you." She sighed and pulled her gloves back on. "It would be for the best if you were to spend the fall with your father and me in Kent. You clearly are floundering on your own. I can give you no more time today, child. Mrs. Dunleigh is expecting me. Her daughter does not share your lack of interest in the married state."

I did not respond to this, nor did I wait until she left to return to my seat at Philip's desk, furious. I would never marry again after having been so completely deceived by Philip. My thoughts turned once more to Mr. Attewater and the museum. Why on earth had Philip done it? If only he were alive, I could have barged into his library and demanded an explanation, knowing quite well he would be unable to offer anything satisfactory. He would have been shocked to hear me shout at him and most likely would have ordered me upstairs until I could control my emotions. I would have refused, of course, and implored him to remember his morals, his values, and to become again the man we both knew him to be. This would move him greatly; he might even break down and confess that he himself was plagued by his actions and did not know what to do. I would have told him that, maybe, I could find it in my heart to forgive him if he were willing to return everything to the museum. He would have thanked me profusely and congratulated himself on finding such a wife. I sighed. Beastly of him to have died before I had the chance to orchestrate a happy ending.

Ivy appeared on my doorstep the next day, earlier than I could have hoped. She was not surprised to hear confirmation of our suspicions; we both knew it was unlikely that there could be any other explanation. We settled into chairs in the library to discuss how we should proceed.

"Are you absolutely certain that Mr. Attewater will give you no further information?" Ivy asked.

"He was very clear on that point," I replied. "I suppose we cannot expect more of him."

"Well, at least we know that Philip did not contact him directly and arrange for the copies to be made. I'm inclined to believe that he heard of the availability of the pieces and snatched them up."

"Perhaps," I said. "But either way Philip did something both illegal and immoral."

"Have you told Margaret yet?"

"I saw her last night and expect her here at any moment."

Ivy paused. "This must be very difficult for you, Emily."

"To put it mildly," I said, and told her about Andrew's proposal and my mother's visit.

"I do not envy you your mother," Ivy said. "Thank goodness you do not have to live in her house. How did you ever manage to survive all those years? Philip clearly deserves our sympathy, if only because he removed you from an unbearable living situation."

"Yes," I said wryly. "Which would put us back to where we were before Philip became interesting."

"Except that you are in love with him now," Ivy said, the slightest hint of a question in her voice.

"Unfortunately so," I admitted.

Margaret arrived, and we all rehashed what we knew, to little result.

"Terrible that it's too early in the day for port." Ivy sighed, glancing at the clock.

"Do you think that Cécile can be of further help to us?" Margaret asked.

"I have already written to her, asking her opinion. In the meantime I thought that perhaps I could do something similar to what she did in Paris: let it be known that I am in the market for black-market antiquities."

"Do you really think that would be a good idea?" Ivy asked.

"It's an excellent idea, Emily!" Margaret cried. "You must let me assist you."

Before I could reply, Davis announced Colin Hargreaves.

Ivy gasped when she saw him. "Has he grown more handsome since Paris, do you think?" she whispered while Margaret smiled.

After a brief exchange of the required pleasantries, Colin turned to me. "Please forgive my frankness, Lady Ashton, but I do not know any other way to broach this delicate subject with you." I closed my eyes, irrationally certain that he had somehow heard about my refusal of Andrew's proposal. I couldn't imagine what he would say to me on such a topic. I was, however, completely incorrect. "I understand that you met with Mr. Aldwin Attewater in the British Museum. Is this true?"

"Yes," I answered, remembering our conversation in Paris concerning Mr. Attewater.

"I hope you do not mind my speaking freely in front of your friends?"

"Don't be ridiculous, Mr. Hargreaves. Say what you came to say," I snapped.

"I had hoped that, upon reflection, you would heed the advice I gave you in Paris. I see that is not the case. Suffice it to say, Emily, that some very undesirable parties have noticed your acquaintance with Mr. Attewater. You appear to be seeking some sort of information from him, and I cannot say strongly enough that you should abandon doing so immediately."

"Really, Mr. Hargreaves?" I asked, not looking at him as I spoke. "Why is that?"

"I am not at liberty to speak further on the subject. Believe me when I say I would never want any harm to come to you and would not issue such a warning lightly."

"Good heavens, Mr. Hargreaves!" Ivy exclaimed. "A warning? I cannot imagine what you mean. Emily's interest in the British Museum could not be more innocent. She hired Mr. Attewater to make a statue for her. Where is the harm in that?"

"In theory there should be none," Colin said. "Please, Emily"—he looked into my eyes—"promise me that you will make no further inquiries."

"I will promise no such thing." I rose from my chair. "You have given me no reason to."

"I ask that you trust me as a friend," he replied, his eyes never leaving mine. "It's more important than you can possibly imagine, Emily. Please."

"I shall take the matter under advisement, Mr. Hargreaves. If there is nothing further, my friends and I were in the midst of a rather important discussion."

"I apologize for the interruption." He stopped partway out of the room and came back to me, reaching for my hand. "Emily, if I could tell you more, I would. You must trust me." He kissed my hand and departed.

"What an interesting man," Ivy said.

"More interesting than either of you know." I told them about the glove. "I see no reason at all to trust him."

"When I think of Andrew telling you to stay away from Colin, I get chills down my spine." Ivy shuddered as she spoke. "Do you think Andrew knows anything of this?"

"He may have surmised that something funny was going on. Andrew is very perceptive when it comes to anything that could be remotely related to gossip. Despite his faults, he is very straightforward. Had he any idea of the specifics of this situation, I have no doubt that he would have told me."

"Do you think Colin is behind the forgeries?" Ivy asked.

"I don't know, but I have every intention of finding out," I said.

―――

Vardakas's collection frankly stunned me. Hardly know what to think and have no intention of writing about it.

Letter from K arrived today. Unfortunately bland, as they usually are, but can expect little else until she knows me better. Agreed to ride on the fox hunt with me—sure to be a capital day. Did not reprimand me for going ahead with plans for safari—said she had no objection to me spending April away, so long as I return to London before the wedding. I will have a most understanding wife.

My Achilles-Alexander project is progressing nicely, although have not written as much as I would have liked. Too distracted, I suppose. This will change once back on Santorini.

21

"LOOK AT THIS," I SAID, HANDING A NOTE TO IVY THE next morning at breakfast. "Arthur Palmer has proposed to Arabella."

"Your mother must be pleased." Ivy smiled.

"Exceedingly." I pushed the rest of the mail away from me and turned my focus to Colin. "I am wondering at Colin's motive for befriending me after Philip's death. I suppose he wanted to keep an eye on me. He sent the man with the scar to follow me. That would explain why he made no attempt to pursue him that day in Paris."

"Do you think he had something to do with the break-in at the Meurice? Didn't he send you a note that very afternoon telling you he was leaving Paris?" Ivy asked.

"Yes, he did," I answered. "Trying to establish an alibi, I imagine. Why do you suppose he would have broken into my room?"

"Nothing was taken," Ivy began, "but I cannot imagine what he would have been looking for."

"I have found nothing in Philip's papers that could be related to any of this. Yet I must be close to discovering something if Colin feels the need to warn me. Perhaps it is time to talk to Mr. Attewater again."

Davis entered the room and presented me with a calling card. "The gentleman would like to see you immediately, Lady Ashton."

"Good heavens, Davis, you look very serious this morning."

"Yes, madam." Davis nodded. "If you please, madam, Mr. Palmer was most insistent that he speak with you concerning an urgent matter."

"Well!" I raised an eyebrow and laughed as I looked at the gentleman's card. "I expected to see the bride before the bridegroom."

"He must be quite pleased with himself," Ivy said.

"I have put him in the drawing room, Lady Ashton," Davis said.

"Very well, Davis, we shall be there directly."

The butler led us up the stairs and opened the heavy drawing-room door. Instead of closing it behind us, he followed us into the room. Arthur looked decidedly ill and rushed toward me.

"Lady Ashton, forgive my intrusion. I have asked your butler to remain, as what I have to tell you is of a most shocking nature."

"We have already heard of your engagement, Mr. Palmer, and wish you great happiness," I said with a smile. "Surely you did not think we would be surprised that you and Arabella will be married?"

"No, Lady Ashton, of course not. I am here concerning something altogether different." He wiped sweat from his brow with the back of his hand.

"I hope your family are all well?" I asked, suddenly worried that Andrew had taken my refusal more badly than I had thought.

"We are all fine. Please, Lady Ashton, Mrs. Brandon, be seated." His voice sounded so strained that I did not object to being ordered about in my own house.

"What is it, Mr. Palmer?" Ivy asked. "It's not Arabella, is it?"

"No, she is in excellent health, Mrs. Brandon. Thank you for your kind inquiry."

"Clearly you are not well, Mr. Palmer. Davis, fetch a glass of brandy," I said, wondering what could have upset the man so. Davis immediately filled a glass but, rather than give it to Arthur, stood behind me holding it.

"Perhaps you could enlighten us as to the nature of your call, Mr. Palmer?" Ivy asked.

Arthur took a deep breath and began to speak. "I hardly know what to say, Lady Ashton. This news is so . . . so . . . unexpected that I am at a loss where to begin. Perhaps it would be best if you read the letter yourself." He thrust at me a tattered, filthy envelope addressed to himself. I recognized the handwriting.

"This is from Philip?" I asked, wondering why Arthur felt the need to share his private correspondence. He nodded. I pulled the letter out and read it.

Palmer—

I do not have time for a formal letter but am in desperate need of speaking to you privately as soon as is possible. Tell no one of this note, especially Hargreaves. You do not need to respond; I shall take the necessary steps to arrange a meeting once you are in Africa.

P. Ashton

I read the letter through twice before looking up at Arthur, pacing in front of me.

"It is very kind of you to bring this to me. Seeing anything from Philip is a great comfort to me." I touched the words on the wrinkled paper gently as I spoke. "Forgive me, Mr. Palmer. The content of this letter does not seem particularly remarkable. Perhaps I am missing something?" I asked.

"Yes, you are, Lady Ashton." Arthur nodded at Davis, who moved to my side. "I received this letter in the morning mail today. It has only just arrived from Africa."

"It must have been misdirected, I suppose." I watched the faces of those around me. "Yet I don't understand," I said slowly, trying to comprehend what this meant.

"I think your husband may still be alive, Lady Ashton," he said softly. "The letter isn't dated, but it was postmarked in Cairo a little more than a week ago."

Davis held out the glass of brandy. "I knew you wouldn't faint, madam, but I thought that a stiff drink might be in order," my butler said. I took the glass from him and drained it in a single gulp. Davis refilled the glass but I refused it, wanting my senses perfectly clear.

"How can this be?" I asked. "Weren't you there when he died, Mr. Palmer?"

"Actually, I was not." He paused and cleared his throat. "I'm rather ashamed to admit it, Lady Ashton, but we left him after he got sick. We all believed the fever to be highly contagious and did not want to be exposed. Hargreaves was the only one who stayed."

"Colin?" I looked at Ivy, my eyes wide. "He alone was with Philip?"

"Yes, Lady Ashton. I can give you no explanation of what happened. You would have to ask Hargreaves."

"You told me, Mr. Palmer, that Philip and Colin argued the night before my husband fell ill. Yet you left them alone?"

"We all thought them to be the best of friends, Lady Ashton. Friends argue on occasion. Given what we know now, I admit that perhaps we were foolish to act as we did."

"What are you suggesting, Mr. Palmer?" Ivy asked rather severely.

"I hardly know," he said. "All I can say is that the rest of us traveled to Cairo, where we waited for Hargreaves and Ashton. As we are all painfully aware, only Hargreaves joined us. He told us Ashton was dead and that the body was being shipped to England. Forgive me for speaking so bluntly."

"There is nothing to forgive, Mr. Palmer," I said, my mind reeling. "But if Philip is alive, why hasn't he returned to London?"

"He was very ill the last time I saw him. Even a man in his excellent physical condition would be greatly weakened by the fever he contracted. It's possible that he was not able to travel."

"I find it difficult to believe that Mr. Hargreaves would abandon his friend," Ivy said.

"As do I," Mr. Palmer agreed. "Clearly we are not in possession of all the facts."

"Is it possible that he left because he, too, was afraid of catching the disease?" Ivy asked. "He may have left Philip in the hands of the natives, who told Mr. Hargreaves that Lord Ashton had died."

"It is possible, Mrs. Brandon," Arthur said, his voice revealing that he did not think it likely.

"This is very troubling," I said.

"I do not know what to make of it either," he replied. "But I felt that it was important you see the letter immediately. I will, of course, share with you any further correspondence I receive."

"Thank you, Mr. Palmer," I murmured.

"You may keep the letter," he said. "I hope it shall bring you some measure of comfort."

We sat dumbfounded as Davis led him from the room. At last Ivy spoke.

"What do you make of this? Do you think it is true?"

"I certainly want it to be, but I do not know," I said slowly. "I am overjoyed at the thought that Philip may be alive."

"Of course you are," Ivy replied. "Do you want to send for Margaret?"

"No," I said, pausing. "I'm afraid she would think me silly to consider such a thing. I'll tell her eventually, but not yet."

"Shall I ring for tea?"

"Please do. This news makes me wonder about Colin."

"What are you thinking?"

"Would Colin, afraid that Philip was going to expose his role in the forgeries, have left his friend to die in an African village?"

"I cannot believe that!" Ivy cried.

"It would have been simple for Colin to convince the others that they should leave. He could have waited a day or two and then gone to Cairo himself, assuming that Philip would die eventually from the fever. Why should he risk his own health waiting to see it?"

"What a terrible thought," Ivy said. "But, Emily, why would he have left? He would have gained nothing by leaving his friend's side."

"Unless he had done something that he thought would ensure Philip's death," I said. "Perhaps the notes I found were meant to warn Philip that Colin planned to do him some harm."

"You don't think that Colin murdered Philip?" Ivy said, clearly stunned by the thought.

"I suppose not, but I think he may have made certain that nothing kept nature from running its course. He could have prevented Philip from taking quinine or something that might have helped him and then left, assured of what the outcome would be yet unwilling to watch the painful end. But Philip didn't die, and now he has recovered enough to reach out to his true friends."

"It seems somewhat plausible," Ivy admitted. "But not entirely. If Philip did not die, whose body was sent home to be buried? And why would the native guides have gone along with the scheme?"

"Perhaps Philip knew what Colin had done and, as he began to re-cover, realized that his life would be in danger as long as Colin thought he was alive. He enlisted the help of the faithful natives—he was the one in the group who could speak their language the most fluently—who pledged their assistance to him."

"But what of the body you buried?" Ivy asked, clearly captivated by my story.

"Maybe it was the body of a member of the local tribe who had re-cently departed life," I said. "Maybe there never was a body in the coffin at all. Colin was the one who arranged for it to be shipped from Cairo, and it was he who brought it to London. We could have buried a pile of rocks for all we know."

"Or a carcass from the hunt!" Ivy exclaimed.

"Excellent suggestion," I said. "Still, it seems unlikely, doesn't it?"

"I'm afraid so, my dear," she said, watching a maid come in with the tea tray. I filled our cups, carried mine to Philip's desk, and sat in his chair. Planting my elbows firmly on the desk, my chin in my hands, I sighed.

"If there is any chance this is true, I ought to confront Colin," I said. "If he did try to harm Philip, his reaction to anything suggesting that my husband is still alive would be most telling."

"But the letter specifically instructs Arthur not to inform Colin," Ivy said.

"Yes, but assuming our speculations are true, Philip most likely wrote that because he did not want Arthur to get mixed up in this forgery business. If Philip is alive, he knows he cannot avoid facing Colin upon returning to England. It makes sense that he would try to protect Arthur. I shall send for Colin immediately," I said, ringing the bell for Davis.

In fact, Colin's reaction to the letter was not at all what I expected. He did not grow pale or worried, nor did he skulk guiltily out of the room. Instead he sat close to me, took both of my hands in his own, and bit his lip before meeting my stare and speaking.

"I wish, more than anything, Emily, that this could be true. Ashton was the best friend I have ever had. Losing him caused me greater pain than any I had felt before. But he is dead, my dear."

"Arthur said you were the only one with him—that you sent the rest of them away. You made them afraid they would get sick if they stayed."

"Yes, that is true."

"Perhaps you were also scared of falling ill," I said, wrenching my hands from his. "And you left him with strangers."

"I would never have done such a thing."

"You must have, because otherwise he could not be alive, writing to Arthur Palmer, desperate to speak to him, and clearly wanting to avoid you. Does that not suggest he feels you betrayed him in some way?"

"No, Emily, I do not think that line of reasoning makes any sense at all."

"Perhaps you could suggest an alternative, Mr. Hargreaves," I said.

"The only alternative that I can offer is the truth." He stood up and walked over to the window. "Ashton had been more tired than usual from the time we left London, something we all attributed, if you will excuse me, to his newly married state." Ivy gasped, and we looked at each other, amazed that he would say such a thing. Colin turned toward us.

"Don't allow us to distract you, Mr. Hargreaves," I said.

"He was not himself those last few days. Irritable, short-tempered, he argued even with me. In hindsight, of course, I realize that he probably had been ill for days. A camp in the African bush, no matter how well appointed, is not a comfortable place when one is sick. At any rate, the evening after Ashton got his elephant, his health began deteriorating quickly. Andrew Palmer brought out some fine champagne to celebrate the success of the day, but Ashton declined a second glass and retired to his tent."

"Very difficult life in these camps, Mr. Hargreaves, with all this sitting around and drinking champagne," Ivy said.

"Palmer liked to have as many of the comforts of home as possible in the bush. It was wonderful for us, but not for his porters." Colin walked across the room and leaned against Philip's desk. "At this point I still did not realize Ashton was ill. A couple of hours later, I decided to go to bed myself, and as I walked toward the tents, I heard my friend calling out in his sleep. I looked in on him and saw immediately that he was consumed by fever."

"I sat with him all night. By the next morning, it was clear that his condition was serious. I spoke to the others. Having no way of knowing how contagious Ashton was, we all agreed that it would be best to minimize everyone's exposure. They were gone before noon. I stayed with Ashton."

"He suffered a great deal of pain, Emily," Colin said, walking toward me and taking my hand. I pulled it away. "He could keep no food or liquid down and was sick repeatedly. He kept asking for you, and eventually I calmed him by reading the letters he had from you."

I cringed to think of anyone, least of all Philip, reading them. Written entirely out of duty, they contained little more than impersonal reports on my daily activities and any news I had of his nieces and nephew. They certainly were not love letters that could have provided him comfort. I hated that Colin had read them, and I glared at him now.

"I do not have the vaguest idea what the letters said. I was exhausted physically and mentally. Ashton's pulse was very weak despite his fever. We both knew he did not have long to live.

"As ill as he was, he kept speaking of you and begging me to promise that you would go to Santorini. But you already know that. Gradually he grew less coherent and spoke as if you were with him, always addressing you as Kallista. By the time the sun had set, he had lost consciousness and never regained it. It was the worst twenty-four hours of my life."

"I'm so sorry," Ivy said softly.

"So you see, Emily," he began, taking my hand again, "there is simply no possibility that Philip is still alive. I never left his side. I watched as he took his final, labored breaths and did not release his hand from mine until his body had grown cold."

"He could have been in a coma, Colin. You are not a physician," I snapped, and pulled my hand away. "I do not claim to have an explanation for what has happened, but clearly if Philip is writing to Arthur Palmer, he is not dead." I did not want Colin to think I suspected him of foul play so did not question outright his account of Philip's last night.

"If, through some extraordinary series of events, he is alive, and I must say again that I cannot even imagine such a circumstance, don't you think he would have contacted you before now? Surely he would write to *you* before Arthur Palmer? Think hard on this, Emily. None of it makes sense."

It wouldn't have made sense had I chosen to believe Colin's version of the story; he was truly a clever man. Logically I still was not thoroughly convinced that Philip was alive, but emotionally I desperately wanted him to be. As I was in possession of no definitive evidence to support either view, I decided to hope for the best.

"None of us knows what Philip has been through," I retorted. "To recover from an illness as severe as the one you claim to have witnessed would have left him incapacitated for some time. He may even have lost his memory. We have no idea who took him in, who cared for him. Whoever it was would have no idea of his patient's identity."

"Emily, it has been more than a year and a half. Be reasonable. I know how much you want to believe that he is alive; I share your feelings." He stood again and turned to face me. "But it is not possible. He died in Africa from a terrible, savage fever. I cannot imagine where this letter of Arthur's came from; most likely it was misdirected, mishandled, and delivered extremely late. I wish it had never happened. You should not be forced to face the loss of a loved one more than once."

Now, as I looked into Colin's eyes, I was certain that he was at the heart of this intrigue. He knew all too well that the first time I had faced Philip's death, I had not mourned my husband. Colin's cool demeanor and soothing voice seemed condescending and patronizing; he was trying to manipulate me.

"I would think that, as Philip's best friend, you would insist upon thoroughly investigating this situation," I said.

"Believe me, Emily, if I thought there was even the smallest chance that Ashton is alive, I would already be on my way to Africa."

"I have no interest in arguing with you, Colin," I said, dismissing him. "Please leave me." I shook my head as the door closed behind him. "I thought perhaps he would show some guilt. Obviously I was wrong."

"Do you think there is any truth in what he said?" Ivy asked.

"Yes, up until the part where he claims Philip died. His calm in facing the subject unnerved me."

"I must admit I find it difficult to believe that he could have harmed Philip," Ivy said quietly.

"Think of what a man of Colin's status would suffer if exposed as having orchestrated a series of major thefts from the British Museum. Desperation has driven many a man to do the unthinkable."

"I know you are right, Emily. Our reasons for suspecting Colin's involvement in the matter of the forgeries are sound, yet the question of what really happened in Africa still troubles me."

"Perhaps all of our questions on that subject will shortly be answered by Philip himself," I said, the smile returning to my face. "Colin's story should not fluster us. We were naïve to have thought he might say anything else. Did we really expect that he would admit to abandoning his dying friend as he praised his own good fortune? Of course he would not. He has merely recounted to us the story he has told everyone since his return to Cairo after the hunt. He has had a considerable length of time to rehearse his performance. I do not think we should put too much weight on it. We would have been better to say nothing to him."

"Well, we do know that the letter does not seem to have ruffled Colin's feathers in the least. Clearly he believes that he still controls the game," Ivy said.

"His confidence will prove his undoing."

5 OCTOBER 1887
GRAND HÔTEL D'ANGLETERRE, ATHENS
εκ της Αγγλιας

Vardakas has introduced me to Pavlos Forakis, the dealer from whom he has made his recent spectacular purchases. Forakis assures me he can easily find objects of similar quality for my own collection. Have not yet decided what I shall do.

The ethics of collecting are sometimes ambiguous, particularly in this sort of a case. I have tentatively agreed to a rather large purchase—hope I do not regret it.

22

"I DON'T THINK I'VE EVER SEEN YOU SO DISTRACTED!" Margaret exclaimed as we sat together in the library discussing Homer. "You just agreed with me that Achilles is a superior male."

"Did I?" My eyebrows shot up. "I'm sorry, Margaret. My mind is not entirely here today."

"Is something wrong?"

"Not at all. I just miss Philip and find myself spending more time than I ought wondering what our life together might have become." I felt more than a bit guilty at not telling my friend what had motivated these thoughts, but I could not bring myself to tell her that I hoped my husband was, in fact, alive. I still did not want anyone to point out the logical implausibility of such a thing's proving to be true.

"There's nothing surprising in that. But focus instead on the reality of the situation, Emily. Take comfort in the fact that no matter how wondrous he seems in death, in life Philip was a typical English nobleman. He may not have reacted well to your having decided to educate yourself."

"Perhaps."

"Don't be offended by this, Emily, but I think that if Philip were still alive, you would be in exactly the same position as Ivy."

"And what is wrong with that?"

"Nothing, for Ivy. She is content with her role. I do not think you would be. Eventually you would have wanted more, and your husband probably would have been shocked, if not horrified, to realize that he had married a woman with an active mind. Was Philip so unlike Mr. Brandon?"

"I cannot say," I said.

"Don't be so melancholy," she admonished me as she took her leave. "Seek solace in Homer. Your plight is far less than Hector's."

Resolved to take her advice, I dove into the *Iliad*, quickly losing myself in the poetry. I hardly heard Davis enter the room to announce Mr. Attewater, who had come to update me on the progress of my sculpture.

"Mr. Attewater, this looks delightful!" I exclaimed, peering closely at the sketches he held out before me and examining the paper on which they were drawn. "I am so pleased that you have already begun work on my commission."

"I am a busy man, Lady Ashton, but I consider you to be one of my most important patrons. I have chosen Aphrodite as the subject of this sculpture because she, alone among the Olympian gods, approaches your own beauty." He executed a perfect little bow as he spoke.

"There is no need to flatter me, Mr. Attewater; I have already agreed to pay you."

"I assure you, Lady Ashton, that any compliments which spring from my lips are entirely genuine," he said, puffing up his chest. "I am a man of high principles." This comment made me laugh despite myself.

"I'm so sorry, Mr. Attewater, I mean no offense."

"It is nothing," he replied. "I realize the contradiction in my person that stems from the nature of my work. But remember, only once have I strayed from my principles. Do not judge me based on the lack of scruples enjoyed by the majority of my patrons."

"Let me assure you I do not, Mr. Attewater," I said, smiling warmly at him. "I am very curious about your other patrons. I believe that I know one of them rather well."

"I would imagine that you know any number of them. My pieces grace the collections of many aristocrats. Not everyone can afford originals, you know."

"Yes, I am quite aware of that and know better than to press you for names."

"I appreciate that, Lady Ashton," he said. "This is a fine library, if I may say so, but shockingly short on art. Where did the viscount keep his collection?"

"Nearly all of it is in our country house. I do have a lovely bust of Apollo in the drawing room."

"Oh, yes, the Praxiteles. We saw mine in the British Museum, didn't we? A very difficult piece to complete," he said, clearly proud of himself. "Not many could have pulled it off. Do you know who did yours?"

"Praxiteles, actually," I said, raising an eyebrow. "It's a bit embarrassing, I'm afraid."

"My dear lady, I assure you that I do not hold it against you at all. I was already aware of that"—he paused, searching for a word—"habit of the viscount's. I can guarantee you not only my absolute discretion but also of my respect for any man who has such a profound appreciation for beauty. A great man with a fortune at his disposal can hardly be blamed for wanting to own the original of such a thing."

"I do not blame him for wanting it. Accepting that he went through with the purchase has been somewhat more difficult for me."

"Had he not, my own work would not be so prominently placed in the museum for the pleasure of thousands," Mr. Attewater replied. I almost pitied him, knowing how much it must bother him that he received no credit for his work by the viewing public.

"Please do not think that I consider your work unremarkable. It is the deception that troubles me."

"I understand completely, Lady Ashton. It is the same concern that keeps my involvement a step away from where I would have to be if I wanted to become really well-off from selling my works."

"That, Mr. Attewater, brings me back to the subject of my friend, the one who I believe is a customer of yours. Mr. Colin Hargreaves."

"Why do you mention him, Lady Ashton?" he asked, looking rather concerned. "I have never told you that he is a patron of mine."

"But he is, isn't he?" I asked, trying to sound lighthearted.

"I'm afraid that I must stay true to my policy of not discussing clients."

"So you admit that he is one?"

"I have said no such thing," he stated, mopping his brow with his handkerchief. "Suffice it to say that he is a man who has a significant effect on my business."

"How is that, Mr. Attewater?"

"Please, Lady Ashton, you will make things terribly difficult for me if you press the issue. I can neither confirm nor deny the name of anyone I work with. Should I start making exceptions, it would undermine my position greatly."

"But you told me that Lord Ashton never contacted you," I said.

"I did that, Lady Ashton, against my better judgment, because I could see the pain in your eyes. Do not ask more of me."

"Did you ever contact Lord Ashton?"

"What makes you think I would?" he replied.

"I have found two notes that warned of grave danger. Both were written on heavy paper—like that on which you sketched your plan for my sculpture," I said, walking over to the desk. I unlocked the drawer, pulled out the notes, and handed them to Mr. Attewater, who turned slightly pale.

"I had heard rumors. Nothing specific, mind you. Although I had no direct dealings with Lord Ashton, I knew of his reputation as an excellent patron and thought that he deserved to be warned."

"What were these rumors?" I cried emphatically.

"People said he had angered a powerful person and was in danger. It had something to do with antiquities he had purchased, but I really know nothing else." Although I pressed him, Mr. Attewater insisted that he was ignorant of further details, leaving me to wonder whom my husband had angered and why.

———

Lord Bromley hosted a magnificent foxhunt to mark the opening of the season. K rode but did not follow the hounds, instead choosing to tear about the grounds with her friend Miss Ivy Cavendish. Told me she hoped the fox would escape—but the spark in her eyes suggested she was teasing me.

I managed to evade our chaperone in the garden for a mere five minutes. Not enough time, but—at last—I have kissed my bride.

23

Ivy left me alone the following afternoon while she called on friends. We had agreed to tell none of our acquaintances of Philip's letter, not wanting to make the news public until we were more certain of its truth. While she was gone, I took stock of my wardrobe and, unsatisfied with it, dashed off a note to Mr. Worth, ordering two more gowns in fabrics decidedly unsuitable for mourning. I say "dashed off," but after signing it, I glanced at the clock and realized that I had spent nearly an hour writing precise descriptions and drawing sketches of what I wanted. I turned my attentions to Philip's dressing room, lamented at having so recently purged his clothing, and wondered if I should order some clothes from his tailor. This led me to wonder if it would be possible to re-hire his valet, who had taken another position some months after Philip's death. Not death, disappearance, I corrected myself.

The only bookshelf in our master bedroom was rather small, and I quickly set myself to the task of filling it with the same titles Philip had in his room in the country. Happily, both of his libraries contained copies of *Troilus and Cressida*, and I added my own catalog from the British Museum as well as the copy of *Lady Audley's Secret* I'd read on our honeymoon. I had lent *A Study in Scarlet* to Ivy but had Davis send one of the footmen out for Conan Doyle's new Sherlock Holmes book, *The Sign of Four*, which I thought would be a pleasant surprise for my husband should he, in fact, return home. The only volumes I did not search for were those on hunting; I rather hoped that his latest experience in Africa would have soured Philip on the subject.

I sat on the edge of our bed and smiled to myself. Perhaps I would not be forced to sleep alone for much longer. Never had I imagined that I would so look forward to the intimacies shared by husband and wife, but here I was, craving Philip's gentle touch, his warm breath on my cheek, and the feel of his strong body on top of mine. I sighed and collapsed into a supine position on the bed, quickly realizing that the pins Meg used to such stunning effect to hold my hair in place dug into my head and made lying on my back wholly uncomfortable. My tightly laced corset made returning upright difficult, and eventually I rolled onto my side and off the bed. These logistical problems quickly broke the spell of my thoughts of Philip, and I became aware of the sound of Ivy's voice calling to me from the hall. The stairway carpet muffled the tap of her heels, but I could tell that she was racing up the stairs, all the time shouting my name. I pulled myself to my feet and met her at the top of the steps.

"Good heavens, Ivy! What is the matter? You look as if you had run through all of London."

"Emily, I have just had the most extraordinary afternoon." She sat on the top step. "Have you met Cyril Elliott?"

"No, the name is not familiar," I answered, my curiosity piqued.

"I saw Arabella and Mr. Palmer at Lady Fielding's. Arthur was rather severe with me for having left you alone. Clearly he has no concept of the strength of your character." Ivy laughed. "But it is kind of him to be concerned, I suppose."

"Yes, Ivy, but that can hardly be the extraordinary part of your afternoon?" I asked.

"No, of course not, merely an interesting aside," my friend said with a wicked smile. "Later, when I was at Victoria Lindley's—" Ivy stopped and interrupted herself. "Have you been to her house since her marriage?"

"No, I haven't," I answered, wishing Ivy would regain her focus.

"Horrid place," she said. "At any rate, while there, I was introduced to Mr. Cyril Elliott. And before you ask, no, he is not related to the dreaded Lady Elliott."

"Good," I said.

"Mr. Elliott, it seems, has only just returned from Africa, where he and a small party of friends were hunting. In the course of recounting his adventures to myself, Victoria, and Jane Barring, who, I must tell you, looks terrible—"

"Ivy! The story. What did Mr. Elliott say?"

"Right. He told us that everywhere they went, they heard rumors about an Englishman wandering through the bush."

"Could it be Philip?" I asked, hoping that this would be the proof I needed to erase the seeds of doubt I harbored.

"He said the story grew more and more fantastic each time they heard it. First they were told that the man was very ill, then that he was mad, then that he had renounced civilization and planned to live like a native. Mr. Elliott gave little credence to the latter two versions but said that it does appear that someone, separated from his party, grew sick and was left to his own devices to find help."

"Where on earth is this man?" I asked. "It must be Philip. I hoped he might be alive after reading the letter, yet I must admit that it alone did not offer indisputable proof. But this story seems to confirm everything."

"It appears so, Emily," Ivy said, taking my hands. "If nothing else, it is without a doubt reasonable to think there is a very good chance that this man may be Philip. Surely it is too much to think that coincidentally there would be two Englishmen in a year who have fallen ill and been abandoned by their friends."

At that moment Davis appeared, announcing Margaret, who had come to study with me. She joined us at the top of the stairs, and I immediately told her all we knew; she reprimanded me for not having shared with her Philip's letter when I first learned of its existence.

"Why didn't you tell me, Emily!"

"I do apologize, Margaret, but please understand that I wanted to tell no one until I had better evidence. You, of all people, would require considerable substantiation of such a claim. I know your standards of proof. I suppose I was afraid you would point out the implausibility of the whole situation when I had no desire to abandon my hopes."

"You have me all wrong, Emily. I've heard of stories like this before—men surviving against unthinkable odds. It's happened more times than I can count in the American West. And think of Dr. Livingstone."

"Dr. Livingstone?" Ivy asked.

"Oh, yes!" I cried. "Of course, Dr. Livingstone."

"He was presumed dead in Africa for at least three years before Stanley went to look for him. And it must have been another two before he succeeded," Margaret said. "Philip's been gone fewer than two years. That he might be alive doesn't shock me in the least."

"Mr. Bennett," Ivy said, grabbing my arm. "Do you remember him from Paris?"

"Of course," I replied, confused.

"He's the one who sent Mr. Stanley to look for Dr. Livingstone because he wanted the story for his New York paper," Ivy said. "I talked to him about it at some length. It was rather difficult to get him to move on to another subject."

"You're clever to remember that, Ivy. I had forgotten," Margaret replied. "And you know everyone believed that Livingstone had been killed."

"He was in poor health when Stanley found him, I recall."

"Actually, more weary than ill," Margaret said.

"All the same, his experience must have been dreadful!" Ivy exclaimed. "How he must have suffered."

"I must go to Philip. I must try to find him," I said, hardly hearing what either of them said, as I suddenly felt almost panicked. "I am going to Africa. I cannot bear the thought of him languishing alone in an isolated village. I want to see him the moment he is discovered."

"Of course you must go. If he is still ill, your very presence will undoubtedly lift his spirits and aid in his recovery. Your reunion must not be delayed," Margaret said, growing more and more excited.

"Perhaps Mr. Bennett would be willing to organize an expedition to find Philip," Ivy suggested.

"Mr. Bennett might be an excellent resource, but I don't think he would agree to let Emily go. Can we think of anyone else to arrange things?" Margaret asked.

"You are right. Furthermore, if Mr. Bennett were to hear of this, he would undoubtedly want the story for his paper. I do not want to attract publicity." I thought for a moment. "I shall enlist the help of Mr. Palmer. It is he, after all, whom Philip chose to contact. He should be able to orchestrate a search party."

"We should remember that Dr. Livingstone was a missionary, Emily. He had chosen to live in Africa and was well established there. Granted, his living conditions were undoubtedly wretched, but they were satisfactory enough that he stayed on even after Stanley found him. Philip was not in such happy circumstances. While we can hope that he may be found alive, I do not think that we can be sure," Ivy said.

"I will believe it until it is proven otherwise," I said with a flourish, utterly captivated by the idea that I would soon find myself in Philip's arms.

"Do you really think you should go to Africa?" Ivy asked. "It sounds awfully dangerous."

"She must go!" Margaret cried. "I wish I could. I cannot believe that my sister's wedding is so soon. There's no way I can avoid going back to New York for it."

"I will need your help, Ivy," I said. "My mother cannot know that I am going. She would do everything in her power to stop me. I would like to tell her that I am with you in the country. Will you corroborate my story?"

"Oh, Emily, I just don't know if this is a good idea. I want Philip to be alive as much as you do, but it is not a certain thing. And the idea of traveling to Africa—it just isn't safe."

"You needn't worry, dearest. You know the Palmers will see to it that no harm comes to me."

"I don't think now is the time to abandon your friend, Ivy," Margaret said.

"Emily knows I only want what is best for her." I could see from Ivy's expression that she thought I was going too far.

"But now you are implying that you know better than she does what that is," Margaret said, rather forcefully.

"Please, Ivy, will you help me?"

"Of course," she said, sounding more resigned than convinced. "If you feel this is something you must do, I will not stand in your way."

"If Mother writes, could you answer the letters for me?"

"Yes, but surely she would recognize your handwriting?"

"True. If she writes, you shall have to send any reply by cable. Say that I'm so very rich that I don't like to wait for letters to arrive by post. She'll be horrified and won't write again," I said. "And, Ivy, you must not tell Robert."

"Oh, Emily, I don't know that I could lie to him."

"Your husband has no right to know her plans," Margaret said.

"Please, Ivy. If he were to find out, he might try to stop me."

"Yes, I imagine that he would." She furrowed her pretty brow. "But maybe not, if you agreed to go only as far as Cairo. You could let the others travel the rest of the way without you and still see Philip more quickly than if you waited in London. No one would object to your going to Cairo, not even your mother. You could stay at Shepherd's—this is the perfect time of the year for it."

"I am not going to Cairo, Ivy—I am going to Philip, if I must travel all the way to Lake Victoria to find him."

"Good heavens! Is that where he was hunting?" Ivy asked.

"To tell you the truth, I have no idea," I admitted. "But Arthur certainly knows."

"Perhaps he should speak with Mr. Elliott to get a more complete picture of these rumors," Margaret suggested.

"Excellent idea." I leaned against the rail at the top of the stairs. "I never liked Arthur much when I first met him, and I still don't particularly enjoy his company. Yet if he agrees to do this for me, I shall be utterly indebted to him."

Within a few hours, I had dispatched a hurried note to Arthur and received a reply. He, along with Andrew, was booking passage to Cairo and arranging for guides to take them south.

"I am most impressed that Arthur rose so quickly to the occasion," Ivy said, reading over my shoulder.

"And Andrew, dear Andrew." I sighed. "I hardly know what to say about him. He is going all this distance to rescue my husband so soon after I callously turned down his own proposal. I do not think many men would do such a thing."

"I think that he loved you more than we realized," Ivy replied. "He certainly must have a deep admiration for you to go to such lengths to ensure your happiness."

"Romantic though that idea is, we should not forget that both he and Arthur were friends of Philip's. Lovely and charming though you are, Emily, they may be doing this for their friend more than for you," Margaret said.

"You are right, of course. Still, I rather like the idea of the rejected suitor moving heaven and earth to bring his love her heart's desire," I said, less than half seriously. "It is awfully good that I turned down Andrew, isn't it? Only imagine if Philip were to return home and find me engaged."

"Thankfully, that never would have happened." Ivy stood up. "I'm surprised that Arthur did not mention in his note any thoughts on your decision to accompany the party. I felt certain he would protest."

"I haven't told him yet," I admitted. "I didn't want him to refuse to go and thought it would be easier for him to adjust to the idea once his own plans were set in motion."

"You are terrible, Emily. Well, if you are to depart for the Dark Continent in less than a week, I think you had better begin packing," Margaret said. "And you will have to break the news to the Palmers. I would love to see their unguarded reactions when they learn of the addition to their search party."

1 December 1887
Ashton Hall, Derbyshire

———

Have spent much of the day reorganizing my collection and labelling objects—activities necessitated by what might be considered excessive purchases made during my recent travels. Forakis has not been able to locate any more of the objects from my list—suggests I will have to return to Paris if I am set on finding them.

Will visit K briefly in Kent next week so that we might see each other before I leave for Africa. How quickly both our lives will change when I return.

24

THE NEXT AFTERNOON I CAME FACE-TO-FACE WITH THE
man I had avoided since refusing his proposal of marriage. I received
Andrew in the drawing room, on this occasion preferring it to the library, the scene of my rejection of him. He looked more handsome than
I expected and behaved so properly to me that I would have thought him
a completely changed man if it weren't for his slightly wry smile.

"Lady Ashton, thank you for seeing me," he said, waiting to sit until I
invited him to do so.

"Andrew, please do not revert to formality with me," I said, smiling
back at him. "That would be unbearable."

"I hardly know what to say, Emily. So much has changed between us
since our last meeting, yet my feelings for you are unaltered." He rose to
stand before me. "The level of my affection leaves me no alternative
other than to do whatever will make you happy. In this case that means
restoring to you the man you never stopped loving, even though my own
heart will break to see you reunited with him."

"Andrew, I am truly sorry. I never meant to hurt you."

"I know, darling." He paused and looked into my eyes. "But I must
not call you that any longer. Had you accepted me, we would still be
faced with the fact that Ashton is alive. I would have been plummeted
from the greatest joy of my life to the deepest despair. It is better that
you never agreed to be mine. That way I avoid the pain of having to give
you up."

There was nothing I could say in response to this, so I remained
silent, staring down at my hands on my lap. Andrew sat in a chair across
from me and crossed his legs.

"My intention was not to come here and make you feel terrible. Forgive me if I have done that; I am not quite ready to abandon the role of rejected lover," he said, smiling again. "But I am also here in another capacity entirely. Arthur and I have everything in place for our departure to Africa. Is there anything you would like me to take to Ashton? A letter or some small memento?"

"Actually, I had something else in mind," I began, hardly daring to look at him. "I want to accompany you. I shall go mad waiting for you to return with him. I need to see him as quickly as possible and imagine I shall understand what he has suffered better if I am there when you find him."

"Are you certain?" Andrew's eyes narrowed as he looked at me. "Africa is a singularly inhospitable place. You would be much more comfortable at home."

"How can I think of my own comfort when my husband has languished near death far from everyone he loves? I must go to him, Andrew."

"I confess I had rather hoped you would say that," he replied. "I would never ask you to do such a thing, but I reckon it would be immensely beneficial for Ashton to see you. We do not know what his physical condition will be when we reach him. Whatever the stage of his recovery, it cannot help being positively influenced by you. I can conceive of no one better to nurse him than you. The sound of his calling for you when he first fell ill still haunts me." He gazed toward the window. "He repeated your name over and over. It was dreadful knowing that we could not respond to his wish."

"Well, then it is settled," I said. "I shall be prepared to depart with you. If you would be so good as to arrange the travel details, I will see to everything else."

"I would be honored, Emily."

"And, Andrew . . ." I paused. "Please do not be offended when I say this. I know enough of your finances to realize that this trip is beyond your means. I have already instructed my solicitors that anything you and Arthur need shall be paid for out of my accounts."

"That is not necessary," he said, looking at me quite candidly.

"Perhaps not, but it is an expense I cannot ask you to bear. If you should like to take the matter up with Philip when we return to England, you may." I smiled. "I shall never be able to thank you adequately for this, Andrew."

"I see the happiness in your eyes, Emily, and that is enough."

There was a soft tap on the door, and Ivy peeked into the room. "I hope I am not interrupting," she said.

"Not at all," Andrew said jovially. "Emily and I are planning quite a trip, and I shall depend on you, Ivy, to ensure that she has an appropriate wardrobe. These trailing skirts of hers would be a disaster in the bush."

"We have anticipated the problem, Andrew, and already have the matter well in hand," Ivy said. "I think you will be most pleased."

"I expect so," he said.

"Emily, I came in to tell you that I'm off to Victoria's," Ivy said. "Are you certain you do not need my assistance with anything else? I should not mind missing tea at all."

"No, go Ivy. I shall be fine. Send everyone my regards," I replied.

Andrew bowed as she left and then turned to me. "Emily." He stopped. "May I beg one final favor from you?"

"Of course, Andrew. What is it?"

"May I kiss you good-bye? I know that when I see you next, we shall be immersed in our search for your husband and that I never again will enjoy the closeness we shared during these past several months. I should like very much to end that wonderful chapter of my life with a kiss. Of course, it is entirely inappropriate, but then so was most of our courtship." He smiled at me, but I thought I could see the pain of rejection in his eyes. What harm could come from one kiss? I walked over to him, took his hands in mine, and raised my lips to his. He kissed me deeply for what seemed like a very long time.

"Thank you, Emily. From now on I shall try very hard to think of you as Lady Ashton, but in the recesses of my heart, I shall cling to that kiss." He raised my hand to his lips and departed.

THE FOLLOWING DAYS FLEW by quickly. I managed to locate several walking suits and two pairs of sturdy boots that I hoped would prove adequate for the African plains. We were to stop in Paris because of a prior business engagement of Andrew's and then continue on to Cairo, where we would meet the native guides who would lead us to British East Africa. Upon leaving Cairo, we would take the railroad as far south as possible and then continue on horseback. Andrew and Arthur had very clearly stated to me the dangers we would meet on our journey; the land itself would provide a considerable challenge, and there was no guarantee that the region would not be in a state of political unrest. Possible danger, rather than deterring me, made me all the more determined to complete my mission and bring Philip home.

Margaret's excitement was palpable, and she lamented daily that she could not join me on the adventure, cursing her sister for deciding to marry at such an inopportune time. She swore to join any safari Philip planned in the future. I pointed out that then it would be *her* turn to be the only female in the party, as I had no intention of ever participating in a big-game hunt. Margaret only laughed and made me promise to write down every detail of the journey so that she might enjoy it vicariously.

Ivy, on the other hand, grew more nervous as the time for me to leave grew near. She hovered over me, wringing her hands, wishing I would agree to stay in Cairo. Despite her worries, she never wavered in her support and promised not to breathe a word of my plans to Robert. She herself wrote to my mother, asking if she thought some time in the country would do me good. My mother, always happy to believe that she controlled me, replied to Ivy that she really must take me away from London; it vexed her no end that I had remained in town after the opening of grouse season. Thus my alibi was established.

Three days before my trip, I put on one of my new traveling suits and walked down South Street to Park Lane and Hyde Park, where I spent the afternoon circumnavigating the Serpentine and meandering through the park's wide paths without any specific purpose. The bright sun did not take much of the chill out of the air, but I walked at a brisk pace, welcoming the turn of season. The freedom brought by a simple change of clothing was extraordinary. With no corset I could breathe deeply, and my sturdy boots did not threaten to twist my ankles every time I increased my speed. I felt as if I could conquer the world. I paused for some time before the great statue of Achilles, contemplating my husband's opinion of the hero. Eager though I was to see Philip again, I was also a bit nervous. His return would once again alter my life; all the independence I had enjoyed for nearly two years would be gone. Philip might prefer that I not walk alone in the park; he might not like my taking over his library and disagreeing with his views about Homer. He almost certainly would not like my drinking his port. I felt a flicker of insecurity as I wondered if he would love this version of his Kallista, but I could not really believe that our reunion could be anything less than romantic perfection.

As I started to walk in the direction of Kensington Palace, a gentleman rushing down the path nearly bowled me over.

"I am terribly sorry," he said, looking up. "Emily!"

"What brings you to the park, Mr. Hargreaves?"

"The same as you, I would imagine. Excellent day for a walk."

"It would appear that you are running. Are you late for some engagement?" I asked.

"No, I've just come from one," he replied tersely.

"In the park? Tell me, Mr. Hargreaves, were you meeting a lady?" I asked, raising an eyebrow. "Am I to wish you joy?"

"Hardly, Emily. You of all people should know that. I've just seen Palmer; he tells me that you plan to accompany him and the others to Africa."

"That's right," I said, lowering myself onto a nearby bench, once again delighted by how much easier even the simplest things became in the absence of a corset. "I want to see Philip as soon as possible."

"Emily, please listen to me," he said, sitting next to me. "I know you hate being told what to do and that when you get an idea into your head you are loath to turn away from it. I understand your need to believe that your husband is alive. Perhaps sending a search party for him is necessary for you to realize that he is dead. But it simply is not wise for you to embark on such a journey."

I looked into his eyes as he spoke, wondering at this choice of words. "I am quite aware of the potential danger."

"I don't believe that you are," he said. "I cannot imagine what Palmer is thinking, letting you go."

"In the first place, he realizes that I may be of assistance to Philip; in the second, he, unlike some other members of my acquaintance, realizes that he has no control over what I choose to do."

"If Ashton were alive, he would thrash Palmer for putting you in harm's way," Colin retorted.

"Well, we shall let him handle the matter himself." I stood up and adjusted my gloves. "I, however, am quite confident that Mr. Palmer and his brother will be able to provide more than adequate protection against whatever dangers we may face. I shall have to beg your leave. There is much I need to do before the trip."

He stunned me by leaping up and taking my face gently in his hands.

"Please do not put yourself at risk, Emily," he said softly. "That is what you will do if you insist on carrying out your plan. I will have no way of protecting you."

"I'm much obliged for your concern, Mr. Hargreaves," I said, removing his hands. "But I assure you that I shall be fine." I started to walk away, then turned back toward him. "I am certain that my husband will wish to have words with you upon his return."

With that I turned quickly on my heel and marched away from him. Clearly, it was in his best interest to keep me in London, away from Philip for as long as possible. Colin's perfect manners, handsome face, and charming demeanor would not deceive me; I would never give in to him. I slowly made my way back to Berkeley Square, where I was surprised to find Ivy opening the door for me.

"Good heavens!" I exclaimed, walking into the cavernous entrance-way. "Why are you answering the door? Has Davis completely taken over the household and made himself master? I would not have thought he had it in him."

"I've been watching for you for nearly half an hour," Ivy whispered. "There is a very mysterious gentleman called Wesley Prescott waiting to see you."

"Are you acquainted with him?" I asked, removing my hat and handing it to Davis, who appeared completely unperturbed by my friend's behavior.

"No, I've never seen him before in my life," Ivy replied, still speaking so quietly that I could hardly hear her. "Imagine his nerve at calling without first obtaining a proper introduction."

"Did he tell you why he came?"

"Not at all. Insisted that he would speak only with you and that he would wait any length of time. Davis wouldn't let him into the house at first, but eventually I felt sorry for the man."

"I have put him in the drawing room," Davis said.

"Thank you, Davis." I nodded. "Come with me, Ivy. We must hear what Mr. Prescott has to say." I marched into the drawing room and found myself staring at a tall, rail-thin, sunburned man who was dressed terribly. He rose to his feet as soon as I entered the room and began apologizing for his intrusion into my home.

"Perhaps you had best tell me why you are here, Mr. Prescott. I do not have much time; I am preparing for an extended trip."

"I am with the Anglican Church Missionary Society, Lady Ashton, and have spent the past ten years converting the unfortunate pagans in eastern Africa. Nearly a year ago, a tribesman brought to us an Englishman who was very, very ill. Apparently the local medicine man had done all he could and no longer wanted the burden of a white man's life on his hands."

"Philip!" I said, clutching my hand to my throat.

"Yes, your ladyship. We did not know his name for some time; he did not speak coherently for several weeks. The best we could tell, he had yellow fever and hadn't been able to rest enough to fully recover. When he began to get better, his memory was not entirely intact, but over the course of the following months, he regained it, along with much of his strength. He carried this with him." Mr. Prescott handed me a dirty envelope, which I opened immediately. In it was a photograph taken of me on our wedding day. I gasped. It was the picture I knew Philip had brought to Africa, the same one he showed to Renoir when he'd commissioned the portrait of me in Paris. There was no conceivable way that this man could have the photograph unless Philip had given it to him.

"I do not know what to say." I handed the picture to Ivy, who rang for Davis and ordered brandy. I could hardly breathe; my hands trembled uncontrollably. "He really is alive."

"Oh, yes, quite alive," Mr. Prescott replied. "When I left the mission, he was still not well enough to travel. I'm afraid he suffers terribly from malaria. Knowing that I would return to England before he could, he asked me to bring this picture to you to reassure you."

"Did he give you anything else?" Ivy asked.

"Yes, a letter to a chap called Palmer, which I posted for him in Cairo. I apologize for not getting here sooner, but I had planned to stop in Dover to see my parents before journeying to London. I only see them on my rare visits to England."

"Of course. Thank you, Mr. Prescott. Could I beg one more favor of you?"

"Certainly, Lady Ashton."

"Could you call on my friend Mr. Andrew Palmer and tell him the precise location of the mission? We have already planned a trip to bring my husband home."

"I would be honored to, Lady Ashton," he said with a rather undignified bow. I quickly penned a letter of introduction for him to give to

Andrew and thanked him again. After he was gone, I hugged Ivy, Davis, and anyone else who crossed my path, delighted by this final confirmation that Philip was still alive. The trip to Africa did not seem nearly as daunting now that we knew where to find him; we might even be home before Christmas.

"Emily, I am so sorry I doubted that Philip might be alive," Ivy lamented. "Yellow fever and malaria! You shall have to take very good care of him."

"I have every intention of doing exactly that," I said, beaming.

———

Anne's son showed signs of great intelligence, I think, when he tried to chew on the statue of Alexander the Great I presented him as a Christmas gift. My sister chastised me for giving the tot such an inappropriate gift—suppose wooden blocks would have suited her better, but I would rather serve as the uncle who inspires the little lord to greatness. Next year shall give him a copy of the <u>Iliad</u> to put under his pillow.

Have given Emory explicit directions on how to handle the impending arrival of my shipments. Much though I would like to supervise this myself, I see no need to alter my plans for Africa.

K has given me a small spyglass for Christmas. She and her friend Miss Ivy Cavendish were quite amused by the gift, which they selected together, and suggested that I take it on safari. I have not heard K's laughter before; it sounds like silver.

25

AT LAST THE DAY OF OUR DEPARTURE ARRIVED. THE weather did not cooperate in the least, but the blinding rain had no effect on my high spirits. My heart was full of the joyous anticipation that should have marked the days preceding my wedding. Instead of picturing my groom at the altar, I imagined finding Philip tossing in a primitive bed, his straight hair damp with sweat. I would rush to his side, place my hand on his forehead, and he would immediately lie still. His eyes would open; the sight of me would give him the strength to sit up and kiss me passionately. After a pleasant interlude, I would admonish him to remember his health and he would agree to rest. I would sit with him, holding his hand until he slept, this time peacefully, with a slight smile on his face. I hoped we would be able to bring him home at once. The remainder of my romantic fantasies would be better executed at home, or at least at Shepherd's Hotel in Cairo, than in a remote African village.

Meg interrupted me before my reverie carried me further, saying, her voice filled with dread, that the carriage was waiting. I had realized that it would be highly inappropriate to travel with only Andrew and Arthur and decided to take her with me as far as Cairo. Beyond that, I hoped that the presence of guides would be enough to satisfy the proprieties. My poor maid had cringed at the thought of having to go abroad once again, but I was determined to turn her into a traveler. I presented her with a copy of Amelia Edwards's reminiscence, *A Thousand Miles Up the Nile*, with the hope that she would read it and be inspired to explore at least Cairo and its environs while the Palmers and I searched for Philip.

"Are you ready for our trip, Meg?" I asked.

"Oh, Lady Ashton, I think you would be much better off taking Mr. Davis or someone else," she said reluctantly.

"Nonsense, Meg. You shall enjoy yourself immensely, and I need you. Davis's place is here." She and my butler were the only members of the household who knew the true nature of my excursion; the rest thought I was going to Ivy's country house. Meg, for all her hesitation at consorting with foreigners, was a model of efficiency under any circumstance. Furthermore, no one else could match her skills in arranging hair. Davis would have been a singularly useful addition to nearly any expedition, but to take him would be unthinkable. Why on earth would my butler travel with me to someone else's house?

"Yes, madam," Meg replied halfheartedly.

I adjusted my hat and, with a final glance in the mirror, swept out of the room, past the commanding portrait of Philip's father in the hallway and down the wide staircase.

"Goodness, Emily, you look as if you could fly!" Ivy exclaimed.

"I am ecstatic at the prospect of some time in the country," I said, winking at Davis, who struggled to maintain his dignified posture.

"I sent your trunks to the station before breakfast, Lady Ashton, with precise written instructions for the porters."

"Thank you, Davis. I shall wire with any news," I whispered to him, patting his arm.

"Take care, madam," he replied. "We hope to have you home again very soon."

Within an hour Meg and I had settled snugly into our train. Margaret went to the station to see us off, and I waved frantically to her until the train pulled far from the station. The cold landscape outside the window made me feel doubly warm and exceedingly comfortable in our cozy private compartment. Andrew and Arthur sat with us for the beginning of the journey and then retired to their own compartment on the other side of the corridor.

"It is an excellent day to travel," I said to Meg when we were alone.

"But the weather is dreadful, Lady Ashton."

"I have always liked traveling by train in inclement weather. One is completely isolated from the elements and whisked away to emerge at a destination where the weather may be entirely different."

"I'm afraid it will be a rough time crossing the Channel, madam."

"I shouldn't worry too much, Meg." I remembered how seasick she had been during our return from Paris and wanted to put her mind at ease. "We shall hope for calm waters. Have you started your book?"

"Not yet, madam. There was no time, what with all the packing to tend to."

"You are free of all such distractions at present. Try to enjoy the journey, Meg." As she picked up her Amelia Edwards, I rummaged through my bag in search of a book for myself. I had taken Philip's copy of *King Solomon's Mines* from the bedroom at Ashton Hall and soon was engrossed in Mr. Haggard's story of adventure in Africa. Presently Meg asked if I was hungry and produced a spectacular picnic lunch, which I invited Andrew and Arthur to share with us. They appeared as unsettled at the prospect of dining with my maid as she was at eating in the company of gentlemen, but I did not pay them any notice.

Soon we reached Dover, whence a steamer would take us to Calais. Meg's face was still tinged green when, hours later, we boarded a train to Paris. My thoughts of calm seas of course had no effect on the Channel, which was at its choppiest, taking away any hope poor Meg might have had for a pleasant crossing. Andrew and Arthur fared no better than my maid; I alone did not fall sick on the ship. My companions staggered onto the train and were all asleep within moments of our departure from the station, leaving me to my reading. Rather than return to *King Solomon's Mines*, I turned instead to my Greek grammar. I had spent sadly little time on my academic pursuits while preparing for my journey and did not want to fall hopelessly behind. After passing nearly half an hour staring blankly at a passage I could not focus on enough to translate, I opened Philip's journal. I had already read the parts that pertained to myself but now wanted to peruse it in its entirety. The volume I carried with me spanned a period from the year before our engagement through the time of Philip's disappearance. I hoped that reading it would provide me with a greater insight into the character of my husband.

The early entries in the volume had been written in Africa and chronicled what evidently was a thoroughly satisfactory hunt. For over a month, Philip, Colin, and their fellows stalked more types of prey than I care to remember. Colin appeared to have spent more time trekking through the countryside than hunting, for which I admired him. Philip was in his element, tracking prey and planning strategies; he filled page after page describing the process in maddening detail. Clearly he loved what he was doing. I, however, found the topic rather boring and had a difficult time doing more than skimming the pages. I was thankful when the party eventually returned to Egypt, where they played tourist for another month. Philip's descriptions of the monuments of Egypt were not particularly inspiring, but for this I could forgive him. Greece, not the land of the pharaohs, was the area of his expertise.

I closed the book and gazed out the window as the train ripped through the French countryside. It had been very easy to fall in love with Philip when I believed him to be dead. Looking at his journal brought to mind the reasons I had never been interested in him in the first place; hunting encompassed a terribly large part of him, and it did not interest me in the least. How would I feel next year if he wanted to leave me home for three months while he cavorted around Africa?

I shook off these troubling thoughts and continued to read. Philip had spent the spring in London; this was the time during which we met. Rereading these passages dissipated my melancholy, and once again my heart filled with ardor for the man who had written so beautifully as he fell in love with me. I found mention of the Judgment of Paris vase and an account of his decision to purchase both it and another vase. To this point there had been not a word of anything that I could interpret as underhanded or suspicious in the least. The only surprising revelation was the fact that he'd brought to the villa an English cook. Despite his love of the Greek countryside, he did not fully embrace the culture.

To this day it distresses me to admit it, but reading Philip's journal in detail proved rather tiring; I began skimming again. Our engagement, a trip to Santorini, another African safari, our wedding, our wedding trip, flew past me in short order. After considerable deliberation he donated the Paris vase to the British Museum shortly before our wedding and did not write about it again. It was just as Mr. Murray had told me. I skipped ahead to Philip's last entries, which unfortunately gave me none of the information I had hoped to find. He spoke of Colin in the warmest of terms, even in his account of their final argument.

"Achilles heard, with grief and rage oppress'd; / His heart swell'd high, and labour'd in his breast. / Distracting thoughts by turns his bosom ruled . . ." Hargreaves *cannot understand what I am doing, and we argued bitterly, but of course he supported me in the end, as he always does. Nonetheless, I shall not let him be my Patroclus.*

I wasn't entirely sure what that last phrase meant. Did it suggest that, although they were friends, he would not consider Colin to be as close to him as Patroclus was to Achilles? Or was Philip attempting to protect Colin, by not accepting an offer of assistance? Achilles allowed Patroclus to fight for him, and his friend died in battle. Although I could not make complete sense out of Philip's statement, I could not but think that it must pertain somehow to the forgeries.

Philip was buying stolen antiquities; that much was certain. Perhaps Colin was the one who had them copied and removed the originals from the museum. Philip, after our marriage, may have decided to stop his nefarious activities and told Colin that he would no longer be a buyer. He may have gone a step further and told Colin to stop the thefts altogether, giving him the opportunity to reform himself. Colin, unwilling to abandon a profitable enterprise, would have argued with Philip, not comprehending why his friend had suddenly changed his feelings about their activities. This made sense to me. Marriage would make a gentleman more aware of the importance of his code of ethics and morals. The two friends may have started down their illegal path together by letting a joke or a challenge go too far. Philip recognized that the time had come to stop; Colin was not ready. His friend, although they had been close for years, would never be his Patroclus.

None of this was of much concern to me at the present; before long I would be reunited with Philip and insist that he reveal everything, but I liked trying to decipher the puzzle. I wondered if the time had come for me to bring Andrew into my confidence. I did not require his assistance but would very much have liked to have his emotional backing in my quest to reveal Colin's thievery. As I considered my options, he opened his eyes and smiled at me. I decided instantly to leave him alone. I had caused him suffering enough.

The conductor tapped on our door and told us Paris lay only a few miles away. Soon I felt the train begin to slow, and I shook Meg gently to wake her. We had arrived. Monsieur Beaulieu greeted us on the platform and escorted us back to the Meurice, where he put me in his best suite, assuring me that he had personally overseen the changing of the locks only that morning. I convinced him that I felt perfectly safe in the hotel, thanked him for his hospitality, and then told Meg to leave until morning what little unpacking she had to do. We would spend only enough time in Paris for Andrew to tie up his business, and I planned to enjoy myself thoroughly while I waited for him.

Cécile's carriage collected me immediately after breakfast the next day. My friend had not yet dressed and received me in her ornate bedroom, where she and her maid were arguing over what she would wear that day and did not even notice me enter. Marie Antoinette herself would have envied Cécile this chamber, with its white-paneled gilt walls whose centers were covered in white silk brocade embroidered with flowers.

"*Non!* Madame! The rose is too soft a color," Odette insisted, stamping her foot and sending Caesar and Brutus running to hide under the tall bed that dominated the room. "A brighter hue suits you better."

"I am not looking for a husband, Odette," Cécile retorted, lying back on a chaise longue, her lacy dressing gown fluttering around her. "I like the rose. Monsieur Worth would not have allowed me to purchase it if it did not flatter me."

"Monsieur Worth is terrified of you, madame."

"I cannot believe that Monsieur Worth is terrified of anyone," I said, raising an eyebrow. "More likely it would be the other way around."

"Except that I fear no one," Cécile reminded me, rising and hugging me emotionally. "I am so pleased to see you, Kallista."

"The feeling is entirely mutual, I assure you."

"Fine, Odette, bring me some other dress. The rose would clash with Kallista's dreadful mauve. How much longer must you mourn, my dear?"

"The moment I see Philip, I shall burn all these clothes," I said. I had written extensively to Cécile; she knew every detail of my present situation.

"*Chérie, chérie,* truly you think too much of this man. I hope his return to you is as joyful as you hope."

"I think it shall be," I replied.

Cécile disappeared into her dressing room. "You do not sound as confident in person as your letters did," she called to me.

"I am quite confident, just a bit tired from the journey."

"Your trip to this point has given you only a fraction of the misery you will suffer on the rest."

"Thank you for your kind support." I laughed.

"Well, at least your bedroom will no longer be lonely. You will be happy of that?"

"Yes, immensely happy," I said, glad that Cécile could not see me blush.

"That is encouraging," she replied, sailing back into the bedroom, grabbing my arm, and leading me into the hall. "If that is your attitude, then Philip cannot be all bad. Come. You must see my lovely miniatures while we talk."

Behind Cécile's drawing room ran a long, wide corridor lined with miniature reproductions of rooms from the palace at Versailles. She began collecting them as a girl, after her father had designed her first one for her. This was the only thing I knew of her father; she gave no further information about him. I wondered if her family had been aristocrats before the revolution and if she still harbored sympathy for the lost monarchy. My mother was convinced that they had been closely connected to royalty. The history of noble families was the only subject on which my mother could claim expertise, so in the case of Cécile's ancestors, I felt inclined to agree with her.

"However did you get that done?" I gasped, looking at the Hall of Mirrors, the latest addition to her spectacular dollhouse. The detail stunned me. Cecile assured me that every bit of tiny gilt trim, the twenty crystal chandeliers, and the seventeen beveled mirrors perfectly mimicked the originals.

"You know better than most people that anything can be accomplished with enough money," she said, adjusting some of the golden maidens holding elaborate candelabras that stood at intervals along the walls. "Your friend Monsieur Pontiero has turned out to be a most skilled miniaturist. He painted the ceilings for me."

I bent down to look at my former drawing master's work and felt duly impressed. "Never having seen the original, I shall have to take your word for the authenticity. That Monsieur Pontiero's work is exquisite cannot be questioned."

"Much has changed in the *palais*, but what can be expected to happen after the revolution?" She shrugged. "Next time you come to Paris, I shall take you there."

"Philip would love that; I know that he wanted to take me to Paris," I said with a sigh.

"None of this romantic nonsense, *chérie*. I said you, not Philip. He will be left with the impressionists or at the Louvre. Love him if you will, but I am not sure that I would enjoy his company."

"You are dreadful, Cécile," I moaned.

"I am too old to be subjected to your foolish sentiments," she said, smiling. "What would I have to say to a man whose prime entertainment is hunting exotic beasts? What conversation could we have?"

"His interests include many other things, Cécile. Be fair." I did not like the fact that she had focused on my only real fear in being reunited with my husband. "Do not forget that he is also an avid collector of art."

"Yes, I had put that out of my mind." She picked up a tiny table and dusted it off with her handkerchief. "Perhaps I shall find that he is not hopeless."

"Thank you," I said, rolling my eyes.

"Do you think he will continue his habit of prolonged hunting trips? It hardly seems fair to you."

"I admit that is a subject that has given me some cause for concern, but there is no use speculating. I shall discuss it with him after we return home."

"I do wish you had chosen a husband who did not enjoy such an odious activity," Cécile said, returning the table to its place in a lovely little receiving room.

"Yes, I know. I secretly hope that he will be put off the entire business after his last safari."

"Somehow I doubt that is likely. But I will try to withhold judgment of the man until I have met him. In the meantime I do have a fine surprise for you this afternoon. I told Renoir that we will bring lunch to his studio."

"That will be marvelous. You haven't told him about Philip, have you?" Brutus and Caesar had followed us and engaged themselves in a battle with the hem of my skirt. Having tired of the skirmish, I removed them one at a time and handed them to Cécile, who put them on a wide windowsill. They seemed to enjoy the view and did not trouble me further.

"No, I have told no one. I did not think it would be prudent until you produced the man himself. You say your evidence that he is alive is good, and I do agree with you, but"—she tapped my arm with her fan—"I am not convinced, Kallista. It all is too fantastical. Do not be angry with me, but I agree with your handsome friend Monsieur Hargreaves."

"Colin! But, Cécile, I am almost certain that he is behind all this forgery trouble. How could you take his side?"

"I would welcome a criminal with his face into any room of my house," she said slyly.

"You are trying to shock me but shall not succeed," I said, smiling and shaking my head. "But really, Cécile, I am afraid we were completely deceived by him."

"I am not sure that it matters," she said, shrugging. "Forget about these forgeries. Leave it to Philip, if you really think he is alive."

"If I did not think he were alive, I would not be traveling to Africa."

"I am not sure that is true, Kallista. Whatever the outcome, I hope that you are not disappointed." She finished rearranging the furniture in one of her tiny dollhouse bedrooms and turned to face me. "Let's speak of something more interesting. Did you know that our infamous cat burglar is still at large? Madame Bouchard, who lives just three houses from me, lost a diamond necklace that had been in her family for generations. It seems the thief will never be caught."

"I hope you are careful about locking your windows, Cécile. I'd hate to see any of your jewelry go missing."

"It would take more than locks to keep out such a clever criminal."

After stopping in Paris for several days to complete some unexpected business transactions, I have at last caught up with my friends. We will reach Cairo the day after tomorrow, where Kimathi, our guide, will meet us to start our journey south.

Palmer outdid himself in arranging the trip, although I fear our porters will suffer carrying the array of comforts he insisted on bringing. Hargreaves gave him a grilling over it, preferring a simpler camp, but I doubt he will refuse to share our friend's hospitality once he has tired of Masai cuisine.

K promised to write me regularly in care of Shepherd's—am anticipating reading her letters as soon as we arrive.

26

CÉCILE SENT THREE FOOTMEN TO ARRANGE HER LUNCHEON at Renoir's, with spectacular results. They created an indoor picnic, spreading thick blankets over the floor and placing vase after vase of hothouse flowers around the room. These blossoms combined with a blazing fire in the stove to give the effect of a lovely midsummer day. Renoir suffered greatly from arthritis and did not have the money to heat his studio to a temperature warm enough to ease his symptoms; Cécile had concocted her picnic in order to give him an afternoon of relief from the damp autumn day. I had no doubt that her footmen had also left sufficient wood to keep the stove burning hot for several more weeks. We sat on the blankets and shared an elegant feast: *mousse de foie gras, pâtisseries génoises, saumon à la zingari,* a variety of *chaud-froids,* and countless other dishes.

"I am delighted to see your work again, Monsieur Renoir," I observed, looking at the canvases that filled the studio. "Your paintings are like the music of Mozart: perfectly pleasing."

"*Merci,* Kallista," he replied, beaming. "I have the most beautiful model; all I must do is imitate her." Aline, who had spent the morning sitting for him, did not blush but instead leaned over and kissed her husband full on the mouth.

"How are Monet and the others?" I asked.

"Fine, fine," Monsieur Renoir answered. "Will you be in Paris long enough to travel to Giverny?"

"Unfortunately not."

"Kallista has merely stopped over on her way to Africa." Apparently Cécile had decided to reveal my secret.

"*Mon Dieu!*" Aline rolled her eyes. "What will you see there?"

"Egypt, Aline. I shall not be satisfied until I have laid eyes on the Great Pyramid." I glared at Cécile, not sure if I wanted to tell Renoir that Philip still lived. "Autumn is a lovely time to go, you know."

"I would imagine so," Aline said. "Seems a hopeless place. Desolate. I suppose a person might recognize a sort of stark beauty in it."

"I should like to go," her husband interjected. "If only to see the sunlight in the desert. The light must bring out a myriad of colors in the sand."

"Well, I shall stay home." Aline shrugged. "Paris is far superior."

"No one questions that," Renoir replied.

"I suppose you could persuade me to join you." Aline stroked Renoir's face. I averted my eyes, not wanting to intrude on a private moment.

"You see, Kallista—that is what marriage should be," Cécile commented. "Will you have it with Philip?" Thankfully, Renoir and Aline, utterly captivated by each other, appeared not to hear her.

"I shall not discuss it, Cécile. Please do not insist upon bringing up the subject," I retorted, quite certain that Philip would emphatically disapprove of such a public display of affection. His behavior in such matters had always been perfectly proper. Unless his near-death experience had changed him significantly, I anticipated that any displays of his devotion would be limited to our bedroom, where they would be warmly returned.

"It is something you should consider, *chérie*, before it is too late." Cécile waved her hand in the air as if fending off an irritating insect and sighed loudly.

"You are surprisingly melancholy today, Cécile," Renoir observed. "Have you been crossed in love?"

Cecile laughed. "Hardly. I am only hoping that our *chère* Kallista is not about to be."

"Ah!" Aline gasped, grabbing my hand. "Have you fallen in love? How delightful! Who is he? I hope he is French?"

"No, no, please, you misunderstand. Cécile, you will force me to address the topic I am trying so hard to avoid." My friend threw her hands in the air as if to indicate that she had no control over the matter.

"Let the child have her secret if she wishes," Aline said. Then, in a tone of close confidence she whispered to me, "There is nothing more glorious than passionate love. When you find it, nothing will compare."

"Thank you, Aline." I did not know how to respond. Truly, I hoped I was passionately in love with Philip, although such a judgment proved difficult to make after having had no contact with the object of my affections for nearly two years. I knew that seeing him again would be exquisite, but I did have some lingering doubts as the moment of our reunion grew nearer by the day. His hunting bothered me, the forgery business plagued me, and I continued to worry that he would not appreciate the changes in my character since his disappearance. I did not question for a moment that he loved me very dearly; his journal proved that. But how passionate could that love have been if he left me so easily after an abbreviated wedding trip? Clearly he preferred the idea of a safari with his friends to the company and comforts of his wife.

"I have found that in love everything falls into place when you least expect it. When you are convinced there is no hope, your heart is saved," Aline said.

"Unless, of course, it is broken instead," Renoir said, sitting behind his wife. "Aline likes to speak in absolutes that are not always reasonable. It is one of the most charming things about her." He hugged her.

"In matters of love, it is preferable to be hopeful rather than a pessimist," Cécile stated matter-of-factly. "I think you are trying admirably to do that, Kallista, even if I do not always agree with your choice of lover."

"I have no lover, Cécile!" I cried with mock indignation.

"Speaking of lovers, Kallista." Renoir turned to me. "I have meant for some time to return this to you." He opened the drawer in a small table standing near him. After rummaging through the contents, he looked a bit confused. "I was certain it was there."

"What is it?" I asked, curious.

He walked over to a chest and lifted its lid. "Not here either." He sighed. "Where on earth could I have put it?" He dug through several painting cases and a large bag, each time coming up empty-handed. He shook his head. "I just had it. I showed it to Monsieur Palmer when he came here not three weeks ago."

"What, Monsieur Renoir?" I asked, my voice growing more urgent. "What is it you seek?"

"The lovely photograph from your wedding day that I used when I painted your portrait. Lord Ashton left it with me when he departed for his safari."

———

Hunting this season so extraordinary—have already made plans to repeat the trip this fall, with sights set on an elephant—the only prey that has had the audacity to evade me. Tracked a great kudu today— an exceptionally large male. Led me through miles of woodlands before at last I found him. I was careful not to alert him to my presence, but he must have sensed something—he stood absolutely still, nearly invisible in the bush as I aimed my rifle. I felled him quickly with one perfect shot. What an animal! Immense twisting horns make it more handsome than any other antelope. Kimathi says mine has the longest horns he has ever seen—more than seventy inches. Between them a spider had woven the most enormous web that shone in the sunlight like a crown, leading Hargreaves to suggest that I had got the greatest of the great kudu.

Tonight Masai guides prepared a feast for us—must confess to preferring English roast beef—but we dined like African royalty. To be among such friends, in such a place—what could be the equal of such an experience? Our camp, in the midst of the flat-topped mimosa trees, lighted by a blazing fire, is as fine a home as any I have known. "Thus the blest Gods the genial day prolong, / In feasts ambrosial, and celestial in song."

27

I EXCUSED MYSELF FROM MY FRIENDS, TELLING THEM that I wanted to be alone, and shot out of Renoir's studio. They followed me to the door, obviously concerned, and I could hear Cécile calling for me to come back as I ran down the rue Saint-Georges, pulling my cape close around me. Although I did not know precisely where I was, I remembered Renoir's saying that the Opéra was only a short distance from him. When I reached the rue La Fayette, I asked the first person I saw which way to turn and soon found myself in front of the grand building. Seeking refuge under its curved arches, I leaned against the wall, my chest heaving from exertion. My heart pounded so forcefully that I could hear the blood rushing in my ears, and I felt as if I would faint. I knew that something had gone deeply, deeply wrong. I opened my reticule and pulled out two pictures from it: the first my portrait of Philip; the second the one for which Renoir had searched.

Clearly Philip could not have sent my wedding picture to England with Mr. Prescott if he had left it in Renoir's possession. Renoir certainly had no cause to deceive me in the matter; if anything, it made perfect sense that the photograph remained with him when Philip left for Africa. It would have taken Renoir longer to paint the portrait than the brief time my husband had spent in Paris on his fateful trip. And what of Andrew? I had no idea that he'd returned to Paris only a few weeks ago; he had not mentioned it to me. The timing would mean that he'd left England soon after I refused his proposal. Perhaps he had traveled in an effort to mend his broken heart. Regardless, it appeared that Andrew must have taken the picture from the studio after Renoir showed it to him. How else could it have come back to England? But what could have motivated Andrew to do such a thing? Surely not petty revenge after my rejection.

Worrying about why Andrew had done it troubled me, but not nearly as much as what it might imply about Philip's current status. My confidence in finding my husband alive began to ebb, and as I felt it drift away, tears streamed down my face. Realizing that I looked rather conspicuous, I decided to keep walking; I did not want Cécile or any of my friends to find me just yet. Most of all I did not want to return to the Meurice, where I was certain to see the Palmers.

I headed away from the Opéra, keeping my head down lest I see anyone who might recognize me, and walked as quickly as I could all the way to the Cité, where I sought refuge at Sainte-Chapelle. The day not being especially bright, there were few tourists inside the church; the stained glass could not be viewed at its best under a cloud-filled sky. I sat on a bench facing the southern wall with its glorious windows, not particularly caring what I saw. Confident that no one would search for me here, I dropped my head into my hands and sobbed quietly.

The sun began to set, and as my surroundings grew increasingly dark, I felt comforted by the absence of light in the medieval chapel. Too soon an elderly man approached me and told me the hour had come for the building to close. Seeing my swollen face and red-rimmed eyes, he suggested that I move to Notre-Dame, where I would find only the choir closed to visitors. I took his advice and spent an immensely soothing length of time in the nave of the magnificent cathedral. My mind somewhat cleared, I decided to walk the length of the Cité to the Pont-Neuf, my favorite of Paris's many bridges.

I stopped near the center of the bridge as it approached the Right Bank and relished the commanding view I had of the Louvre. The moon's brightness as it slipped out from behind a cloud shocked my eyes after the easy candlelight of Notre-Dame, and I considered returning to the cathedral. Before I could make up my mind, I heard a man's voice calling my name. I turned around, startled, and was utterly astonished to see Colin Hargreaves striding toward me.

"Emily!" he cried, grabbing both of my arms. "What are you thinking, standing here by yourself in the middle of the night?"

"Good evening, Mr. Hargreaves. It's quite delightful to see you, too," I quipped. "It is hardly the middle of the night. I don't think it's later than eight o'clock."

"It's already dark, so the hour is irrelevant. Have you no regard for your safety?"

"At present, no, I do not. I thank you for your kind inquiry." I turned my face from him and looked back at the river.

"Thank God I happened upon you. What on earth are you doing? You've been crying. Pray, tell me what is the matter. Have your friends abandoned you?" He placed his gloved hand gently on my cheek; the sensation was so comforting that I did not ask him to remove it.

"Quite the contrary, I assure you. They are most likely mad with worry after my hasty departure," I said, trying to smile. "So much has happened today."

He put a hand to my lips and pulled me close to him. "My poor girl. There is no need to discuss it if you would rather not." I let my head rest against his chest in a most inappropriate fashion. He said nothing further until I pulled away from him.

"Thank you for solacing my wretchedness. Truly, I have had a most disturbing day."

"Can you trust me with your worries?" he asked, his voice deep. I tilted my head and looked into his dark eyes. A funny choice of words, I thought. *Can* I trust him? Not knowing the answer to that question, I remained silent.

"I do not want to pressure you into a confidence, Emily. You are too dear to me." This revelation should have startled me, but I found that it did not; in fact, it seemed completely natural. I met his gaze and parted my lips to speak. Before I could utter a sound, he embraced me and began kissing me with an urgency I had never before felt. Despite myself, I relaxed in his arms, returning his kisses at least as passionately as he bestowed them on me. Soon I touched his hair and tried to pull him closer to me, as if that were even possible. Then, all at once, I thought of Philip. I pushed Colin away from me and slapped him soundly on the cheek, aware of the unfairness of my action even as I did it. He did not flinch.

"I deserve that," he said calmly, looking me straight in the face. "But I am afraid that I cannot apologize to you. Kissing you is, without a doubt, the most ungentlemanly thing I have ever done. However, to beg your forgiveness would be completely dishonest, because, given the same opportunity, I would do it again."

"How could you do that when you know Philip may be alive?" I cried, trying unsuccessfully to slow my breath to a normal rate of respiration.

"I would never have done such a thing if I thought there were even the slimmest hope of such a possibility. You know that, Emily. He was my best friend."

"I do not know what to think," I said, my head spinning. The only thing of which I felt certain was the intense anger inspired by the man standing across from me.

"I shall not pretend to know all that is troubling you at the moment, although I think I have a fairly good idea. I can only offer clarification of my own actions. I am very much in love with you, Emily," he said huskily, raising my chin in an attempt to force me to look at him. "I have been since I had the good fortune to escort you home from Café Anglais during your last visit to Paris. I adore the fact that you have so willingly shed the restrictive mantle of your upbringing, and love absolutely the woman you have become. I want to argue about Homer with you, help you learn Greek, take you to see Ephesus."

"And what do you expect me to say to that?" I asked, finally able to meet his eyes.

"I expect nothing. Forgive me if I have offended you. I would never want to bring you any discomfort."

"That is precisely what you have succeeded in doing, Mr. Hargreaves," I said, my heart pounding. "I have never sought love from you, and your conduct tonight has ensured that my feelings on the subject shall never be any different. Would you be so kind as to hail a cab for me? I should like to return to my rooms." He did as I asked immediately and helped me up to my seat.

"Know that you can call on me at any time if you are in trouble. I could not live with myself if anything happened to you, Emily."

"I hope I should have better sense than to put my trust in you ever again, Mr. Hargreaves."

Much to my chagrin, he kissed my hand very sweetly, looking intensely into my eyes the entire time. I had nothing to say.

I DID NOT RETURN to the Meurice but instead directed the driver to take me to Cécile's house. As the cab took me across the river to the Left Bank, I could not stop thinking about what had transpired between Colin and myself on the Pont-Neuf. Try though I did to redirect my thoughts, my mind remained full of the memory of his body pressed against mine. It horrified me that a man whom I believed to have played a significant role in the disappearance, if not demise, of my husband could elicit such a physical response from me. I shuddered, wondering if our encounter had been an attempt by Colin to distract me from my purpose. The cab approached Cécile's grand house on the boulevard Saint-Germain, where my friend opened the door for me herself. I was thankful she had remained home for the evening, and after she scolded me violently for running off so thoughtlessly, she embraced me and sat me down next to her in the blue drawing room.

"I don't think I've ever seen you so flushed, Kallista. I know that my reprimand cannot have affected you so greatly. Pray, what is going on?"

"Oh, Cécile, it's just the photograph—" I stopped.

"You don't fool me for one second, *chérie*. It's been hours since you left Renoir's studio." She narrowed her eyes and scrutinized me. "Have you been alone this whole time?"

"Yes. No. I saw Mr. Hargreaves briefly and do not wish to discuss it."

Knowing Cécile and her seemingly clairvoyant ability to detect clandestine romantic interludes, I felt certain that she knew exactly why my face had turned red. I sighed, resigned to the fact that I had little hope of escaping from a conversation during which I would be coaxed into revealing every detail of my encounter with Colin.

"Ah." Cécile looked at me knowingly. "We shall discuss it later. Do not think that I shall forget; Monsieur Hargreaves fascinates me. But for the moment I am infinitely more concerned with your reasons for rushing out of Renoir's. It is obvious, of course, that your missionary friend is not all that he appeared to be."

"Clearly not." I walked over to a dainty eighteenth-century desk and seated myself in its matching chair. "I think the time has come to consider very carefully what is going on. There are two problems before us: the first being the question of Philip. Is he alive or dead?" I did not look up as I said this. Despite having spent a great deal of time that afternoon trying to come to terms with the probability that my dear husband was in fact dead, I had failed miserably. "Second is the issue of the forgeries and thefts from the British Museum."

"I fear this discussion calls for very strong coffee," Cécile said, ringing for a servant. I frowned. "I realize that you despise it, but it will fortify you."

"I suppose," I replied, pulling a piece of paper from the desk's drawer. "I shall take notes. Let us begin with the question of Philip."

"What evidence do we have that suggests he is alive?"

"The letter Arthur received, the rumor Ivy heard, and the story Mr. Prescott told when he delivered the photograph to me. Obviously we cannot precisely trust Mr. Prescott. Philip did not give him that picture."

"No. If anything, your good friend Andrew did," said Cécile, directing her footman to place a large coffee tray on a table near her. I added an extravagant amount of cream and sugar to the hot brew she gave me, the end result being almost drinkable.

"I find it difficult to believe that he would do such a thing, but I must admit to the possibility," I said. "I cannot imagine what would motivate him."

"Did he have any other reason for desiring to go to Africa?" Cécile asked. "He certainly agreed quickly to making the trip. Could he have been too short on funds to go on safari this year? Perhaps he hoped to combine purposes, knowing that if he went to find Philip, you without question would insist on paying his way."

"I suppose it is possible. But doesn't it seem an extraordinary thing to do? I had already told him I would pay for everything."

"He could have set the plan in motion before you told him, or he wanted to ensure that you wouldn't change your mind."

"Maybe he thought that my getting the picture in such a circumstance would put my mind at ease during what he knew would be a difficult trip. He may be reasonably confident that Philip is alive, and hoped to reassure me."

"From what you have told me, it appears that Andrew is the type of man who likes drama and extravagance, so your explanation could be true. But it does seem unlikely."

"I am going to wire the Anglican Church Missionary Society immediately, asking for more information on Mr. Prescott. Whatever the explanation, Andrew has not been truthful."

We sat quietly for several minutes before Cécile interrupted the silence. "I am afraid that I do not trust Andrew much at this point, Kallista," she stated flatly, shaking her head.

"Nor do I, and I do not wish to travel into Africa with a man whose motives are not perfectly clear." The knowledge that Andrew had so deliberately deceived me hurt me deeply. I hardly knew what to think. "I don't want to abandon Philip, but I cannot depart for Africa until I know why Andrew has lied to me."

"Of course not, *chérie*. But for now there is nothing to do for Philip. And do you not find it strange that you have been thrust into the center of *two* mysterious situations? Perhaps they are connected," Cécile suggested.

"It is possible," I admitted.

"Perhaps solving one question will lead toward the answer to the other." Cécile fed a small biscuit to Caesar, who swallowed it before Brutus could attempt to steal the treat. Brutus begged for one of his own, but she refused him, doling out what she believed to be a small measure of justice against the dog's namesake.

"There may be some sense in that, Cécile. At any rate, you are right that we cannot prove anything about Philip as long as I am in Paris." I crumpled the piece of paper that I had filled with random scribbles and placed a clean one in its place. "I think we must determine from whom Philip purchased his stolen artifacts. That person may also have directed Mr. Attewater to make the copies."

"You must try to get more information out of this Attewater character."

"He's in London. I shall send him a letter, but I do not expect him to give much assistance. He has made it perfectly clear that he will not reveal his contacts."

"It is understandable, I suppose. His discretion ensures his commissions as much as his talent does," Cécile said. "Have you any other ideas?"

"I believe Colin to be involved." I shared with Cécile my theory that Philip had decided to stop his involvement while Colin had insisted on continuing. She did not take to my hypothesis as readily as Ivy had.

"It is, of course, possible. We have no evidence to the contrary." Cécile shrugged and then smiled. "Perhaps it is time for you to expand your own collection of antiquities. I should hate to waste all those fascinating contacts I made in the black market. Could you lure Philip's contact to you?"

"Yes, but if Colin is at the heart of all this, he shall recognize me and protect his own identity."

"True. Well, I shall have to do it myself. About what piece do you think I should inquire?" Cécile asked, looking rather pleased with herself.

I realized immediately that she had never intended to allow me to rob her of the pleasure of returning to the nefarious world of illegal antiquity trading. I envied her the adventure and wished that I could conjure up something equally interesting to undertake myself.

"What would you say to an entire panel of the Elgin Marbles?" I asked, a wide smile spreading across my face. "You're very rich, Cécile. No one would doubt your ability to pay for it. And such a purchase surely would attract the attention of whoever runs the whole show, don't you think?"

"Is it too much?"

"No. Mr. Attewater told me that he began the project once but never completed it. It sounded as if the money had fallen through."

"Money would be no object here." Cécile clapped her hands and the little dogs leapt to her lap. "I rather like the idea. Where do you think I should put the piece? It would be quite large, I suppose."

"You shan't actually get it, Cécile," I scolded, knowing full well she was teasing me. "You must find out who could acquire such a thing for you and then insist on meeting with the man himself; no underling can be trusted to handle such a transaction. Once the appointment is set, all we shall have to do is wait for our man to show himself for the thief he is."

14 April 1888
Hôtel Continental, Paris

———

Never before so willingly left Africa earlier than planned. There is so much I must do before my marriage—so much work to finish—do not know how I shall ever accomplish it. Saw Fournier today; excellent talk with him, although have not yet forgiven him for owning the discus thrower. Offered me little help on my latest quest. Thought of marrying K within two months put me in such a generous frame of mind that I let him have a fragment of an Etruscan frieze without countering his offer. Monsieur LeBlanc very disappointed I did not drive up the price.

Have found my wedding gift for K. It is more simple, perhaps, than what she may expect: a brooch of ivory flowers, delicately carved. To my mind it captures her elegant innocence, and I hope she prefers it to something more ostentatious. Lord knows she will have enough of that sort of thing once my mother's jewellery is sent to her. To date, our relationship has been less personal than I hope it will be in the future; another diamond necklace would only be more of the same.

28

Cécile had promised to contact me as soon as she returned from her black-market adventure, but as the morning passed in what seemed to be geological time, I grew tired of waiting for her in my room and decided to go to the lobby and sketch. I was comfortably settled in a quiet corner when I heard two gentlemen conversing as they walked past me.

"I'm sorry not to have more time to talk," Colin Hargreaves said. "I'm late for a rather important meeting."

This piqued my interest. As soon as Colin walked out of the hotel, I followed him, keeping a careful distance between us. It quickly became apparent that he was going to the Louvre. Once inside, I hung back as he walked purposefully up the Grand Escalier. I waited until he was out of sight to ascend the staircase myself. Unfortunately, before I got there, I saw Monsieur Pontiero.

"Lady Ashton! What a delight to see you back in Paris."

"Thank you, Monsieur Pontiero."

"How is your drawing?" He motioned to the sketchbook I was holding. "May I see your work?"

"I'm afraid I don't have time at the moment. I'm in a dreadful hurry."

"Very good, very good. Perhaps we can meet soon?"

"I shall send you a note," I said, rushing up the steps, hoping that I was not too late to figure out where Colin had gone when he reached the top. As soon as I reached the landing on which stood the Nike of Samothrace, one of the most beautiful statues in the museum, I saw Mr. Murray, the keeper from the British Museum, speaking excitedly to Colin.

". . . removing a piece from its gallery is no small undertaking." He stopped immediately when he spotted me and bowed politely after I nodded to him. Colin turned around, clearly surprised to see me. Never before had I seen him look unruffled in the slightest; now, however, I detected a trace of color on his cheeks and something less than his usual cool demeanor.

"I'm sorry to have interrupted you," I said, fervently wishing I had heard more of their conversation.

"Not at all, Lady Ashton!" Mr. Murray cried. "I had no idea you were in Paris. I'm pleased to see you." Colin said nothing, nodding almost imperceptibly to acknowledge my presence.

"I am only here for a short time and thought I would take the opportunity to revisit my favorite pieces at the Louvre. Incomparable beauty to be found here."

"Quite," Mr. Murray replied as Colin stood motionless, looking rather irritated, his arms crossed over his chest.

"Don't you think that this statue is terribly displayed?" I asked. "It is most difficult to view." No one replied. "I should think a piece like this would merit an entire room, not a mere landing."

"As always, Lady Ashton, you make a keen observation." And that, apparently, was all I was to have from Mr. Murray on the topic of the Nike of Samothrace. I waited for him to comment further, but he said no more. Obviously his thoughts remained with the subject he and Colin had been discussing.

"I shall leave you two to your conversation," I said, aware that I would learn nothing more from them today. I descended the staircase and walked back through the Rotonde and into the Salle Grecque. After pausing to admire the lovely panels from the Temple of Apollo on Thalos, I hired a cab to take me back to Cécile's.

"Where have you spent the day?" she asked, patting Caesar. I wondered where Brutus was hiding.

"The Louvre. And I was not the only person of your acquaintance there." I quickly told her of my encounter with Colin and Mr. Murray.

"Monsieur Hargreaves again." She sighed. "Such an interesting man. What a coincidence to find him speaking to a keeper of antiquities about removing artifacts."

"I don't see how even you can defend him now." Brutus emerged from under the chair in which I was sitting, darted beneath my skirts, and started to chew on my shoe. I unceremoniously removed him and dumped him in his owner's lap. "Perhaps I should buy you a cat."

"I will refrain from passing judgment on the gentleman, having had great success on my own today. You may remember that when I made inquiries for you about Philip, I met a Monsieur LeBlanc, a man through whom some black-market dealers sell their wares. He is of interest to me at present because he has the means of passing on messages to a man who goes by the sobriquet of Caravaggio."

"Caravaggio?"

"I cannot explain the rationale of these criminals," Cécile said with a disinterested shrug. "That he chooses to style himself as an Italian is of no concern to me."

"Perhaps he *is* Italian?"

"No, not at all. Even LeBlanc knows that he is English."

"Is he Colin?" I paused. "Colin Caravaggio. It does have rather a ring to it, don't you think?"

"Hardly. I have no indication of Caravaggio's identity, but Monsieur LeBlanc assured me that he is currently in Paris and would respond to me quickly." Cécile reclined on her couch. "I also learned much more regarding your husband's illegal dealings."

"From Monsieur LeBlanc?"

"*Non.* After leaving my note for Caravaggio, I visited three more shops and managed to bully a good deal of information out of a weasely little man. When Philip wanted something, he informed the appropriate parties in the black market. These dealers, if we can call them that, scoured private collections and records of recent sales to locate the object. Whoever could find the object in question first received a handsome bonus. Your husband always made it clear that he had absolutely no interest in the provenance of any of the pieces, saying that he didn't care whence they came, only that they wound up in his collection."

I sat silently for a considerable time, pulling at my handkerchief. Caesar tugged at my skirts; I did not bother to push him away.

"'What are thou, boldest of the race of man?'" I paused. "I realize that this information provides details of things we already know, but somehow it makes his actions sound worse, doesn't it?" I asked.

"Kallista, you have built the man up too much in your head. He was an adventurer who hunted animals and antiquities. If he is still alive, you will have to accept him for what he is, not what you have styled him to be."

"I know you are right."

"I think it is perhaps time for you to tell me of your mysterious meeting with Monsieur Hargreaves after you fled Renoir's. Shall I ring for coffee or champagne?"

"Coffee," I said severely. "There really isn't anything to tell."

"Then bore me. I do not mind."

"I was upset. He consoled me, as is his style. Then he had the audacity to kiss me without first asking permission or begging my forgiveness afterward."

"How exciting! Philip grows less attractive with each passing moment," Cécile mused.

I glared at her. "Exciting is not how I would describe it."

"I would, after having seen your face when you arrived at my house that night."

"I shall not dignify that with a response," I said. "Can we please return to the subject at hand? Did you learn anything else this afternoon?"

"Only that no one I spoke to is familiar with Mr. Palmer or his unfortunate brother."

"Of course that doesn't mean much," I said. "Especially if either of them is Caravaggio. Did you ask about Colin?"

"I did. Only one person recognized him, and he laughed when I mentioned the name Hargreaves."

"What on earth could that mean?"

"If Colin is Caravaggio, I may have unearthed someone who knows his true identity. On the other hand, he may not have known him at all. He may have laughed because I described Colin as having the face of Adonis."

"You are impossible, Cécile." I frowned. "I should very much like to speak with that man."

"Do not consider it, Kallista. The people with whom I spoke this afternoon are not the sort with which you would want to trifle. They are dangerous. I have a certain reputation for idiosyncrasy that made my entrée into their society possible. You would not have such an easy time at it."

Before I could protest, a footman entered and handed Cécile a note from Caravaggio, requesting a meeting the following afternoon. Barely pausing before starting to dictate her reply, Cécile agreed that her mysterious contact could come to her house on the boulevard Saint-Germain at three o'clock. I felt strongly that the meeting should take place in a public location where we could easily get assistance if matters took a dangerous turn. Cécile, however, insisted that would seem suspicious.

"I am, as far as he is concerned, merely an eccentric old woman who wishes to buy some very famous, yet-to-be-stolen art. Would it make sense for me to conduct such business in public? Never. He shall come here. Besides, it will be much easier for you to observe us unnoticed. I shall receive Monsieur Caravaggio in the red drawing room, and you can listen from the back hallway."

"Will I be able to hear you through the door?" I asked.

"Yes. I did the same thing numerous times myself when my dear departed husband received lady visitors there. Discretion never was his strong suit," she said with a shrug. "I shall attempt to get Caravaggio to tell me as much about his operation as possible. If I am lucky, I will get enough evidence to bring about his arrest."

"And if you do not?"

"Then I shall have to go through with my purchase of the panel of the Elgin Marbles and turn him in afterward."

"That could take months!" I cried. "I cannot wait that long to depart for Africa."

"Well, then I shall have to do my best to collect information," Cécile observed. "I do rather hope Colin is Caravaggio; it would delight me to use all my wiles on him."

"You are terrible, and I am leaving," I teased, rising from the table.

The day had given me much to consider. My thoughts turned to Philip. Could he escape prosecution for his own crimes? A good barrister could probably argue that Lord Ashton knew nothing about the source of his prized collection and was guilty of nothing more than poor judgment and ignorance. I sighed, wondering what it would be like to live with such a man as my husband on a daily basis.

Thoroughly disheartened by the time I reached the Meurice, I ignored the telegram Meg handed me as I walked into my suite and headed straight for the bathroom, desperate for a hot bath. After a satisfactory soak, I stepped out, slipped into a lacy pink tea gown entirely unsuitable for a woman in mourning, and told Meg to bring me tea as quickly as possible. Back in my sitting room, I opened the telegram.

I read it through twice before storming to my desk and scrawling a brief note. I shouted for Meg and thrust it at her, filled with an anger I had never before experienced.

"Take this to Mr. Palmer and tell him that I expect to see him immediately."

———

K greatly surprised that I arrived back in London before expected. She is more lovely than when I last saw her. Am delighted that she has no objection to my returning to Africa in autumn—it is a fortunate man who finds such a bride.

My mind is still full of Africa and plans for the next safari. I've yet to do a Masai lion hunt with spears. Wonderfully primitive—and a decided challenge after growing used to the ease of rifles. Perhaps in autumn . . .

29

"I AM SURPRISED AND DELIGHTED TO SEE YOU DRESSED IN such an inappropriate color!" Andrew cried when he saw me.

I ignored his good humor. "Sit, Andrew." I handed him the telegram. "Could you please explain this?"

"I don't understand," he began. "How is this possible? We shall have to change our course of action, but that is not—"

"I do not think it is quite so simple, Andrew. The Anglican Church Missionary Society states rather clearly that they have never heard of Mr. Wesley Prescott. Whoever that man is, he obviously is not recently returned from the mission at which my husband is recovering."

"Yes, I am quite stunned."

"I find that rather hard to believe," I said, looking directly at him. "After all, aren't you the one who gave Mr. Prescott my wedding photo?"

"Emily . . . how could you think—"

"Spare me the lies. I know you removed it from Renoir's studio. Enlighten me, Andrew. What is going on?"

He closed his eyes and sighed before speaking. "All right, you have found me out. I should never have done it. I don't know any better than you whether Philip is alive or dead. When you told me you wanted to go to Africa with us, I realized that if we discovered that Philip is in fact dead, I would have the perfect opportunity to renew my suit for your hand. If you could only imagine the hope this brought to my heart! But I began to fear that your friends would convince you that the trip would be too dangerous, too hopeless. I thought Prescott's story would ensure that nothing could keep you from traveling with me. I never meant to hurt you, Emily. You already had good reason to believe that Philip is alive. I only wanted to give you further confirmation."

"You have manipulated my emotions in an unforgivable way, Mr. Palmer. The game is up, and you may as well accept the fact that I shall never marry a man of so little principle."

He bristled visibly when I said this and leapt from his chair. "I admit that what I did was wrong. Obviously you have never desperately loved someone who did not return the emotion. You may insult me if you choose, but I will suggest that you consider your husband more carefully before you call *me* unprincipled. Perhaps you did not know Philip so well as you think."

"I can assure you that I am painfully aware of his shortcomings."

"And should I assume that you are prepared to overlook his blatant disregard for all things decent?" He flung the telegram to the ground. "Of course you are! Rich aristocrats will do anything to avoid scandal."

"I do not like your temper."

"Forgive me. It infuriates me. People like Ashton, Hargreaves—they always get what they want. He never deserved you."

"You feel this way, yet you were prepared to travel to Africa to rescue him?"

"You know my feelings for you. I would do anything to bring you joy. Lord, what a fool I have been!" He stomped out of the room without a word of good-bye.

Thirty minutes later I received an impassioned note from him begging my forgiveness and informing me that he planned to leave for Africa in two days' time, with or without me.

AND SO MY ADVENTURE in Paris began to draw to a close. Cécile's meeting with Caravaggio would confirm the identity of our villain. Then I would figure out a way to stop the thefts and return Philip's stolen originals to the British Museum. Much though I hated the idea of letting Andrew and Arthur go to Africa without me, I could not travel with them. I drafted a letter to Lord Lytton at the embassy, giving him what information I had about Philip's possible survival and asking him to help me organize an official search party. I considered the possibility of having my husband's body exhumed but did not think my evidence sufficient to merit such a thing. Furthermore, the scandal that would ensue from such an occurrence really would terrorize the entire Ashton family. This thought made me wonder if I should write to Philip's sister, informing her of the recent events and begging her husband's assistance.

By six o'clock, having completed neither letter to my satisfaction, I decided to go out to the parts of Paris that Philip, if he were still alive, would almost certainly forbid me to see. I dressed in a fine gown of black silk and headed straight for Montmartre, with every intention of visiting the Moulin Rouge. Reality struck me less than halfway there; I could not go to such a place unescorted, not to mention while I was still in mourning. Confining though society could be, I did not want to abandon it completely. Instead I went to the Café Mazarin. Being on the north side of the boulevard Montmartre, it technically would not have been appropriate for a lady, but my Baedeker's guide assured me that the clientele at this particular café were perfectly within the bounds of propriety.

I ordered the blanquette de veau, which was delicious, and ate slowly. Afterward I had an absinthe, which seemed a bit daring, and began to plan what I would do after Cécile's meeting with Caravaggio. The liqueur was rather awful, but I choked it down nonetheless as I contemplated my future. It would be preferable to stay in Paris rather than London while waiting for news of Philip. I had no desire to answer to my mother, deal with social obligations, or pretend that nothing was wrong until I knew my husband's fate. Then, if he was alive—and I did, despite my misgivings, desperately hope that he was—I would of course defer to his wishes. Most likely he would want to return to England immediately.

And if he was dead, I would not go back to London; I wanted to go to Santorini. There I could determine my true desires free from any outside influence. I would apply myself to learning Greek and explore every inch of the island while I mourned the loss of Philip for a second time.

Fortified by another absinthe, I thought of Aline Renoir and her marriage. Never again would I marry for less than the happiness she enjoyed, nor would I do it before I knew better what I wanted from my life. If Philip was alive, I would devote myself entirely to him, confident that together we could capture more than an adequate amount of passion. I hoped that he would support me as I tried to discover what a woman in my position could be other than a society wife. If he would not—I pushed the thought out of my mind, sat back, and spent the rest of the evening reveling in the Parisian atmosphere.

———

My last night as a bachelor. Hargreaves and I marked the occasion with a magnificent '47 port.

K's things have been sent from Grosvenor Square. She will find all in good order—Davis saw to the details rather than letting the maids do it. I hope she will be happy in my house.

It is far too late, yet I cannot seem to sleep. Must try, though, as I have no intention of getting much tomorrow night.

30

I SLEPT FAR LATER THE FOLLOWING MORNING THAN I HAD intended to and wound up having to rush to get to Cécile's in time for *le déjeuner*. I wore a new dress, a deep midnight blue rather than black or gray. Mr. Worth and I never reached agreement as to whether it was technically appropriate for my last month in half mourning, but I did not care. It fell smoothly over my hips, flared as the skirt reached the floor, and had no bustle. On Cécile's recommendation I'd had it fitted with my corset tied extremely loosely and was well pleased with the results. The bodice still had a smooth appearance, but I could breathe, bend, and very nearly slouch. Happy with my appearance, I hurried through the lobby and slammed directly into Colin.

"Good day, Mr. Hargreaves," I said, ignoring my pulse's instant reaction to him. I flew past him toward the door, feeling rather excited that at last I would know the identity of Caravaggio. The thought caused me to pause and turn, taking another look at Colin. My eyes met his, and I raised one eyebrow, wondering if I would see him in a considerably different setting this afternoon. If Colin was the head of the forgery ring, I might get to slap him again; I smiled despite myself.

I greeted Cécile cheerfully and hugged her before joining her at the dining room table.

"You're in a fine mood for someone who obviously stayed up far too late," Cécile observed. "What was so interesting?"

"Absinthe," I said with a smile.

"I am impressed, Kallista. Paris will make an *artiste* of you yet."

"Terrible stuff. I could barely get it down." I dove into the vol-au-vent placed before me. "I am glad to have tried it, though. You should read this," I said, handing her the telegram denouncing Mr. Prescott.

"Not much of a surprise," Cécile admitted.

"I confronted Andrew."

"*Mon Dieu!* What did he say?"

I recounted our conversation.

"Do you believe him?"

"Does it matter?"

"I suppose not," Cécile said, feeding Caesar and Brutus, who sat patiently on her lap waiting for scraps from her plate. "I presume you will not be accompanying him to Africa?"

"Of course not," I replied, applying myself to the rest of my luncheon. "I wrote to Lord Lytton requesting his assistance. I shall not withdraw my financial support of Andrew and Arthur's trip, but I do not believe that I can entirely rely on them. I wonder how long it will be before I know the outcome."

"Try not to think about it too much, *chérie,*" she said, rising from her seat. "Come help me with my miniatures. I want to rearrange the queen's bedroom furniture."

We passed the next hour tending to Cécile's Versailles. The closer the time came for Caravaggio's arrival, the more tense I grew. Any residual excitement that remained deep inside me vanished when the footman announced a visitor.

"Put him in the red drawing room," Cécile said. She took my hands. "Remember, the most important thing you can do is try to identify the voice you hear. Listen carefully to what he says and take notes if you can. I had Louis leave paper and pen in the hallway." She handed me off to Odette, who had appeared out of nowhere to lead me to the back passageway, where I stood, trying not to pace. Soon I heard the door open and close and the click of Cécile's heels as she entered the room.

"Monsieur Caravaggio, I am delighted to meet you," she said. "You are not, I believe, Italian?" She laughed. I held my breath and waited for the reply.

"Not at all, Madame du Lac," he said. "I am English to the core. The Italian name lends a nice touch, though, don't you think?"

"I shall not offend you by insulting your country, monsieur, especially when I have such great hopes for our business relationship. Will you please sit?"

"If you will forgive me for being crass, madame, it is clear to me from your home, your jewelry, and your reputation that you are indeed in a position to afford a panel of the Elgin Marbles. That you want such a thing is a testament to your excellent taste. That you knew to contact me indicates that you possess a superior intelligence. There is no one else who could arrange the procurement of such a famous work."

My head was spinning; I sank to the ground. It was not Colin Hargreaves. Only Andrew would speak in that arrogant tone; I recognized his voice at once. There could be no mistake. The same anger that prompted me to confront him the previous day started to surface again. Every suspicion I had about Colin was now redirected to Andrew, the man who wanted me to travel to Africa to rescue Philip. I pushed my hands against the cold marble floor and put my ear against the door, not wanting to miss a word uttered by the abhorrent man.

"My connections at the British Museum are above reproach. Access to the piece will not be a problem. The artists I use produce excellent copies. Not a single object I have replaced has been suspected."

"Even if it were, Monsieur Caravaggio, I would not expect my name ever to surface in an investigation. I really have no time for such things," Cécile said, sounding marvelously bored with the entire subject.

"Of course, of course." Andrew laughed, disrespectful as always.

"How long until I receive the panel?"

"I will have that information for you as soon as I discuss the project with my artist. Mr. Attewater works quickly, but a piece of this caliber will be rather time-consuming."

"You are quick to reveal the names of your minions, Monsieur ˜aravaggio."

"I have little concern for insignificant information. Mr. Attewater can take care of himself." Of course. Andrew excelled only in looking after his own situation. Poor Mr. Attewater. He deserved better treatment. "We should discuss the financial arrangements."

"The price you quoted in your note is perfectly acceptable," Cécile said. "I presume you prefer cash?"

"You are most gracious, Madame du Lac. I have brought you a token to acknowledge our agreement." I could hear someone open a parcel. "It is Greek, of course. The figures on the vase depict the Judgment of Paris."

"I am familiar with the story. It is an excellent copy."

"It is the original, madame. I would not dream of presenting a customer such as yourself with anything less."

I shook my head as I listened to him lie so coolly. The original Judgment of Paris vase was safely hidden in my butler's pantry in London.

"I am afraid that I shall have to cut our meeting short today. I had not intended to take on any more projects for the moment, as I am preparing to leave town, but did not want to delay meeting with such an important client."

"Are you going back to London?" Cécile asked.

"No, to Africa on the most urgent business." I seethed as he spoke.

"Will you be able to handle my request before you leave?"

"I will push back my departure long enough to ensure that I have all the arrangements set in motion before I leave. My trip will not be an extended one; I assure you that our transaction will not be affected by it in the least." I wondered at this comment. Did Andrew know he would not be able to find Philip?

"I would expect nothing less." I heard the rustle of her silk skirts as she rose from her seat. "I will leave you to your work, Monsieur Caravaggio."

I sat motionless, listening to the echo of his boots disappear down Cécile's staircase. Only after having detected the snap of the brass latch in the front door did I cautiously enter the red drawing room, where Cécile was inspecting the Judgment of Paris vase.

"It's a copy," I said.

"*Bien sûr.*" She shrugged. "Did you recognize our malefactor?"

"Andrew Palmer." I paced angrily in front of the room's tall windows. "No wonder he was so keen to get Philip's papers for his father. He must have been looking for some record of the stolen objects Philip had."

"He was probably afraid there would be some clue that could implicate him."

"I wonder if Philip was more than just a customer," I said, still pacing. "And what about Colin? Do you think he is also involved?"

"*Je ne sais pas,*" Cécile said. "I had rather hoped that Caravaggio would turn out to be someone wholly unrelated to you. It would have made for a neater resolution."

"Would that we were so lucky. We must stop Andrew before he leaves for Africa."

"I wonder if he will really go without you," Cécile mused.

"He insists that he will."

"Yes, but why? Can he really believe that Philip is still alive? I'm very sorry, Kallista, but I find it more and more difficult to believe that he is."

"I have not yet given up hope entirely but must admit that I'm inclined to agree with you." Before I realized it, a tear slipped down my cheek. I brushed it away and turned to look out the window.

"Let us focus on capturing Andrew, *chérie.* There is no use in contemplating Philip's fate until we have more facts."

"Do we have enough evidence for the police to arrest Andrew?" I asked.

"I do not think so. We shall have to think of a way to persuade him to give us something more."

"I want to force him to tell me whether my husband is alive."

"I am not sure that two women could force Caravaggio to do anything; he could easily overpower us if confronted. He must be tricked."

"And tricked in a manner that will result in his immediate arrest. Once their leader is in jail, perhaps Mr. Attewater and the others involved in the crimes could be persuaded to give evidence."

I picked up the vase Andrew had left for Cécile and examined it. Suddenly an idea struck me. "This vase is a forgery."

"I know, Kallista. I did not doubt you when you told me the first time."

"No—look." I pointed to a fold on the fabric of Paris's tunic. "What do you see?"

"Cloth?" She peered at the vase. "Are those letters? Alphas?"

"Precisely!" I exclaimed, growing excited. "They are Mr. Attewater's signature. He hides them on every copy he makes."

"But this proves nothing more than that Andrew did not bring me the original."

"In this case, yes. Andrew's success depends upon being able to replace stolen objects with copies. If we could trick him into stealing something and giving us the original before he could get it copied, we might be able to drive him to exposure."

"*Intéressant.* It would be difficult for him to get something copied in Paris when Monsieur Attewater is in London. What object shall I tell Caravaggio I want?"

"This, Cécile, will be my adventure."

"You cannot let him know that you've identified him as a thief. How would such a man react? It would be too dangerous."

"I have no intention of letting him know. Tomorrow when he comes to tell me of the delay in his departure—as he must, now that you've hired him to acquire the frieze—I'm going to tell him that I'm no longer eager to sponsor the trip because of some disturbing information I've learned about Philip."

"That he was collecting stolen antiquities?" Cécile asked, smiling.

"Exactly. It will lull him into a sublime sense of security. If the entire plot of the thefts were ever revealed, he could blame it all on Philip, who is not here to defend himself." I began pacing again. "And as for me, would I look forward to being reunited with a husband of such low principles?"

"And how will this lure Andrew to steal something for you?"

"I must identify some object that I shall pretend to want desperately. After our conversation Andrew will have been led to believe that he would be welcome to renew his suit if only he could find me the thing that I so desire. It is very difficult being a lonely widow, Cécile."

"At which point, if Philip really is dead, it would be in Andrew's best interest to inform you immediately."

"Precisely."

"You assume that he will not be satisfied by having achieved what he will view as immunity from his crimes? A smart man would allow you to think Philip was the only guilty party and remove himself from further suspicion."

"Regardless of whether Andrew is a smart man, it cannot be denied that he is a poor one. And I am exceedingly wealthy. I do not doubt that he started this business with the antiquities as soon as he had run through his own fortune. If he were to marry me, he could abandon the enterprise entirely."

"A perfect solution to all his problems." Cécile sighed. "And now that you suggest it, does it not make you wonder that the news of Philip's possible survival reached you only after you had refused Andrew? I wonder if your money has been his object all along?"

"I am counting on it, Cécile. If he is as greedy as I suspect, he will be easily trapped, so long as I can be persuasive enough." I sat at a desk and began to compose one of two notes that would be crucial to the success of our plan.

"What will you have him steal?"

"A lovely object currently in Monsieur Fournier's collection."

"And you are sure he will be up to the challenge?"

"Andrew has never lacked confidence. I'm sure he views all this as a wonderful game."

Cécile and I were awake much of that night formulating the details of our plan, so I did not return to the Meurice until the following morning.

I had hoped Andrew would come to see me early in the day, but luncheon passed without his appearing at my rooms. At last, tired of waiting, I took matters into my own hands and sent Meg with a note for my traveling companion, requesting his presence at his earliest convenience. Much to my chagrin, Meg returned twenty minutes later with Andrew's reply; he was indisposed until nearly dinnertime. Could he come to me at six? I did not like having to wait to set my plans in motion any more than I liked the fact that he made my maid wait nearly half an hour for his answer. I had no choice but to agree, and I sent Meg with a second note, saying that I would expect to see him promptly at six.

Once again I found myself in the unhappy position of watching the hours pass with very little to do. I picked up my Greek but could not concentrate enough to translate two words together. My mind wandered hopelessly, and I began to think about Philip. Although the chance of his being alive seemed very unlikely at present, I could not help but wonder what our reunion might be like. Obviously, as I no longer planned to go to Africa, I would have to revise my fantasy of finding him helpless in a primitive tent at the mission. If he were discovered, I could be ready to travel to Cairo at a moment's notice. The thought of our reunion occurring outside of London appealed to me; an exotic locale surely would inspire passion more effectively than would the house in Berkeley Square.

Further thought on the subject ceased when I heard a forceful tap on the door, which I opened with a flourish, wondering if Andrew had decided to see me earlier than planned. Instead I found Colin standing before me.

11 June 1888
En route to Amsterdam

————

Married life proving more delightful than I had ever dared hope. K spends much of her time reading the worst sort of popular fiction (novels that have much amused me, so I cannot reprimand her), periodically raising her head from her book to make wry comments about the heroine. Emerged from her dressing room last night—such a vision of beauty I could hardly speak. ". . . Such celestial charms . . ." What will she think of her husband when—as eventually I must— I regain my ability to speak coherently in her presence? Will she recognize the man she married?

Much accomplished on Achilles-Alexander. Good thing K frequently buried in her reading, or she might take offence that I spend so much time writing.

31

"Good day, Mr. Hargreaves. I did not expect to see you."

"I would imagine not," he replied curtly. "May I come in?"

"Only for a moment. I was just preparing to go out," I lied. "Did you enjoy your visit to the Louvre? I've always found Mr. Murray an excellent guide, at least at the British Museum. Does he know the collection here as well?"

"I spent only a few minutes with him discussing a matter of business."

"I had guessed as much," I said, looking at him skeptically. "Have you come with a specific purpose, Mr. Hargreaves? I'm afraid that I am not at liberty to spend much time sitting with you."

"I would like to know when you plan to leave for Africa."

This surprised me. If he were working with Andrew, I would have expected him to know that I no longer planned to accompany his friend to the Dark Continent. Unless . . . could Andrew have sent him to determine if the suspicions that led me to cancel my trip went deeper than concern about the deception played on me with my wedding photograph? I considered my options briefly before answering.

"I have decided not to go," I said, meeting his eyes. "My friends have convinced me that Philip would prefer to see me in Paris, so I've agreed to stay here and wait for news from the search party."

"I'm glad to hear it and wish that *I* had been so persuasive. My efforts to alter your plans seemed only to make you more intent on your purpose."

"You do prompt extreme reactions from me," I said with a laugh. "But I suppose I shall forgive you for that."

"I can ask for little more. Where are you off to this afternoon?"

"I have an appointment at six o'clock and thought I would go to Frascati for some pastry in the meantime."

"May I walk with you?"

"I don't see why not," I agreed, nearly certain now that Andrew had sent him. Clearly Caravaggio was busy this afternoon and wanted to be confident that I would not stumble on anything that might disrupt his plans. "So long as you promise to make no mention of the topic on which we cannot agree."

"Ashton?" he asked.

"Yes. I am not so naïve as to think that it is entirely likely he is alive. Until it can be proven otherwise, however, I would prefer to have hope rather than despair as my companion."

While Colin and I strolled along the *grands boulevards* of the city, I made every effort to learn from him as much as I could about Andrew. My success was somewhat limited, although I could not say whether this was due to his unwillingness to be forthcoming or to my own lack of focus. A trip to Frascati, the best patisserie in the city, is never wasted, however, and we passed an agreeable hour there discussing Greek grammar over *tourte aux confitures*. Colin was quite sympathetic to my complaints regarding my tutor's choice of texts, and he reassured me that after a bit more work on Xenophon, I would be able to start on Homer. Occasionally when our eyes met during a lull in conversation, he would look away abruptly, leaving me to wonder if he now regretted his actions on the Pont-Neuf, not that it really mattered.

The afternoon had grown cold. I rejected Colin's suggestion that we take a cab back to the Meurice, a decision I regretted before we had walked two blocks. The occasional savory aroma drifted from cafés, bringing the temptation of a bit of comfort to passersby. I had taken Colin's arm and was happy for the warmth of him next to me, but I must admit that I was not entirely comfortable with him. The more I thought about it, the more justified my suspicions of him seemed, a fact that disappointed me greatly. I imagined that Colin, Philip, and I could have spent any number of pleasant evenings conversing in the library. Why had my husband had the misfortune to choose his friends so poorly? Or had he been no better than the men with whom he surrounded himself?

Being cold, we walked quickly and soon reached the hotel. I bade Colin farewell and rushed upstairs to prepare for my meeting with Andrew. While changing my dress, I shared my plan with Meg, who reacted with a mixture of alarm and excitement. That Mr. Palmer would acquiesce to my slightest whim, she did not doubt, but that her mistress was going to entangle herself with a criminal left her rather unnerved. By the time Andrew rapped on my door, Meg was so anxious that she squealed. I was more than a little apprehensive myself, but the effort of trying to calm my maid had a better effect on me than her; I was ready to begin.

Andrew looked very polished, dressed in evening kit, smiling wryly as he walked toward me. I could tell by his expression that he expected me to return to the topic of my wedding photograph. He kissed my hand quickly, meeting my eyes only for a moment, and waited for me to speak. I sat motionless, noticing for the first time that he truly did fill the role of master criminal well. The initial impression with which he left one was that of an impetuous gentleman who did not take his position in life very seriously. Observing him now, however, I saw beneath that to the calculating way he looked around the room, the studied manner in which he carried himself. I began to believe that everything he did had been meticulously planned and rehearsed. I wondered what he had practiced to say to me tonight, quite certain that whatever the script, he would find it inadequate.

"Are you quite well, Lady Ashton?" he asked, tired of waiting for me to speak. His voice had an edge to it I had not heard before.

"Yes, Andrew," I said, deliberately addressing him informally as I looked in his eyes. I bit my lip and shook my head. "No. I have demanded honesty from you; I should offer you nothing less in return."

"Have I done something else to offend you?" He was angrier than I had expected.

"You?" I said. "Oh, Andrew, what you have done to offend me now seems so trivial. I would, perhaps, apologize to you, were I not still the slightest bit annoyed at having been so readily deceived." He looked at me more directly now, clearly surprised.

"What is it, then?"

"I am having such misgivings about the trip to Africa."

"You have already told me you do not plan to go. While this is of course a source of great disappointment, I understand why you made the decision."

"Please, Andrew, do not take such a formal tone with me. I—" I paused for effect. "I am afraid the entire trip must be canceled."

"You do not trust me to find your husband?"

"I do not know that he is worth finding," I said, burying my face in my hands. "I have learned the most dreadful things about Philip. I am afraid to tell them to anyone."

This statement caused him to warm up immediately, and he sat next to me on the settee. "What, Emily? You must tell me. I know I have not always been truthful with you in the past, but you know that was only—"

"I know, Andrew. It was because you loved me. You do not have to say it." I hoped I seemed forlorn. "What must you think of me now?"

"What has Philip done?" he asked, looking at me quizzically. I decided to answer his question directly, not wanting to waste any time.

"He is a thief. His collection of antiquities is full of objects stolen from the British Museum."

"Are you sure of this?" He sat perfectly still, hands folded in his lap, his eyes fixed on me.

"Quite sure." I had decided to tell the truth as much as possible, lest my fabrication become too elaborate to remember, and told Andrew how I had learned that the Praxiteles bust of Apollo was an original. "Imagine my surprise when I visited Ashton Hall and found it full of more questionable artifacts that were all familiar to me from my own visits to the museum. I hoped they were merely excellent copies. I brought with me on this trip several notebooks Philip had left in the country. I thought they were volumes of his journal and wanted to read them because I missed him so keenly. Instead I found that one was filled with records of his illegal transactions."

"Are you sure you did not misunderstand what he had written?"

"There can be no doubt. He wrote that he did not care about provenance, only that there were certain pieces he would do anything to acquire. All that is followed with details of how he came to get each artifact. Apparently the pieces from the museum were replaced with copies."

"Let me look at the journal—perhaps it is not so bad as you fear. Where is it?"

"You will hate me," I said, averting my eyes.

"Where is it, Emily?" His voice was strained, as if he were trying too hard to control it.

"I burned it. I shouldn't have, and I am certain that you will judge me severely for doing so. I can't bear the thought of facing such a scandal, Andrew. Haven't I suffered enough?"

"My dear girl," he said, moving closer to me. "I hardly know what to say." He managed to keep his countenance fairly well composed, but I recognized in his eyes a glint of joy that was wholly inappropriate to the situation.

"I know I should try to return the stolen items to the museum, but how could I do so without drawing attention to my husband's crimes? Perhaps I am not as principled as I once thought, but I am inclined to suspect that if the keepers at the British Museum cannot recognize a fake in their own galleries, I am hardly obligated to point it out."

Andrew laughed. "You are very, very bad." His voice grew serious. "I must make a confession of my own."

My muscles stiffened. Was he going to tell me of his own role in the intrigue?

"I knew that Philip was involved in such a scheme. It had come to my attention before your wedding. I confronted him with my knowledge when we were in Africa—the morning before he fell ill. I begged him to stop. He was very upset, very angry at first, but then became melancholy. By the end of the day, he was horribly depressed, almost despondent. He knew I would never have turned him in to the authorities, but I had spoken rather harshly about the consequences his activities might bring for you were he ever to be exposed."

"Now it is I who do not know what to say."

"When Hargreaves told us Philip was dead, I was filled with guilt, wondering if he had done himself harm."

"How awful for you! But, Andrew, it could not have been your fault, even if he had done such a thing." I wondered if there was any truth in what Andrew was telling me. Had Philip been Andrew's partner?

"Perhaps you understand now why it has been so important for me to go to Africa to find him. If I can find my friend alive, I will be relieved of this pressing feeling of guilt."

I was astounded at the lengths to which this man would go, twisting facts to make himself appear nobler than he could ever hope to be.

"I have one more confession to make," he said. "When we returned from Africa, I learned that when Philip died, he owed money to at least one of his unsavory associates. You and I weren't acquainted, and I did not feel right imposing upon you while you were in mourning, so I hired a man to watch you, lest someone come after you. I apologize for infringing upon your privacy but could think of no other way to protect you without causing unnecessary alarm. I fully expect Philip to rebuke me upon his return for my having done it."

I wondered what he had hoped to achieve by doing such a thing. I could only imagine that he feared I would somehow learn of his role in this intrigue, and shuddered to think what he might have done if he thought I was prepared to report him to the police. I had seen the man with the scar just once following my return to London—the night he had met with Colin, whose role in this still confused me. After I had allowed Andrew to befriend me, he could easily have kept an eye on me himself, and I thought of the hours I spent in his company, all the time being watched. Despicable man! I forced my attention back to our conversation.

"I think, Andrew, that it is very unlikely Philip is alive. You and I have both fallen victim to putting too much faith in rumors and coincidences because they suggest something we wanted to believe. The best evidence came with the wedding picture, and we know it was not true."

"I'm sorry, Emily."

"Don't bother to apologize. I know that your intentions were the best," I said, glad to find I could speak such drivel without giving myself away. "Philip is the one who deserves my anger. Have you ever read Balzac?"

"No."

" 'Behind every great fortune there is a crime.' I do not think I would have agreed with such a statement before now."

"You have suffered greatly, Emily." I tried not to openly seethe watching his eyes dance as he spoke.

"I would find it easier to forgive Philip if he had not presented himself as a man of such high principle. I shall never forget on our wedding trip— Oh, but I shall make you late for dinner. I cannot impose on your goodwill, forcing you to listen to my lament."

"I don't mind at all. It is such a relief to know that I do not have to hide all this from you any longer. Tell me whatever you wish. It may help you feel better."

"We were in an antiquities shop, and I saw the loveliest ring—gold, of course—with a picture of a horse on it. You know how I love to ride?"

"Better than most," he said. I could see he wanted to take my hand.

"I begged Philip to buy it for me, but he refused. Because the horse in question was apparently the Trojan horse, he felt the ring too significant a piece to be relegated to the role of bauble to a society wife. He actually said that—can you imagine?"

"I'm afraid I can," he said, shaking his head. How I would have loved to slap him.

"We argued for some time about it, even went back to the shop on more than one occasion, but he would not alter his position. In the end he said that he would consider buying the piece only to donate it to the British Museum. At the time I decided it was an inconsequential incident and actually admired the way he adhered to his principles."

"And now?"

"Now? Now that I know he was a common thief? That he took whatever he wanted for his own private collection while denying me a petty ring? I'm furious."

"You shall have to find the ring and buy it."

"It's in the private collection of a gentleman here in Paris. He'll never sell it."

"Everything has its price, my dear." At last the man spoke the truth. I gazed into his eyes and knew that I had him.

"If only that were the case." I sighed. "I would be eternally indebted to anyone who could convince him to sell. I'm sure it must seem trivial, but knowing what I now do about Philip, the ring has become something of a symbol to me."

"I do not think it is trivial in the least, Emily. The ring has taken on great significance to you."

"Angry though I am, I cannot abandon Philip in Africa. But given that it seems very unlikely he is alive, I do not want to risk your health or that of your brother in the venture. I have written to Lord Lytton asking him to arrange for an official search party of sorts. I'm not sure what he will be able to do, but I do not doubt that it will be adequate." I took his hand. "And so, my dear friend, I have called you here to relieve you from your duties as expedition director and to beg your forgiveness for my own shortcomings."

"There is nothing to forgive. I shall never breathe a word of this to anyone."

"Thank you, Andrew. I know that I am asking a great deal of you."

"Do not mention it again," he said, still holding my hand. "Will you return to London immediately?"

"No. The thought of going back to Philip's house no longer appeals to me. I think I shall stay in Paris and take on the role of eccentric widow." I looked in his eyes. "Although I will admit that being a widow is not quite as appealing to me as it once was. I didn't think it would be this lonely."

"You feel lonely because you have suffered so great a betrayal. It will not last forever."

"You are right," I said, forcing my face to brighten. "There is no cause for despair. I shall enter the Parisian social scene with a vengeance, announcing my intention of marrying the first gentleman who can produce for me the Trojan-horse ring."

Andrew laughed but met my eyes with a steady gaze.

"Of course, it would be rather embarrassing if Monsieur Fournier took the opportunity to offer it to me himself."

"Oh—it's in Fournier's collection?" Andrew said, his voice returning to its usual bored drawl. "I shouldn't think his wife would let him part with it."

9 JULY 1888
FLORENCE

I have taken to combing the city's antiquities dealers when not sightseeing—K not troubled at all when I leave her. She seems immensely gratified by her ability to speak Italian like a native. Think she must have something of a flair for languages, but she insists that her German is atrocious. We laugh often now, and her presence in my room no longer renders me speechless. I may not yet know her heart but am certain that we will spend our years together happily.

Although she does not invite me to take her in my arms, neither does she shun my advances. If I may flatter myself, I think she enjoys them, as it is one of the few times she abandons her reserve and allows her eyes to meet mine—". . . the many-colour'd maid inspires / Her husband's love, and wakens her former fires . . ."

32

T HREE DAYS PASSED WITH LITTLE INCIDENT. C ÉCILE AND I agreed that my discussion with Andrew had gone as well as we could have wanted; now we could only hope that the lure of my fortune would be great enough to tempt him to steal Fournier's ring. There was nothing more we could do.

Margaret sent a wonderful letter describing her sister's wedding in the most humorous detail. American socialites, apparently, are at least as silly as their English counterparts, and their antics made for delightful reading. Also enclosed were some simple passages in Greek from the *Iliad*. Mr. Moore be damned, she said, I was ready for Homer. Expecting that I would not receive her letter until my return from Africa, she suggested that I have my husband assist me with them. I succumbed to a brief moment of melancholy, knowing that the translation would be done without Philip's help, then fell to work, feeling uncompromised satisfaction when I had succeeded in translating the first, despite the fact that it was, not surprisingly, a passage lauding Achilles.

That same afternoon Cécile came for tea, and we were in the midst of discussing plans to visit Versailles when Meg told me that Andrew was at the door. This was wholly unexpected. He had made a great point of going on at length about how the demands of his business affairs would allow him little time to see me. Not wanting him to realize that she and I were acquainted, Cécile hastened to my bedroom, where she left the door slightly ajar.

"Are you expecting someone?" Andrew asked, glancing at the tea table, which contained far too much food for only myself. I gave him my hand, which he kissed with far more attention than I would have liked.

"I've just disposed of a most unwelcome guest," I lied. "A French acquaintance with perfectly dreadful manners. I thought she would never leave."

"I'm glad to have found you alone," he said, sitting too close to me on the settee. "I have some news that I'm afraid will be most distressing. I've just had a letter from our ambassador to Egypt. He wrote that he has learned that the Englishman rumored to be wandering about in the bush turned up in Cairo nearly a month ago. He was a missionary by the name of Thomas Tresham."

I did not speak for several minutes, first, because I felt that it lent a certain credence to my position as widow with ambivalent feelings toward her husband. More important, I needed to control my anger. I had talked to Lord Lytton not four hours earlier. He had told me in no uncertain terms that it would be months before anything could be determined about Philip's fate and that I should not count on ever receiving confirmation from Africa. Rumors, like the ones I had heard, had very little chance of being either proved or completely discounted.

"Philip is dead," I said at last, matter-of-factly.

"Yes, my dear, he is." I had no doubt that on this point he was telling the truth. Although this was not entirely a surprise, hearing the words spoken made me feel as if I had received a violent blow. There was no small hope left to which I could cling. I had been led to believe that my husband was alive because it furthered Andrew's plans, whatever they had been. Now that he believed he might have a chance at marrying me, it served his purpose to leave Philip dead. I wanted to sob, to mourn again the man whose love I had never appreciated, but knew that I could not do so at present. Instead I raised my head slowly, looked at Andrew, and smiled.

"Will you think me very bad if I tell you that I am most relieved?" As I said this, I could not help but remember that relief was in fact the emotion I had felt when I had originally learned that my husband was dead.

"I understand your reasons completely," he assured me, taking my hand in his. "You have already mourned him once, Emily. You need not feel further obligation to such a man."

"Yes, such a man," I said, wondering at the ease with which Andrew disparaged his friend. "I am glad you were the one to tell me, Andrew. I'm afraid I find myself most obligated to you."

"You owe me nothing," he said, looking at me in a most unnerving fashion. Clearly he felt I owed him everything. I did not like how close he was to me, and I rose from my seat.

"I must turn again to Balzac. 'When women love us, they forgive us everything, even our crimes; when they do not love us, they give us credit for nothing, not even our virtues.' I have been guilty of overlooking your true character, Andrew. My misguided love for Philip kept me from seeing it."

"Do you credit me my virtues now, Emily?" he asked, walking toward me. I backed away.

"I believe I do, Andrew," I said, almost whispering, trying to ignore an overwhelming feeling of nausea. "When I think of the opportunities I have thrown away . . ." I let my voice trail off and daintily placed a hand on my forehead. "I think I shall make plans to visit Margaret in America as soon as possible. Traveling always makes it easier to forget." My head still lowered, I raised my eyes to look at him. His expression brought to mind a hunter readying to fire at his prey.

"I did not plan to give you this so soon," he said, removing something from his coat pocket. "I needed more time—" He stopped abruptly. "But perhaps it is best that you have it now, if you will agree to accept it."

I took the small parcel he presented to me, knowing full well what I would find when I opened it: Monsieur Fournier's lovely ring.

"Oh, Andrew! How did you ever persuade Monsieur Fournier to part with it?" I gushed, hoping I looked appropriately awestruck.

"I can claim no great skill in the matter. He sold it to a dealer several months ago. All I had to do was track it down. Dare I hope that you will take it?"

"I don't know how I could refuse," I said, slipping the ring onto my finger.

"Of course," he said, pausing, smiling in his most devilish manner, "you cannot expect to have it for nothing." I laughed nervously, recalling a time when I had taken great pleasure in that smile.

"Are you going to beg another kiss?"

"No, Emily, I will not be satisfied so easily. I want you to be my wife."

I had expected this and knew how I must respond, but the thought of entering into any arrangement with this man, even a false and temporary one, revolted me.

"Marry you, Andrew?"

"You said only three days ago that you would marry the first man who could present you with this ring."

"Surely you didn't think I was serious?" I was not going to allow him to get his way so easily.

"As you can see, I did," he said. I saw anger begin to cloud his good humor. "I assure you I wouldn't have gone to such lengths to satisfy you if I did not." I let him stand there, stupidly, for a moment before replying, watching him wonder whether he was going to succeed in getting my fortune.

"I had little hope that you would renew your suit after having been so abominably refused," I said coyly.

"Did you think my feelings so fickle?"

"I feared you would despise me after you learned what I know about Philip and how I have hidden the facts."

"I would forgive you anything, even your crimes," he said, smiling once more.

"Again, you tell me news that brings me great relief," I said, looking at the ring and twisting it anxiously on my finger. "I would like very much to keep the ring."

I let my eyes meet his and smiled demurely, tacitly accepting his odious proposal. He took me forcefully by the shoulders and kissed me hard on the lips. I could barely keep myself from pushing him away. Happily, he did not pursue the endeavor for long, stepping back from me and sitting down.

"It would be best, my dear girl, if we did not tell our general acquaintance of our understanding at present. Wear the ring as much as you like when you are with me and when you are alone, but not in public. Such a striking piece would be certain to draw attention, and I do not want anyone to think I have sought to win your affections while you are still in mourning. I would not have your reputation so tarnished."

My reputation? He did not want me to wear the ring where Fournier might see it; he had not been able to get it copied.

"I am nearly out of mourning, Andrew—it's only a matter of weeks. I don't think anyone would take notice."

"You are not to wear it in public, Emily." I did not like his tone.

"Already you consider yourself my master?"

"Yes," he said, smiling and coming back to me. "I shall have to take a firm hand with you. Give me the ring until you can be presented as my fiancée." I could not risk letting him get it from me.

"If you remove it from my hand, I shall not kiss you again until I can be presented as your fiancée," I said, simpering. "Can you wait that long?" I pulled him close to me. He took the bait and kissed me in the most horrendous way, all the while clumsily fondling my neck. My head throbbed.

"I am going to enjoy taking you as my wife," he said, his breath distressingly heavy. I stepped away, backing against the wall. "Your modesty suits you," he said, looking at my crimson face and neck. "A woman should not be too eager." The sound of breaking china came from my bedchamber.

"Oh, dear," I said, my voice trembling. "I'm afraid my maid must have broken something. Will you excuse me, Andrew? I really must see what she has done." Afraid that he would try to kiss me again, I walked quickly toward the door. He picked up his hat and his stick and followed me, kissing only my hand as he took his leave.

"I look forward to seeing you wearing my ring again. I shall call on you tomorrow."

I could not bear the thought of being alone with him. "Not tomorrow, Andrew. I've planned a trip to Versailles."

"Let me know as soon as you return." I locked the door after he left.

Cécile immediately appeared from the bedroom. "That man is more dreadful than I would have thought," she said. "You should not have been alone with him."

"There was no other way, Cécile." I called for Meg, wanting her to run a burning-hot bath for me as soon as possible. "I will not, however, repeat the experience. I shall be forever grateful to you for breaking whatever unfortunate object you did in order to rescue me."

"Something had to be done," she said, "and it was a very ugly vase."

———

Lord Palmer dined with us tonight—made a point of steering conversation to things that might interest K, rather than letting us fall into our typical arguments about Achilles. Capital evening. K was a vision of perfect elegance and an excellent hostess. Imagine she will want to entertain on a grand scale next Season.

Hargreaves less than enthusiastic about hunting with spears. Says he'll spend his time trekking instead. Andrew Palmer's game for it, though. Wonder what Kimathi will think of my plan?

33

BEFORE ENTIRELY SUCCUMBING TO WRETCHEDNESS THE previous evening, I had the presence of mind to send out a note, requesting an immediate reply. When it came, I sent another two; I would have to wait only a short while longer for the resolution of this dreadful business. When I had told Andrew I planned to visit Versailles, I had no intention of actually doing so. Cécile, however, insisted that we do exactly that. It was too soon for the final stage of our plan, and I could not very well go anywhere in Paris, where Andrew might see me.

She was right, I knew, so we spent two days at the Sun King's spectacular palace, where I furiously sketched rooms that Cécile wanted to add to her collection of miniatures. The act of drawing calmed my restless mind, allowing me to think rationally about the pieces of the forgery scheme that still eluded me. I wondered who Andrew's connection at the museum was and how Colin was involved. Most worrisome, what part had Philip taken in the abominable crimes?

Upon our return to Paris, I found answers to the notes I had sent; everything was in place for Andrew's ruination.

The following afternoon he met me in the lobby, putting his arm around my waist in a manner most unwelcome to me. I gently removed it and gave him my arm instead.

"Really, Andrew, you are the one who was so insistent that our engagement remain a secret," I admonished him.

"You are difficult to resist."

"I must say that it shall be all I can do to keep from laughing when I see Monsieur Fournier today. To think that I now have his ring and that he has no idea. Promise me you will not tell him, Andrew. I so want to see the surprise on his face when he notices it on my hand."

"You're not wearing it, are you?" he asked, grabbing both my gloved hands.

"Of course not. I meant after our engagement is announced. I carry it with me at all times to remind me of you but will wear it only when we are alone." I smiled at him and raised an eyebrow. "You're beginning to make me question your sincerity, Andrew. Are you quite certain you plan to marry me?" I said, squeezing his arm lightly.

"Don't be ridiculous, Emily." We took a cab to Monsieur Fournier's house, not far from Cécile's. I would have preferred to walk, but Andrew could not be persuaded. I was thankful that the ride was a short one, leaving us little time alone in the closed carriage.

"I do not know how I allowed you to convince me to accompany you on such a tedious excursion," he said. "Must we really spend the afternoon looking at Fournier's dreary antiquities?"

"His collection is marvelous, Andrew. I don't see how your father's love of archaeology and Greece did not rub off on you at all."

"That, my dear, is because you were not subjected to innumerable tedious conversations on the topic from your earliest days. I am quite at a loss to see why you have any interest in such things. I shall have to find something better to occupy you once we are married."

The cab stopped at our destination before I had to answer this preposterous suggestion.

"I warn you that I shall tire of this endeavor quickly," he said as he helped me down from my seat. "Hargreaves and I are riding at three. If we are not done before then, I will excuse myself with little remorse."

"And leave me alone with Monsieur Fournier and the Lyttons? That hardly seems fair!" I cried, taking note of the fact that he planned to see Colin.

Now that we were at our destination, my heart began to pound so loudly I was afraid my companion would hear it. Monsieur Fournier greeted us and immediately led us to the room that housed his impressive collection. Lord Lytton and his wife were already waiting, sitting on heavy leather sofas whose slight smell of tobacco suggested that it was here that Monsieur Fournier and his close acquaintances retired after dinner to smoke. The ambassador rose to greet us, and I realized that my hand was shaking as he raised it to his lips. Why was this, the simplest part of my plan, causing me such anxiety? I clutched the small silk reticule that contained the ring as I conversed politely with Lady Lytton, barely aware of what I was saying. Before long, Monsieur Fournier suggested that we begin our tour.

His collection surpassed any that I had seen before, but my distracted frame of mind prevented me from appreciating the beauty of the pieces that filled his impressive gallery. Sofas and oversize chairs were placed intermittently through the chamber, strategically located to allow a person to sit, happily contemplating the lovely works before him. Unlike Philip's collection, which contained only objects from ancient Greece, Monsieur Fournier's spanned the whole of ancient history. Cuneiform tablets, Egyptian ushabti, and Roman mosaics adorned the walls and cases, along with spectacular pieces from Greece and Assyria. A small, partially reconstructed chapel that he had ordered moved, stone by stone, from Egypt stood along one wall, eerily backlit by the light streaming through the large windows lining the wall behind it.

I paid little attention to what Monsieur Fournier said as we admired all that we saw until we came to a case made of highly polished wood. It contained piece after piece of the most exquisite ancient jewelry, artfully displayed on a background of rich purple velvet. There were several spaces within the cabinet where objects were obviously missing. It was time for me to begin.

"I see that not everything has been left safely in its case," I said, smiling. "Your wife must be adorned in a way that would make fair Helen jealous."

"Unfortunately, I have fallen victim to the cat burglar," Monsieur Fournier replied. "The pieces were stolen several nights ago. The police believe that the thief lowered himself from the roof to one of my gallery's windows."

"How dreadful!" I cried. "I remember very well the beautiful ring you were wearing at Mr. Bennett's earlier in the fall." Andrew glared at me; I looked at him with innocent eyes. "It is neither in the case nor on your hand. I do hope it was not stolen."

"It was, Lady Ashton."

As he spoke, I worked the wedding band Philip had given me off my left hand and let it fall, the gold clinking loudly as it hit the marble floor. Andrew immediately dove to the ground in search of it, nearly knocking over Lady Lytton in the process.

"Goodness, Mr. Palmer!" Lady Lytton exclaimed. "Why must you move with such rapidity? There is no danger that whatever Lady Ashton dropped would be lost here."

"I do not think that is what concerned Mr. Palmer," I said, stepping toward Lord Lytton. Andrew rose to his feet and handed me my ring. "I believe he thought I dropped something else." I pulled Monsieur Fournier's ring out of my bag. "Were you looking for this, Andrew?"

"I have no idea what you are talking about. What ring is that?"

"Monsieur Fournier's Trojan-horse ring, of course. The one you stole for me in an attempt to secure my affections." Andrew looked entirely nonplussed, smiled, and turned to Monsieur Fournier.

"The poor girl doesn't know what she is saying. Is that something from your husband's collection, Emily?"

"No. As you well know, it's from Monsieur Fournier's." Andrew laughed; Monsieur Fournier's eyes fixed on the ring in my hand.

"I'm afraid she is trying to protect the memory of her husband, who had an unfortunate habit of stealing antiquities."

"Are you suggesting, Mr. Palmer, that the Viscount Ashton stole this ring?" Lord Lytton asked. Andrew made no attempt to answer the question.

I handed Monsieur Fournier his ring. "Is this yours?" I asked.

He examined it methodically for a moment before nodding. "It is one of the pieces that was stolen from me," he said.

"Mr. Palmer presented it to me several days ago after having proposed marriage."

"I assure you I did not take it," Andrew said, the edge returning to his voice. "I was foolish enough to propose, but I did not give her the ring."

"Cécile du Lac witnessed the entire exchange. Would you care to enlighten these gentlemen regarding the relationship you have with her? I'm sure Lord Lytton would be particularly interested in your plans for the Elgin Marbles."

"You forget that the Elgin Marbles are safely in the British Museum, Lady Ashton. Again, I refer you to your own husband's crimes. Perhaps you are confusing him with me. Or are you trying to blame his wrong-doings on me?"

"Madame du Lac spoke with me this morning about the meeting you had with her," Lord Lytton interrupted. "It would appear you have quite a bit of explaining to do, Mr. Palmer."

"I would like to know how you came to give my ring to Lady Ashton," Monsieur Fournier said forcefully. "Did you steal it yourself or hire someone to do it for you?"

"Given the short period of time in which he needed to acquire it, I imagine that he took it himself," I said. "Although I confess I am somewhat shocked that he is clever enough to have pulled it off. I heard every word of your meeting with Madame du Lac, Andrew, and was devastated to learn of your true character. I quickly realized that greed motivated you above all else, and I knew that the lure of my fortune would be too much for you to resist. I suggested that you find Monsieur Fournier's ring for me, knowing full well you would do anything you thought might induce me to marry you."

Andrew looked like a man who was slowly beginning to realize that his plans had been thwarted. Anger clouded his eyes, his expression similar to the one I had seen after refusing his first proposal of marriage.

"I admit to stealing the ring. It was the foolish action of a man in love. But it was an isolated incident."

"It was nothing of the sort," I said with conviction. "Aside from the evidence you have already provided for us during your conversation with Madame du Lac, do not forget that I am in possession of all of my husband's records."

"You said you burned them."

"And you said that you confronted him about his illegal activities. Both of us lied. Philip kept meticulous track of your own involvement in the forgeries."

"Aren't you a clever girl, Emily? I underestimated you," he said, crossing his arms and methodically tapping his fingers against them. "But why would anyone believe what Ashton wrote? His character will not stand up to scrutiny."

"I find it interesting that when faced with evidence, you attempt to discredit the source rather than proclaim your own innocence. Whatever Philip's faults, he was not a criminal." I hoped this was true. If it was not, I fully expected that Andrew would quickly blame everything on his accomplice. "I must admit it surprises me to learn that you managed to orchestrate such an extraordinary series of thefts; I would not have thought you capable of pulling it off."

He bristled visibly at this comment. "I will not respond to such preposterous accusations," Andrew snapped, his cold eyes fixed on me.

"And I, Mr. Palmer, have heard quite enough," Lord Lytton said, motioning to Monsieur Fournier, who pulled a bell cord.

The two gendarmes I had arranged to have waiting in the house entered the room and bound Andrew's hands. "You are under arrest for having stolen Monsieur Fournier's ring. Do not doubt that further charges will be filed. Madame du Lac's testimony was quite compelling."

16 September 1888
Hôtel Continental, Paris

———

Left K most reluctantly yesterday morning, after a decidedly sleepless night. Had I not such expectations, both for the hunt and for the conclusion of this game in which I have become involved, I think I would not have quit England. Hope she will be grateful for a less distracted husband upon my return.

Have arranged for Renoir to paint a portrait of my darling wife; I do not think another artist could so accurately capture the brightness residing in her.

34

THE HOURS THAT PASSED AFTER ANDREW WAS TAKEN AWAY slipped by me unnoticed. Madame Fournier put me into one of her sitting rooms, sent for Cécile, and plied me with tea and more than a little cognac. Needless to say, her husband was delighted to have his ring returned, but he was even more pleased at having had a hand in the downfall of Caravaggio. Lord Lytton congratulated me heartily and told me that he would send someone to speak to me about the case as soon as possible. Sometime later Colin Hargreaves walked into the room. Cécile, considerably more composed than I, spoke at once.

"I must say, Monsieur Hargreaves, that your arrival is completely unexpected. Am I to assume that this means you are not in league with Caravaggio? I hoped that such a face would not be wasted on a criminal."

"I'm afraid I have a significant amount of explaining to do," he replied.

"I have no plans for the evening, monsieur," she said, motioning for him to sit. "Perhaps if you begin now, you could finish before dinner."

He ran his hand through his hair and looked at me. "I have been looking into the matter of Caravaggio for some months."

"How interesting," Cécile exclaimed. "Are you a spy, Monsieur Hargreaves?"

"Not at all," Colin said, laughing. "I am occasionally called on by Buckingham Palace to investigate matters that require more than a modicum of discretion. Rumors of forgery and theft at the British Museum have circulated for some time, and it had become clear that some involved were members of the aristocracy. Her Majesty, as you might imagine, prefers such things to be dealt with as quietly as possible."

"So you have been following Andrew all this time?" I asked.

"Partly, but I have also been following you, Emily, in a vain attempt to keep you out of danger. Shortly before the Palmers joined us on that last safari, Ashton confided in me that he had discovered their involvement in some sort of underground activity. He would tell me no details, insisting that he had the situation well in hand, and that he planned to confront them when they arrived in Africa."

"Perhaps he wanted to give them a chance to end things honorably?" I suggested.

"Yes, he unfortunately assumed that they would hold to a code of gentlemanly behavior similar to his own. He rather liked the idea of handling everything alone, imagining himself as some sort of classical hero."

"But when did you learn of the thefts?" Cécile asked.

"Shortly after I returned to England following Ashton's death. I did not connect him or the Palmers to any of it until Andrew started to show such an interest in you, Emily."

"Is it so astounding that a man would fall in love with Kallista, Monsieur Hargreaves?" Cécile said, arching her eyebrows.

"Not at all, I assure you," he replied. "It was, however, astounding that a man of Andrew's decided lack of intellect would show any interest in investigating Ashton's papers."

"He did that for his father. Lord Palmer asked me for them himself," I protested. "I have seen the manuscript."

"If you knew Andrew better, you would know that he never, on any other occasion, has done anything on behalf of his father. His adult life has been spent deliberately vexing the poor man, squandering his fortune, and generally causing him as much grief as possible. He had no respect for his father's passion for antiquities. In fact, all this began when Andrew sold pieces of Lord Palmer's collection to cover gambling debts. He replaced the originals with good copies. His father never suspected a thing.

"Pleased to have a new source of income, Andrew began spending more and more. Once his father's collection had been copied and sold, he and Arthur, confident in their success, decided to expand their operation. His father's reputation enabled the son to get whatever special access to the museum he requested, even after hours. The forger would then make sketches, molds, whatever he needed to copy the piece Andrew had decided to steal. Once the forgery was complete, Andrew could switch it for the original when the museum was closed. If he ran into trouble, he found an obliging night guard who was easily bribed to let him in. The artifact would be sold on the black market. It seems there are endless unscrupulous buyers willing to purchase such things."

"I am afraid that I thought Philip was guilty," I admitted, telling him what I had found in the library at Ashton Hall and of the information Cécile had gathered about my husband's black-market activities.

Colin sighed and shook his head. "I admit that I, too, suspected him initially, when I first learned he was well known on the black market. That is why I questioned you about purchases he made on your wedding trip. The day when you confessed to me your . . . er, feelings toward Philip, I thought you were going to tell me that you knew something about his illegal purchases."

"Why did Philip collect all the stolen pieces?"

"He wanted to have all the originals in his possession before he confronted the Palmers. When they joined us in Africa, he told Andrew all he knew and asked him to put an end to the scheme and return what had been taken from the museum."

"How did you learn all this?"

"As I said, I've been investigating the matter for some time. I suspected that both the Palmer brothers were involved, but unfortunately they left very little tangible evidence. When Lord Lytton told me that Andrew had been arrested, I confronted Arthur. He told me that Ashton had asked for nothing more than Andrew's word as a gentleman that they would stop."

"Andrew gave his word?"

"There are few other things he would give away so easily."

"But surely he knew that Philip would expose them if they did not stop. Perhaps he did mean to abandon the enterprise."

"Andrew is not the type of man to give up what he views as an easy source of income."

"And once Philip fell ill, there was no incentive for Andrew to stop." I paused and looked at Cécile. She held my gaze and nodded almost imperceptibly. "What a convenient coincidence that Philip did not return from Africa." Colin began to step toward me, then stopped. Cécile took my hand as the reality of what had happened slowly seeped into my consciousness. "Andrew killed him, didn't he?"

"I'm so sorry, Emily. I do not think we would ever have learned of the murder had Andrew not been arrested before Arthur. The Crown is indebted to you. Arthur, it seems, is much concerned with his own fate and wanted to make it perfectly clear that he was only an accomplice. He told me that on the way to our safari camp he acquired from an obliging tribesman a poison used on blow darts. Andrew must have slipped it into Ashton's cup when he was pouring champagne for all of us. I had never suspected that he died of anything but natural causes. As I have told you, Ashton had been tired for most of the trip, but I suppose that was due to his worry over confronting his friends."

For some time I could not speak, able to think only of my poor, murdered husband. I knew that Philip had left no records that implicated Andrew; I had lied about finding them in an attempt to goad him. Philip, true to his own code of ethics, had wanted nothing more than for his friends to stop their thievery. He never had any intention of bringing them to justice. A sob escaped from my throat, and Cécile took me in her arms while Colin politely pretended to look out the window. My tears were short-lived, however; I had already mourned the death of my husband.

Cécile wiped my face with her handkerchief, smoothed my hair, and marched over to Colin. "And why did this contemptible murderer try to forge a relationship with Kallista? He would have been better to avoid her entirely," she said.

"Andrew believed that Ashton had records that would prove his guilt. Ashton had said as much in Africa. The Palmers tried on numerous occasions to find them, but to no avail. Andrew bribed a servant—a footman, I believe—to search Philip's papers in the library but met with no success. Arthur broke into Emily's suite at the Meurice."

"While I spent the afternoon at the Bois with Andrew," I said. "And when Arthur found nothing, their strategy was to convince me to marry Andrew?"

Colin continued. "At first. It would have given him free access to all Ashton's papers and, more important, a certain level of control over you. When you turned down Andrew's proposal, the scheme changed again. Arthur suspected that you had started looking around when he saw you at the British Museum with Attewater, so he and Andrew decided to change their strategy lest you uncover the information before they did. They fabricated all the evidence to suggest that Ashton was still alive, knowing that you would insist on coming to Africa."

"And what then?" I asked.

"Obviously you would not find Ashton, and Andrew would be close by to console you. Arthur said that Andrew expected to marry you in Cairo, but shortly thereafter you were to have fallen ill, just as Ashton had."

"Leaving the heartbroken widower to return to London and collect your fortune," Cécile said. "Vile man."

"I hope that the queen realizes that this incident can no longer be quietly hushed up," I said.

"I dare not anticipate what she will say. The Palmers, of course, will have to go to trial. As for the matter of the forgeries, I imagine it would be greatly appreciated if you would agree to quietly return the stolen items to the museum."

"I never intended to do anything else." I pressed my hand to my forehead. "This is all so awful. Poor Lord Palmer. He will be devastated.

And Arabella! What a disappointment to learn that her fiancé is no better than a common thief."

"And an accomplice to murder," Cécile added. "I shall discuss the matter no further; I have had enough of this dreadful business. Will you dine with us, Monsieur Hargreaves? I am certain that Kallista would enjoy your company."

"I am afraid that I must refuse your kind invitation, Madame du Lac. I am long overdue at the police station and must also make a full report to Lord Lytton."

"*Oui, oui.*" Cécile sighed. "Will you excuse me? I must find Madame Fournier and thank her for her hospitality," she said, giving me a meaningful look and leaving the room.

I turned to Colin. "I must apologize. I have thought the most terrible things about you. I am ashamed."

"My own conduct has left much to be desired," he replied. "I am afraid that I have offended your sensibilities on more than one occasion."

"Not at all," I said, thinking of our meeting on the Pont-Neuf. "Quite the contrary."

"You are very generous, Emily," he said, pacing in front of me.

"I am sorry that I did not trust you more. But I had reason to doubt you. Why did you meet with the man Andrew hired to follow me?"

"How do you know I did?" I told him about the glove. "It was reckless of you to have run after us. After I left your party that night, I went to Lady Elliott's soirée. She lives in Albemarle Street, an easy walk to my house in Park Lane. As I crossed through Berkeley Square, I saw a man watching your house and confronted him. He denied any wrongdoing, of course, and before I could push further, he heard a sound and ran off. I chased him, but he got away from me."

"I shouldn't have run into the park."

"If I had been more straightforward about Attewater and this forgery business, you might not have found yourself trying to uncover matters by yourself. But I was under strict orders from the palace to reveal no details to you."

"Nothing would have convinced me to abandon uncovering the truth myself."

"I'm not sure that I approve of your wanton disregard for your own well-being. Andrew is a dangerous man. If he had discovered your intentions, you would be dead now. On the way to Frascati, you asked me so many questions about him that I feared you had fallen in love with him. When I think that you pretended to be engaged to that man—the liberties he must have taken . . ." He sat next to me and picked up my hand. "I am more than relieved that you came to no harm in the end."

"So am I." I kissed him lightly on the cheek. He smiled and touched his hand to my face. Before he could speak, the door opened and Monsieur Fournier entered the room.

"You have earned this, Lady Ashton," he said, handing me his beautiful Trojan-horse ring.

From that day I wore it on my right hand. Philip, I suspected, would have donated it to the British Museum. Once again I found that my opinions differed greatly from those of my husband. I preferred the feel of it on my hand to seeing it in a case.

27 November 1888
East Africa

———

Despite my best attempts, this season's safari has not lived up to the expectations raised by the previous one. We are finding less game, but I think that is due more to my own cluttered mind than any change in the animal population; I fear I am virtually useless to the party. Hargreaves has had more success on this trip than the rest of us, an accomplishment that he can rarely claim, because of his habit of wandering off to investigate terrain rather than focusing on his quarry. That he is doing so well is a testament to the situation at hand.

"The man who suffers, loudly may complain; / And rage he may, but he shall rage in vain." I do not rage, of course, but the general effect remains the same. Everyone is aware I am dissatisfied. I am aggravated even by the howler monkeys, whose antics in camp used to amuse me. Now their sole purpose appears to be dumping out every cup of tea I pour for myself. I will not tolerate this nonsense again tomorrow.

I do not, however, despair completely, and insist that I shall get my elephant and return triumphant to England and my wife. Am very much looking forward to the arrival of the rest of our party tomorrow. I hope that conversation with Palmer will put my mind at ease.

35

THE CASE AGAINST THE PALMERS PROVED TO BE FAIRLY
straightforward. Arthur admitted everything to anyone who would listen, but Andrew stubbornly refused to speak again on the subject after
he left Monsieur Fournier's, not that it mattered. They would both be
tried in England for the thefts of the objects from the museum as well as
for Philip's murder, because he had died in a British colony. In France
they would be charged with the illegal sale of antiquities. The crime of
murder being a capital offense, Andrew at least would probably never
make it to trial in Paris. Lord Lytton accompanied me to the police station when the time came for me to give my own detailed statement, after which I felt a pleasing sensation of relief. Finished with my part of
the administrative aftermath of the affair, I realized that I really ought to
return to London; I wanted to speak with Lord Palmer and Arabella
Dunleigh in person.

Mrs. Dunleigh had already planned a trip to Cairo, where she hoped
her daughter would be more successful in catching a husband than she had
been in London. She appeared rather affronted that I called on Arabella,
seeming to hold me responsible for exposing Arthur's criminal past. The
fact that he had participated in such terrible crimes did not trouble her
nearly as much as the fact that all of society had learned about it. Arabella,
eating as many tea cakes as ever, exhibited few signs of a broken heart.
Knowing that one man had proposed to her improved her confidence immeasurably, and it was clear that she looked forward to the Season in Cairo.

More distressing was my visit to Lord Palmer, whose life had been
profoundly affected by the turn of events. The dear old man seemed to

have aged a lifetime since I last saw him. I asked him to assist me in orga-
nizing the return of the stolen pieces to the British Museum, a request
that he gratefully accepted. Together with him and Colin, I took everything from Ashton Hall to Mr. Murray after the museum had closed for
the day. Having completed this task that I knew to be so important to my
late husband brought me great satisfaction. Afterward Lord Palmer presented me with the monograph on Achilles and the great Alexander, published on Philip's behalf. Mr. Murray, feeling keenly Lord Palmer's
distress at having Andrew and Arthur betray him so completely, gave him
a lovely small statue of Athena from his own collection. Unfortunately, it
was now the only authentic piece in Lord Palmer's possession; we found
none of the pieces stolen from him among those recovered by Philip.

When she learned all that had transpired in Paris, my mother flew
into a rage that has since become legendary. I did not tell her myself, instead leaving the unpleasant task to my father, whom I had called to my
side as soon as I arrived at Berkeley Square. She came to me the instant
he finished relating the story to her, and I was subjected to a solid hour
of her ranting; like Mrs. Dunleigh's, her primary concern was the scandal raging through society.

"It is insupportable that you should have exposed your own husband
in this dreadful manner." She took a seat at last, indicating that the end
of her lecture drew near.

"Philip did nothing wrong, Mother. No one suspects him of wrongdoing."

"You have turned him into a murder victim instead of a gentleman
who met a noble death on safari," she said. "Why would you want to
bring such notoriety to the family?"

"You would prefer that his killers go free?" I asked.

"It is impossible to speak with you, Emily." She wrung her hands. "I
fear for your future more than ever."

"There is no need to worry, Mother. I have no interest in remaining
in London at present and plan to depart for Greece as soon as possible;

you will be glad to know that I have found a most excellent traveling companion."

"That, at least, is a relief. Who is she?"

"Cécile du Lac," I replied. It had taken some considerable arguing to convince my friend to leave Paris, but eventually she agreed to accompany me, on the condition that she could bring Caesar and Brutus. I firmly believe that her unwillingness to accept my invitation was merely a ploy to trick me into allowing those odious little beasts to travel with us.

"Perhaps there is hope for you, Daughter," my mother said, sighing. "I am certain that Madame du Lac can present you to any number of very eligible young men. But must you go to Greece? I do not know of any society to speak of there. Why not Italy instead? Perhaps Florence? I believe that the Duke of Middleton's son plans to travel there with a large party after the New Year."

"I am going to Greece, Mother. I want to see the villa and, frankly, would prefer to avoid society entirely."

"What on earth can you possibly mean by suggesting such a thing? Avoid society?"

"I am going to spend a considerable amount of time determining what it is I want from my life, and the villa will provide the right amount of seclusion required for serious contemplation."

"What you want from your life? Emily, I have lost all interest in attempting to understand you." She sighed again and fluttered her eyelids. "Well, I can assure you that a woman like Madame du Lac will not suffer to sit around at some tedious villa for months on end. I shall quite depend upon her to see to your return to society. I shall write to her today."

"Thank you, Mother," I said through clenched teeth, taking comfort in the knowledge that Cécile's version of society was infinitely preferable to that of my mother. "If you will excuse me, I have much to attend to if I am to have any hope of being ready to receive you and the rest of the family at Ashton Hall for Christmas."

"I have several other errands to run and have already tarried here for longer than I intended," she said as she rose from her seat. Unfortunately, before she could leave the room, Davis entered to announce the arrival of Colin. As soon as she heard his name, my mother sat back down and smoothed her skirts. "I believe I would like to speak with Mr. Hargreaves." I dropped my head into my hands, barely looking up when Colin entered the room.

"Good day, Mr. Hargreaves," my mother said. "I am forever in your debt for saving my darling daughter from the clutches of that dreadful man."

"I assure you, Lady Bromley, that Emily had the situation well in hand herself," he replied. "I was not even there when she exposed Mr. Palmer."

"It's lovely to see you, Mr. Hargreaves." I smiled as he kissed my hand.

"And it is even more lovely to see you out of mourning, Lady Ashton." I could hardly take my eyes off his handsome face as he lingered over my hand.

"My mother was just preparing to leave, Mr. Hargreaves," I said with a wicked grin. "I am certain that you will take no offense if she stays with us no longer." My mother scowled at me and tapped her parasol on the floor.

"Of course not." Colin bowed politely to my mother. "As always, Lady Bromley, it has been a delight to see you."

"Thank you again, Mr. Hargreaves." My mother rose from her seat once more, not willing to argue with me in front of an extremely eligible gentleman. "Will we have the pleasure of seeing you at Mrs. Barring's tonight?"

"Unfortunately not; I have a prior engagement." He bowed again, and my mother left, shooting me a cutting glance on her way out. Colin closed the door behind her and leaned against it with folded arms. "I am afraid that I am here on business."

"You look dreadfully serious," I replied.

"I've read the statements you gave to the police. You made quite a point of telling them that Aldwin Attewater had nothing to do with the thefts."

"That is true. Mr. Attewater is a frustrated artist who sells his work to whoever will buy it. He does not deceive his clients. They are fully aware they are buying copies."

"Surely you do not believe that?" Colin asked, looking at me skeptically.

"Why shouldn't I? I imagine that if you investigate Mr. Attewater's financial concerns, you will find that he is a man of very limited means. Surely he would be much better off if he chose to present his copies as originals."

"Is it true that you have commissioned a work from him?"

"I have."

"I know that you have conversed with him at great length and that it was he who identified for you the fakes in the British Museum. Are you certain that he showed you all of them?"

"Quite certain."

"And you would swear that he never was involved in deceiving the museum?"

I paused for an instant to consider my answer. "A lady, Mr. Hargreaves, should never swear."

"Is that all the answer I am to expect?"

A smile was the only response I gave him. Frankly, I liked the idea of Mr. Attewater's fragment staying in the museum. Perhaps, in the very faraway future, it would be identified as a copy and appreciated in its own right, like the Roman versions of Greek originals.

"Very well. I am not convinced that Attewater is the innocent you believe him to be, Emily, but have no evidence to prove it. He does not appear to have the sorts of connections that would enable him to continue the Palmers' work, so I shall leave him alone for the time being. You, however—" He stopped. "No. I shall never again warn you off an acquaintance."

"Thank you, Mr. Hargreaves," I said. "I appreciate your respect for my judgment."

"Think nothing of the kind. I make it a practice not to waste my time on futile endeavors."

"Then we shall abandon the subject entirely," I said. "I'm sorry you shall not be at Mrs. Barring's tonight. It's sure to be a tedious evening. I should like to have danced with you, though."

"I've grown rather fond of dancing with you in sitting rooms." He reached for my hand and pulled me from my chair. He wrapped his arm around my waist and brought me close to him; the feeling of him so near caused me to tremble as I looked up at his face. I am certain that we would have started to waltz had our eyes not met, but they did. Neither of us moved, and we stood for some time staring silently at each other. Finally he lifted my chin gently with a single finger, bringing my lips to his and kissing me softly.

" 'Andromache! My soul's far better part,' " he murmured against my neck. "I cannot adequately explain the effect you have on me. Your slightest touch ruins my self-control."

"I know the feeling very well," I whispered, kissing him back.

"I am the worst type of cad to do this without asking your permission first and fully expect you to slap me again." He touched a curl that had escaped from my pompadour.

"I don't think you shall be slapped today," I replied, burying my face in his chest. "If pressed, I would admit to having liked it very much when you kissed me on the Pont-Neuf."

"I should never have done it, Emily. Not then." He lowered me onto the settee and sat next to me. "I hope you can forgive me."

"My recent behavior suggests that I have." I smiled. He leaned closer, as if he would kiss me again, and then stopped.

"Is it too soon? I know that you are out of mourning, et cetera, et cetera, but the emotional upheaval of the past months must have taxed you greatly."

"No, I assure you, I am all right now. I am happy to have suffered what I did. If I had not, I should have been consumed with the guilt of neither having loved my husband nor grieving the loss of him. In the end I truly mourned him. He deserved nothing less."

"He was a most excellent man, Emily."

"I know. It is a pity that I did not realize it sooner, but it would be foolish for me to dwell on romantic fantasies of what our marriage could have been like. I did grow to love him after his death, but I might never have if he were still alive." I shrugged and caught myself feeling suddenly French. "At any rate, that chapter of my life is over, and I have no regrets."

"I am glad," he said, sighing, as he looked at his watch. "I'm afraid I really must leave. My brother is expecting me in Richmond. When do you go to Ashton Hall?"

"Tomorrow. I shall return to London only briefly before I journey to Santorini."

"I should not have arranged the trip so well for you." He smiled and rose from the settee. "I wish I had thought of delaying your departure so that I could see you again before you go."

"When will you return to London?"

"Most likely not until the spring. I have business in Berlin and will travel there soon after the New Year."

"What sort of business, Colin? Anything that might interest me?"

"Not in the least," he replied firmly, and pulled me to my feet. "I shall miss you, Emily." He kissed me lightly and slipped a small box into my hand. "Happy Christmas."

He took his leave before I opened the gift and thus cheated himself of seeing my expression as I realized what he had given me: a golden apple inscribed *"Tê kallistê."*

"I ALWAYS KNEW I liked Mr. Hargreaves!" Ivy cried, holding the apple as we sat in the library after dinner that evening. "What a marvelous gift! And you, Emily, seem quite in danger of falling in love with the gentleman."

"I shall make no attempt to deny the possibility."

"It seems ridiculous now that we ever thought he was the ringleader of the forgers."

"Given what we knew at the time, it was a perfectly reasonable hypothesis. His behavior made him appear quite suspicious."

"I am glad the whole business is over." She grinned wickedly. "But it was rather exciting. It is shocking, though, that Andrew and Arthur should have turned out to be so awful."

"'So fairly form'd, and only to deceive.' Lord Palmer has suffered greatly," I said.

"I am glad to see that he is not being cut by society."

"His own character is spotless. He deserves all our sympathy."

Ivy nodded in agreement and leaned close to me. "Is Davis really bringing port to us, Emily? I don't know that I shall have the nerve to drink it in front of Robert." She glanced at her husband, who sat across the room from us contentedly reading the newspaper.

"There's no one here but the three of us, Ivy. What better occasion to get him used to the idea?"

"He is a very conservative man," she whispered.

"There may be hope for him yet," I replied. "Perhaps someday we can get Colin to sponsor him at the Reform Club."

"That, my dear, is going too far, even for you," Ivy said, smiling.

Davis came in with a decanter of port and three glasses, which he placed on a table. I asked him to pour for us, and Ivy reluctantly accepted the glass he handed to her, glancing at her husband, who sighed loudly and turned his attention to me.

"Emily, darling, I cannot tolerate this. If you are going to continue with your attempt to corrupt my wife, I am afraid I must insist that you advise her correctly. It's very bad form to have your butler serve port. The decanter should start with the host and be passed around the table to the left, each gentleman . . . er, person pouring for whoever is seated on his right. In this case, because we are in the library instead of the dining room, the rules may be relaxed somewhat, I suppose, but the basic form stands. Always pass to the left. When your glass is empty, never ask directly for more. Instead inquire if the person nearest the decanter knows the bishop of Norwich. Any educated chap will know what you mean and pass you the decanter."

"Robert, I knew from the moment I first met you that you were a man of much possibility," I said, laughing.

"Do not think, Ivy, that I shall stand for this in any but the most private situations. However, I look forward to having you join me for port when we dine at home." He tried to appear severe as he said this but did not succeed. Nonetheless, I couldn't help but wonder if it would be possible to find an English gentleman who would allow his wife to do what she truly wanted.

3 December 1888
East Africa

Am excessively tired—think I have caught some blasted fever—but must record the day's conquest. I have my elephant—never before has a man felt such exultation. What a story this will be to tell K. Am rather hoping she has one of her own to share with me upon my arrival home. News of a future heir would be most welcome.

More tomorrow.

36

THE HOLIDAYS PASSED QUICKLY AND WITH REMARKABLY little incident. Soon after the first of the year, I departed for my Cycladic villa, stopping in Paris to collect Cécile, Caesar, Brutus, and an enormous pile of Cécile's trunks. Meg, who had actually been disappointed not to have the chance to go to Cairo, looked forward to our journey with great enthusiasm. My plan to turn her into a traveler had worked; evidently she found Amelia Edwards perfectly inspiring. By the time our boat docked at Santorini, she and Cécile's maid, Odette, had become fast friends, and later I heard Meg tell one of the Greek housemaids that she thought Paris was a lovely city.

The villa completely surpassed my expectations. It sat near the village of Imerovigli on top of a tall cliff overlooking the caldera and the remains of the volcano that had sunk the center of the island in ancient times. Inside, the house, with its bright, white rooms, wide arches, and huge windows, was unlike any building I had seen. As I had suspected, Philip chose to display his collection of impressionist paintings here; the simple surroundings set them off perfectly. The furniture in the house combined an odd assortment of traditional Greek pieces with a number of ill-fitting English ones that I quickly banished from my sight. The villagers gladly took them off my hands, happy with the novelty of the chintz settee, skirted tables, and other assorted monstrosities. My bedroom on the second floor opened onto a balcony with a view of the caldera. On warm nights I left the bright blue doors open so that I could feel the air and watch the stars as I fell asleep.

As when the moon, refulgent lamp of night,
O'er heaven's pure azure spreads her sacred light,
When not a breath disturbs the deep serene,
And not a cloud o'ercasts the solemn scene,
Around her throne the vivid planets roll,
And stars unnumber'd gild the glowing pole,
O'er the dark trees a yellower verdure shed,
And tip with silver every mountain's head:
Then shine the vales, the rocks in prospect rise,
A flood of glory bursts from all the skies:
The conscious swains, rejoicing in the sight,
Eye the blue vault, and bless the useful light.

Weeks flew by as we quickly adapted to Greek culture. Unlike Philip, I did not hire an English cook. Instead we found ourselves surprised and delighted by the cuisine prepared by Mrs. Katevatis, who the villagers in Imerovigli had assured us was the finest cook on the island. Kreatopitakia, seasoned meat tucked into a flaky pastry, became a favorite food, and we were enthusiastic supporters of several of the local vineyards. Cécile threw herself with abandon into the Eastern habit of napping every afternoon, and neither of us particularly missed the cosmopolitan society to which we had been accustomed. We did not, however, entirely abandon our Western European ways; I still took port after dinner, and Cécile had champagne shipped to her by the case from France. Although we tried, neither of us liked retsina, the resinated Greek wine.

While continuing my study of the ancient language, I decided also to learn to speak modern Greek in order to better communicate with our servants and neighbors. Mrs. Katevatis's fifteen-year-old son, Adelphos, spoke excellent English and was soon persuaded to tutor me. I picked up the language quickly and before long was able to respond in her own language to Mrs. Katevatis's cry of *"Kali orexi!"* Good appetite!

Unfortunately, finding someone to school me in ancient Greek was not as easy, so I had to tackle the subject on my own, which proved to be no small effort. Margaret planned to join us later in the spring; until then the notes in her lecture books would help me immensely. My interest in Homer had not faded, but I began to expand my readings in translation to include Plato and, when I was in a light mood, Aristophanes. I don't know when I have laughed so hard as while reading *The Clouds*.

For entertainment we invited large groups of our neighbors from the village to dine with us. Never before had I mingled with such a varied group of friends. Cécile's dearest compatriot was a young man called Aristo Papadakos, a skillful woodworker. After she described to him her miniature Versailles, he carved for her a tiny Parthenon and presented it to her. From that day on, they set about re-creating Athens in its golden age, complete with small figures of Pericles, Socrates, and Plato.

I spent much of my time alone, sketching or reading. In the afternoon I liked to walk along the cliff toward Fira, the largest city on Santorini. Often I would stop at the summit of a rocky outcrop with a book and enjoy perfect solitude while seemingly everyone else on the island napped. The weather that spring was extraordinary, bringing day after day of sunshine following a rainy February.

Perched on a rock one fine day in March, I sighed with satisfaction as I looked at the caldera before me and wondered what lay in ruin beneath its waters. I had been reading Plato's *Timaeus*, a dialogue in which the great philosopher describes the destruction of the ancient civilization of Atlantis, often thought to have been located on Santorini. I had just decided that I must find someone to take me across to the volcano tomorrow when I heard a person approaching from the path behind me. I turned around and saw Colin smiling at me.

"It looks as if you have found paradise," he said.

"What a surprise!" I exclaimed, rising to meet him. "I should not have thought Santorini a convenient excursion from Berlin."

"I assure you it is not." He kissed my hand.

"Then I am most flattered that you made the trip." He was dressed more casually than I had ever seen him and looked extraordinarily handsome with his hair disheveled by the wind.

"You should be," he said. "You are reading Plato?"

"Yes."

"*Timaeus?*"

"I felt this the perfect location for it."

"I adore the way your mind works." He kissed my hand again. I touched his face and leaned forward to kiss him. After a short embrace, I pulled away and looked at him, relishing the warmth I found in his eyes.

"How are your studies coming?" he asked.

"Very well for the most part, although I have stalled a bit on my Greek—difficult to learn on one's own."

"Hmmm . . ." he agreed, softly kissing my neck.

"Now that you are here, you must help me. I'm so pleased to have someone who can answer my grammar questions. I'd begun to fear that I would be stuck reading in translation until Margaret arrives." He did not seem to be paying much attention to my plight, so I lifted his head. "You will help me, won't you?"

"Yes, but not before you feed me—there was nothing edible on the boat." He took my hand, and we walked slowly back to the villa, where Cécile rejoiced at his appearance. She insisted that we celebrate his arrival and immediately began discussing plans for a feast with Mrs. Katevatis, who, in typical fashion, had soon invited the entire village to dine with us. The food was, as always, incomparable, and the amount of ouzo consumed led to some particularly raucous dancing. Colin took to Greek folk dancing well, cutting a fine figure with Cécile and the villagers. The festivities did not break up until late in the evening, and although I was exhausted by the time I fell into my bed, I found that I could not sleep. I paced restlessly on my balcony for some time, calmed by neither the stars nor the sound of the ocean. Suddenly my eyes caught something below me; I had left a book on the white wall at the edge of the cliff and decided to get it before the wind blew it into the water.

I went downstairs, stepping quickly, the stone floor of the veranda cold on my feet. The book, my poor abandoned *Timaeus,* collected, I paused for a moment to look at the caldera, when I saw Colin sitting in a chair only a few feet away from me.

"Why aren't you asleep?" I asked as he stood and walked toward me.

"Morpheus seems to have eluded me completely tonight," he said. The skirts of my nightgown and my long hair billowed around me in the wind as I took his hand. "You are cold."

"A little," I admitted. "I couldn't sleep either. Your arrival has forced me to realize how much I have missed you, when all this time I thought I had found perfect contentment. I shall never forgive you for disillusioning me."

"What can I do to redeem myself?" he asked, putting his arms around me.

"I cannot say. You might start by kissing me again."

He obliged me immediately and thoroughly. "I hope that was satisfactory."

"Perfectly," I murmured, resting my cheek against his.

"The difficulty, of course," he continued, "is that it does not address the long-term problem."

"Is there a long-term problem?"

"Of course. Now that I know you shall miss me, how can I possibly leave you again?"

"There's no need to think about leaving; you've only just arrived."

"But eventually I shall have to go, and I have found being without you a severe impediment to my happiness. I am afraid there is only one solution to our predicament."

"What is that?" I asked, kissing him. He was unable to respond for several minutes.

"I want you to give me your heart, Emily. I want you to marry me," he said. "But I know your views on that subject. I would not want you as my wife unless you truly believed that marrying me would complement a life you already find perfectly satisfying."

Although the idea of spending my life with Colin struck me as very attractive on a number of levels, I was not willing to commit to something that would so radically affect my personal freedom. Perhaps later, when I had a more precise idea of how I wanted to live my life, I would be in a better position to judge how he could fit into it. For now, though, I was not prepared to abandon my autonomy and did not want to feel obligated to anyone. An odd thought crossed my mind.

"Whom do you prefer: Hector or Achilles?" I asked.

"What kind of a question is that?"

"Hector or Achilles?"

"Hector, of course," he said, looking confused. " 'Sprung from no god, and of no goddess born; / Yet such his acts, as Greeks unborn shall tell, / And curse the battle where their fathers fell.' "

"And you did express an interest in taking me to Ephesus, if I remember correctly. I believe it was on the Pont-Neuf?"

"So long as you are willing to uphold your pledge to leave your evening clothes behind."

"Cécile is right," I said, laughing. "She has always told me that you are a man of great possibility."

"Perhaps I should propose to *her*," he replied, raising his eyebrows.

"She undoubtedly would accept you." I rested my hand on his cheek. "I, however, have no intention of marrying again." He did not take his eyes from mine, even as they exposed the pain my statement caused him. I paused. "But, faced with such a suitor, I am willing to allow for the possibility."

"What does that mean?"

"I am giving you permission to court me, Mr. Hargreaves," I replied, placing my fingers lightly on his lips. "But I can offer you no promises." He pulled me close and kissed me passionately, apparently satisfied with my response.

"Perhaps just one promise?" he asked, brushing my hair from my eyes.

"What?"

"Promise that you will not be too hard on me. I've no goddesses lining up to help me convince you."

"No promises, Colin," I said, and kissed him very sweetly before returning to my bed.

THE HISTORY

BEHIND

THE STORY

ON WRITING
And Only to Deceive

ONE DAY, WHILE I WAS ENGROSSED IN DOROTHY L. SAYERS'S wonderful *Gaudy Night*, a sentence leapt off the page at me:

> *If you are once sure what you do want, you find that everything else goes down before it like grass under a roller—(all other interests, your own and other people's.*

I had been saying for as long as I could remember that I wanted to be a writer. Now I realized that if that was truly what I wanted, I had to sit down and write a book. No more excuses. At the time, my son was three-and-a-half years old and had reached the age where he stopped napping. I had to take advantage of every free moment I had—and in bursts of fifteen minutes, a half an hour, whatever time I could steal—I spent the next two months writing the first draft of *And Only to Deceive*.

I knew I wanted to write about an English woman in the late Victorian period and had a strong image of her standing on the top of the cliff path on the Greek island of Santorini, one of my very favorite places. Once I started asking questions about how she came to be there, the story started to invent itself.

I was determined not to create twenty-first-century characters, drop them into bustles and corsets, and call them historical. Fundamentally, we may have much in common with those who lived before us, but sensibilities have changed greatly. A strong-minded young woman in 1890 would not think in precisely the same way one would today. Emily's search for independence had to make sense in the context of the society in which she was raised. So she rebels in small ways at first, gradually becoming more steadfast in her convictions, more confident in herself, but she's vulnerable because she's not prepared to absolutely renounce her position in society. And, really, I think it's that sort of compromise for which we all search: How much of our culture, our society, do we accept? How much do we reject? Can we live according to our principles without sacrificing anything? It's very easy to have strong opinions when holding them does not threaten the comfort of our daily life.

The paramount goal for an aristocratic woman in Victorian England was to make the best possible marriage, one that would preserve fortunes and estates while increasing her standing in society. The marriage market was a competitive one. A family might have many eligible daughters but could only have one eldest son, who, alone among his brothers, stood to gain a significant inheritance. A young lady would feel a great deal of pressure to catch a respectable husband in as few seasons as possible after making her social debut. If two or three years passed and she was not engaged, she would be considered a failure.

Emily, coming from a wealthy, titled family, would have been in an excellent position to make a good match, and although I wanted her to be independent, it would have made no sense, historically speaking, for a girl in her position to avoid marriage. Her parents would never have allowed it. As an unmarried woman, she would be subject to her mother's rule, a situation, that, given Lady Bromley's character, would hardly have allowed her to do the things I wanted. But I did not want her to be married. A Victorian gentleman, even an enlightened one, would still have a decidedly Victorian view of marriage. To make her a widow seemed the perfect solution. I would be able to give her a certain degree of freedom without having to sacrifice historical accuracy.

Once I had Emily's character and situation firmly in my mind, I started to consider what might inspire in her an intellectual awakening. I've always been struck by the graceful beauty of classical art and fascinated by the enduring nature not just of Homer's epic poems, but of

Greek mythology in general. It's astounding to me that these stories, first told more than two thousand years ago, still resonate with people. Can you imagine writing something that could permeate Western culture for that long? I'd be afraid even to try!

Regardless of how many times I've read *The Iliad*, I always hope, hope, hope that *this* time Achilles won't kill Hector, even though I know it's impossible. I fling the book across the room every time I get to the part where Hector dies. I can't help it. It slays me. But that's part of the brilliance of the story; even though we know what happens, we still care desperately about these characters.

(If you like Hector, read the lovely, heartbreaking poem Irish poet Valentin Iremonger wrote about the night before the Trojan hero's death.)

As I was concocting the plot for the novel, I decided to have part of the intrigue involve art forgeries, which can be immensely difficult to detect. Two of the pieces I've mentioned in the book, both pointed out as fakes by Mr. Attewater, were actual objects found in the museum. The first, a bust of Julius Caesar purchased by the British Museum in 1818 for approximately thirty pounds, was not only exhibited, it was reproduced extensively as well, becoming one of the most famous images of the great Roman. It is not an ancient piece at all, dating instead from approximately 1800.

Second, the fragment Mr. Attewater confesses to having sold under false pretenses is based on an object that came to the museum in 1889, a piece depicting a boy's head. It was not until 1961 that it was determined it had been copied, sometime after 1840, from a slab of the North frieze of the Parthenon.

Bernard Ashmole, a former Keeper of Greek and Roman Antiquities at the British Museum and Lincoln Chair of Classical Art at Oxford, recognized that both of these items were forgeries, and they were included in a marvelous exhibition staged by the British Museum called "Fake? The Art of Deception."

To me, the most fascinating thing about forgeries is that they make one think about the true definition of art. If a work is copied so perfectly that no one can detect it as a fraud, why isn't it art? Why does only the original count? Yet, of course, the original is *different* somehow. But how can we quantify that difference?

FACT VS. FICTION

I HAVE TAKEN THE LIBERTY OF USING SEVERAL HISTORICAL persons as characters in *And Only to Deceive*. Pierre-Auguste Renoir, who once said, "Why shouldn't art be pretty? There are enough unpleasant things in the world," and his wife, Aline, are of course real. They were married at a city hall in Paris on April 14, 1890.

Emily's friend, Alexander Murray, was named Keeper of Greek and Roman Antiquities at the British Museum in 1886. His *Manual of Mythology* was recently reprinted as a facsimile of the original edition.

Lord Lytton was the British ambassador in Paris from 1887 until his death in 1891. He published fiction and poetry under the pseudonym Owen Meredith, his most successful work being a novel-length poem called *Lucile*. His father, Edward Bulwer Lytton, wrote *Last Days of Pompeii*, a book that was wildly popular in the nineteenth century.

Gordon Bennett, the publisher of the *Paris Herald* and son of the founder of the *New York Herald*, was responsible for financing Henry Stanley's famous search for Dr. David Livingstone. He immigrated to France after a scandalous drunken incident at his then-fiancée's house ended with him challenging her brother to a duel. No one was killed, but Mr. Bennett found himself no longer welcome in New York society. His behavior did not much improve upon his arrival in Paris, where he would pull tablecloths off restaurant tables if he found the service to be lacking. Nonetheless, he was handsome enough that the ladies were willing to overlook his shortcomings.

Charles Frederick Worth, though not precisely a character in the novel, was a man near and dear to the hearts of the nineteenth-century women fortunate enough to be in a position to afford the elegant dresses he designed, using the most luxurious fabrics and trims. He is often called the father of *haute couture*.

LOCATION, LOCATION, LOCATION . . .

I HAVE TRIED TO USE ACTUAL PLACES AS OFTEN AS POSSIBLE in *And Only to Deceive*. Sadly, many of the mansions that lined Berkeley Square in the nineteenth century were pulled down in the twentieth, but in 1890, the square was one of the most fashionable in London. Hyde Park and the British Museum are of course familiar to those even casually acquainted with the city, and all of the objects Emily sees in the museum were there in 1890, with one notable exception: The Judgment of Paris vase is, alas, fictional.

Travel to Paris was common for wealthy Britons, many of whom would come in January after they'd tired of country house life and before the start of the Season in London. Carriage rides in the Bois de Boulogne, strolls through the Jardin des Tuileries, trips to the Opéra, parties, and balls filled the days and nights of Englishmen abroad.

The Hôtel Meurice still offers some of the most luxurious accommodations to be found, although extensive renovations completed in 1907 have altered it since the time of Emily's visit. The Café Anglais closed in 1913. As with the British Museum, everything Emily sees in the Louvre would have been found there at the time the book was set.

It is impossible to overstate the glow that comes from hours spent walking through the lovely streets of the French capital. Emily's solitary wanderings in the city come at a difficult and sad time for her, but even in such circumstances, the solace one could find in Notre Dame or Sainte-Chapelle is unparalled. If one must be miserable, it might as well be in beautiful surroundings.

Although Emily did not make it all the way to Africa, it was not unheard of for women in the period to travel extensively. Some went on tours, some traveled with male guardians, but a not insignificant number traveled with female companions, letting their own interests guide their itineraries. There are a number of fascinating travel memoirs written by Victorian women, including Amelia Edward's *Thousand Miles Up the Nile*, Gertrude Bell's *Persian Pictures*, and Mary Kingsley's *Travels in West Africa, Congo Français, Corisco, and Cameroons*.

A widow in Emily's situation would find herself in a very different London from the one she occupied while her husband was still alive. Wealthy women had social schedules that could exhaust even the heartiest of souls: rides in the park, luncheons, garden parties, afternoons making calls, tea parties, dinners, soirées, balls, the opera, theater. The death of one's spouse brought an immediate stop to such activities.

When Prince Albert died in 1861, Queen Victoria entered a period of mourning that would last the remainder of her life. No one was expected to emulate the queen's devotion to the memory of her dear departed, but at least a year of deep mourning was required of widows, a time during which they would dress in unrelenting black and wear jewelry fashioned either from jet or from the hair of the deceased. Thank heavens that Colin Hargreaves did not have the presence of mind to snip some of Philip's hair to return to Emily!

An article that appeared in *Harper's Bazaar* on April 17, 1886, comments on women who were not devastated to lose their spouses:

> *A heartless wife who, instead of being grieved at the death of her husband, is rejoiced at it, should be taught that society will not respect her unless she pays to the memory of the man whose name she bears that "homage which vice pays to virtue," a commendable respect to the usages of society in the matter of mourning and of retirement from the world.*

Once she entered the period of half-mourning, the widow would start her gradual return to society. Black gowns gave way to grey, mauve, and lavender, and could now be made from silk instead of crape or bombazine. To alert the members of her circle that she was ready to face society, a widow would leave calling cards at the houses of her acquaintances. She would begin to accept more invitations, always being careful only to attend events that were not *too* joyful and to behave in ways respectful of the memory of her husband.

It is during this phase of Emily's life that the action of *And Only to Deceive* takes place. I wanted her to be somewhat isolated from society so that she would come to see that she did not, in fact, miss it as much as she might have thought. Because she, like the heartless wife of *Harper's Bazaar*, is not truly grieving Philip; it's an awkward and uncomfortable period for her, and a perfect time for her to look for intellectual stimulation.

SUGGESTIONS FOR FURTHER READING

Private Palaces: Life in the Great London Houses, Christopher
    Simon Sykes

The Bourgeois Experience: Victoria to Freud (five volumes), Peter
    Gay

The Decline and Fall of the British Aristocracy, David Cannadine

Victorian and Edwardian Fashion, Alison Gernsheim

Age of Opulence: The Belle Epoque in the Paris Herald, 1890–1914,
    Hebe Dorsey

Fake? The Art of Deception, Mark Jones (editor)

Parallel Lives: Five Victorian Marriages, Phyllis Rose

The lighter side of HISTORY

AND ONLY TO DECEIVE
A Novel of Suspense
by Tasha Alexander
978-0-06-114844-6 (paperback)
Discover the dangerous secrets kept by the strait-laced English of the Victorian era.

DARCY'S STORY
Pride and Prejudice Told from Whole New Perspective
by Janet Aylmer
978-0-06-114870-5 (paperback)
Read Mr. Darcy's side of the story.

PORTRAIT OF AN UNKNOWN WOMAN
A Novel
by Vanora Bennett
978-0-06-125256-3 (paperback)

Meg, adopted daughter of Sir Thomas More, narrates the tale of a famous Holbein painting and the secrets it holds.

REVENGE OF THE ROSE
A Novel
by Nicole Galland
978-0-06-084179-9 (paperback)
In the court of the Holy Roman Emperor, not even a knight is safe from gossip, schemes, and secrets.

THE CANTERBURY PAPERS
by Judith Healey
978-0-06-077332-8 (paperback)

CROSSED
A Tale of the Fourth Crusade
by Nicole Galland
978-0-06-084180-5 (paperback)

ELIZABETH: THE GOLDEN AGE
by Tasha Alexander
978-0-06-143123-4 (paperback)

THE FOOL'S TALE
by Nicole Galland
978-0-06-072151-0 (paperback)

THE KING'S GOLD
by Yxta Maya Murray
978-0-06-089108-4 (paperback)

PILATE'S WIFE
A Novel of the Roman Empire
by Antoinette May
978-0-06-112866-0 (paperback)

A POISONED SEASON
A Novel of Suspense
by Tasha Alexander
978-0-06-117421-6 (paperback)

THE QUEEN OF SUBTLETIES
A Novel of Anne Boleyn
by Suzannah Dunn
978-0-06-059158-8 (paperback)

THE SIXTH WIFE
She Survived Henry VIII to be Betrayed by Love...
by Suzannah Dunn
978-0-06-143156-2 (paperback)

REBECCA
The Classic Tale of Romantic Suspense
by Daphne Du Maurier
978-0-380-73040-7 (paperback)

REBECCA'S TALE
by Sally Beauman
978-0-06-117467-4 (paperback)

THE SCROLL OF SEDUCTION
A Novel of Power, Madness, and Royalty
by Gioconda Belli
978-0-06-083313-8 (paperback)

A SUNDIAL IN A GRAVE: 1610
A Novel of Intrigue, Secret Societies, and the Race to Save History
by Mary Gentle
978-0-380-82041-2 (paperback)

THORNFIELD HALL
Jane Eyre's Hidden Story
by Emma Tennant
978-0-06-000455-2 (paperback)

TO THE TOWER BORN
A Novel of the Lost Princes
by Robin Maxwell
978-0-06-058052-0 (paperback)

THE WIDOW'S WAR
by Sally Gunning
978-0-06-079158-2 (paperback)

THE WILD IRISH
A Novel of Elizabeth I & the Pirate O'Malley
by Robin Maxwell
978-0-06-009143-9 (paperback)

Available wherever books are sold, or call 1-800-331-3761 to order.